THE NIGHTINGALE FROM SINGAPORE

Harriet Geary

PublishAmerica
Baltimore

Softcover 9781627723428
eBook 9781629075983
PUBLISHED BY PUBLISHAMERICA, LLLP
www.publishamerica.com
Baltimore

Printed in the United States of America

CHAPTER ONE

It was with a certain degree of smugness that Archie and Clive Chance said goodbye to their school chums. Not for them the leafy lanes of the English countryside, or 'the boring back of beyond,' as Clive ungraciously described the sleepy, rural landscape; but, rather, these two fellows were setting sail for far more exotic climes.

And, so with his thin, little chest puffed out to its fullest, Clive told them, 'we're off to the other side of the world.' Then with a final whoop of excitement he shouted from the train, 'Fortress Singapore, here we come! Yippee!'

Apart from one boy who was going to Canada, and another, who had already left school the previous month to stay with an aunt in Australia, the rest of their classmates would join the hundreds of other London children heading for evacuation that late summer of 1939.

Grandma Chance anxiously scanned the long line of people hurrying from the train. At the best of times she was edgy among crowds, and now she felt tendrils of panic rising through every fibre of her being. Her grandsons were nowhere to be seen.

Suddenly she heard a bellowing cry. 'Mind your backs, please! Mind your backs.'

She glimpsed the top of the navy-capped porter, and frantically sped towards him. He likewise moved at a goodly pace even though he was loaded down with luggage. Panting furiously to keep up, the old lady pleadingly asked if he had noticed two young school boys getting off the train. However, he was most unhelpful, and all he did was to roll his eyes, and scathingly tell her that the place was crawling with school boys. She began to think that she had muddled up the time, or worse, the day. With shaking hands she opened her bag to check the letter. She became even more flustered. Her eyes were misting over and she couldn't make

out the writing. Someone bumped into her, almost knocking her off her feet. An impatient apology was thrown at her. There were so many people rushing towards her, men in khaki uniforms, women in khaki uniforms and children in a blur of school uniforms. Suddenly she heard her name being shouted.

'Grandma! Grandma!' It wasn't just one voice, it was two.

'Darling boys! Oh! Oh! Oh my goodness. What a relief that you're here, safe and sound.'

'Of course we are, Grandma,' said Clive, unperturbed.

She gripped her ample chest, and then gripped the boys. 'Travelling all that way on the train on your own and so many people—'

Archie said, 'it's alright, Grandma, really it is. You see, matron took us and some of the other chaps to the station, and waited until we got on the train.'

'Did she? Well that is something to be truly thankful for. Now, give me your hand Archie, and you too Clive, and when we get out of the station you must help me look for a taxi.'

By the time the children reached their grandmother's house in North London, it was almost dark. To Archie and Clive that didn't matter. Having spent many school holidays with their grandmother, they knew every nook and cranny in the lovely old Victorian house. The only thing they found odd was the black shutters which covered all the windows.

'Its regulations,' she told them, noticing the looks. 'Everyone has had to have them fitted. But never mind that. Come through into the dinning room and let's eat.'

Later, Clive casually, asked, 'where's Millie?'

'She'll be here tomorrow. Now it's getting late. Give Grandma a kiss, both of you, and quick, quick, quick, hop into bed.'

'Grandma,' Archie said, with infant-like concern as the elderly woman held the youngest of the brothers, 'Grandma, come with us. We'll take care of you. You'll be safe with us in Singapore.'

'Why, bless you, my darling,' she said. 'Don't you worry about Grandma she's as tough as old boots.' And she hugged Archie until he fell asleep.

Early the next morning before the boys had got out of their beds, Millie, their sister arrived. A little out of breath, she struggled up the steps with two heavy suitcases. Taking a key from around her neck, she let herself in.

Setting the cases beside the barley twist banister, Millie called out, 'it's me, Grandma.'

'I'm in the kitchen, *chéri*.'

Millie went down the three steps into the kitchen-cum-breakfast room.

'Morning Grandma—' was all Millie could say before large tears welled up and her throat tightened.

'There, there now, my darling. Don't get upset or you'll start me off. Here, sit down and have some tea and toast. It's freshly made. Let's take it together before the rascals come down.'

Millie smiled and nodded and attempted to eat the warm, crusty bread.

'Grandma, it feels like we are abandoning you—'

'Don't say such a thing, Millicent.' Only Grandma Chance called her Millicent. 'I've been over and over this with your mother and father and I am not going to change my mind now. The Germans are not going to shift me,' she said, defiantly. 'This is my home and this is where I'll stay. They're not going to put me out this time. Not like they did in France in the last—' she patted her favourite grandchild's hand. 'Don't get alarmed. There is nothing for you to worry about, my dear. Now chin up, all will be well. The boys have got their cases ready and I have the documents that your father wants taken to him. And,' holding a finger to her lips, she went to a drawer in the sideboard, 'this is for you.'

'Grandma, no it's far too much money, I can't—'

'No cants, Millicent. Put it away quickly before—'

They both looked up. The sound of feet racing down the stairs got louder. Grandma Chance smiled and set about getting the boys their breakfast.

'Millie! Millie!' They both cried in unison.

'Hello Archie boy, hello Clive.' She stared at Clive. 'Crumbs, you've grown.'

Millie tousled their already sleep dishevelled hair, and pulled out chairs to show that there was no time to be wasted simply because they hadn't seen each other for six months. And indeed within a couple of hours, Millie was arranging a taxi to take them to the station. Before leaving, however, Grandma had a surprise for the boys.

'The other day I searched and searched all through the book case because I knew I had this.' She untied the string and took the brown paper wrapping off a slim A4 volume. 'It was your grandpa's—God rest him—but he would want you to have it. So, I thought this is now the best time to pass it on, because you can study the maps while you are on the ship. And perhaps it will help the voyage go quicker.' She handed a beautiful gold embossed Geographical Atlas to the oldest boy, Clive.

Fingering the atlas, Clive said, 'gosh, it's real leather, too. Grandma, thank you very, very, very much. I'll put it in my satchel and we'll take great care of it, won't we Archie?'

Archie nodded enthusiastically wishing it had have been handed to him.

She reached for two other packages on the sideboard. 'Tuck, for the journey,' she chuckled, and out of Millie's hearing, lovingly whispered, 'and some pocket money'.

'Oh thank you, Grandma,' both said, trying to smother their delight.

In spite of their excitement at leaving there were a few tears. Poor Mrs Chance did her best to remain in control of her emotions, at least until the taxi was out of sight, and then she sank down in an armchair holding a large handkerchief over her face. In a sudden wave of that mercurial thing called hindsight, she now felt guilty. She thought they were all so very young to be making the long journey on their own, especially with war breaking out. Millie was still only seventeen. She sobbed some more, regretting that she had not gone with them to keep them safe. In the past they had always been accompanied either by herself or one or other of their parents. And now she told herself it was too late, they'd gone.

It was only when the ship set sail, and was well out of sight of land that Millie decided to unpack their cases. Somewhat earlier, the siblings had joined the pulsating lines of passengers to watch old England disappear in the distance. Subdued, Millie opened her own cases first, enjoying the privacy of a single cabin. It would have been unbearable sharing with those two live wires, she thought. It was, however, with ill-humour that Millie fitted hangers into some of her garments. Her mother had advised against extravagance and insisted she bring practical wear like the cotton dresses she'd just closed the locker on. She'd had to leave behind a good many lovely ball gowns, managing to squeeze in only two. Her friend Janet who had agreed to keep on the flat said she would post them out at a later date, or keep them until the fracas blew over. Millie regretted having to give the flat up, she was just beginning to enjoy her new found freedom and now everything has changed, again. She thought, lucky old Janet, she was still there. But Janet was her best friend and she knew the flat was in good hands.

Quite a number of clothes she decided to leave in the case. Shorts and bathing costumes and canvas sandals wouldn't get much use until they were well out to sea, so maybe she'd just leave them where they were, until reaching Singapore. Then she gave a smile as she admired the distinctive pattern of a long dead reptile. She was very glad that she'd manage to wedge in her favourite crocodile-skin handbag. Her unpacking finished, for now; she went to the adjoining cabin to help Clive only to find him and Archie peering at a page in the atlas.

Annoyed, Millie was quick to admonish. 'Haven't you done anything, Clive? And Archie you could at least have hung up those blazers.'

They appeared not to hear.

'You'll see,' Clive said to Archie, 'the Germans won't get through the Maginot Line. Mr Phipps said so in class, the other day, and if he said it, you can take it as gospel.'

Archie was impressed. 'Did he?' Then perplexed, he asked, 'er, um, what's the Ma-Ma-Mano Line, Clive?'

'Maginot, Maginot Line, you clot. Archie you are a Saracen numskull. Don't you know anything?'

'Look here,' exclaimed Millie, getting impatient, 'if you two think I'm hanging around waiting for you to finish your argument, you are very much mistaken.'

'Alright, we're coming. Archie, undo your case,' Clive directed. The order got passed along the line to the youngest.

Millie knelt beside her brothers as lids were raised. Then she let out a gasp.

'What in the name of heaven is this?'

'What?'

'Where are your clothes?'

Millie was bent over rummaging through Clive's case.

She asked again. 'Where are you clothes?'

Clive said, 'Matron told us to pack what we needed so I—'

'Didn't she do it for you? Didn't she help you?'

'No, er, you see she was er, awfully busy with the ones who were being evacuated. She had these lists of-of things-things that they had to take—'

'But you were leaving too couldn't she…Oh never mind. It's too late now.'

To ascertain just exactly what Clive had put in his case, she had to delve beneath something foul. Millie wrinkled her nose as she uncovered a pair of smelly, mud encrusted football boots. She quickly wrapped them up again and put them at the bottom of Clive's suitcase along with his cricket bat and torch. There was only one pair of trousers and there was a rip in one of the legs, and a jumper, which happened to be his sort of white, cricketing pullover. She thought Mother will have a fit. By now Millie had even less confidence of what she'd find among Archie's belongings.

'Archie, what on earth did you put these old conkers in for?'

'Because Millie, they are not just any old conkers. One of them, this one,' he fondled the treasured nuts, 'this one is a niner, and this one a sixer and this one, look, this one with the red spot is a tener.' Archie breathed over the seasoned, mahogany coloured skin of the champion conker, and gave it a rub.

However, Millie had no interest in discovering what niners or teners or even sixers were. Aside from the fruit of the chestnut tree, Archie had a brown paper bag filled with neatly tied lengths of string, as well as a catapult, and marbles stuffed in a sock, along with some rolled up comics. And carefully protected in a tin biscuit box, was his favourite collection of toy soldiers. Sighing, Millie considered that at least he had sense enough to bring his pyjamas and slippers.

Keeping her brothers occupied on the voyage was not as difficult as Millie had thought it would be. The pair studiously poured over the handsome atlas, tracing out their sea route each day. And, contentedly, they would spend hours setting up imaginary battles with lines of Dragoons and regiments of foot soldiers, bringing up the rear. Archie had a particularly splendid piece, a general, on a white charger. Archie loved the General so much that it often got slipped into his pocket, keeping him separate from the others.

Then as a need for something different to do, the brothers would have a mad half hour running round the deck, expending their energy. As she watched them, Millie did have one niggling concern, though. She was wondering how on earth she was going to get Archie and Clive all the way to Singapore with only the shirt and trousers they stood up in. Fortunately, along came help, in the form of Mrs Elliott and her daughter, Grace. The ladies, Millie learned, were returning to the Far East to join Mr Elliott, a Baptist Church missionary. Grace was a nurse and newly registered midwife, and they had plans to set up a mission hospital at their new posting outside Kuala Lumpur. They met Mrs Elliott and Grace one afternoon while getting some exercise on deck. Archie and Clive were doing their usual racing up and down, when suddenly Archie let out a wail of a cry.

'Clive, Millie, it's gone, it's gone! It must have fallen out of my pocket.' He and Clive retraced their steps but the General was nowhere to be seen. 'Millie!' Archie pleaded. 'Millie, please do come and help me look for him.' Tears were not far away.

The General had indeed fallen out of Archie's pocket. Unbeknown to Archie, the toy soldier bounced and rolled some distance away to land beside Mrs Elliott's shoe. Grace fortunately spotted the brightly coloured model.

'Don't move your foot, Mother,' she warned, 'or you'll tread on that young boy's little soldier.'

Grace walked over to Millie and the two boys, now on their hands and knees searching behind deck chairs.

'I think a famous battle could be lost without this handsome fellow.' Grace held out her hand.

'Aaa you've found him,' exclaimed Archie, clambering to his feet. 'Thank you. Look Millie this-this lady had found the General.'

'What a bit of luck! Thank you,' Millie said. 'The toy soldiers are his most prized possessions. He usually takes better care of them than he does his clothes.'

'Well, that's boys for you.'

'No it's not just that.' Millie began to explain. 'They were left to their own devises when it came to packing, and you should see some of the things that they brought.' She shook her head. 'I wouldn't have minded if they had have put some clothes in.'

Grace smiled sympathetically. 'My name is Grace and this is my mother, Mrs Elliott.'

Mrs Elliott, having being shown, and admired the General, came alongside her daughter and heard Millie's tale of woe.

'I think we may be able to do something for Archie and Clive. What do you say, Grace?'

'Yes, Mother, I'm sure we could find something.'

Wondering what to expect, Millie and her brothers were taken down to the ladies cabin, to where a huge travelling trunk stood. Inside, it was filled with clothes that Mrs Elliott and her daughter were taking out to the mission station, for the poor children.

'Now,' Grace said, 'I am sure we shall find some shirts and at least one pair of trousers each, among the clothing that has been donated by the good people of the borough of Islington.'

They had to plough through layettes of knitted baby bootees and bibs, vests and bonnets, to girl's liberty bodices and cardigans and leggings, until they reached the boys wear. Millie did wonder if liberty bodices would have been worn by little native girls. She also remembered her mother telling her that baby girls used to have their feet bound up, but she couldn't quite recall if that was perhaps in China.

'Yes, these will fit, wonderfully well,' said a grateful Millie, as she held up a pair of trousers against Archie's knobbly knees. 'It really is so very kind of you. I'm sure Mother will happily pay for them when we land in Singapore.'

Mrs Elliott said, kindly, 'that will not be necessary my dear. I'm glad that the problem has been solved and that Archie and Clive won't come in for a scolding for ruining their school uniforms.'

Then, Millie asked Mrs Elliott, 'where are you staying in Singapore? Are you staying at Raffles Hotel?'

'Good gracious, no. We poor missionaries couldn't possibly afford to stay in somewhere as grand as Raffles.' With a smile, she added, 'no, no. We will have to find accommodation that is considerably more modest before embarking on the next leg of our journey. As well as that, we do have a couple of old friends that we must look up while we're in Singapore.'

'Then you must stay at our house,' Archie told her, big-heartedly. 'There are bags of room. Mother would insist on it. Wouldn't she Millie?'

'Absolutely,' Millie replied eagerly. 'We shall send a telegram in advance.'

And so, it came about that the matter of Mrs Elliott and Grace's Singapore lodgings were promptly settled.

CHAPTER TWO

Mrs Chance, Millie's mother, needed little persuading to be convinced that Singapore would be the safest place on earth, for them all to sit out the war. It was, in fact, common knowledge, both back in England and in Singapore that their island fortress was impregnable. Mr Chance pointed out, more than once, to his wife that absolutely anything attempting an assault, would be blown out of the water by the massive guns trained out to sea. And for city dwellers, there was an additional aura of comforting British protectiveness in the form of machine-gun bunkers, which were positioned all along the southern coast line.

Looking through her husband's binoculars, from one of the offices of the Straits Steamship Company, Mrs Chance could just make out the vessel's flag, with its distinguished blue background and white cross on the red diamond. It flew from the ship nearing the harbour. She left her accountant husband, at his desk, while she joined a throng of people at the quayside, waiting for the ship to dock. In spite of the delight at seeing her children, she had mixed feelings. She was unhappy that her mother-in-law had dug her heels in and remained in London. But she was a stubborn lady, and they had to respect her decision and abide by her choice to stay.

In keeping with many colonials who had lived in Singapore for a long time, Mrs Chance had seen the island's economy and social standing within the Empire, flourish. In the thirties, hundreds of far eastern workers were drafted in help construct the massive, floating King George V1 Graving Dock. High demand for tin and rubber production grew, as did the need for domestic workers to service the hotels and homes of the burgeoning white population. Excellent sport facilities and cinemas had been built to entertain the colonials who enjoyed a hugely thriving and convivial life style. And added to the already large number of British forces stationed on the island, the arrival of the Australian army lent a certain sense of panache to the mix of people now in Singapore. The islanders benefited from first-class medical facilities, which included the well equipped Singapore Civil Hospital, only a mile or so from the Chances comfortable six bedroom bungalow.

Mrs Chance dwelt for a moment on the interruption of her sons' education. It hadn't caused her too many sleepless nights, considering the reason for them fleeing England; anyway, there were enough decent English schools to choose from in Singapore. She gave a sniff. Obviously not in the same league as the establishment that they had just left, but she took comfort in the knowledge that there would be no difficulty placing the boys in a good school. With Millie, however, things might not be that easy. She wondered how her only daughter would settle in Singapore, for what might be years, of a stay. Millie often seemed such as restless spirit with a tendency to flit from one thing to another.

It brought to mind the cycling holiday, when Millie and her friend, Janet, had gone from Dover to France for two months. In spite of her father advising against it, and indeed she expressed her concern to Millie for going on such a precarious mode of transport as bicycles. Yet old Mrs Chance overruled them, in the nicest possible way, by pointing out that their daughter was a fit young person and fluent in French. And once they got through Paris they knew the girls could stay with relatives, en route. But it was the molly-coddling bit that clinched it. Grandma Chance said it was not a good thing to wrap Millicent up in cotton wool. And then there was the flat that they had found her, so that she'd be near her new job, and which now both had been given up.

Then Mrs Chance remembered the telegram they'd received. Two women, Millie had seemingly formed an acquaintance with, on the ship—did she say they were missionaries? And wasn't there something about them travelling to Kuala Lumpur, and needed to be 'put up?' None of the family doubted that Millie was good at organising. She gave a smile when she recollected the name that Clive had given her—Miss Bossy Boots. Well, for a start there were plenty of clerical positions that needed filling, even within the Straits Steamship Company. Mrs Chance cogitated; a word in the right place would do it. Her thoughts were interrupted when cheering broke out as passengers began to disembark. She too joined in the mood and waved as she spotted Millie. She was hatless, her brown hair blowing hither and thither in the breeze. How pretty she looks, thought Mrs Chance, but I must remind her to keep her head covered in this climate.

Millie greeted her mother a little formally. It had been over six months since the whole family was together.

'Mother, it's good to see you. Thank you for meeting us. How are you?'

'Very well, dear, and I'm delighted to see you all. My! Boys, how smart you look in your school uniforms.' Archie and Clive smiled at their mother, looking the picture of innocence. Behind her back, they pulled faces.

'Mother,' said Millie quickly, as she saw the grimaces, 'let me introduce you to the two very kind ladies who were of great help to us on the journey. This is Mrs Elliott and Grace, her daughter.'

Mrs Chance extended her gloved hand. 'It's so nice to meet you. Did you have a good journey? Sea crossing wasn't too rough, I trust?'

'No, it wasn't at all, Mrs Chance. Grace and I are well used to being tossed about on our travels. But do please forgive us, we would not presume to intrude on your hospitality without—'

'It is no intrusion whatsoever, Mrs Elliott,' Mrs Chance responded grandly. 'You are very welcome to stay for as long as you wish. And we are looking forward, tremendously, to hearing the latest news from home.'

Just then a car horn blared.

'Hey, Father! There's Father,' shouted Archie. 'Come on Clive, 'I'll race you over.'

'Stop boys, stop running so wildly,' Mrs Chance ordered. But the two lads were already sprinting towards the car. She shrugged her shoulders and followed a grinning native wheeling their luggage in the direction of the car.

Mr Chance embraced his sons warmly, and kissed and hugged Millie. After welcoming Mrs Elliott and Grace, he gathered everyone up and got them into the car.

'Well now,' he said, starting up the engine of the sleek Rolls Royce motor. 'Let's move from the crowd and on the way home boys, you can tell your mother and I, all about the voyage. And Millie dear, we want to hear how Grandma is.'

Unlike Millie, Grace and Mrs Elliott travelled light. Apart from the large trunk which was put into the Chances store room; they each had brought only an average sized suitcase of personal belongings. Grace went into her mother's bedroom to ask if she needed help. From the doorway she saw her mother holding a framed photograph. She came in quietly and put her arm around her mother's shoulder.

'Mummy, don't worry about Christopher, he can take care of himself.'

'I know he can, Grace. It's just that we are going to be such a long way away.'

'I know.' Tactfully she changed the subject. 'Doesn't he look splendid in his uniform?'

Christopher was as fair-haired as his sister Grace, who wore a thick plait coiled round her crown, like a halo of a latter-day saint. On his head, her bother wore the cap with the insignia of the Royal Air Force.

Ten days had passed and Mrs Elliott had thought that her stay with the Chance family would be two, perhaps three days at the most. However, due to an unexpected hitch, they were unable to move on to Kuala Lumpur as quickly as they had hoped. Their friends at the little Baptist Church at the North end of the city had not received the expected consignment of medical supplies and bibles which the minister, Mr Elliott had previously asked for. And all Grace and her mother could do was to wait until they arrived. They could not leave without the valuable provisions—one to treat the body the other to treat the soul, so Mrs Elliott said.

Meanwhile, Archie and Clive had hoped to have escaped going to school until after Christmas, but their luck ran out. In the eyes of their parents, schooling was a number one priority. To a large extent, Millie had continued to keep a watchful eye on the boys' capers. She took them on outings and trips up the mountain, and their meandering round old haunts, greatly amused them all. Without a fixed purpose, Grace was at a bit of a loose end, so she joined in the excursions. After barely two weeks of lovely freedom, however, Millie came bounding in one day carrying an armful of new school uniforms. Fun for the boys was over.

When it looked as if the hold-up on the missionaries' delivery was going to run into weeks, Grace, innovatively, offered her services in the maternity section of the Military Hospital. On discovering just what her friend was doing, the prospect for Millie of a bustling hospital all seemed so much more exciting than the job that her mother had secured for her—clerk in the city office of the Straits Shipping Company. And so, a touch irked, Millie turned up her nose at her mother's endeavours, because, suddenly she had found her vocation. Millie wanted to be a nurse. After some telephone calls to the Military Hospital, she obtained an interview with the Matron. From Millie's point of view, the interview seemed to be going well, especially when Matron rang the bell for tea. Matron seemed very eager to hear how the war situation was developing in London; being a Londoner herself. When she was offered seedy cake, Millie thought she had it in the bag. Then came the let down. Matron told her that she wasn't old enough to start nursing training. If she applied again in six months time she would consider her application then. She hadn't meant to be unkind but the Matron could see by Millie's face, how disappointed she was. Not wishing to see the possibility of a new student nurse, vanish, Millie was asked if she would like to be shown round the hospital itself, to get a feel for the place.

This suggestion brought Millie a little crumb of solace, and later in the week she received a letter inviting her to a tour of the hospital premises. If Mrs Chance had gotten annoyed at Millie's blatant refusal to even consider the clerical post that she had secured for her daughter, she would have been forgiven. This was because Mrs Chance was quite used to Millie's somewhat frivolous outlook, and simply accepted it; almost as nonchalantly as she would have accept another after dinner gin and tonic.

Dressed in a very smart, new suit, that her father had bought her, and a hat, to please her mother, Millie set out with a feeling of great importance. Matron was going to give her a conducted tour of the hospital. What she didn't know was that the task was delegated, as always, to Home Sister, a sprightly middle-aged lady called Sister Graham. And in addition, there were ten other girls, all eagerly waiting at reception to meet Sister Graham. If Millie was a little crest-fallen, it was only momentarily, for there came such a babble of chatter and giggles that the youngest prospective recruit soon felt quite at home.

Like a knife slicing through butter, silence descended, instantly, when Sister Graham made her entrance. In a business-like manner she ran her eyes down the list of the new intake of student nurses, smiled at the group and indicated for them to follow her. To reach the start of the jaunt, they had to walk through beautifully tended grounds. Here they might have noticed a couple of dark-skinned youths who instantly swept up any stray leaf or twig, that deigned to rest on the lush, manicured lawns. And as the morning wore on, Millie became captivated. Everything was so bright and clean, and in the few selected wards that they saw, there seemed hardly any really sick people. And at the maternity wing she was acknowledged by Grace who came toward the group holding a sweet, chubby-cheeked little baby.

Finally the small assembly was taken to the Preliminary Training School, or PTS as Home Sister called it. It was in this building that Sister Graham informed them that here they would spend many weeks confined to the serious business of study. Anatomy and Physiology would be taught by Sister Tutor whom they would meet at a later date. She herself would teach the Theory and Practice of Nursing. Millie liked the class room; she thought it had a lovely atmosphere. Regimental rows of polished desks faced two expectant blackboards. Hanging on a frame, every bit like a hangman's gibbet was a life-sized skeleton, going by the name of Charlie. Mysteriously, some mischievous person had placed a dunce's cap on Charlie's cranium. This caused a little nervous hilarity. Sister Graham had undoubtedly seen it done before because she made no comment and simply placed the hat in a bin.

Millie wished she had been born six months earlier. Those girls, she thought, were in for such a jolly time. When the session had ended they all drifted away in ones and twos. Calls of 'good luck, see you after Christmas,' echoed down a long corridor. With a forced air of merriment, Millie found herself responding, similarly. Yet, watching them all disappear, she felt a wave of loneliness, which rooted her to the spot. She thought she was alone until a cough at her elbow, made her jump.

'You are Miss Chance, I believe.'

Millie swung round. 'Yes Miss, er yes, Sister Graham.'

'Will you come into my office for a moment, please?' A few yards past reception was Sister's office. 'I was speaking to Matron earlier.' Oh Lord, now I'm for it, thought Millie. 'We understand how very keen you are to start your nursing training. But of course, as you know, you are not old enough.' Millie nodded. 'We do, however, have something—' she hesitated while she picked up a sheet of paper, 'something which might interest you. Nothing in the nursing line, I must stress.' Millie thoughts were whirring. Please not a clerk, please not filing, please not… 'We run a service for our patients, very modest in some respects, but greatly valued, nevertheless.' Millie was silently shouting, what what? 'The service is a trolley-shop and mobile library.' Millie had to smother a laugh; Sister Graham appeared not to notice. 'It is run by the Red Cross, and it operates along voluntary lines. Miss Palmer is the person in charge, and she usually has an assistant. However, we see her last one has moved on.' She set the sheet of paper aside and gave Millie a smile. 'So, what do you think, Miss Chance? Fancy a spot of volunteering?'

Of course the trolley-shop and mobile library was a poor second to actually donning a pristinely starched apron over a nurse's uniform, but at least Millie sensed she had her toe in the water, and it kept her out of her mother's hair.

Miss Palmer was a likable, cheery spinster lady, in her late fifties. She catered for the material needs of the infirm as if it were her life's calling. Each commodity on the wooden trolley was arranged with military-like precision. Miss Palmer meticulously stacked the trolley with sweet smelling toiletries that included damask rose and lavender soaps. Tooth powder and brushes could be found on the lower shelf, along with ladies hair nets. These hair protectors came in a skin tinted fine or coarse mesh, which cost one penny and could be bought singly or by the half-dozen, at a half-penny cheaper. Stationery and jars of Brylcreem and combs were popular with male patients, as were sweets such as barley sugar and cough candy. It rarely happened, but occasionally if it were not on the trolley, the odd item that patients might need, Miss Palmer did her utmost to get for them. The trolley-shop was wheeled round the wards on alternate days to the mobile library. It wasn't taxing by any means and Millie enjoyed meeting the patients, and it meant that quite often she saw Grace. They had become good friends, Grace and Millie, regularly going to the pictures together, or getting in a game of tennis or a bit of swimming.

Millie might have easily spent the next six months leisurely biding her time, and happily pushing the trolley-shop and mobile library around with Miss Palmer until she could start PTS. However, an unusual incident curtailed Millie's purposeful strolling and her simple daily routine was changed by the fortunes of a ship belonging to the French Navy. The vessel, a light cruiser, had limped into Singapore harbour damaged, with a jagged hole in her stern, just above the water-line. There were a number of casualties on board, which included some of the officers and several of the ratings, who were in need of urgent medical attention. For security purposes, they were taken to the Military Hospital. The light cruiser, had, according to speculation, been torpedoed, somewhere off Africa. Some said that rumour was a bit of baloney, because she was too far south to have come in contact with U-boats. While the truth remained to be discovered, the conjecture continued.

On first contact, Millie thought she had done something terribly wrong by talking to the French sailor. All he wanted from the trolley-shop was writing paper and envelopes. But he was such a nice young man and Millie had leisurely idled away a good thirty minutes with him. Naturally, when he couldn't speak English she started up a conversation in his native tongue, to help him out. She even sat on the edge of his bed—an unforgivable breach of nursing protocol, had Millie but known—when they started reminiscing about Paris, in spring time, and the ambience of a meander along the *Champs-Elyées.*

'Bring that girl over here!'

The loud shout, bellowed forth from a man in a British army uniform. It gave Millie such a fright that she dropped a jug of flowers clean out of her hands and it smashed unto the floor. It gave the poor sailor an equally nasty shock as half of the contents of the water-jug spilled down his chest and left his bed bestrewn with mimosa.

Pale of face, Miss Palmer, who had been down the far end of the ward, came hurrying towards the offending kafuffle.

'Whatever has happened, Millie?' She asked, again. 'What have you—?'

'I-I dropped—'

Their conversation was interrupted by the ward Sister. 'Quickly, Miss, come here,' she said. Millie made to pick up the broken glass. 'Do leave that, there's no need—' she waved to a ward orderly, to clean up.

Millie practically ran to her. But not another word was spoken to Millie until the door of Sister's room closed.

Then the man in army uniform said to the Sister, 'there was someone here all the time! Why did no one tell us, *she* speaks French?'

'Well, I'm very sorry, Colonel, we had no idea—'

He asked Millie, 'what's your name, girl?'

'Millie. My name is Millicent Chance, sir.'

'How well do you speak French?'

'I beg you pardon?'

'I said how—' he was losing patience.

'Excuse me, Colonel,' the Sister interjected, 'let me explain to her.'

'Miss Chance,' she said, placing herself between Millie and the colonel, 'we need someone to act as an interpreter, someone who can translate French into—'

'Oh yes, I see. Why yes, I understand French perfectly well. My grandmother is French. We went for lots of holidays to France, and I lived there with her and Grandpa, for two years, while Mother and Father were in Hong Kong. But since Grandpa died, she now lives in London. Of course we wanted her to come with us to Singapore but she wouldn't budge—'

'Yes, yes, Miss Chance that's-that's fine,' Sister said, brusquely cutting into Millie's long-winded retort. 'We um, you obviously know about the ship that got er damaged, and which resulted in a number of casualties.' Millie nodded, perceptively. 'Some of the injured men are capable of talking to us now, but as you can appreciate we are not fully able to always understand their language. I myself have no knowledge of the spoken French.'

Millie was beginning to sense that it wasn't just their wounds that were of paramount importance. There was something else, something more sinister, and the authorities had to know. It was, nevertheless, going to take longer than the colonel thought, with all the to-ing and fro-ing with a mere slip of a girl. He stuck to Millie like her shadow as she tentatively approached the ward where most of the French men were. The sailors seemed to perk up at the sight of a pretty young girl, and they were greeted with wolf-whistles. Millie coloured and the colonel cleared his throat. At the first bed, Millie and the sailor gabbled away in French, until the colonel stepped in and spoke.

'What is he saying, what is he saying? Can you understand him? Were they sailing round the coast of Africa when they got hit?'

Millie said, '*oui* um wee.'

'Yes! Yes!' The colonel rubbed his hands. 'I thought so.'

Because of the secret nature of the mission, the colonel had not as yet received word, officially, of Churchill's intention to destroy all French vessels, to prevent them falling into German hands.

'No,' Millie said, 'you don't...Colonel, he is saying, he needs to wee, pass water, you know, urinate!'

CHAPTER THREE

Christmas was celebrated in a big way on the island, and for Millie and Grace it was a very special occasion. They had invitations from two French navel officers to attend the Christmas Eve Ball, held at the very popular, Raffles Club. Happily, Millie had at last got a chance to air her favourite ball-gown. Grace did not possess anything remotely wearable for such a grand affair and was all set to decline the invitation. Millie would not hear of Grace not going just because of a dress. So without a second thought, she gave her friend the other ball-gown that she had brought with her from London.

For some families, and members of the Allied forces based on Singapore, being away from home at Christmas was something of a nostalgic time. With Britain and Germany at war, the season brought particularly poignant thoughts and concerns. For many youngsters though, Archie and Clive included, 1939 ended on a high note. School was closed for another week, and with jamboree-like parties running for days, and along with concerts and fireworks to entertain, there was much excitement to fill the long, sunny days. To mark the end of the old year, the social life of a colonial population buzzed with cocktail parties and dances, and the usual rousing rendition of *Auld Lang Syne* echoed well into the early hours. For Mrs Elliott and Grace, they had the additional good news that the consignment of medical supplies and bibles had at last arrived, and was awaiting collection. This meant that Grace's short stint on the maternity wing came to an end, as did the stay at the Chances lovely home. Millie was very sad that Grace was going; they had got on so well together. To help with the move, Millie and her father went to the warehouse to lend a hand with loading the goods. Mrs Elliott had organised a truck as a means of transport and was collecting the vehicle from a garage, just a mile or so away from the warehouse. It was a good arrangement as the truck would carry a load of jute back to a wholesaler in Singapore, thereby halving the hire cost of the vehicle. They knew that to get to Kuala Lumpur a rough ride lay ahead, but Grace and her mother were going to share the driving and didn't consider the task too daunting.

However, it was on the drive over from the garage to the warehouse that Mrs Elliott met with an untimely accident. Everyone said how lucky she was to have come out of it relatively unscathed, even though she ended up with two broken ribs and a sprained wrist. The unfortunate mishap occurred when Mrs Elliott was negotiating a sharp bend and another car, coming in the opposite direction, took the corner too fast and clipped the truck's right wheel. The collision blew out the tyre and sent the truck careering into a tree. Once again the Elliott's journey was beset with further delays while repairs to the truck and to poor Mrs Elliott's injuries got attended to. It was the first time that anyone had seen Mrs Elliott looking so glum. As a solution for getting under way, Grace said that she would drive but her mother wouldn't allow it. Too much of a responsibility, she said, for one person to drive alone, especially after what had happened to her. It looked as if the journey was to be postponed one more. A little later, while Mrs Elliott was resting on the Chances veranda, Millie came up with a plan.

'I'll go along,' she said, to Mrs Elliott. 'If you'd like me to, that is.'

'Go along, go along with us?'

Everyone gravitated towards the veranda.

Looking swiftly at her mother, then back to Mrs Elliott, Millie said, 'yes of course, and why not? I can take over from Grace, give her a bit of a break when she gives the say so, and all Mrs Elliott has to do is to sit back and enjoy the ride.'

Millie's suggestion and casual turn of phrase caused a little wry amusement.

'Why thank you for that Millie, my dear,' said Mrs Elliott. 'But I don't think...and besides, how will you get home?'

'Oh I can hitch a ride back when the jute is ready, or I could get the train back. We did the journey last year, didn't we Father?'

Mr Chance was leaning against the door, puffing hard on his pipe.

'Um, oh yes, that's right we stayed a few days with the Barnet family.'

'No, Millie,' Mrs Elliott said firmly. 'It's asking too much and what about the work you do in the hospital?'

'Oh don't worry about that. Under the circumstances I'm sure Miss Palmer will be fine about it. Anyway, I won't be gone that long; and the other thing is there are fewer patients in the hospital, what with most of the French Navy blokes gone back to their ship.' She suddenly changed the subject. 'By the way, I never did get to hear what caused their ship to nearly sink. In spite of my certain *je ne sais quoi* with the French lingo, I couldn't make much sense of all that naval jargon they were rattling off. All the same, they've kept the incident pretty hush-hush. Mind you, one of the officers told the colonel he was pretty sure that the Japanese had a hand in it.'

'Stuff and nonsense, Millie,' retorted Mrs Chance. 'The Japs couldn't have launched an attack on anything as powerful as a French light cruiser.' She turned to her husband. 'They would not dare…and not only that, they have no navy to speak of, isn't that so, Freddy?'

Freddy Chance sucked on his pipe, thoughtfully, but would not commit himself one way or the other. Not to be excluded from this interesting grown up talk, Clive and Archie rudely pulled their eye lids apart and squashed their noses with a finger. Millie was about to give them both a cuff when they made a bolt for it into the bushes.

Word got around among the local community that Mrs Elliott's plans were once again thwarted by sheer bad luck. Concern for her predicament soon became evident. To her great astonishment, so many people showed such kindness. She was showered with all manner of wonderful gifts for the new mission hospital. A large quantity of mosquito nets and fold-up camp beds were donated by a more than apologetic driver who admitted he was to blame for the crash, and as such wished to make amends. And a crate of tinned fruit and bags of rice were given by the owner of the warehouse. Miss Palmer even sent down a selection of slightly dog-eared books, and Mrs Chance gathered up sacks more clothes from the ladies at the Bridge Club. When all these unexpected, but nevertheless most welcome contributions were piled into the truck, there was no space at all left, not the merest whisker's breadth that even a very tiny grey mouse could fit into.

A little later, and with Millie now on board, the three ladies set off early in the morning to make as much headway as they could, before the heat of the midday sun would force them to rest up in the shade. They were all in excellent spirits; as if they were setting off on a wonderfully big adventure, which is what Archie called their venture. Travelling at a virtual snail's pace it took three days to cover the two-hundred odd miles. In places the road conditions were bad, with great pot-holes to be steered round and because they had a full load to contend with as well as a somewhat fragile Mrs Elliott, they rarely exceeded thirty miles. Millie was fairly inexperience and drove only on good stretches. At one point they took a short diversion and stopped the night at the home of a church contact, that Mrs Elliott had been given. And very glad they were for a good meal and comfortable beds. Then they had another two miles of a narrow winding road to do once they got through Kuala Lumpur. This stretch was undertaken by Grace.

At the end of the long journey and looking forward to somewhere pleasant to rest up, they were all shocked to find how little progress had actually been made on the hospital building. Millie especially was taken aback, having just left a sterile, shiny hospital, where not a speck of dust lay for more than a second. And now they were confronted with virtually a wooden shell, and even then, under a partial makeshift roof, there were three patients lying on rough beds. Trying to disguise their disappointment, all three stiffly climbed out of the vehicle and went in search of Mr Elliott. Thick exotic flowering bushes and rubber trees prevented any sighting of another human being. However, they headed for the noise of chopping and found the minister overseeing the felling of trees. No one at the plantation had heard the truck pull up.

Grace shouted as loud as she could. 'Daddy, Daddy!'

It took several more loud calls before one of the natives tugged Mr Elliott's shirt sleeve.

Mopping his brow with a handkerchief he exclaimed, 'ah, there you are, so you have at last arrived.' He swept his arms around as if he were about to swim the breaststroke. 'Welcome, welcome.' He kissed Grace, and embraced his wife tenderly. She tried not to wince, her ribs were still very sore. Then spotting Millie, he asked, 'And who is this young lady? Another helper! How marvellous, how absolutely marvelous, just what we need.'

'Well er no, Daddy, not exactly. But do come down. Can you please leave attacking the trees for a bit and let's all get a cup of tea. That's what we need.'

'Certainly, certainly, my dear, I'll lead the way, follow me.' He called to the nearest worker, 'Chinglee, let the boys take five.' Removing his hat Mr Elliott wiped the sweat from round the band. Not in the least crestfallen, he announced, 'we're not as far on with the hospital as we might have liked. The rain hasn't helped. Still the house is fairly sound. It might need a tidy, you know, a woman's touch.' He chuckled, child-like.

As for the house, built typically on stilts, a tidy was more than a slight understatement. Inside it really was bordering on the chaotic. Packing cases were stacked crate upon crate in one room. And in other rooms, furniture was hidden beneath dust sheets. These grey drapes lent a weird ghostly feeling which accompanied swirls of diaphanous cobwebs. Suppressing a shiver, Mrs Elliott though, was never the one to flinch in the face of adversity, and so she stoically put on a brave countenance before speaking to her husband.

'Well, at least we are here safe and sound, and once we get a nice cup of tea, we'll make a start and get some semblance of order in this, um,' for a second Millie thought she was going to say, this God forsaken place, instead she mumbled, 'this mother of muddles.'

Exuberantly, the minister said, 'now, my dear, you mustn't tax yourself, remember your bones are attempting to mend.'

Millie and Grace couldn't help smiling when Mr Elliott said that to his wife, especially after giving her a right hearty squeeze.

It was the following day before the arrivals could properly take in just what had to be done to both the house and the hospital. And it was formidable. Moving off to one side, to take stock of the situation, Millie made some quick calculations and came to a decision. She told her friend, Grace, that she would stay and lend a hand for a month or so, or until such times as Mrs Elliott was feeling back to normal. With her arm in a sling Millie knew that that would be the first thing to be discarded, if she started to tackle the mountain of jobs in the house. Mrs Elliott and Grace didn't bother to explain this bit of good news to Mr Elliott, but they were delighted.

For days, Millie and Grace worked like coolies, from morn till night, to get everything in the house shipshape. Then they went flat out to tackle as much as they could in the hospital. Without a doubt, it was starting to slowly take shape, especially when the donated beds and mosquito nets were put into what would be the four small wards. However, two months down the line Millie realised just how much she had underestimated the amount of work that was involved in the mission project. There was though, one definite piece of good news. She learned that once the hospital was established, the London Missionary Society was to send a doctor out from England.

Mr Elliott had an old wreck of a car, which, when it worked, just about made the few miles into Kuala Lumpur. Nevertheless, the old banger was desperately needed for carrying their essential supplies. At the first opportunity, Millie went into the town with Grace, to do some shopping. While her friend made her purchases, the store keeper allowed Millie the use of his phone. On reaching her mother, Millie told her that she was going to stay with the Elliotts until she heard from the hospital Matron, hopefully with the offer of a place at the Preliminary Training School. At the same time a letter was dispatched to Matron explaining Millie's unexpected change of plans. Before signing off, Millie, with gushing enthusiasm, wrote of how much she enjoyed being taken round the hospital, and was looking forward enormously to starting her nursing training.

CHAPTER FOUR

While 1940 found the whole of Europe heaving and sick, amid the throes of a tumultuous war, it could almost be said, that 'Fortress' Singapore bathed in an extraordinary atmosphere of sublime tranquillity. The military bods were constantly reinforcing the concept that an island invasion was impossible. With a huge garrison of troops, and heavy fifteen-inch guns defending the port, and the city, the effectiveness of the island defences were, in their eyes, truly sound. Consequently, this air of assured confidence coming from the top brass was extremely heartening for the population. After all, Singapore was a major imperial force, and with her powerful navel base, was strategically, a vital part of the British Empire. The adamant proclamation that ships of his majesty's navy would see off all challengers, undoubtedly bolstered any possibility of flagging morale.

Isolated, to an extent, and away from Singapore, helpers at the missionary station were clearly out of earshot for most of the usual war propaganda. And news on the home front was also sketchy. As fate would have it, things were to change with the arrival of the doctor. It was at the end of June that he appeared at the mission hospital, loaded down with luggage and equipment. For the hard working quartet eagerly awaiting the newcomer, he at least would have some reliable and up-to-date news of what was happening back in Europe. However, this medical man wasn't at all what the missionary folk were expecting.

'He-he's ancient,' gasped Millie, her eyes widening as Mr and Mrs Elliott gave Doctor Elder—that was his name—a tour of the growing, but still incomplete building.

'Hush, Millie, he'll hear you,' said Grace, smothering a giggle. 'I heard him telling Daddy that the Islington committee brought him back out of retirement. Apparently, the doctor that was originally coming to us got his call up papers and enlisted with the Royal Army Medical Corp.'

Ancient he might be, but Doctor Elder was able to bring them all kinds of interesting, albeit alarming developments on the war front. It was while sharing their dinner, round the bamboo kitchen table, that he started to tell them of the unimaginable and terrible defeat that the British Expeditionary Force had suffered, at Dunkirk. They all listened in stunned silence when he went on to tell them of how both the Belgium and French Armies had collapsed, allowing the Germans to overrun France. While the demoralised remnants of the BEF were sent packing, back to England.

'Our whole army in France is defeated, in what is being called a *Blitzkrieg.*'

Millie asked the doctor, 'what's a blitz-blitz what?'

'*Blitzkrieg, Blitzkrieg,* Millie, it's German for lightening war. I believe that is the proper translation. It means when things-events happen so fast, or words to that effect.' He shook his head. 'They all said it was impossible to get through the Maginot Line, that great line of concrete fortifications that was built to stop everything in its tracks.'

Mrs Elliot started to ask, 'but how—'

'That is what is astounding everyone. And stupidly, they're still asking how did they do it?' His faced creased as if in pain. 'The Nazi's have overrun Europe and the Low Countries, and they're asking how did they do it? Well, the answer to that is simple. They drove their tanks through the Ardennes Forest, thus they by-passed the Maginot Line, and ploughed on with highly trained infantry, so it's being said.'

Unable to grasp what she heard, Millie blurted out, 'never! Not through that massive forest. My friend Janet and I tried once to cycle through the Ardennes but we could only do a little bit, it was so dense. Then we had to turn back—'

'Yes, Millie, I'm not surprised on mere bicycles. But German tanks simply flattened all in their path. Flora and fauna, man and beast, crushed like a tuppenny bag of digestive biscuits under a rolling pin. And the last I heard as I was getting off the ship was that Paris had fallen to the Germans.'

Still sceptical Millie cried, 'no! Not Paris, my poor Grandma, she'll be heartbroken, she's French, you see. They couldn't. It's not possible, is it?'

Doctor Elder nodded, his lined face, serious.

Then more to himself, Mr Elliott said, 'I suppose it was inevitable that Chamberlain had to go.' He asked the doctor, 'what about Churchill, how's he shaping up? Can he handle it?'

'It's hard to say. A new man in the job and all that, but I don't think many will envy his position, just at present.'

Thinking of the lovely holidays to Venice and Naples that the family went on, Grace asked, 'and what about Italy, we've heard so many different rumours.'

'Mussolini has shown his hand and sided with the Germans. He has declared war on France and us.'

They stared at their half eaten meal. Suddenly no one had much appetite. Then Doctor Elder shook them out of the sudden wave of despondency when he said, 'eat up; it would be a sin to waste such wonderful food. The government in London has started to ration all sorts of commodities. Petrol, well that was one of the first things, and then coal of course, and now there are food shortages, and they'll be a whole lot more rationing before long. I know it's hard to believe it out here, but people are beginning to feel the pinch, back home.'

While the Battle of Britain was being fought over the green fields and sun kissed meadows of old England, the battle to build a new hospital in the tropics, was being won. At the same time, two little Malaysian babies successfully strove to come into a world far away from the bombs and bullets of war-torn Europe. They were the first of a number to be born at the mission hospital. Doctor Elder stood in attendance while Grace delivered the infants, without complications, and Millie, as a prelude to her nursing career, was allowed to be present at the births. The babies, a boy and a girl, were given the names Grace and Elder, by their respective mothers, in honour of the English doctor and his midwife. In the weeks and months that followed, the small hospital treated an assortment of minor accidents, ranging from a septic finger, to a snake bite— fortunately not a venomous one, as it turned out—to broken bones and a woman with a badly scalded hand returned often to have her wounds dressed. More serious, an appendix operation was performed by Doctor Elder, with the result that the offending, little worm-like appendage got removed, successfully.

Mrs Elliott was no slacker, either. Once the soreness wore off her ribs and wrist, she got down to visiting some of the nearby villages. Chinglee, the resident head boy, offered Mrs Elliott a not uncommon method of travelling in those parts—the rickshaw. By riding in the rickshaw, pulled along via this willing helper, parcels of clothing were tactfully distributed to many of the village women. This frequent social interaction allowed Mrs Elliott to get to know the children and their families better. And quite soon the mission had a respectable little group of children; curious enough to want attend the Sunday bible class. Extraordinarily, the quantity of liberty bodices that had travelled over the seas in Mrs Elliott's seemingly bottomless trunk, were adapted and re-sewn by Grace, to make wonderfully soft swaddling clothes.

It very soon became clear that Doctor Elder had a mine of information at his bony fingertips, and his experience in many fields of medicine, proved invaluable, to everyone. Although he never actually disclosed his age, he was a tireless worker who gave of his time and knowledge, unstintingly. Watching the skill and dexterity with which the elderly doctor and his young colleague, Grace worked, their accomplishments positively served to heighten Millie's resolve to be a good nurse. And in due course the long awaited letter from Matron did arrive, offering Millie a place at the PTS, starting on the 9th January 1941. It was a little later than she had hoped but what excitement it brought all round, when the precious epistle was read.

*

At the start of her nursing training, it had always been Millie's intention to go back and visit the missionary hospital. For practical reasons, however, her wish to do so did not materialise until almost the end of her first year as a student nurse. Over the months, letters from Millie were exchanged between Grace and Mrs Elliott, and even Doctor Elder wrote some little anecdotes and words of encouragement, from time to time. Still, Millie often did wonder where those first ten months went to. To her, they seemed to fly by like a dream. Although they were tough months of hard work, they were also very rewarding ones. And before she knew it, the first round of exams was almost upon her. Then it was off to study block, head down with Sister Tutor cracking the whip and rattling the bones of old Charlie, the skeleton. She did this out of exasperation whenever a nurse incorrectly named one of his bones. After the last set of examinations had finished, the student nurses were given their first short, but welcome holiday.

There was a consensus of opinion between Mr and Mrs Chance that Millie had at last grown up and settled down. It came as quite a relief to both her parents that she didn't change her mind and give up half way through the nursing course. By way of a reward for having done so well, they were on the point of suggesting a boat trip up to Penang Island. Their friends, the Barnet family had a holiday home there, near Georgetown, which they let out occasionally. Before Mrs Chance could mention it, Millie announced that she was taking the opportunity to go and see her friends, at the mission hospital. As well as that, Millie also asked if Archie and Clive would like to go with her to see Mrs Elliott and Grace, and meet Mr Elliott, and the mission's Doctor Elder. There was no contest when it came to choosing, for they both jumped at the chance to venture into the 'wilds of the jungle,' as Clive put it. And so it was all settled. Mrs Elliott had been sent a wire to say they were coming, and the plans were, that Millie and the boys would be back in Singapore to enjoy another Christmas with their parents. To Millie, after all the hard work she'd put in for exams, it sounded like a heavenly break. As a special treat, she had told her brothers that they could visit the shops in Kuala Lumpur for Christmas presents.

On the train ride up, Millie tried to describe to Archie and Clive all the work that was involved in getting the little hospital off the ground, so when they did eventually see it for themselves they were most impressed.

'Golly gosh, Millie,' said an amazed Archie, 'it was frightfully clever of your to turn your hand to building all this.'

Millie hugged Archie, and kissed his head. 'Silly boy, I didn't do it on my own. Everybody helped. But even so, all this is new, and so is this, and this.' She pointed to things that were built since she left. There was also another structure that resembled an old fashioned tree house, though it was strung together on a much larger scale.

'Golly gosh,' Clive repeated, parrot fashion, he too was impressed.

For Millie, it was wonderful to see Grace, and Mr and Mrs Elliott and dear old Doctor Elder, again. Ever the dapper, not a silver hair on his head moved out of place as he raised his hat to Millie, and shook hands with the boys. To be able to compliment her friends face to face, on such great strides they had made to the hospital, got everyone beaming with satisfaction. In the house where the Elliott family and Doctor Elder lived, little had changed. However, there was not sufficient space to put up extra visitors so to Archie and Clive's delight it was to the so named, tree house that they were to bed down in. And adding to the excitement, they had to climb a rickety bamboo ladder to reach the living quarters. Millie declared she would sleep there as well; just to be sure she was within earshot of what the boys were getting up to.

It was a wonderful holiday for the visitors, and things were going swimmingly. Then as a special treat, on the tenth of December, Doctor Elder borrowed a car from the neighbour, Mr Barnet, and took Archie and Clive on a mystery trip up-country, heading in the direction of Kuantan. His purpose for the expedition was to collect plants and herbs that grew just below the mountain. The doctor was something of an amateur apothecary and would often mix up his own medicines. He decided he would take the young lads away for the day and let them see a bit of the mountain terrain, and this would give Grace and Millie some time together. Coincidentally, Grace had an appointment in Kuala Lumpur to see a friend. Not wishing to appear rude, she asked Millie if she wanted to go with her.

Grace suggested, 'it might be an ideal time to get the boys those Christmas presents that you were talking about. And you could hide them away somewhere without them being seen.'

'Yes, that is a very good idea, Grace. I'll take you up on that.'

While Grace was driving her father's old jalopy, Millie sensed that there was something slightly odd in Grace's manner. And she threw her friend a series of sly looks, out of the corner of her eye. Instinctively, she sensed that there was something different about Grace. It wasn't her hair, beautiful though it was Grace still wore the thick blond plait high on her head. And unable to keep totally out of the sun, her skin glowed in an all over golden sheen. And yes, she had a very pretty short-sleeved frock on, but Millie remembered having seen the dress before. Suddenly, Grace became conscious of Millie's glances. She tried to ignore them, until feeling downright uncomfortable, she pulled the car over. A pink flush came to her cheeks.

A short silence followed. Owning up, Grace said, 'yes I am meeting a male friend, to answer your unspoken question.'

'Ah-ha, I just thought as much. Come on spill the beans, old girl'.

Grace laughed. 'He's a really nice chap—'

'He'd better be. So, how did you meet him, pray tell. And does you mummy know? And—'

'Yes she does know, and if you give me a chance, *Miss Chance*, I'll tell you how we met.'

Pre-emptively, Millie rushed in with, 'well listen here, I don't want to play the gooseberry—'

Grace laughed, loudly. 'You won't have to play the gooseberry. He's bringing a chum. There's a bit of a shortage of female company as you might have guessed.'

Millie said, 'yes I know.' Then she boasted, outrageously, 'I could have taken my pick and gone out with any number of handsome doctors from the hospital. In fact,' she added, haughtily, 'I did. I could have and did go on any number of dates, you know.'

Pretending impatience, Grace asked, 'hey, do *you* want to know or don't you?'

'Oh yes, I want to know. Yes, yes do go on, please.'

Grinning from ear to ear, Millie removed her sun glasses, in an attempt to study Grace's features, more earnestly.

CHAPTER FIVE

Clive got the awful news from the Malayan fishermen, and word began spreading like wild-fire through the small, fishing village, situated just a few miles from Kuantan. The men had turned and looked, strangely disturbed, at the curious, young English boy, now peering down at their catch. Clive was absorbed in studying the unusual assortment of fish brought up from the depths of the South China Sea. They were the weirdest looking fish he'd ever seen. Some, were as bright red as a sunset, some as black as Dante's inferno, and some had fierce spines, which when he touched the spikes made him draw back his hand in pain. Poking one big fish that was in its last death throes, he was oblivious to the fishermen's agitated chattering. Then, in pidgin English they told him what had happened. Clive's face became a mirror image of the poor fish he'd just prodded. The muscles of his mouth slackened, and his jaw fell open in silent disbelief. They shook him and told him again. This time it registered. Fleeing the little huddle of stunned Malayans, Clive dashed off to find Doctor Elder and Archie.

Almost unable to speak from a stitch in his side, Clive, between gasps, spluttered, 'Doctor Elder, Doctor Elder, Archie, the *Prince of* the *Prince of Wales* and-and *Repulse* have been sunk! They've both got sunk, sunk by the Japanese!'

'Steady now, Clive, get your breath,' said Doctor Elder, gripping him by the shoulders. 'Who told you that? Come now. You've got it all muddled, surely, you must have. The *Prince of*...no, no, that's nonsense. Weren't you telling Grace, only the other day, how you and everyone watched the *Prince of Wales* sail from Singapore?'

Yes, that was true. On the second of December, Archie and Clive had indeed watched from the jetty in Singapore as HMS *Prince of Wales* glided, effortlessly in. She looked magnificent. Splashes of bright colours streaked across the sky, her line of flags, fluttering in the breeze like a ballerina's seductively flouncing can-can skirt. With his father's vast shipping knowledge, Mr Chance, proudly informed his sons that the *Prince of Wales* was the Empire's newest battle ship, commissioned just back in March. Amid the loud patriotic cheering, he added, that she is the pride of the Royal Navy.

Clive was in tears of anger when he sobbed, 'and now they are both at the bottom of the bloody sea.' He cursed, bitterly, 'bloody, bloody Japs.'

The incident, like the demised of both fish and ships, brought an end to the party's little expedition, so they swiftly made preparations to return to the mission base. They were some hours away but most of the time was passed in silence. Archie talked non-stop to begin with until overly tired, and low in spirits, he fell asleep. Doctor Elder seemed preoccupied with his own thoughts and responded out of character, in a monosyllabic way to Clive's unanswerable questions. Gradually, Clive too, went quiet. They both wondered if anyone on the mission base had heard, or would they be the first harbingers of bad news?

*

Around the same time and blissfully unaware of the tragedy, Grace and Millie were drinking a weird concoction of cider and iced mango juice, while their companions, two British army officers, drank ice-cold beer. The girls had arranged to meet them at the *Lotus Hotel*, after that is, Millie had taken in all of the shops in Kuala Lumpur. However, Grace had anxiously kept looking at her watch. She could see Millie just wanted to be shopping while she just wanted to be with Captain Gordon McGregor. As luck would have it Grace managed to tear Millie away and they were only fifteen minutes late.

When Grace had made the introductions she asked Gordon, 'how's you arm?'

He replied, cheerfully, 'good as new. Look!' And with that he reached for Grace's hand and with exaggerated politeness, kissed it.

Grace blushed. 'Aren't you ever the charmer, Gordon?' She turned to Millie. 'Do you remember me telling you, Millie, that's how I met—?'

'And wow, what a meeting!' Gordon turned to his fellow officer. 'Just imagine, if that tiger hadn't had me in his jaws,' he nudged his companion, 'you remember, Philip, when he almost bit my arm off. Why, I might never have got nursed by this darling of an angel.'

Millie rolled up her eyes in mock derision. But she liked Grace's friend, he had a nice face with an easy smile, and it was instantly recognisable that they were both in love. Millie pushed her glass aside. She was sensitive enough to realise it was time to make an exit.

To the young man sitting beside her, Millie said, humorously, 'right then, Captain Philipo, what do you say we leave these two love birds to bill and coo, and you help me get all these bags into the car?'

Captain Philip Hendry drained his tankard, and kept up the banter by throwing an equally witty rejoinder. 'That suits me just fine. Lead on Millipede.' He gathered up four of Millie's packages and pretended to stagger under the weight.

Millie said to Grace, 'we'll meet you back here in what, a couple of hours of so?' Grace nodded and smiled her agreement.

As the parcels were being put into the car, Philip asked, 'would you like to go to the pictures?'

'Um, actually no, it's a bit hot for the cinema. I wouldn't mind getting something to eat, we didn't get round to thinking about food, and I'm really rather hungry now.'

'Good, well, there is an unusually civilised little place just about ten minutes away, and there might even be a band playing.'

'Fine, let's eat.'

He gave Millie his arm, which she took in a nonchalant, matter of fact kind of way.

She asked, casually, 'what are you doing down this neck of the woods? Or are you stationed in Kuala Lumpur?'

He told her he was stationed near Alor Star, which Millie knew was further north about sixty miles from Penang, and not far from where the Barnet family holidayed.

'Got a couple of days leave owing, and heard that there was some young thing in need of chaperoning, and thought I'd give her the benefit of my company.'

Millie gave him a dig in the ribs. Philip knew of the missionary hospital as he drove Gordon there for emergency treatment to his arm, when he had the accident, due not to the ridiculous story about a tiger but rather it happened while their unit was out on manoeuvres. And it was there that they met Grace and Doctor Elder. But it puzzled Philip to find another English girl so far up-country. It also caused him some concern. He was relieved to know that Millie was only visiting and was going back to Singapore in a week or so. He decided not to say anything about the growing reports of large numbers of Japanese forces landing at Singora and Patani.

The restaurant was as Philip said, all rather civilised, with a very British atmosphere. As if to emphasis the point, the restaurant had a large portrait of the King hung on a wall, which was clearly visible as diners walked through the entrance. On a raised podium, a small band was playing popular dance music. Gradually, more couples were taking to the floor. By the time Millie and Philip finished eating, the waiters had begun to move tables back to make a larger floor space. And soon they had joined the other dancers in a waltz. Millie hadn't been in the least bit bothered about meeting anyone else, but she went along with Grace's arrangement to please her friend. It surprised her then, just how much she liked the company of Philip Hendry. He was tanned, and fit from his spell in the Far East. And he had the bluest eyes Millie had ever seen in a man. She found the sensation very nice, being held in his arms. And after a few more numbers he held her so close that their faces were touching. Once or twice she felt his lips brush the tip of her ear. It was electrifying, and gave her a deliciously warm tingle, all over. Annoyingly, this pleasant mood was shattered by someone banging into a microphone. Philip cursed under his breath, and couples came to a standstill.

'Please, ladies, ladies and gentlemen. Ladies and gentlemen, I must insist on having your attention.' Disconcerted, the musicians hiccupped to a stop, one by one. Festooned in flashes of red and gold braiding, the officer shouted into the microphone, again. 'Ladies and gentlemen, I must have your attention!' The room was sufficiently quiet for him to proceed. 'I am sorry to interrupt your evening, but we have just been given some shocking information. Two ships, I repeat, two ships of His Majesty's Navy, the *Prince of Wales* and *Repulse* have been torpedoed, and sunk by Japanese bombers.' For a few seconds there was a jagged silence. Then the officer announced, 'all military personnel are commanded to return to their units, forthwith.'

Philip cried, 'Christ!' 'Both ships sunk! *The Prince of Wales*! And the veteran cruiser, *Repulse*! I can't believe it.' People were gawping at their partners and then saying virtually the same thing. Once galvanised into action, Philip grabbed Millie's hand. 'Come on. We need to get back to the *Lotus Hotel* to see if Gordon and Grace know about this.' Philip's adrenalin was running high, whether it was the close proximity to Millie or from the fury at hearing of the latest outrage committed by the Japanese, it was difficult to distinguish, though probably it was due to both causes. In spite of that, Philip had to let her know how he felt about her, and he tried to explain. 'Its dammed bad luck our meeting like this, Millie, just when…' He couldn't go on, there were too many bodies pushing and scrabbling to get out. 'Sorry.' He had to give up. 'But-any-anyway, duty calls, and we must get back to Alor Star.'

Once clear of the mass exodus, they thought they could get a taxi, but they were out of luck, they had all gone. They couldn't even grab a rickshaw. There was nothing else for it but to go to the hotel on foot, as fast as they could.

They weren't far from the *Lotus Hotel* when Philip stopped abruptly. He said, 'listen Millie, I've been thinking as we've been going along. You should get back to Singapore as soon as you can.' She frowned. 'I'm serious, Millie. Don't wait until next week or whenever you planned. Things are hotting up pretty fast here. Although there's a great deal of uncertainty as to exactly what's going on, it's damned clear the Japs are getting more and more hostile towards us and the Allies. Believe me, Millie; the situation is not looking good.' By now they reached the steps of the *Lotus Hotel*. Philip took her arm, and said, in a low voice, 'get Grace and the rest of her party to leave as well. The mission station is far too remote and isolated for comfort. God knows what could happen.'

Millie stared at Philip as if he'd gone demented. 'Grace and her family would never leave the mission. They've worked so hard and besides, the hospital, small though it is, has only recently got finished. And my young brothers are having such a good time—'

'You've got your brothers there?' Philip took off his cap and ran his hand through his dark, wavy hair. 'Darling girl, listen to me, get out, and don't delay. Get everyone out and go back to Singapore, for your own and everyone else's safety.'

Millie and Grace arrived at the mission house barely an hour before Doctor Elder and the boys. Their departure from the *Lotus Hotel* was made with such haste that a quick kiss and a few exchanged notes, jotted down on a *Lucky Strike* cigarette packet, were all the personal details Millie had of Captain Philip Hendry. Nevertheless, Millie felt there was something very touching in his concern for her, and then the way that he called her "darling girl", kept echoing in her brain.

The two officers had first to get to a camp a few miles outside Kuala Lumpur to pick up their truck and spares, and then they had to drive the long trek up to their unit near Alor Star. Occurring a few days before the treacherous sinking of the *Prince of Wales* and *Repulse*, men and women of the armed forces serving in Malaysia had barely begun to digest the staggering news of the horrendous bombing attack on the American Fleet at Pearl Harbor. An anxious Philip and Gordon got back in time for an impromptu briefing on the state of the Japanese hostilities. They were given the latest update on the growing numbers of Japanese air attacks on British aerodromes in Northern Malaya. To their growing consternation, the men were also told that the nearest RAF airfield at Kota Bharu had to be evacuated, and was now in the hands of the Japanese army.

*

Meanwhile, the Minister and Mrs Elliott, along with Grace and Millie were all grouped in a little huddle, around the bamboo coffee table that Chinglee had so kindly made for them. While they were mulling over the dreadful events, one of the frequent downpours, fell with such deafening ferocity, that they didn't hear Doctor Elder pull up in the car. It was the sound of his horn tooting that brought everyone out of the house. He knew straight away from their expressions that they had heard about the two ships being sunk. Very gently, so as not to disturb him, Reverend Elliott lifted the still sleeping Archie out of the back seat of the car. Through the rain-soaked night they carried him straight into a bed in the main house. There would be no excited climb of the ladder to the tree house this time. A sullen Clive was comforted, and given a cup of warm, sweet milk. And unduly quiet, he crawled into bed beside his brother, and pulled the sheet right up over his head.

CHAPTER SIX

Just as dawn was breaking, the following morning, a visitor turned up at the Elliott's house. It was a very distraught Mr Barnet. The sparse strands of hair that grew on the pate of this tall, gangly plantation owner, flipped from side to side as he raced about trying to raise someone. Tie-less, and unusually unkempt, his bedraggled appearance gave an indication that he'd not slept in a long time, and in truth, Mr Barnet had not. He had driven like a maniac through the early hours of the morning to reach the mission hospital. Earlier, there had been a frantic rush to shut and secure the Barnet home, on Penang Island. Mr Barnet then gathered up a neighbouring family, and packed them together with Mrs Barnet and the two girls, along with their old amah, onto his motor launch and sent them back to Singapore. It was quite a squeeze with luggage and four adults and three children on Mr Barnet's modestly sized boat. As he left them, they looked clearly shocked, yet his wife bravely waved a miniature Union Jack. The farewell brought a lump to his throat. Whilst Mr Barnet fervently prayed that the neighbouring islander, a capable yachtsman, would get them all safely to Singapore, he tried to banish the possibility of them getting sunk. Unprovoked, the Japanese had inflicted a heavy air raid attack on Georgetown, the island's capital, which resulted in many civilian casualties. Fortunately, their house was on the South side of Penang Island and none of the family or their neighbours were hurt. They were among the lucky ones.

It was so early that only Doctor Elder was up and about, getting ready to make his way to the hospital. He had never met Mr Barnet before and was not prepared for the agitated spectre suddenly confronting him.

'I say', gasped Mr Barnet, with all the coherence he could muster, 'would you mind awfully, giving the Minister and his wife a shout, and-and Millie Chance, of course. She is still here with you?' Without waiting for a reply, he added, 'I know it's frightfully early but you see it is most urgent.'

Doctor Elder hesitated for a second. Everyone had gone to bed so late the previous night he thought to let them rest a bit longer. However, the man before him was clearly familiar with the Elliott family and in his disturbed state the Doctor decided it best to rouse Mr Elliott at once. Except for Clive and Archie, who were fast asleep, everyone else emerged to the sound of the Doctor's knocking. They stumbled out, a might sleep-laden, and still in their night attire and dressing gowns. Millie was the first to speak to Mr Barnet.

'Mr Barnet! What are you doing here? Mr Barnet, whatever is it? What's happened?'

He clutched her arm. 'Millie, I've just come from Penang.' He stared, his eyes wide with fright. 'The Japs have bombed the island. Georgetown was attacked by dozens of fighter planes. The oil refinery has gone up in flames, and petrol depots have been abandoned. Hundreds of civilians have been killed—'

'Mrs Barnet and the children they're not…?'

'No, no, they are alright, thank God. I've sent them back to Singapore. But Millie, I have come to warn you, and everyone. It is too dangerous to stay here.' He let go of Millie's arm and turned to face the others. 'You must all go back to Singapore. Before I left the island I managed to contact your father. Millie, you are to leave at once with your brothers and go home. Those are your father's orders.'

'I-I can't just—'

'Millie, you don't understand. The Japanese are at war with us. They have made us their enemies. You must have heard about Pearl Harbor, and the sinking of our two ships.' Glumly, Millie nodded. 'Well, before our telephone lines were cut, I promised your father that I would drive down here and bring you all back with me to Singapore. Don't you realise it's…no I suppose there was no way anyone could have…no, we had no idea either.' He was beginning to sound confused.

'Mr Barnet, Mr Barnet,' Mrs Elliott interrupted, quickly realising his frail state of mind, 'do come inside, and get a drink and try and tell us exactly what has gone on.'

Millie took his arm and virtually led him into the house. She guided him to a chair and told him, 'now then, Mr Barnet, you sit there, and-and have a nice cup of tea and everything will be alright.'

'You really are a silly, silly girl, Millie!' He shouted at her. 'Everything won't be alright! That's what I'm trying to tell you. It's what I'm trying to tell you all, if only you'd listen. The Japanese have gone power crazy. They are taking over the towns and villages, whole countries, even. They are killing anyone who stands in their way. Man, woman or child, it makes no difference to them.'

His outburst stopped Millie in her tracks. Grace was quick to go to her friend's aid.

'Millie,' she said, 'to be on the safe side why don't you go and get your brothers things together?'

Millie threw Mr Barnet a scathing look as she left the room. Nevertheless, by the time Clive and Archie began to stir from their night's sleep, Millie had their clothes as well as her own garments packed in suitcases, and all her Christmas parcels were gathered up as well. Then to keep them temporarily out of Mr Barnet's way, Millie got the boys a hastily thrown together breakfast. She left them while they were eating and went back towards the main room where everyone was. Pausing at the thin wicker door she could hear a heated discussion going on. Statue-like, Millie held her breath and listened.

She overheard Mrs Elliott say to Grace, 'you must go with Mr Barnet. Millie and the children are our responsibility, Grace. Yes, I know you are concerned about the patients, but we have Chinglee, who is turning out to quite the little medic. And Doctor Elder said that the other two orderlies have shaped up nicely. So, along with me and Daddy, we should manage very well. The Japanese will obviously respect that this is a hospital and will know of the good work that English missionaries do. I'm-I'm confident that they won't bother us. You must—'

A hush fell as Millie creaked opened the door.

'Millie dear, come here,' said Mrs Elliott. 'Now, we have rapidly been making plans while you were out. Mr Barnet has told us…well um… we won't go into that all over again as time is pressing, and um the thing is, we are committed to staying. Mr Elliott and myself, and of course

Doctor Elder is going to remain at the hospital…' Suddenly, much to everyone's surprise, Mrs Elliott started to cry.

The Minister went and tenderly fussed around his wife, concerned at her distress.

Grace kissed her and said, 'there Mummy, there, sit down dear, don't go upsetting yourself. I'll talk to Millie.' Grace opened the door. 'Come on outside for a moment while Mother regains her composure.' She sighed. 'It's very upsetting for them; you know all the work that we've all put in—'

Just then Millie craned her neck and held up her hand. 'Listen! What's that? That's-is it?'

'Oh my-oh my goodness, yes, it is, it sounds like guns and mortar fire. They must be closer than we thought.'

With a gasp, Millie told her friend, 'you don't have to come, Grace, we'll be OK. You are needed here.'

'Millie, it's been decided. And besides, my mother is right, we have to make sure the children are out of harm's way.'

*

Despite better roads, the nearer they got to Singapore, progress slowed down to barely more than a walking pace. Troops and vehicles and civilians arriving from the mainland were clogging up these arteries and adding to the congestion and mayhem. The car engine was overheating and so was Mr Barnet. Grace and Millie were thankful that the Barnet's house was the nearest port of call. It put everyone out of their misery to find his family had arrived safely and unscathed after the boat journey. And once satisfied that no one had come to any harm, Mr Barnet perked up no end while driving Millie and Grace and the boys to the Chances' house. To Grace, and especially Millie's way of thinking, considering how emphatically her father stressed that they should return to Singapore, and in the light of the narrow escape that they'd had, their welcome home seemed strangely restrained. After a formal shake of his sons hands, and a light kiss for Millie, Freddy Chance and Mr Barnet disappeared, along with the whisky decanter, into the study, and they stayed there until Mr

Barnet was ready to go home. Although Millie's mother made more of a fuss of her children, she seemed in no way unduly worried about what was happening on the mainland.

'Well, I know,' said Mrs Chance, a little later, 'it's hardly what one might call a storm in a tea cup, what with Pearl Harbor and the sinking of our two ships, but we have no need to worry, those little yellow men will never get across the Jahore Strait.'

'Mrs Chance,' said Grace, trying not to sound impatient, 'I must get back to the mission hospital.'

'My dear, there is plenty of time for that. Take a few days off. Go shopping with Millie. She'd like nothing better. Isn't that right, Millie?'

Millie looked somewhat incredulously at her mother.

'No, really, thank you, Mrs Chance, I must return, as soon as I can.'

'Oh well, just as you wish, dear.'

CHAPTER SEVEN

They were never to see Grace, or her father, the Minister, again. Instead, a few weeks later, it was a broken-hearted Mrs Elliott that the Chance family took into their Singapore home, once more. And for the two whole days before Christmas, under the care of Doctor Elder, Mrs Elliott remained heavily sedated. Unlike the previous year, at the Chances' household, this was a very different Yule-Tide, and one that was without cheer or merriment, and, some felt, even hope.

It took some time before the usually calm and mild mannered Doctor Elder could communicate fully the whole tragic series of events that caused the deaths of Grace, and Mr Elliott.

At one point Mrs Chance screamed, 'we should have stopped her! We shouldn't have let her return!'

Amid floods of tears, Millie screamed back, 'be quiet, Mother!'

Trying to keep control, Freddy Chance told him, 'if you'd rather, Doctor Elder, it can wait until tomorrow.'

'No, no I've got my second wind, and Mrs Elliott is dead to the world. And after the horrors that we've both had to witness, bed's the best place for her, right now.'

'Here, Doctor Elder, would you like—'

With a grateful nod he took the brandy glass from Millie. After a swig he began to relate the happenings of the previous few days.

'Ha,' he began cynically, 'we thought we'd be OK, especially Mrs Elliott. We all assumed as it's a hospital, we'd not come to any harm, and our patients would be protected. We knew Japan was not part of the Geneva Convention, but we never dreamed…' He finished the brandy in one gulp, silent for a minute. 'Grace told us she'd had the devil of a struggle to get to the mission, but we were all so relieved and happy to see her. She wasted no time in changing and getting into the hospital.

One of the women was about to give birth and it was a difficult one, a breech you see. Grace was marvellous, so gentle, and so patient. That all went well, baby fine, and so too was the mother. But after the birth, they wouldn't stay. We tried to persuade the villagers to get the mother to rest for a few days, but she was frightened, they all were, all the patients, and not just in maternity. They didn't say it in so many words, but they felt vulnerable, we could tell. The ones who were not seriously ill, fled with their families to their villages, and some took to the hills. They were scared, so scared of the Japanese. They had heard terrible stories, well, so had we, but we tried to tell them otherwise, tried to calm their fears. It didn't do much good, they left just the same.' His shoulders slumped. 'Only the three patients, who were too sick to move, remained in their beds.'

While he was struggling to get his thoughts in order, Millie refilled his brandy glass. Momentarily distracted, he traced circles round the rim before setting the glass down. Then screwing up his eyes he ploughed onward.

'It is a strange thing in a way, for we watched, cool as you like, as the Japanese planes flew overhead. They seemed to be heading in the direction of Penang. We knew the fighting was getting close, it even got so that we could distinguish between our guns and theirs. Then we caught our first sighting of the Japs. Chinglee called me to the high ridge above the hospital.' He turned to Millie. 'You know where I mean, Millie, you and the boys climbed up that way many times.' Millie nodded. 'Chinglee said there was an artillery detachment making its way through the jungle. He was scared stiff, poor boy. I should have paid more attention to his distress, thinking back to how the Japs treated the Chinese, back 1937. He said we should all go, leave, before they came. He was warning me, but foolishly I was transfixed. They laid these sorts of duckboard things, down on the floor of the jungle while their troops manhandled huge guns across them, with nothing more than brute force. I watched through my binoculars to see there were men carrying bicycles. There were whole lines of Japanese soldiers carrying bikes through dense jungle undergrowth. It really was the weirdest thing.'

Puzzled, Mr Chance said, 'bikes?'

'Yes!'

No one said anything more, just waited until the Doctor was ready to continue. It surprised them all to be told what happened next.

'I wasn't expecting it, but the next thing I knew the binoculars were knocked from my hands, and I was shoved into Archie and Clive's hide-hole.' He looked again at Millie. 'You remember the one they built while they were out playing that time. Anyway, once inside, what did Chinglee do, he tied me up and gagged me. I couldn't understand it. I thought, what's he up to, how could he do such a thing? But you know he saved my life. He might have gone about it in a muddled sort of way but he knew what he was doing, and he knew what the Japs were capable of, not like us stupid, gullible English missionaries.'

Mrs Chance started to sob. Millie gave her a glass of brandy. 'Here, Mother,' she said, gently.

'I'm not sure exactly how long I sat there strung up. Then, suddenly the sacking covering the den was flung back and Mrs Elliott was thrown in alongside me. She could barely get a word out before Chinglee was tying her up too.'

'My good God!' Freddy Chance exclaimed, loudly. 'The rotten bloody swine!'

'No, you don't understand, Freddy. He was trying to save us falling into Japanese hands.'

'What! Well, I-I, well what happened next?'

'I think his idea was to get us all up there, Grace the Minister and… but there just wasn't time. From where we were hidden we could hear the enemy approaching the mission. We didn't know what was going on. We were tied up too tightly to wriggle free. Then, we heard two shots ring out. I can't say how long it was, but we began to smell burning. There were several explosions, followed by an eerie quiet. All we could do was to wait. I expected to see a Jap soldier when the sacking was thrown back. I thanked God, it was Chinglee. Poor fellow, I think he was half out of his mind. At first I couldn't understand a word he was saying. He was chattering in Cantonese, and at the same time his teeth were chattering as he was untying Mrs Elliott. She was released first and was about to box him round the ears until she went outside. He tried to stop her but she ran down towards the hospital. Then he got round to undoing me. This time I made sure he spoke in English. How I wish he hadn't for he told me,' Doctor Elder swallowed hard, 'he told me that they had shot Grace and her father and decapitated our two orderlies.' At hearing these graphic details Millie gave painfully choking gasps, and a horrible animal-like howl broke forth from Mrs Chance. The Doctor didn't stop; he daren't, he had to get it all out. 'As for the hospital, we don't know exactly what happened to the three sick patients. But before the Japs left they set the hospital alight. We suspected the worst, and you don't have to use too much imagination to draw your own conclusions as to the fate of our last few patients.'

Millie knew she should have been comforting her mother, but at that moment in time, she was too caught up in her own grief to have any crumb of compassion left to spare for anyone.

Just then, her father asked, 'how, I mean, if you can, if you are alright to go on, can you tell us how you and Mrs Elliott and the boy—'

'Chinglee, you mean?'

'Yes, that's right, Chinglee. How did you manage to get past the soldiers?'

'There was nothing else that Chinglee could do for Grace or her father. The Japs had already seized them by the time he got off the ridge, and so he hid and waited. It was as if it was all in a day's work for those murderers, for they just passed through. Apart from taking all our food supplies they cleared out, and never stopped to hang around once their dastardly work was finished. Chinglee told us he thought they were heading in the direction of Kuala Lumpur.' Doctor Elder held his hand to his brow. 'It was a terrible sight for us to come upon. Oh dear God, that poor, poor Mrs Elliott. We said we would bury Grace and Mr Elliott but she said she needed to help, it was her loved ones. We didn't argue with her. Grim and tragic though it was, we let her do that last final thing for them. Chinglee and I tended to the bodies of the orderlies, poor souls. That was something we could not let Mrs Elliott do. I never witnessed such an atrocious act in all my life. And it felt like I had peered into the evil, putrefying abyss of hell.'

Shocked, Mr Chance cleared his throat. 'Ahem-ahem. Doctor Elder, where did our chaps pick you up?'

'Aye?' Um yes. Well of course the Japs stole Mr Elliott's car so we had to start out on foot. Chinglee said he saw an officer commandeer the vehicle and was driving it, triumphantly away. There were people that Mrs Elliott knew three or four miles south of the mission and we headed in that direction. It was slow going, and our route took us through some dense rubber plantations. Poor Mrs Elliott looked all in and we often had to rest. And our nerves were strained in case any other Jap patrols were about. So when we heard the sound of a lorry behind us we had to get off the track pretty sharpish. As luck would have it, it was one of ours. Instantly, I recognised the young man who climbed down. It was Captain McGregor, Gordon. We treated him when he came in injured, some months ago. Grace liked him…'

Hearing the name McGregor seemed to shake Millie out of her moroseness, and she went and knelt at the Doctor's side.

She dried her red and swollen eyes, and asked, 'McGregor, did you say Gordon McGregor?'

'Yes, that's right. Actually it was Grace who stitched up a bad gash to his arm.'

'Was-was there any other officers, was there a-a Captain Hendry with him?'

'No Millie. There were five RAF chaps in the back of the open top lorry, and some English women, who were trying to get to Singapore. Captain McGregor had orders to pick up any waifs and strays and get them to Singapore, with all haste. He told me he had intelligence reports that the Japanese army were advancing towards Kuala Lumpur. Captain McGregor purposely made a detour to assist in the evacuation of the mission.'

'Did he see—?'

Doctor Elder answered, unable to hold back the bitterness.

'Oh yes Millie, he saw. He saw the burnt out hospital and the burnt out shell of the house. Oh yes, he witnessed the fathomless barbarity of those Japanese soldiers. He saw the devastation, and how our whole project got wiped out in one fell swoop.' Exhaustion was beginning to show on the brave Doctor. Quieter now, he told Millie, 'he was dreadfully cut up, poor fellow. But it was when he found the freshly dug graves, with the names of Grace and Mr Elliott and the orderlies, carved on rough crosses, Captain McGregor knew he was too late.'

Doctor Elder wrapped his arm around Millie, as her head fell on his knee.

CHAPTER EIGHT

Travelling for what seemed like hours, on a very slow train, Flight Lieutenant Christopher Elliott arrived in the London borough of Stoke Newington. He was enveloped in an aura of happy anticipation. Feeling immensely grateful to escape the sleeting snow, he stamped his frozen feet at the entrance of a small block of flats, not far from the open space of Clissold Park. Then bounding, expectantly, up the stairs, two at a time he went to the window at the end of the landing. He hesitated, fractionally, to take in a gloomy picture of bombed-out homes. The sight threw up an alien landscape which resembled a jigsaw with some of the pieces missing. Tatters of once private wallpaper now exposed to the world, fluttered, pathetically in surrender. It shocked him, as it was just a month ago that he stood in exactly the same spot admiring a perfect piece of architectural magnificence—a fine crescent of Georgian houses. Now they too had become victims, deformed and broken wrecks amongst the growing debris of war.

Yet glancing along the street, in the opposite direction, Christopher had to admire the salvage and clearance squads. Often drawn from the ranks of the unemployed, they were toughened men of the Pioneer Corps. He could see them, hard at work amid the chaos of an earlier raid. And due to their colossal effort, they managed to keep roads clear for people to get to work. They were also in part responsible for ensuring the continued running of the red London buses. And beneath a fragile veil of quasi-normality, black taxi cabs still conducted the lucrative business of lifting fares.

The elevated height of the flats gave him a sense of being in the air. Only a couple of nights ago, he'd flown with his squadron of Avro Lancaster bombers. Their mission was to ensure the accuracy of the hundreds of tons of bombs that got dropped on the heavy industrialised region along the Rhur Valley. Aimed at the heart of the German war industry, in its wake, this type of strategic bombing undoubtedly caused the deaths of countless civilians. So Christopher knew he was, in part, responsible for a similar picture in Germany. He shuddered, involuntarily. Coming from a Christian background his actions held significant poignancy and he tried to shake off the reality of such inhuman actions. Turning away, he felt for a key at the bottom of the aspidistra pot. At the same moment, he couldn't help but smile as he tweaked its drooping leaves, weighed down with paper chain decorations. She'd told him, the tenant on the ground floor, who was an experienced gardener, called the aspidistra the Cast Iron Plant, because of its ability to withstand neglect, draughts and shade. Well, he felt all of that was undoubtedly true. Two panes of glass had got blown clean out, and this side of the flat was practically always in semi-darkness. And its soil was as dry as his mouth felt at this moment. But the plant served its purpose, admirably, and kept their secret wonderfully hidden. Retrieving the key, Christopher opened the door and let himself in. He called out, expectantly, 'anyone home?' There was no reply. Slightly downcast, he picked up the post and without glancing at the letters he tossed them, along with his gas mask and cap, on a table, and made for the kitchen.

The small functional, but pleasant enough kitchen had the basics: gas cooker, sink, table and chairs and a painted pale blue cupboard was fitted between the sink and another door that led into the bathroom. Christopher bent down and opened the cupboard. Inside was a poorly stocked larder, bordering on what some might call starvation rations. A tin of spiced ham looked at him, as did two tins of Heinz soup. The lid of a jar of marmite dangled from its rim like the broken neck of a hung-man. He shook a packet of dried peas and said, aloud, 'God, in heavens name, what does the girl eat?' Reaching over to the other side, behind some teacups and various items of crockery, he took out a tumbler and a bottle of whiskey. It was the same bottle that he's bought, under the counter, last time he was in London. Pouring a generous measure, he took the drink into a larger, more airy room.

Feeling unsettled, he walked round the furniture, twice. The lounge was neat and tidy apart from newspapers strewn across the sofa. Seeing them that way, he assumed she'd left in a hurry. There was the odd china vase which got filled when he remembered to buy flowers, and a few Christmassy ornaments were arranged on a low table beside the telephone. Though it was comfortable, on the whole it was an impersonal, room, not really what he would call overly feminine. Her bedroom, however, was quite the opposite. He went in. A flimsy negligee draped itself over a fuchsia pink-padded chair. This unexpected image of erotica stirred a desperate longing between his loins, and he stroked his hand along the length of the gossamer material. Her fragrant perfume floated in the air, seductively, while an array of scent bottles, and hair brushes and combs almost covered the surface of a dressing table. A soft, fluffy powder puff had tumbled out of the compact, spilling some of the powder. Thoughtfully, he replaced it in its box. Then in the sweet-smelling dust, he romantically traced an arrow pierced heart and the letters J and C. A wardrobe door lay open revealing a plethora of sensuous gowns and clothes. He checked his wrist watch then sucked his teeth, impatiently, and turned on his heel. The flat wasn't the same without her.

There was another bedroom which was kept locked. He understood this to be merely a store room, but in a fit of annoyance he rapped his knuckles on it. He cursed her for being late. She knew how little time he had, how little time they both had, when it came to it. Instantly, he was ashamed for he realised how important her work was. All at once an image of his father flashed through his mind. He couldn't account for the reason and he suddenly went cold. Feeling in his pocket for matches he lit the gas fire. It coughed and coughed until it spluttered into life. He considered there must once have been coal burnt in the grate, though by the looks, the chimney had been blocked up for some time. Probably can't get the coal, he decided. He rested his hand on the marble mantelpiece then drew away quickly. Its touch added to the chill of the room. He loosened his tie in front of the mirror and flicked back the blond strands of hair that had strayed out of place. A ticking clock kept accurate time, while a pair of tarnished silver candlesticks stood sentry-like either side. These were the only decorative items here. Then his glance fell to where something was resting behind the time piece. Curious, he slid it out and saw that it was a greetings card with a view of Singapore. He turned it over and read it. It was written last June, six months ago. Then he remembered when he saw the signature, of course, the school friend, Millie.

Christopher gathered up the newspapers and put them in a pile on the floor, then sank down on the sofa to finish his whiskey. His thoughts strayed again to his parents, and Grace, away in some bloody God forsaken spot, somewhere in Malaysia. His father had admonished Christopher for taking the Lord's name in vain when he referred to Malaysia as a bloody God forsaken spot. He felt he was a disappointment to his father who had wanted him to go into the Ministry. But he had his own views on religion, and rather arrogantly, he'd told his father that he couldn't pretend, even for the family's sake. On this topic, there were sometimes, heated arguments between Christopher and his father. His mother, wisely, said little, while Grace, dear darling Grace, she was the peacemaker. She would smooth things over, and all would be well. Yawning and feeling warmer now, he stretched out and stuck a cushion behind his head and gave in to the tiredness that was creeping over him.

A well trained eye enabled Janet Marsh to observe that her arrangement of paper chains had been disturbed, and had fallen from the aspidistra plant. Being on the top level of the flats, only the postman had any reason to come along the landing and occasionally, Olive. Of the six flats, just four were occupied. The flat adjacent to Janet's had suffered damage when a bomb fell nearby. Apart from doing remedial repairs, the landlord had not got round to putting any other tenant in. This suited Janet, and with the irregular hours, that she kept, she rarely saw the neighbours. The flat immediately below was empty, and the one on the ground floor was let to two elderly spinster sisters. A Mr Young, the gardener, who was in a reserved occupation, and worked on the railway, rented the flat opposite the elderly spinster ladies. The only other tenant was a war widow, Mrs Unwin, or Olive as she preferred Janet to call her. Her husband, who had been in the army, was killed during the evacuation of Dunkirk. They had no children and Janet had felt rather sorry for her. Olive was only a little older than Janet and out of pity Janet had struck up an acquaintance by asking her on the odd occasion to the cinema or a concert. The young widow woman snapped up the invitation to accompany Janet on these outings. And seeing no harm in it, Janet was glad she had been able to do her another good turn by offering the spare bedroom for Olive to use as storage.

Leaning her dripping umbrella underneath the window ledge she replaced the fallen Christmas decorations. She just hadn't had time to get a Christmas tree and the chains were the best bit of festive cheer she could come up with. Plonking down a bag of groceries on the floor, Janet began searching in her handbag for the door key. When this was found she was careful to cover up a long heavy implement. When she got the chance, she would hide it in its usual place—behind the gas meter—out of Christopher's sight. In spite of being a little nervous to get the device away, she opened the door excitedly. What with his ops, and her work, this was the first time in four weeks that their leave had coincided. Then Janet saw his familiar cap and gas mask box. The flat was quiet, too quiet, not even the radio was playing. She peeped round the door of the lounge and with a relieved sigh she found Christopher spark-out on the sofa. She took her groceries into the kitchen and wrapping a cloth around her weapon she stuffed it behind the gas meter. The next thing she did was to fill the kettle. While she waited for the water to boil she went round each window to comply with the blackout regulation, and as quietly as she could, she drew the curtains. She hadn't bargained on the kettle boiling so fast and its screaming whistle woke a startled Christopher.

'Sorry, sorry darling,' Janet cooed over Christopher's pink face. 'I didn't want to wake you. I meant to take the whistler off the kettle. Sorry, forgot, force of habit. Anyway, now you're awake, happy, happy Christmas, darling.'

He drew her down, into his arms and kissed her, passionately.

CHAPTER NINE

They were glad to see the back of Christmas, 1941. It came with great sorrow and went in much the same way. And such was the heartache that many of Millie's presents that she had so carefully chosen, whilst happily shopping in Kuala Lumpur, remained unopened and forgotten. She did try to make an effort for Archie and Clive's sake, they all did, but the hurt was too raw and the loss for poor Mrs Elliott too great for any remote desire to celebrate. And without her friend, Grace to share it with, even Millie's excellent exam results brought no enthusiasm for rejoicing.

The earlier fall of Penang on December 18th saw growing numbers of civilians and Australian and British troops flooding into Singapore. Terrified casualties caught up in Japanese bombing raids, quickly filled up beds and vacant floor spaces in medical institutions. Doctor Elder wasted no time in offered his services at the hospital where Millie worked. He was assured by desperate and short-handed staff that in spite of his age, they were very glad to have him with them, and he was thankful to be needed. For the work helped to keep his mind from constantly reliving the horror of that mindless, though nonetheless evil slaughter.

It was on January 11th, and Millie had just started back into her second year of nursing training when the grim news came through that the Japanese had captured Kuala Lumpur. For the army and the colonial population as well as native Singaporeans, this additional loss brought intense panic, and disbelief at the speed with which the enemy were advancing. Mrs Chance's flippantly, ignorant boast, that the little yellow men would never cross the Johore Strait, now struck an empty note with a cord that was beginning to sound less and less in tune with reality.

In the boardroom at his place of work, Freddy Chance had had a lengthy meeting with officials and the directors of the Straits Shipping

Company. The impromptu gathering was to discuss the hitherto unthinkable prospect of a Japanese invasion of their island. One or two of the old staunch die-hards tended to dismiss out of hand, even at this late stage, the possibility of 'Fortress' Singapore succumbing to an invasion by what they considered an inferior army, from the land of The Rising Sun. However, Mr Chance shook them all up by giving a first hand account of the evidence, as he saw it. Afterwards, when the meeting ended, and without consulting his wife, Freddy Chance set in motion plans for evacuating the family, which included the newly widowed, Mrs Elliott. Because there was no time to waste Mr Chance drove directly to the hospital to see his daughter. When Millie was told of her father's arrangements she was seething.

'You have absolutely no right, Father, to—'

'In this instance, Millie, I have every right.' He spoke with an air of authority which he rarely used on his children.

Intimidated by his stern attitude, Millie backed down a little, then told him, 'Father, I am needed at the hospital.'

'You are needed with the family, Millie. I know your mother well enough to realise that she will never be able to cope with the boys on her own, on such a long and dangerous journey back to England. And then there's Mrs Elliott. Look at the state she's in, poor soul. She'll need a great deal of care if she is ever to recover from what has happened to her.'

'But Father, what about you and Doctor Elder. You'll be with us and—?'

'No Millie, that's just it, we won't.'

'What! Who won't? Doctor Elder? Don't be silly, of course you both will. If things look so bad then you can't possibly stay.' She watched the expression on her father's face. 'Father, you and the Doctor can't stay behind. I-we-we won't go. We most definitely won't go without you; it's as straight forward as that.'

Freddy Chance couldn't fail to take in the stubborn tilt of his daughter's chin. In any other circumstance she would have had him laughing and giving in, but not this time.

'Listen to me, Millie. Every able-bodied man in Singapore, must stand up and be counted. Take the old Doctor, for instance, he's at the hospital every day, mending broken bones and performing operations and God knows what. Many of my colleagues have joined the ARP and the auxiliary services. We-I too have to do my bit. The island must be protected, the shipping company must be protected, and-and...' he considered for a moment if he should tell her. 'We've heard on the grape vine that General Wavell has orders from Churchill that he must defend Singapore to the death. Which means surrender can not be contemplated. My God,' he mopped his brow with a handkerchief, 'there are even plans to execute a scorched-earth policy.'

'Oh Father, no!' Millie threw her arms around her father's neck.

'There, there now, where's my brave girl?' He held her now at arms length and stole a moment to appreciate the transformation of his beautiful daughter. Gone was the wayward teenager, Millie had matured into a spectacularly confident young lady. Freddy Chance took a deep breath. 'It's doubtful, well let's say hardly likely that it will come to that. However, in the light of the worst happening, the Board of Directors has agreed that passage to England will be a priority for the families of senior British staff. I shall need you to be strong. It is a lot of responsibility to take on your shoulders, but I know you can do it.'

Ships leaving Singapore harbour did so without air protection. Flown by the RAF, until recently, the old Brewster Buffalo fighter aircraft was a stubby-looking, chunky plane, with poor manoeuvrability. But disastrously, because they lacked speed, they were quickly shot down by the faster Japanese Zeros and Nakajima or as the British knew it, the 'Oscar'. Terrified families lining the quayside had watched in horror as two ships carrying British women and children got blown out of the water by Japanese bombers. These aircraft took off from across the causeway that separated Singapore from Malaya. Zeros and Oscars would circle the waters around the harbour and inlets, waiting like sharks, to dive in for the kill. And worse, much worse was the fate of the hospital ships. Marked clearly with red crosses, they made easy targets for the Jap pilots, who without conscience, sank and killed all on board—regardless.

At the Chance's residence, what started out to be fairly composed preparations for leaving, soon turned into a franticly desperate rush to get aboard, what was understood to be the last boat sailing out of Singapore. Mrs Chance, unable to take in the implications or the seriousness of their predicament left it far too late to get herself organised. Unavoidably, Freddy Chance had to dash back to his office. There was a last minute matter which he had to attend to. He knew he'd not be gone for very long, taking comfort in the knowledge that they'd be all packed and ready by the time he'd come back. He had to collect some documents from the safe for Millie to take with her to England. What he returned to was a dithering wife trying to decide which shoes to take and which to leave behind. An air of vagueness still clung to poor Mrs Elliott and she simple scooped up an armful of garments, dumped them in a single suitcase and closed the lid. As far as Mr Chance and Millie were concerned, she at least was ready.

Millie had been preoccupied with her two brothers and her own packing, to have got round to helping her mother. Fortunately, she was almost done when her father arrived. Freddy Chance was beside himself when he saw how little progress his wife had made. Getting near the point of exasperation he fled from her dressing room.

'Millie,' he cried, 'in heavens name! Do something with your mother, please. I've just looked in and she is nowhere near ready. This really is too bad. Doesn't she realise…can you go and sort her out? And Millie,' he was beginning to get desperate, 'if we don't get to the docks within the next half hour, it will be too late.'

Millie took charge and gave the order, 'boys, go and take mother into the kitchen and fill a thermos flask. Then make plenty of sandwiches to take with us.'

Archie asked, 'can we take biscuits and—'

'Yes, yes, anything you like, just hurry up. Hurry! For goodness sake, get a spurt on, Clive. And you too, Archie, do buck up your ideas.'

It took Millie precisely six minutes to fill a suitcase and hold-all for her mother. Then throwing the entire luggage into the boot, and with the lid slammed thunderously shut, Mr Chance finally drove off. He put his foot down on the accelerator so hard, that he sent the locals scurrying out of his way. And at times the passengers held their breath when they were only inches from tipping over into the monsoon ditches.

Unfortunately, Millie and her father's all out efforts were not enough, they were too late. As the car speed towards the ship, a change of gear at the top of a hill slowed them down, and allowed them enough view of the harbour to see that their endeavours were all to no avail. They could only watch, aghast, as the gangplank was hauled up. And within minutes the ship had set sail.

Driving aimlessly through the harbour, if the Chances had but noticed there were dozens of wealthy Eurasians, who had been milling around for days in the hope of securing a passage—to anywhere that would take them off the island. All were very well dressed and respectable looking. Despite their affluent persona the terrible truth finally dawned. They realised they hadn't a hope in hell of getting on board a vessel. Precedence was, of course, given to the colonials. The fate of these Eurasians looked sealed. Clearly, the island of Singapore would very soon be at the mercy of a far less lenient, or humane invader than the British.

Millie sat in the front seat, feeling totally miserable. It surprised her then that instead of driving back to the bungalow, her father took the narrow side streets away from the harbour that lead up to his office. In due course he drove through the familiar stone-pillared archway that opened out onto a fan shaped series of spice and jute and grain warehouses. He pulled up sharply, jolting them forward.

'Wait here,' he said, sternly. 'Clive and Archie stay in the car, and don't get out. Do you understand?' They nodded, obediently. 'Millie, come with me.'

The car doors closed on a sobbing Mrs Chance. Millie had to run to keep up with her father. She was about to ask him what he was going to do, but thought better of it, and kept silent. They climbed two flights of stairs, and then Mr Chance flung open the first door he came to.

'Freddy! Freddy, what the hell...' A startled Mr Jones saw Millie behind her father. 'I thought the family would be long gone.'

Without going into detail, Mr Chance asked, 'Thomas, can you help us? We—' he gulped, 'they couldn't get on the ship. I-I'm really stumped now for what to do to get them away. Is there anything else left?'

'Um, er, well I-no.' He looked doubtful. 'Everything that we have has gone, Freddy.'

'Is there nothing, man?'

'No, we don't have a thing. But, but,' he scratched his beard. Rising from his desk Thomas Jones looked hard across the harbour. 'Wait a minute. I got something in this morning.' As the man shuffled some papers Freddy Chance loosened his tie. 'It's the old *Dover Castle*. She's tried to get out once but had to come back, just last week. Engine problems, I gather. Hem, oh dear, she's not in her prime, um, she's well past it actually.'

'Is she sea worthy?'

'Sea worthy enough, I should think. She's had a quick refit and she should at least make it to India. From there your family could either stay put till the dust settles, or they can transfer to another ship that'll get them to England.'

Freddy Chance breathed a sigh of relief. 'Thanks, Thomas. When does she sail?'

'I'll need to make a few phone calls. Come into the other office and I'll look at some charts at the same time.' He nodded to Millie now crouched in a corner and asked automatically, 'hello Millie, how are you?'

'Hello, Mr Jones,' she said, flatly. Mr Jones, she remembered, was the gentleman that her mother had spoken to about an office job when she first arrived in Singapore.

Once a couple of phone calls were made, Freddy Chance was told, 'Captain Bristow will slip anchor and get away under cover of darkness, tonight.'

'Did you say tonight?'

'That's right. Captain Bristow said there's no way that they can make it in daylight with the Nips patrolling the waters. His old tug is too slow, and he reckons its suicide to try until it gets dark. So, all I can suggest is that you get your family over to the bay and get them on the ship as soon as you can. It could be their last chance.'

CHAPTER TEN

Janet Marsh spat out a mouthful of dry toast in order to let out the loud expletive, 'Oh bloody, bloody hell!' Holding in her hand was the only letter to arrive in the post, all week. So on seeing a postage stamp from India, her curiosity she was greatly aroused. However, a little way into the missive it dawned on her exactly who it was that had sent it. Then curiosity turned to hard, cold panic. Snatching at a page to establish the date only brought forth a further, 'Oh my…sod, sod, sod.' Instinctively she looked towards the bedroom. Unlocking the door didn't help. It just made her gasp and she slammed it closed. She strode into the other bedroom and began to hastily throw on some clothes. All the while she was making calculations. Allowing for the long journey back to England the family should be…Janet froze. The jumper was stuck in mid-air halfway over her head as she counted. She realised her friend could be in England, no London—already! Janet's thought was that's put the bloody cat among the bloody pigeons.

*

Millie Chance had indeed arrived in London. The passage from Singapore had been fraught with danger practically every nautical mile. The journey started without incident. The old sea dog, Captain Bristow, had, miraculously, under the very nose of the Japanese patrol boats, safely steered the *Dover Castle* out of the harbour. With skilful navigation, Captain Bristow hugged the coast line like a favourite overcoat, for as long as he could. When the land disappeared, he ordered full-steam ahead and pointed his ship out into the open sea. As far as Millie remembered that probably was the only stretch that went without a hitch. Once out of reach of the land, her mother succumbed to the most dreadful bout of sea sickness. To the unaccustomed Mrs Chance, the ever present fumes and rank smell of oil that an old boat gives off did nothing to ease the plight of the wretched traveller. Their friend, Mrs Elliott helped Millie to tend to her needs; however, it fell on Millie's shoulders, once again to provide for her brothers welfare. And in so doing Millie noticed a change in them, at first she couldn't quite put her finger on what it was. She thought possibly it could be due to everything they had all gone through. And the shock had somehow dulled their spirits, dulled their very souls, even, more than she thought, for the lads had grown really quiet. They both appeared more amenable. And Archie was definitely more willing and really quite biddable in most things, and there were virtually no grumbles from Clive. There was another thing that Millie noted; Clive had become very protective towards Archie. She recollected he even went so far as to stuff Archie's toy soldiers safely into the tin box, before they left Singapore. She wondered, was it possibly all to do with the difficult and insecure business of growing up?

The *Dover Castle* was never designed to carry passengers; she was an ancient and well-worked cargo ship, a camel of the sea that had spent all her life ferrying freight across the oceans. So the passengers that Captain Bristow had kindly granted permission to come aboard, had to put up with makeshift quarters as best they could. Nevertheless, no one complained, not even Mrs Chance, they were only too thankful to be escaping from the jaws of a terrible enemy.

For a time, the crew was very edgy, on account of still being within range of the Japanese fighter planes. Then to everyone's great consternation, on the second day out, the captain gave the order to stop engines. Milling about among the ship's ropes and tackle, the boys were the first to discover what was going on. Then spotting the boys nearby, Captain Bristow barked out orders to them. Obeying, Clive and Archie fled below to tell Millie and Mrs Elliott to get blankets and any medical supplies that they could lay their hands on, and then come with all haste on deck. It soon became apparent as to why the *Dover Castle* had suddenly cut her engines. The first mate had seen a life-raft drifting on the port bow with men on it, waving. The Captain made the decision to stop and pick up survivors. It wasn't an easy task. A scrambling net was lowered over the side for those that could climb unassisted; only two sailors were able to haul themselves up by that means. There were two other badly injured sailors and three soldiers who looked in poor shape. The Captain was later to learn that these men were the only survivors from a Royal Navel patrol boat that was torpedoed by the Japanese. Getting the injured on board proved difficult. A hastily cobbled together stretcher had to be lowered, and a large basket used for lugging produce, lifted the rest of the men up. While the *Dover Castle's* crew was working flat out to get the survivors out of the sea, Captain Bristow grew ever anxious, constantly scanning the horizon through his binoculars. After what seemed an eternity, the ship got under way.

Little Archie willingly fetched and carried, for whoever asked him, Clive arranged tea and Millie treated the injured servicemen as best she could. They had no morphine on the ship. All that could be found in the way of stopping pain was aspirin. Along with rum, it had to do. There was no doctor on the ship, so the Captain was relying on Millie's expertise. As she had been taught, she made a quick assessment of the most seriously injured, and they were treated first. Some were covered in oil and one of the sailors died the instant he was hauled up. When blown into the water his lungs became filled with the oil slick that seeped on the surface. There was nothing anyone could have done for him to prevent his death. It was still shocking and heartbreaking for Millie, and the others to witness. Another young sailor was also smothered in oil and although deeply shocked, he appeared to have no other physical injuries. Millie was quietly confident he would survive, with careful nursing.

It was while she was going from one man to another, issuing instructions and treating her patients as best she could, that a low mumbling began to distract her. She forced herself to focus on applying a dressing to a soldier's burnt arm. Once this was done she finished off by bandaging the whole arm. Disconcertingly, the utterance persisted.

Shaping itself into a voice, a word broke forth from the incoherent babble.

'Milliepead,' it called, no louder than the capricious sound of the wind. She raised her head and took stock. It came again, stronger, 'Millipead.'

Millie turned and blinked in bewilderment. At first, all she could see among a heap of bodies were members of the crew, moving in and out of the injured. The first mate had found a can of industrial oil cleanser. He was going round inspecting each man's condition. Then dipping rags soaked in the solvent he gently rubbed the oil stained skin of each casualty. He was kneeling beside a soldier, making circular movements over the man's head and face. The soldier held out a limp hand in Millie's direction.

She screwed up her eyes. 'Philip? Philip, is that you?'

'Millie!'

Millie nearly fainted at the shock of Philip's presence. He was barely recognisable, but with the efforts of the first mate the oil has gradually got loosened off. He was exhausted though spirited enough to give her a faint smile.

'Philip, just rest now, and let me look at you—'

'Darling Millie,' he whispered, 'you can look at me any time.'

In spite of it all, he still had that endearing, chirpy sense of humour, and it brought a lump to Millie's throat. She ran her hands over his body looking for broken bones. He moved his arms and legs when she asked.

'Philip, I don't think you have broken anything. Do you have any pain?'

He answered, wearily, 'no, I'm OK, just a bit tired. We've been in the sea for—' he stopped to think, 'I guess it must be a couple of days. I don't know how the Nips didn't see our raft. They would have finished us off if they had, the bloody evil bastards.'

Millie didn't want to tax him, so she told him, 'you rest now, and we'll catch up with things later. And I need to see to these others. Here's something to help you get some sleep.' She took the tot of rum from the first mate and watched while Philip drank it down. He coughed, yet Millie was relieved to see he'd not brought up any oil. This was a good sign that his lungs were clean.

As if Captain Bristow hadn't enough problems to contend with when the helmsman shouted, 'mines! Mines ahead on the starboard bow!'

Seamen ran to starboard and the Captain shouted his orders down to the engine room. Every breath was held as the ship approached dangerously close to the deadly sea porcupines. Suddenly a tremendous explosion threw up great spews of water, drenching those unlucky seamen by the rail. One of the mines had hit the abandoned raft as the waves floated it away. But, alarmingly, another mine was getting sucked ever closer to the ship. They all stared, mesmerised as the mine was about to bump the ship's helm. They tensed themselves for the inevitable bang. Then to everyone's huge relief the ship turned just in time for the swell to sweep the mine out of the ship's path. For the next few hours everyone except the ladies, took turns on watch, even Clive and Archie stood alongside the crew. Only when it was deemed safe did the boys stand down from their post. They underwent a good deal of back slapping from the crew and got kisses from Millie.

Over the next few days Millie had her hands full with her first aid and nursing duties. Mrs Elliott came and assisted when she could. Then Millie got help from an unexpected source—her mother. Mrs Chance had recovered well enough from the spell of sickness to be of some use now. By giving assistance in this way it freed up Millie's time so that she could talk more to Philip.

'We've suffered a terrible loss,' he told Millie, dejectedly, 'poor old Singapore.'

She knew their island had fallen to the Japanese, but she couldn't understand why it happened.

'Philip,' she asked, 'how-how in God's name, was it possible?'

'How? That is what will be chewed over and over, probably for years to come.'

'Everyone said Singapore was impregnable. And-and all those guns that we had along the coast line. We'd go and look at them. I'd take Clive and Archie down to the sea—'

'Yes, Millie, and all the guns were pointing *out* to sea, utterly useless, utterly bloody useless. The sea is not where the invasion came from but from overland. How could we have so underestimated the warped ingenuity of the Japs is beyond comprehension.'

Incredulity too still clung to Millie so she voiced what she had seen with her own eyes.

'Philip, there were thousands of British and Australian soldiers on the island how—'

'Numbers we had, yes. But many of the Allied and Empire troops were raw, untrained and unfit for battle purposes. Most of them had never fired a shot in action; they'd never even seen action. And we'd grumble among ourselves that the line of fighting men was spread too thinly, if the worst were to happen. Which of course it did, and so inevitably inexperience told on the day.' He threw in the derisory observation, 'and a cock sure attitude of invincibility possibly contributed to our downfall.'

Millie listened, silently now, while he recounted the last few days before Singapore fell. He told her of the heavy bombing raids that they had to endure without any fighter planes. And when the main Japanese attack was launched along the ridge to the west of the city, Philip explained that the Malay Regiment heroically held their ground until suffering massive losses, they had to yield to a superior force. He tried to spare her from the knowledge that many thousands of troops faced the dubious prospect of being detained by the Japanese, probably in the British Army's own Selarang Barracks. And he knew untold numbers of civilians faced death or possibly worse, for some, being locked up in Changi Prison.

Philip rang his tongue over dry lips and braced himself. 'I um I saw Doctor Elder in the hospital. He told me what had happened at the mission station and…I'm-I'm so, so sorry.'

Millie closed her eyes at the memory, then said, 'did you-I don't suppose you happened to hear anything of my father, by any chance?'

He shook his head, 'sorry, no.'

Mindful she asked, 'and, Grace's friend, your colleague, Captain McGregor, where is he? Did he get out?'

'I've no idea where Gordon is. I saw him briefly at the hospital. He was in a bad way, I don't mean that he was injured, no, upset, dreadfully upset, bitter, you know…'

She grew thoughtful and then said, almost to herself, 'I wonder if the Barnet family managed to get away.' Then thinking a bit more clearly she asked, 'how did you manage to find yourself at sea?'

'I was ordered to arrange the evacuation of some VIP's, staff officers, technicians, bods like that, whose specialised knowledge would be of value to the Allies. There was even a Rear Admiral among the party. We were told that Lieutenant General Percival was going to sign the terms of surrender, and they had to be got away. I had to escort them onto a patrol boat which would transfer them to the *Empire Star*. Then my orders were to return to shore and await further instructions. But a Jap destroyer pursued us and sunk the boat. I think it was only the fading light that saved us little lot on the raft.' He finished in a whisper. 'I don't hold out an awful lot of hope for anyone else's survival.'

It was some days later, and just when the condition of the injured men started to improve, Captain Bristow made an announcement that their water was running low and had to be rationed. He told everyone that he couldn't take the risk of stopping off at any of the islands to get a fresh supply, in case there were Japs there. This meant such things as bodily washing was out. Not unnaturally, it was one restriction that didn't upset Clive and Archie. In fact they quite enjoyed helping the crew draw up buckets of sea water and slosh around the deck in their bare feet.

As was the tradition, the crossing-the-equator rites got marked by the travellers on the *Dover Castle*, and the success of the occasion was in part thanks to Mrs Chance. Before leaving Singapore, Clive had put several tins of biscuits into his rucksack. Mrs Chance had kept them as emergency supplies, but decided this was the time to break them open and they were dished out to everyone at the point of crossing. And on the say so of the Captain, a measure of rum was issued all round. Even Archie and Clive were allowed a sip. Then they had their faces painted white, and afterwards buckets of sea water got poured over them.

The soldiers' injuries were healing well. Only the condition of one sailor was still causing Millie concern. Nevertheless, along with the others he was made comfortable on deck to mark the significance of the moment, and it was then that they could really take stock and reflect on how lucky that they were all still alive. At this little gathering Clive took his precious atlas up to Captain Bristow. He was able to tell the Captain how many miles he thought they were from India. Captain Bristow commended him on his detailed calculations and allowed him and Archie to spend some time at the wheel.

Undoubtedly, they were the most unusual, motley bunch of seafarers that had ever sailed on the *Dover Castle*. However, like newly released cows with the smell of fresh pastures in their nostrils, once India was sighted on the distant horizon, excitement among the passengers grew to almost fever pitch. Clive and Archie could barely stop from dancing up and down with glee. Unfortunately their euphoria was short-lived when the ship's engines, quite out of the blue, suddenly stopped. This time, it wasn't so much danger coming from Japanese planes as the awful frustration of more delays while the ship floundered, naked-like and vulnerable. Once the trouble was identified, it took a further day while the ship's engineer carried out a temporary repair to a broken axel.

However, not everyone was as upset as Clive and Archie. The delay gave Millie and Philip a little longer together. They talked fondly of England, she found out that he was a Hertfordshire man; his family mostly living around the small town of Letchworth. She told him that their plans were to get to London as soon as there was another ship to take them.

'I don't suppose they'll let you come back with us, would they?' She said, not really in the least bit hopeful.

'You know there is nothing I'd like better.' He took her arm and out of sight, kissed her longingly. Then he gave a derisory laugh. 'No, it's hardly likely. I'll have to get the chaps to hospital, not,' he hastened to add, 'not that you haven't done a good-wonderful job, but you know army procedure and then—'

'Thank you, Philip. But no, you are quite right. The sailor, all that oil, he'll not be back sailing the high seas for a long time.'

They kissed again, and then drawing apart Philip became serious. 'I'll have to put in a report on what befell our party. Give them as much information as I can. Then I'll be hanging around waiting for orders, wondering where I'll be posted to next. You know what the army's like.' He sighed. 'By which time you will have sailed off into the wide blue yonder.' He looked into her eyes. 'What will you do Millie? Will you carry on with your nursing work?'

'Well, I have been giving that some thought, and yes, I expect that's what I'll do.'

CHAPTER ELEVEN

Gritting her teeth, Janet decided she had done enough procrastinating, for, whichever way she looked at it she could see no path out of the dilemma. She would have to tell Olive, explain, however embarrassing. So pulling on a cardigan, Janet went down the stairs and knocked on the door. A beaming Olive greeted her.

'What a coincidence, Janet. I was just on my way up to see you. Come in, do.'

Janet groaned inwardly, feeling even worse. She thought, oh no, Olive has some tickets or has made plans and is going to ask me to go to a concert.

Plunging in, Janet began, speaking softly, 'I-I'm most—'

'Janet, I've just had some wonderful news. Come and sit down and I'll tell you all about it. What do you think?' Before Janet could answer, Olive told her, 'I've got a job on the land; I'm joining the Women's Land Army.'

'You're what?'

Olive went on excitedly, 'I went down to the WLA Head Quarters, in Chesham Street, and I've joined the Women's Land Army. You know, Janet, I'm really glad. At last I feel I shall be doing my bit and I'm pleased to get stuck into something tangible.' Olive smiled, 'you might have guessed I was always a country girl at heart.'

'Well er well jolly good for you. And...' Janet glanced around Olive's tiny one bedroom flat.

Olive followed her gaze. 'Oh yes, that's what I wanted to say. It has been really kind of you to store the rest of my furniture in your flat. We,' she gulped, her eyes grew misty, 'we did always intend to move, get a house, but Dunkirk put paid to that.' Stoically she blinked away the tears and went on. 'I've told the landlord that I shall be moving out at the end of the week. I'm being sent to a farm in Hampshire, along with a couple of other girls. We'll live in, you see, and we'll have a proper uniform. My mum and dad have said they will store all of my furniture and things in their barn, they live out Essex way.'

'That's marvellous news.' Janet went and put an arm around Olive's shoulder and gave it a squeeze. 'And your husband would have been very proud of you.' For other reasons, Janet felt like dancing for joy, but she had to stay in control or Olive would get the wrong end of the stick. Yet Janet wanted to be helpful so she said, 'Olive, you just say when, and I'll help you down with the boxes and stuff.'

'Thanks very much, but no, you have done enough already. And besides, I have a big strong brother home on leave and he's bringing a van tomorrow. So if that suits you, we could move everything in one fell swoop.'

Ecstatically, Janet raced up the stairs thinking it suits, it suits, and it couldn't suit better. Reaching her front door, she was just in time to hear the telephone ringing.

She answered, out of breath, 'hello.'

'Hello, Janet, this is Millie. Hello, hello, is anyone there?'

'Yes hello. Hello Millie darling!' Janet gulped. 'I've just run up stairs to answer the telephone, and I'm puffed. Let me get the chair.' Her heart was racing. 'How are you?' Are you back here yet? We heard about poor old Singapore. It must have been terrible.'

'It was bloody awful. We're all quite shattered. I can't tell you over the line just how awful it was.'

'No, no of course you can't. We've also had it pretty bad here, too.'

'Yes, Grandma has told us.'

Janet gave a gasp. 'So, so you are in er North London, at your grandma's?'

'Yes. We've been here for a few days now. Poor Mother, she's totally exhausted. It took us absolutely ages travelling from India. Did you get my letter?'

'Yes, yes I did. It gave me quite a shock, reading it.' She bit her lip.

'Yes, well I can tell you shock is a slight understatement. Nobody in Singapore expected the bloody Japs to invade us.' There was a pause.

'Still, it's happened, and it seems no one can do anything about it. I'll fill you in when I see you.' Millie quickly changed the subject. 'It's lovely at Grandma's, she's making us all so welcome, a proper mother hen. But it's a bit of a squeeze as we've brought back a friend, a dear lady. She went through a very bad time in Kuala Lumpur.' Millie didn't go into the details. 'So I'm beginning to get a longing for my own space, well our space, as it were. The boys have been very good considering what they've gone through, except there's nothing like the thought of a little bit of distance from two lively youngsters. And I'm longing for a good old girlie chat and catch up on what you've got up to.' Millie had a sudden thought. 'Oh Lord! I should have asked sooner. I suppose the flats are still standing. Well of course they are or I wouldn't be talking to you, silly me.' They both laughed.

Janet told her, 'we've been lucky.' She didn't mention the flattened houses opposite, which, bizarrely, now gave way to an uninterrupted view of the park. 'There's a little bit of bomb damage to our building, some window panes on the landings need replacing. And downstairs, the garden had to be dug up to take the Anderson shelter—'

'I don't mind. I just can't wait to see you and get moved back into the flat. Oh, and by the way, I'll bring some food with me. We heard of your tough food rationing when we were in Singapore. So we were advised before leaving South Africa—'

'South Africa?'

'Yes. We had to stop off there coming from India. Phew, what a horrendous journey we all had. Anyway one good thing, we got stocked up with sugar and dried fruit and nuts and lots of other useful things. So, I'll bring some groceries over.'

With as much nonchalance as she could rally, Janet asked, 'er, when do you think that will be?'

'Um, it will probably be next week sometime. We're all still a bit fagged. To cap it all, it was a terribly, long train ride down from Liverpool. We discovered to our horror that all Pullman services are suspended.' There was another short silence, before Millie reconsidered. 'I suppose we were lucky to get seats at all with the train packed to the gunnels with troops. And now, apparently, we have to register at the local Food Office to get our ration books.'

Janet wanted to tell her to stop moaning; instead she breathed a sigh of relief. Thinking next week, that's wonderful. 'Great! That will, um, give me time to have a tidy up.'

The following morning, as arranged, Janet fished out her spare key from the aspidistra pot, and dropped it through Olive's letter box, and went off to work feeling very happy. By the time she got back tonight all of Olive's stuff would be gone. And then she could put her own things into what was originally her bedroom. She would probably have to sponge down the gowns she'd borrowed, but Janet was confident Millie would be none the wiser. The dresses were only gathering dust and Millie did say she might use them for special occasions. She knew she was stretching a point by actually moving into Millie's room, but it was much more spacious than her bedroom and she was after all being neighbourly by helping Olive out.

The two school friends were not good letter writers, mainly because the war made it difficult to fit non-essential things in, and even then letters went astray. So, Janet never got round to telling Millie, that for long periods the flat was never actually lived in. The lovely times that she and Christopher spent there gave her a somewhat mischievous guilty feeling, but she thought what the hell. She knew that Mr Chance paid the rent yearly, in advance. She considered it was an odd arrangement, but she certainly had no reason to complain. Perhaps it was done at Millie's insistence. Anyway, Olive kept an eye on the place which was why she let her store some of her pieces of furniture in Janet's bedroom. Given the choice between living under active service conditions in Nissen huts or in tents without electricity, of course she would have preferred to stay in the comfort of the flat. However, her WAAF training took her to sites all over the country. Now at least she was based in London.

Her blue beret firmly in place, she ran through the park, enjoying the freshness of a beautiful spring morning. A couple of elderly men were already hard at it, digging patches ready for planting vegetables. They shouted a greeting to her and Janet waved back at them. Now that things were settled, she was in a really cheery frame of mind and looking forward to seeing Millie again.

Unfortunately the reunion did not go as well as Janet had hoped. Olive's brother could not get a van until the end of the week, something, Olive said, to do with petrol coupons. Then worst of all when the van did turn up, and furniture was being loaded, Millie too turned up.

'What in the blazes is going on,' she shrieked at Janet.

'Millie! Heavens, I didn't think-expect you, um let me explain.'

'Yes, I think you had better explain. What's all this stuff doing—?'

'Millie, come into the kitchen and I'll make you a nice cup of tea.'

Like an obstreperous child, Millie told her, 'I don't want a bloody cup of tea.'

This was a very different Millie that had left England over two years earlier, thought Janet. In spite of her refusal Janet put the kettle on and closed the kitchen door so that the furniture shifting could be done quickly. Millie was about to protest when Janet took her arm and sat her at the table. For a second she thought Millie was going to hit her. To explain in a few coherent sentences the nightmare things that had happened during bombing raids in London while she was away; to speak of friends they had both known and were now dead or missing, to tell Millie of poor Olive whose husband had got drowned at Dunkirk trying to get to the rescue boats, to make clear how many people are struggling, sometimes from day to day to make ends meet, must have touched a sensitive spot, because to Janet's amazement, Millie burst into tears.

'Millie, Millie dear. I'm sorry to have sounded so brutal.'

'No it's OK it's just me. I think I expected everything to be exactly as I left it. Poor London, poor London.' She got up and looked out of the window and pointed. 'That beautiful Georgian crescent we looked out on has gone, it's just rubble now.' Janet came and stood beside her. Millie searched her face, oddly, expecting some answers.

Janet said, 'I think I've got something with a bit more of a bite than tea.'

She rummaged at the back of the cupboard for the bottle of whisky. They sat opposite each other at the kitchen table. Millie opened a handkerchief and covered her face with it.

'Janet,' she said, hiding behind the piece of cloth, 'Janet, tell me this is all a bad dream. Shake me, wake me up and tell me we're riding our bicycles through France. Tell me we can go back, back to that lovely summer.'

Janet took her friend's hands from her face and held them, and gently rubbed them. Then in a small voice said, 'there's no going back, Millie, dear, if only there was a way, but there isn't.'

CHAPTER TWELVE

When Janet told her friend what her job was, Millie doubled up with laughter, and in truth, Janet saw the funny side and they both got a fit of the giggles.

'You mean to say you send those great fat balloons up, and then you take the bloomin' things down again?'

It was the effect of a little too much whisky when Janet explained, still a tad giggly, 'there's a dash more to it than that.' Putting her glass down and folding her arms Janet said proudly, 'you know Millie, they said we couldn't do it.'

'Couldn't do it? Couldn't do what?'

'Oh they prattled on about us not having the physical strength; they said we weren't bright enough to master the mechanics of a barrage balloon. And as if to prove their point, do you know what they did?' Millie wobbled her head. 'They took a group of us who worked in the manufacturing of the balloon fabric and put us through a ten week course in balloon maintenance and handling techniques. To their astonishment, we became skilled repair operatives as well as truck drivers and winch handlers, and what's more, we flew those beautiful, great whales, every bit as competently as the men.'

'Gosh!'

'Oh yes, we showed 'em, Millie, and...and,' she straightened up, ''course I'm not one to blow my own trumpet, as you know.' More laughter followed. 'However, we all got through the course with no one dropping out, and we scored better than the blokes.' She nudged Millie, 'another favourite old guard whinge was that females would be incapable of stopping anyone intent on sabotaging the balloons. So they gave us—'

'Guns?'

Janet smirked. 'No not quite.' She went to the meter cupboard and returned with a package.

'It's a truncheon! How very clever, useful even.' Curious, Millie fingered the truncheon and asked, in all seriousness, 'have you ever had to use it?'

'No. Mind you that's not to say I haven't felt like it once or twice. I won't mention names but there was one beastly NCO, whom I'd like to have given a tickle.' She whacked the air and more titters followed.

It was beginning to feel a little like old times. Laughter made them both feel good. Then Janet got round to asking about the escape from Singapore. No more whisky was taken as Millie related the sequence of events that hastened their departure from the once thought impregnable fortress, Singapore.

'Have you had any information about your father, and Doctor-Doctor—?'

'Doctor Elder. No, I haven't. We can only assume that they are prisoners of war.' She clenched her fingers. 'Japanese prisoners of war— Oh God help them.'

Janet added quickly, 'the thing is Millie, your father is a professional man and the Japs will need sound men to administer, liaise and that sort of thing, and you said he speaks Japanese, so that's an advantage. And Doctor Elder, well he's a medical man and his skills will be invaluable.'

'Chinese, Father speaks Chinese, Cantonese actually.' Millie knew her friend was doing her best to cheer her up.

'What about that nice chap you met in Singapore?'

'Philip.'

'Mmm, Philip, have you heard anything from him?'

'No, we said goodbye in India. He was waiting for orders. He said he'd write.'

'Well. There you are. It will only be a matter of time before you get a letter. But Millie, I think the best thing that you can do is to get back into work. Do you think you will return to nursing?'

'I thought I would, but now I'm not so sure. I had just started into my second year when we had to leave.'

Janet suddenly chipped in with, 'there's the First Aid Nursing Yeomanry, that's the FANY's. They have all sorts of posts other than your common or garden nurse. Excuse me, but no disrespect intended.'

Showing a mere spark of interest Millie asked, 'posts, such as?'

'Um, telephone operators, ambulance drivers, admin work, and don't forget you speak French like a native, that could be very useful in some sectors.'

Millie puffed out her cheeks. 'I have to go the Labour Exchange on Monday, more forms to fill out, I expect.'

'It's all red tape, I know. Afraid there's no way round it.'

Over the weekend Millie made several trips from Grandma Chance's house and gathered up what she thought she'd need for the flat. Clothes and food were the main priority and by good fortune Mr Chance had got them a substantial lump of money when he made the dash back to his office in Singapore. With some cash now in her purse, Millie set out early Monday morning. She was heading for the Stoke Newington Labour Exchange. Before she got there Millie heard the ominous wail of the air raid siren. For her, it was an alien sound, but it still sent shivers down her spine. She looked around for somewhere to run to, and then she saw a sign pointing to an air raid shelter. She quickly decided to follow other people all making a beeline for the shelter.

Suddenly, someone bellowed in her ear, 'where the hell is your gas mask?'

She jumped. 'I-I haven't had—'

'If you carry your mask you are an asset, if not you are a bloody liability to all ARP services. Your sort makes me sick. I've seen some of you women stuffing lipstick and cigarettes in with the gas masks. Don't you know you'd stand no chance if that was bleedin' gas they were dropping and not bleedin' bombs?'

'I haven't had—'

'Come along, come along everyone, move down move down.'

The stressed ARP warden wasn't going to listen for an explanation. He was waving his arm about to attract the attention of a few stragglers. Unused to the procedure, Millie was getting shoved and bumped rather unceremoniously towards the end of the shelter, and in the crush she dropped her handbag. Flailing about, trying to reach it only knocked the bag further away.

'Let me help,' a voice said, from behind.

After Millie managed to squeeze round, a man in a trilby hat gave her the bag.

'Thank you,' she said.

'They can be rather tiresome some of these ARP officials, but he is right about the gas mask.'

'What a pompous little man. I was trying to explain to him that I haven't been issued with one yet. I've only just got back from Singapore.'

'Indeed, Singapore. That must have been a bit hairy.' He had noted her colouring, and deduced she obviously had arrived from somewhere hot. 'How did you get out?'

Millie was about to answer, when just above his head was a poster in bold writing, almost shouting, *Careless Talk Cost Lives*. The man followed her gaze, nodded and gave a wry smile.

When the all clear sounded everyone filed out of the shelter. Somewhat dazed, Millie automatically lifted her eyes skyward.

'Why haven't they…where are they going?'

The man in the trilby, said, 'who knows? Maybe they are heading for Coventry, or Birmingham. It's a little unsettling. We've had it relatively quiet of late. Still that's not to say…' He raised his hat to Millie. 'Don't forget about the gas mask. Good morning.'

'Good morning and thank you.'

People went scurrying in different directions, intent on getting on with their business in spite of what was going on above their heads. Millie lost sight of both the uppity ARP and the gentleman in the trilby. He on the other hand adjusted his hat in the reflection of a shop window, and hurriedly retraced his steps, keeping Millie just within his sight. It was only when she went through the door of the Labour Exchange that the man veered off in another direction.

Millie had to join a small queue of mostly young men; she counted only two women all sitting passively. Excruciatingly slowly, the whole line moved up a seat at a time until eventually it became Millie's turn to see a clerk behind the counter. The female civil servant took a form from the top of a pile and began to fill it in. Barely into the first page she suddenly looked at Millie, accusingly, and asked her rather loudly, as to why she hadn't registered before. Millie was saved from giving any kind of a reply when another clerk shoved a sheet of paper in front of her face. After reading at length, what was on the page the clerk looked again at Millie and said, perfunctorily, 'take her up, then.'

Bemused, Millie followed the second clerk in silence, down a long corridor and up a flight of stairs. Then he knocked on a door and told Millie to go in.

'Please take a seat, Miss Chance,' a man's voice said.

'Good heavens! It's you-who are you?' Millie asked, quite unabashed.

In a firmer tone he told her, 'if you please, Miss Chance.' He indicated to the chair.

Away from the gloom of an air raid shelter, Millie thought he looked better wearing his hat, for he had not much hair to speak of.

'My name is Graham Bain, and I work for the Ministry and—'

'Which Ministry did you say?'

'I didn't say, Miss Chance.' He cleared his throat. 'And you are here to answer the questions we ask you, not the other way round.'

'Well I just—'

'Yes, well, this interview may seem somewhat unorthodox, I grant you, but one must seize an opportunity when one sees it.' Millie hadn't the foggiest notion what he was talking about. Then unexpectedly he asked, 'tea, Miss Chance?'

'Green please.'

With his hand in front of his mouth, Millie didn't see or hear his almost silent laugh.

By the time a summons for tea was made, Graham Bain had most of the information he needed for Millie's file. He knew even before she set foot into the building there was a strong possibility that she spoke French. When he picked her bag up, in the air raid shelter, he was quick to notice that tucked in a side pocket of the expensive crocodile-skin handbag was a menu card, printed in French. This got slipped into his pocket, without Millie seeing. He considered she would probably come from a middle class background to have afforded to dine in a classy,

French restaurant. She had said in the air raid shelter that she'd come from Singapore. Her healthy golden tan, confirmed she had recently come from a hot country, for she was unlike many of the young English girls who emerged from the British winter, pasty-faced and bleary eyed. In fact, he thought Millie an unusual character who might prove ideal for…his musings were interrupted by a knock on the door. An NCO poked his head in.

Graham Bain said, with sarcastic humour, 'no green, Sergeant, I suppose?'

The NCO asked, 'what's that, sir?'

'Nothing, just bring the usual. That will be all, thank you.'

'Thank you, sir.'

The sergeant shot a sly glance at Millie and closed the door.

Graham Bain gave Millie her tea. There was no sugar, and only a tiny milk jug.

'Sorry, we have no green,' he said.

'Oh that's quite alright. I don't mind, really I don't.' He grinned as she poured. He liked Millie's directness. 'I can drink anything, so long as it's not rum.'

'Rum?'

'Heavens, yes, and I hate being reminded. I had to pour it down the throats of those poor chaps on the ship. And then Captain Bristow would insist on me having a 'wee tot,' as he called it. Yuk, I never want to sample that taste, ever again.'

Bain became sympathetic for a moment. 'Ah, yes, well I can understand. However, now we must push on. We need to get you into one or other of the services.' He thumbed through some papers then said, 'with your background, the FANY's might be a way—'

'Be a way of continuing my nursing career. Why yes, that sounds just up my street.'

'Miss Chance, that wasn't exactly what I had in mind.' He broke eye contact, and under his breath, muttered, 'no, no, no. It's not nurses that we're short of.' Then fixing his gaze again on Millie, he said, 'you see it's-it's a question of…um, by the bye, how's your German?'

'It's passable, I suppose. Though I have to say it's only school girl German. Accents wouldn't be all that but...' Millie was now beginning to wonder where all this was leading.

He sensed her slight unease. 'I'll-um, I'll be frank with you, Miss Chance. For certain work we need people who have some languages under their belt, so to speak, and er in particular French. Nevertheless, a smattering of German is always advantageous. I see you spent many years actually living in France-Paris, with your um yes, grandparents.' Millie had already told him all this, so she made no comment but gave a discernable nod. He glanced at the file again, and scribbled, "Put her French to use. Send on crash course for German?" Quite out of the blue, he fired at her, 'Miss Chance, there's something else I'd like to clear up. Cast your mind back, if your will, back to Singapore.' He hastened, 'I don't wish to cause you any more unnecessary distress, but that um that French light cruiser,' he studied Millie's face, 'did the colonel-did they-anyone, ever tell you or did you ever discover what damaged her?'

'No,' was all Millie said, though she could tell he was being cagey.

'No, no, um, right-oh. I see.'

Bain misconstrued her laconic reply, for something else, possibly secrecy, but in fact that was all Millie could say, because no one ever did tell her what caused the accident, if accident is what it was.

Satisfied, Bain told her, 'Miss Chance, go home, spend some time with your family. Get them and you, of course, registered with all the required authorities for food rationing books, and so on. Relevant forms can be obtained downstairs. That mundane sort of thing will take a bit of time. However, we will be in contact with you very soon. Let me see now, we have the address for your grandmother and mother, that's North London, so—'

'Please send any correspondence to my flat, in Stoke Newington, if you wouldn't mind.'

He felt her request was more in keeping with an order, and he was a little surprised at her haughtiness. Yet he smiled his agreement, and said, 'yes, yes, we'll do that.'

When Millie had gone Bain looked again at her file and wrote in the word, PROCEED.

Huge confidence in one so young, he thought. He put her bold, self-assured manner down to ingrained Empire values, along with that indulgent, relaxed life style, which had previously been enjoyed by so many of the wealthy colonial population. And yet, he sensed that there was something else, something innately noble about her. Bain drew out a word that came to mind, a word which Winston Churchill often bandied about—mettle. Churchill would bark at him, "Have they got the mettle for it, Bain, that's what I want to know?" Yes, he'd describe Miss Chance as having mettle. Graham Bain closed the file with a sigh, knowing she'd have to call on more than that virtue to get her safely through where she was going.

Then with conviction, Bain pressed a bell, and immediately the NCO came in. The soldier picked up the tea tray and waited for his orders.

'Get me a car, Sergeant.'

'Yes sir, straight away, where to sir?'

'Baker Street, Sergeant.'

'Very good, sir.'

This was an address that the sergeant knew well. It was the Head Quarters of Churchill's Secret Army, or The Ministry of Ungentlemanly Warfare, as the sergeant often heard it called.

CHAPTER THIRTEEN

To Christopher Elliott, there was a synonymous connection between Kent and hop-pickers. He remembered they always arrived every summer, in their char'-à-bancs, or by bus, and even the railways recognised the popularity of the annual summer event by running the hopping specials. Sometimes, for fun, he and Grace were allowed to join the seasonal folk, and in no time at all, their skins would be as brown as any hop-picking urchin, from the East End of London. Grace used to say his aunt and uncle lived in one of the loveliest villages in the South of England, and they were so lucky to get staying there. But today, as he got out of the quiet, honeysuckle scented station, his heart felt like lead. The memories came flooding back of the happy holidays he and Grace spent with their relatives. Another stab of pain shot through him. Grace, Grace would never come here again. And Father, dear God! Why did they have to go? Tortured by these thoughts, they continued to rattle round his brain and he couldn't stop them.

When he came to the familiar bend in the road, he saw the three, pretty thatched cottages. The dwellings were so typical to that part of the country, and all were still enclosed by low white picket fences. He was glad they hadn't got pulled up and chopped for fire wood. He knew the names without having to think, Primrose Cottage, and Lilac Cottage and then Rose Cottage, which is where his auntie May and uncle Jim Elliott live. As a child, Christopher thought the thatched roofs magical. His uncle always said the same thing each time they visited, that thatch wasn't just beautiful it was practical too. It was, he'd say, cool in the summer and warm in the winter. And as children, whenever they stayed, he'd have a different animal, cut and shaped from local grown reed and standing proudly on the roof of the thatch. Uncle Jim would not say a word until they noticed. But it pleased him, for that was the first thing that Grace, excitedly, looked for.

Now, his mother would be inside, expecting him, probably worrying that he was late. The Wing Commander had informed him of the deaths and of his mother's return from Singapore, and he had been given compassionate leave. At this moment part of him wished he was in the cockpit of his Avro Lancaster bomber, keeping company with her seven man crew, listening to the steady, comforting sound of the Merlin Engines. Instead he would be listening to the sound of…

His uncle opened the door to him. He's aged, thought Christopher. Solemnly, they shook hands.

'Welcome, lad, welcome. Though, I'm right sorry to see you under these circumstances.'

'Thank you, Uncle Jim.'

Then his uncle led him into the sitting room to where his mother and aunt were waiting. Instantly they got up.

'Christopher,' his mother whispered barely audible. They held one and other in a long embrace. Mrs Elliott had regained enough self-composure to valiantly hold back the tears. However, when Christopher looked into her eyes they were red-rimmed and bloodshot. She patted his hand. 'It's so good to have you here. How long have they given you?'

'Just the two days. The Wing Commander was sympathetic and very sorry that he couldn't be more generous. It's all so dreadfully manic at the moment. But tell me, how are you?'

Mrs Elliott shrugged. 'What is it they say, as well as can be expected? Auntie May is making us tea, so lets you and me go round the garden, it is lovely just now, so very-very English-like, with all the beautiful Spring flowers. Quiet different to the ferocious heat, and giant tropical plants and endless rubber plantations that we had in Kuala Lumpur.'

Outside in the soft, evening sunshine, Christopher laid a comforting hand on her shoulder, and asked, 'what happened back there, Mother?'

As they sat, hardly aware, that the song of the birds were creating a background symphonic cacophony. And with male Blackbirds vying for a mate, and trilling Robins, intent on retaining old territories, it all got told, the whole horror. The loss and the pain were described. And awash with incredulity, Christopher found such terrible cruelty hard to accept. After a while, his aunt May brought out a tea tray with tiered plates, full of dainty little sandwiches and fairy cakes. And an apple tart partnered a jug of clotted cream. A veritable feast that she hoped would tempt them both. Occasionally, the aunt would peep through the little cottage window and go out and refill the tea pot. Then she'd leave as unobtrusively as she came. Nevertheless, with her own tears chasing her, she couldn't fail to see Christopher's face contorted with pained, emotional agony.

Swallowing the remainder of a cup of tea, Mrs Elliott swilled the fine leaves at the bottom, and added, 'I don't know how I would have managed without the help and support of that dear family. Poor Mr Chance was very brave and said he had to do his duty so couldn't be persuaded to leave. And Doctor Elder went to a hospital in Singapore, to tend to the sick.' She grew downcast. 'As yet, we've received no news on either of them.'

Christopher was bent double with his hands holding his head.

His mother went on to tell him, 'very soon I shall go back to London, Islington, to the Mission—'

'No,' he flashed. 'No! No!'

'Now, let me finish, dear. I must let people know what occurred. I don't know if the Missionary HQ, in Islington has been informed, they may have been, but I owe them the courtesy…anyway it is something that has to be done. And besides, I want to do something-something useful.'

'Please, Mother! Please, tell me you aren't thinking about going back to—'

'No, no dear.'

'Thank God for that.'

In spite of everything awful that got talked about, Mrs Elliott gave a dry chuckle, and said, 'God and I have had a falling out.'

However, Christopher scowled. 'Father and I had many a falling out over God. But how I wish he were here to chastise me once again.'

They were quiet for a few minutes, watching a lone Spitfire silhouetted against a blushing sky. Unexpectedly, Mrs Elliott came out with, 'I thought I might do some work with the Salvation Army. When I was in London, staying with the Chances, I saw what a truly worthwhile job the Sally Army does for people, bombed out in the Blitz. There are all those bereaved and homeless families, needing not only shelter but clothing and food. In those terrible raids, many people lose all their personal possessions, money, ration books, everything. And of course so many lives are lost, too. Families fall apart.'

Christopher understood the poignancy of that statement. He wanted to get rid of his spittle. He glanced at the sky. The Spitfire had gone, probably back to its base where the pilot would gulp a stiff whiskey or two in the mess, before going off on another sortie. Mrs Elliott poured out more tea. Christopher thought, in spite of all she's gone through, my dear mother, still had this innate urge to help others. He couldn't help admiring her.

Mrs Elliott went on, 'the government seems quite unprepared for the vast numbers needing succour. My dear friend, Mrs Chance, said I could go back and stay with her as her daughter, Millie, has gone to live in a flat. I probably wont, I don't like to intrude. Also, I know I can get accommodation at the Missionary Society, without any difficulty.'

'Mother, who-who-what was the name you just mentioned?'

'Mrs Chance, the family, you know, the family from Singapore. We all travelled back together.' She was very patient; she knew how hard it was to take it all in.'

'No, I mean, did you say Millie?'

'Yes dear. Millie Chance. The young nurse, she was Grace's friend.'

'Ah yes, I seem to recall...the postcard...Singapore. What a coincidence.'

'What's that dear?'

'Oh just thinking aloud.'

The scraping of coarse hobnail boots was heard on the stone pathway. It was Christopher's uncle Jim. He wore his Home Guard uniform, and slung over his shoulder he carried a formidable-looking weapon.

He waved, and called out, 'I'm off to the shooting range for riffle practice, and then it's out on patrol with the unit tonight. I shan't see you till later, Chris, lad. Cheerio.'

They gave him a wave, and Christopher made the V for victory sign.

'Jim took it hard, losing his only brother. May told me it was the only time she'd ever seen him cry.'

Christopher plucked at a strand of couch grass and wound it tightly round his fingers. 'They do a great job those old chaps. There they go, constantly out patrolling our coast line, it frees up the regular army, no end.' He grew thoughtful. He was just beginning to realise how little his mother knew about what went on while she was away. 'Eighteen months ago, we in England were all geared up for a German invasion being almost inevitable.'

Mrs Elliott gasped at what he said. 'Until Doctor Elder came out to Kuala Lumpur we heard almost nothing about what was going on back in England. We really had no idea. And I'm ashamed, in a way, but we lived in a vacuum, wrapped up with our own beliefs and ideals, and sheltered in a bubble of comfortable ignorance.'

'You weren't to know. Don't blame yourself, Mother.'

She shook her head in disbelief. 'How on earth did we pull back from the edge?'

He started to count. 'Winning the Battle of Britain, thankfully, the Spitfires were swifter, and could outstrip the Heinkel, and if they got close enough, the Messerschmitt. And then of course, getting Radar made it easier to detect approaching planes. We also had some excellent Polish pilots from 303 Squadron. Even before they got here, they were well trained, those chaps. So, gaining air supremacy undoubtedly won the day for us, albeit by the narrowest of margins.'

He was careful to say nothing of his own bombing missions. Just the other month, March the tenth, his Lancaster took part in the first night time bombing operation, over the largely civilian populated city of Essen.

Bending another finger he went on, 'then by good fortune there was a change in Luftwaffe tactics. Instead of bombing our airfields, they took to obliterating our cities. Terrible though the change of strategy was it gave us a chance to repair our airfields, retrain more pilots and get more planes off the ground and in the air.' He gulped some tea down. 'Nevertheless, Mother, it has to be said, we had luck on our side. Of course it will be a long time before the threat of invasion goes away entirely. Still with the Russians now as our Allies and with the Americans in—'

'You know Christopher; when I think about it, we never imagined the Japanese would invade us. It was only four-five years ago that your father and I went out to that conference, in Tokyo, and they couldn't have been more welcoming. We thought they loved us.'

He sucked his teeth in disgust. 'But the fucking, murdering bastards invaded all the same.' He didn't excuse himself for his use of, what his father would have considered, foul language, but he modified his tone. 'When you think about it, the situation was not so different to the German *Blitzkrieg*. We were caught napping, simple as that, and could easily have lost the whole British Expeditionary Force. And in Singapore it happened again. We just did not learn. Too much bloody complacency and that is possibly why we were unprepared for that enemy. I heard losing that precious part of the Empire was a hard pill for Churchill to have to swallow.'

Pulling her shoulders back, Mrs Elliott said, 'well, now, talking of swallowing,' she put on a smile, and picked up a plate of sandwiches, 'let's do try and eat something, Auntie May will be most upset if we don't make an effort. She has gone to so much trouble.'

CHAPTER FOURTEEN

Millie had done exactly what Graham Bain had suggested that she should do. She went home, home to her grandmother's house, and was greeted by her grandmother, as always, with warm affection, and with a kiss on each side of her cheek. However, she found the house unusually quiet.

Millie cocked an ear. 'Grandma, things aren't normal. Where is everyone?'

Old Mrs Chance clapped her hands together, 'well, the reason for that is because Archie and Clive have started at their new school, just this very morning. And…and I don't quite know what to do with myself. So my darling Millicent, I am very pleased to see you.'

Gazing, lovingly at the elderly lady, Millie said, 'and I am very, very pleased to see you, Grandma. And Mother, what about Mother?'

Grandma pointed upwards and smiled a funny little smile. She had a twinkle in her eye as she told Millie, 'your mother will be down presently.'

'And where is Mrs Elliott?'

'Oh, yes, we didn't get round to letting you know because Mrs Elliott decided quite on the spur of the moment and has gone done to Kent, for a while. She is staying with some close relatives, while she recuperates. We wanted her to remain with us. However, as things went, she found it difficult to settle. We did our best to help, of course, but I think she had to be with her family, and I understand her son will be following on.'

Just then the old floor boards on the stairs could be heard creaking, and Mrs Chance came in.

Her first words to Millie were, 'I want no funny remarks from you, Miss.'

Millie's mouth fell open, but she was quick to retort, 'Mother I-I wouldn't dream of it. I er I think you look so chic, really. You look marvellous.'

'Well dear, I wouldn't go so far as that.' She straightened her tie and pulled down the tunic of her London bus conductress uniform. 'The hat's not bad. I think it suits me. What do you think?' She adjusted the peak so it sat dead central.

'Mother, you look very smart. Doesn't she, Grandma?'

'Indeed, indeed she does. But the important thing is your mother is doing a very worthwhile job. Mind you, I think she would have preferred to drive the bus, but nevertheless, your mother is going to earn money, as well as getting other people to their place of work. And that is all for the good of the country, so that's what counts.'

Millie circled her mother, hardly able to believe that just months ago she had servants to tend her every whim. And furthermore, she had no end of leisure time at her disposal. Millie wondered if her mother knew just what type of work she was letting herself in for.

'Satisfied?' Her mother asked, smugly

Millie nodded, enthusiastically, 'um oh yes, you look just the ticket.'

Grandma Chance nearly choked and had to smother a laugh at Millie's choice of words.

'And what about you, Millie,' her mother said, 'what have you got lined up?'

'Oh me, yes, well it seems that they have got me ear-marked for the FANY's. I'm waiting to get called up, anytime now.'

Grandma Chance raised her eyebrows on hearing this, and was about to say something when her daughter-in-law, in a sudden flurry of excitement said, 'must rush, darlings, can't be late on my first day.' She grabbed her coat and bag and the boxed gas mask, and then halfway down the outside steps, added, 'Millie, dear, I have to go over to Tottenham for my training thingy-session, or whatever they call it. I'm not sure what time I'll get back. Will you stay and see the boys when they come from school?'

'Gosh, yes. Cant go without seeing the terrible two.'

Millie waved her mother off and went back down into the kitchen.

On a more solemn note Millie said, 'I didn't like to spoil Mummy's excitement by asking, but I don't suppose there has been any news of Father.'

'No Millicent, darling, there hasn't been a word. We telephone the Embassy on a regular basis, but there is nothing that they can tell us.'

'Even after all this time?'

'Even after all this time. We just do not know what is happening out there.' It would have been easy to have wrung her hands and sobbed, just thinking about her only son. But she had to be strong for Millicent. Instead, Grandma Chance filled the kettle and intended to make the most of a few hours alone with her favourite grandchild. 'I'm going to make a pot of real coffee with some of the beans that your mother brought back from South Africa.' Looking round, she whispered, 'Millicent dear, please close the window otherwise we will have the neighbours coming in if they get a whiff of the coffee.'

It was the most beautiful aroma, and two cups were sipped and enjoyed slowly.

'Wonderful,' Millie exclaimed, with all honesty. 'The taste of this lovely coffee makes me appreciate just how much we used to take for granted.'

After some light hearted chit-chat, Grandma Chance said, 'Millicent, dear, what do you know about FANY, the service that you are going to join?'

'Well, I suppose all the services are a much of a much-ness. FANY may be a way back into nursing, but I'm not sure what they've got in mind for me. It wasn't decided at my interview. Or at least no one has thought fit to inform me, yet.' Then Millie told her grandmother about the bizarre meeting with Graham Bain.

Old Mrs Chance listened intently, if somewhat nervously to Millie's account of the interview.

'I know you will probably have to be careful about what you say—'

'Oh no, Grandma, it's nothing like that—'

'Millicent,' she gripped her granddaughter's hand. 'It's everything like *that*. You don't know. You won't know, just yet. Gradually, you will in time. They…the FANY's have been going for a long time and they are highly respected.' Unable to keep up the show of bravado, old Mrs Chance suddenly became emotional, and had to get out her handkerchief. 'Pay no attention to me.'

Now Millie began to understand. 'Oh Grandma, you were in…there, there you mustn't get upset.'

'No, dear, I mustn't. You are quite right. But there is just one thing I want to remind you of, and then we won't speak of it any more, unless you need to. OK?' Millie nodded, slightly puzzled. 'Of course you will still remember Paris that goes without saying. But it will have changed from the friendly, lively city we knew so well. The gay theatres and the shows we took you to. And the little cafés where we would sit outside and watch aspiring artists ply their trade.' Her mood changed with a warning note. 'People will not be the same. Now they live in fear, always having to watch their backs. It's a terrible thing to have the Germans in ones country again.' She finished the remains of the coffee, and then said, 'my darling, do you remember when you and your school chum cycled up through to Picardie, remember, and stayed with the Blanc family?' She asked again, while Millie looked thoughtful. 'Millicent, you do remember where they live, don't you?' Millie was thinking, but looked vague. 'Millicent,' her grandmother repeated, sharper, 'Millicent, do you remember where they live?'

'Yes, yes, of course I do. Why?'

'Don't ask, Millicent, just remember, they are good people. There are not many of my family left in France, but Jules and Florence Blanc, are good people. Do you understand what I am saying, darling?'

'Yes, Grandma, I think I do, I do.'

*

When Millie got back to the flat she found Janet washing her hair and preparing to go out. She handed her friend a towel.

'Do you know, Janet; Clive, my brother is as tall as me, now, and Archie is not far behind him. I hope this awful war will end before they get…' She didn't finish her sentence because she didn't want to think about the possibility of them being conscripted, in a few years time.

'Anyway, I have to tell you Janet, I could hardly believe it, but what do you think, my mother has a job.' She described her mother rushing off to work in her conductress uniform. 'I can't get over my mother working on the buses, and she really is quite chuffed about it.'

'Well good for her, that's what I say.'

Three frocks already lay discarded on Janet's bed. Plucking out another one she held it up in front of Millie. Millie frowned and shook her head. Then going in to her own bedroom she riffled through her wardrobe rail and pulled out a stylish turquoise and silver number.

'Here, try this,' Millie suggested.

'Oh Mills, I love it, I love it. Mills, you're a darling, you really are.'

'You'd better try it on first.'

It was the frock Millie wore when she first met Philip.

'Right, now that that's settled, tell me about this wonderful chap, this wonderful dashing blonde, who steers a Lancaster Bomber. How did you meet him?'

'Pilots, Mills, pilots, he's the pilot. And I met him…' She had slipped the dress over her head and was studying her image in the mirror. 'I met him at a dance.' She giggled. 'It was love at first sight. He said I took his breath away. I won't say what he took away!' Millie let out a squeal. Janet smoothed the front of the dress down. 'H'mm,' she coughed. 'It's lovely, Millie. Thanks ever so much. I'll try not to spill any soup or champers down it—if I should be so lucky.' For a moment Janet's expression changed and she said, 'he sounded a bit, sort of down, quiet. Not his usual self. I know we won't have an awful lot of time as he's coming up from Kent, and then he has to go back to the air base. He'd said something about compassionate leave. But I'm sure he's meant that as a *double entendre,* because I think he's kidding. He knows it's my birthday soon, so I feel sure he's going to surprise me.'

Millie was about to put the other frocks back on hangers when suddenly she stopped, and clutched them tightly. She was feeling light-headed and slightly sick.

'What…what is his name?'

'Christopher. I told you.'

'What's his other name?'

'What?'

'What's his bloody surname?'

'For God's sake Millie don't be so…It's Elliott. Flight Lieutenant Christopher Elliott.'

'Oh God. Janet! Oh God. This is awful.'

'What! What are you talking about?'

CHAPTER FIFTEEN

For moral support, Millie had told Janet that she would go with her when she went to meet Christopher at the station. Then they could both offer their sympathy. At the same time it would give Millie a chance to tell Christopher what a wonder person his sister was, and how well and how brave all the family thought his mother was bearing up over the loss of her husband and daughter. It wasn't something Millie was looking forward to but she felt she had to do it. However, things didn't go according to how they would have wished. As the two girls were putting final touches of powder and lipstick on, the telephone rang. Janet answered it, thinking it might be Christopher.

'It's for you, Mills.'

'Hello, Millie Chance speaking.'

Not wishing to listen in while Millie was thus engaged, Janet went to her bedroom and busied herself collecting up her hand bag and making sure she had plenty of cigarettes. Then while adding a final dab of perfume, she became aware of silence in the lounge. Thinking that Millie had put the phone down she came out, only to find that her friend had sat down and seemed to be still engrossed with the caller. It was a bit of a one way conversation as all she could hear from Millie was the occasional grunt, or yes and no. Still not wishing to seem rude, Janet went back into her room.

In a short while Millie knocked on Janet's door.

'Is everything alright?' Janet asked.

'Um, oh dear, well, I'm not really sure. That was someone from the War Office. I have been told to go to the Harley House Hotel, in town.'

'Whatever do you have to go there for?'

'It's for some sort of an interview. But it's odd, as I didn't expect to hear anything so quickly, considering I've not long got back from the

Labour Exchange.' Millie's face showed a flicker of displeasure when she scathingly added, "spend some time with your family," is what that Mr Bain said. Humph, he didn't give me much time, did he?'

'Goodness. No he certainly did not. 'When did they say you had to go to this hotel?'

'I have to go today, now.' She looked at the clock, 'straight away, actually. Janet I'm most terribly sorry, but I can't go with you. I have to keep this annoying appointment; it seems if I don't, I'll get into hot water.'

'Of course you must keep the appointment. There's a war on, and we have to jump to it. I can explain to Christopher that it was through you that I have heard about the family tragedy.' Janet went up to her friend. 'And actually, it's possibly a way of gently broaching the subject, just in case he doesn't feel able to. I know it was tough for you having to repeat all that horrible business again, for my sake, but thank you, Mills. At least I'm prepared, and won't go in making a total fool of myself, when I see the poor boy.'

*

Since arriving from Singapore, Millie had seen so little of London, and that evening, she was taking in the West End for the first time in nearly three years. The dire state of the city pained her, dreadfully. Nevertheless, she was glad she'd changed her mind about taking a taxi and decided to go by bus, because she was able to experience first-hand just what sort of work her mother would have to do. From the top deck she had a good view of streets that she had known so well from shopping trips with Mrs Chance, which now with the constant Luftwaffe bombing, had in places, changed beyond recognition. The bus chugged along one stretch by Piccadilly Circus. She craned her neck looking for Eros, only to discover it had gone.

'They've taken him down, ducks,' the conductress, intuitively, told her, 'to stop the bloody, fucking buggars blowing 'im to bits.'

Somehow, she couldn't see her mother using that turn of phrase, yet it expressed well enough the bitterness one worker felt for the enemy. She watched the clippie rhythmically churn out several fares on the ticket machine strapped to her ample chest. Then rather comically, with her bottom pressed against the front of the bus, she gave two heel stamps on the deck floor, as if she were about to burst into a tap dance routine. The bus shivered before moving off. Exhibiting fitness and with her bosom bouncing, the conductress ran down the stairs to check on her passengers. Follow that little pantomime, Mother, thought Millie, with dry humour.

For all the wrong reasons, Millie had expected to be met at the entrance of some grand hotel. She'd no time to eat before leaving the flat. And with her imagination running away with her, she was all but salivating at the prospect of having dinner served in an atmosphere reminiscent of a pre-war Savoy. Disappointingly, for Millie, the reality of it was that standards fell well below even the humblest hotel that she had ever dined in, back in Singapore. Prepossessing, Harley House was not. In fact, the dowdy façade of the three-story building, in Berkeley Square, reflected obligatory Blitz precautions. Doorways and walls, in common with all the surrounding properties, got blanketed in ubiquitous, beige sandbags, thus making a gloomy vestibule even darker.

There was, however, a little glimmer of lightness. A smiling, elderly gentleman at the reception desk set his newspaper aside the instant she approached. He must be expecting me, Millie, thought. Even before she told him her name he was already ushering her along the corridor with pleasantries about the fine weather they were enjoying. Boldly, his arthritic knuckles rapped the door; opening it he announced her name to two men seated at an oblong, mahogany table. Behind the pair, faded wine-coloured drapes were drawn. Already a fug of smoke clung around the men. Still smiling, benignly, the old chap stood aside for Millie to enter, and then firmly closed the door after her.

Graham Bain had taken the tube train over from his HQ in Baker Street and had already arrived at the hotel almost an hour before Millie. He was joined by a recruiting officer from Special Operations Executive. They got down to business straight away. One major concern that the SOE officer had was the issue of Millie's age. Bain had some months ago processed a small number of eighteen year girls as potential wireless operators, shunting them initially into the FANY's. However, most were working in the relative safety of a highly secret establishment, in Buckinghamshire, and in all probability that is where they would stay. What they had in mind for Millie was something far more dangerous— if she could be persuaded to volunteer.

'OK, I see where you're coming from,' said Bain. 'Still, don't be taken in by that. Yes, true, she has a certain h'mm what shall I say, a school girlish look about her, that might fool even Hitler himself.' He gave a self-conscious chuckle. 'But I can vouch for the fact that she's tougher than she appears.' He tapped his finger on sheets of paper. 'You've read of her recent escape from the Japs, you'll agree, no mean feat that. And, let's not forget,' he added, unable to hide his derision, 'thousands of our chaps are there for the duration.' Bain endeavoured to drive home his view point concerning Millie's slender years. 'Consider again how she got to India in something not more than an oversized tugboat. That leaky vessel had to break free from under the nose of the Japanese Navy. Then as our information tells us, there was the incident of rogue mines to contend with. I'd say she showed sheer grit and determination to get her party to safety. And-and let's not forget the rescued servicemen. I've had it on good authority that some would not have survived had it not been for Miss Chance's nursing care.' He drew out more paper work. 'This is the official report on that evacuation. You can read how the VIP navel launch was sunk, leaving Singapore, with the loss of all but a handful of her crew. Most unfortunate, I'd say. There were some top brass among the numbers killed.' His mouth twitched at the thought. 'Anyway, there's no point dwelling. Her story is backed up by the officer in charge of the evacuation, a Captain Philip Hendry.'

The SOE officer asked, 'where is Hendry now?'

'He's back in England, and has recently joined the Royal Corps of Signals. He's stationed up in Doncaster. But it would be easy enough to get him in.'

'The Signals, right, yes, yes, I think at some stage we'll get him down, he could be of some use to us, what do you say?'

Slightly impatient, Bain said, 'yes I agree.' He did not want to get sidetracked so he pressed on. 'What also impressed me was the girl's tight-lipped stand on the incident relating to the damaged French light cruiser. Of course now, it's practically common knowledge within Churchill's inner circle that he'd issued the orders to scuttle ships of the French Navy, to prevent the vessels falling into German hands. However, by some sort of a fluke, that light cruiser escaped being sent to Davy Jones's locker.'

'H'm, you're talking about Operation Catapult.' He'd read the intelligence reports on the sinking of the battleship Bretagne. Over one thousand hands lost on that ship alone. He cringed. 'Yes that was a hard, and unenviable decision Churchill had to make.' The SOE officer concurred. 'It made for bad propaganda, and it does cause one to wonder if de Gaulle and the French will ever forgive us. He can be a touchy blighter, that general.'

'Yes, quite.' Bain again agreed. Then he slammed his fist down. 'Except, let me say, this girl has seen more action than some of those mandarins in Whitehall, who are sitting on their fat backsides, and have never witnessed a shot fired in anger.'

'Right, let's be having her in, then.'

They made it abundantly clear that the meeting was definitely not going to take the form of a cosy tête-à-tête. Millie was not even offered a cup of tea. Instead she had a through grilling, initially about her attitude towards the Japanese. When asked by Bain what her views were on the loss of Singapore, and her feelings about the invading Japanese, Millie told him in no uncertain terms.

'They are nothing short of murdering bastards,' was her unambiguous answer. 'My father could not be persuaded to leave with us. He and Doctor Elder, who worked at the missionary hospital, stayed behind, along with many of our friends to help save our island. And a fat lot of good it did. Father is not in the army, he is a civilian, employed by a shipping company. And our dear friend, the doctor, went, voluntarily, to work in the military hospital.' She leaned towards the two men, accusingly. 'Answer me this if you can, where was the British Army when we really needed it? We were led to believe our island was impregnable.' She gave a scornful snort, 'Ha! My father and Doctor Elder could easily have come with us to safety, but out of loyalty they chose to stay and do their duty.'

'Miss Chance,' said the SOE officer, ignoring her question, 'now that you are back in England, where does *your* loyalty lie, and what do you consider is *your* duty?'

Without hesitation Millie responded. 'I'll do anything it takes to get my father and Doctor Elder home safely.'

The officer was sharp to tell her, 'I didn't ask you that. What I will ask is what have you got to offer that no one else has?' He gave Millie no time to reply. 'Nurses are two a penny, to come by, and practically everyone speaks French and German. You don't speak Japanese so it's not likely that you'll get back to Singapore for years.' He glowered at Millie. 'What the hell do you think you can do with your limited experience?'

It slipped out before she had time to pick her words. 'Well, heaven blast you, you insulting little man. If you're not interested in my skills, or my desire to do something for my country, I'll damn well go to others who are.' With a growing loathing for the bumptious two men, Millie was already off her chair.

Stony-faced, he said, 'that's entirely up to you, Miss Chance,' and dismissively he bid her, 'good day.'

Enraged, Millie stormed out. However, she had no idea that she was being tested for her spunk and commitment. She didn't realise either, that Special Operations Executive were desperate to make contact with people fluent in French and German. Recruitment of SOE volunteers, often by word of mouth, had started back in 1940 on Churchill's instructions when he declared he wanted to *'set Europe ablaze.'* His plans for sabotage and subversion had been undertaken by infiltrating secret agents into areas of Eastern Europe and in the extremely hazardous regions of occupied France.

The instant the door slammed behind Millie the officer grinned broadly, and said to Bain, 'she's got just the type of gung-ho spirit we need. What do you say, Bain?'

Bain stood up, and blew out his cheeks giving a hearty chuckle. 'We're well used to unusual characters, I have to say, but that young lady has spirit in abundance. By escaping from Singapore she's proved her capacity to endure physical hardship, and I'm pretty sure she's not the type to crack under pressure. The training programme will iron out any little foibles and tone down her somewhat irascible attitude. On the other hand, we wouldn't want to destroy that little idiosyncrasy, altogether.'

Satisfied, the office nodded. 'Get her back in, Bain. If she's agreeable we'll put her on a crash course in German, straight away.'

Graham Bain found he was actually running down the corridor to catch up with Millie, and he did not miss the thunderous look she gave him as he grabbed her arm and drew her aside.

'Miss Chance! Miss Chance,' he kept hold of Millie's arm, 'will you please return with me? Forget all that was said in the last half hour by the officer back there.' Millie didn't budge. 'Please, it-it is very important, I can assure you.' Feeling awkward now, he released his grip. 'I-we will explain why we had to conduct things, er the interview, in the way we did.' Astonished, yet intrigued, at this change of tactic, Millie found she was doing as he asked. Anxious to reassure her, Bain said, 'in an ideal situation we would not have been so brutish. It was underhand, I know, definitely not very British. But it was necessary. You see, we have to be sure—'

Millie glared at Bain as he opened the door of the interview room, and demanded, 'be sure of what?' Perplexed at their duplicity in attitude, she was growing suspicious. Bain picked up on this and condescendingly offered her the chair, keen to explain.

However, hearing Millie's remark, the SOE officer told her, 'we had to be absolutely sure of where your loyalty lies, is the answer to that question, Miss Chance, before—'

'There is no question of my loyalty. I am a patriot, through and through.'

'We do not doubt your patriotism. And that is why we have selected you for something-something special and ultra, ultra secret. It is so secret, in fact, that you must not tell anyone about it. Not even you family or your closest friends. Not even your grandmother.' Millie's eyes narrowed. 'Yes we have to make checks, in the light of security, you understand. We have to be sure. There is so much at stake. Of course you don't have to undertake the task, which is why we always ask for volunteers.' He scrutinised her carefully. 'Miss Chance, you have told us you want to serve your country. At present, getting back to Singapore is out of the question, naturally. But what do you think, in the line of duty, to going to France?' Not waiting for an answer, he added, 'oh not right away, you understand. No, no, no. You will have to undergo rigorous training in what we call—'

He caught Bain's eye, who offered, 'trade craft. For instance, you have just come from the Far East and understandably, could not have seen many pictures of Germans in uniform.'

'I haven't exactly come from another planet,' Millie fired at Bain.

Patiently, Bain made light of the quip. 'No, Miss Chance, you haven't. However, let me show you what I mean.' He opened a thin dog-eared note book and handed it to Millie. 'Identify these uniforms and weapons, and point out the German planes, that you can name, please. The reason being, that in France one's safety and even one's life would depend upon instant recognition.'

Millie turned over pages which had drawings of German guns and German military figures of various ranks. Finally, all she could recognise were sketches of French police.

It didn't take long before Mille blushed at her lack of knowledge. Humbly, she said, 'I do beg your pardon.'

Bain nodded and took the book from Millie. He appreciated her honesty in acknowledging her ignorance.

'In time, identification will become second nature and you will live, breathe and smell the enemy, in uniform and out. In Britain, and around our Isles, special schools have been set up; these are highly secret schools, naturally. In these establishments you will be taught the trade skills that will keep you alive in occupied France. SOE instructors will strive to cover all aspects of—'

'What's—'

'SOE?' The other officer took over from his colleague, and told Millie, 'SOE is short for Special Operations Executive. Let me give you some background information on the organisation.'

He went on to tell Millie how Prime Minister Churchill, back in July of 1940, began to wage a clandestine war against Hitler's armies. The outcome was that Churchill created an elite force which immediately came under the direction of Hugh Dalton. Men, and women, with unusual talents were selected for SOE, from a small number of hand-picked volunteers. Of paramount importance was language skills, yet these special people were chosen from various backgrounds. Just as significant, Millie was told, an audacious attitude and an aptitude to think quickly on one's feet were some of the traits regarded as essential factors in choosing, what high ranking SOE officials considered, the right candidate for the job.

The SOE officer stressed, '*if* you get through your training, you will be invited to join this secret service as an undercover agent, carrying out clandestine missions in France. But I must warn you Miss Chance, it is a very dangerous undertaking. And it would be perfidious of me not to point out that a number of fine agents have been captured and tortured by the Gestapo, and some we know, have been executed.' He shot a glance at Bain, and then cleared his throat. 'Going to France will be entirely your decision. However, Miss Chance, you will not be thought any the less of should you—'

Millie answered, without hesitation, 'of course I'll go.'

CHAPTER SIXTEEN

Clad in the uniform of a FANY, Millie found herself billeted in a room at one of the colleges in Cambridge. She'd come up from London to attend the German language course that had been organised for her, by Graham Bain. It was very late in the day when Millie finally arrived at the designated college. After collecting her room key from the bursar she saw an arrow pointing to the refectory. A notice on the door, however, told her it had closed, hours ago. There was nowhere to even get a cup of tea, but she didn't care, not a bit. She had something much nicer to look forward to. Prolonging that moment of ecstasy, Millie whipped up a flurry of energy and unpacked her small suitcase, in a trice. Then she threw on pyjamas and leapt into an unwelcoming narrow bed. She had to be up early for the class, but thoughts of that got pushed aside. Carelessly, draped over a chair Millie delved into her uniform jacket pocket. She got out Philip's letters and began to finger the torn envelopes. Thumping the pillow signalled the start of the moment of pleasure. Maybe she would find something she might have missed, earlier, while trying to read them amidst the chaos of a crowded train. She held the tissues of love, next to her heart, her breath quickened, as she thought, how awful it would have been if she had decided not to go back to the flat to get something to read on the train. She would have missed Philip's telephone call. Her gaze flickered to the precious volume resting on the bedside locker—*A Tale of Two Cities*—it would, forever, be her favourite book.

Philip had said he was in London, for a couple of days, and asked if they could meet up. Breathless, and excited, she told him yes, yes, yes. She had peered at her flushed face in the mirror, and then at the FANY uniform she was wearing. It couldn't be helped, she'd have to go as she was, there was so little time, and she didn't want to waste a minute by changing into mufti. Her case would have to be lugged along, as well, but, too bad. She was rearranging things in her mind. She would get a much later train up to Cambridge. She would have plenty of time to get there, if she forewent the sightseeing walk she had planned. The choice was blatantly easy.

When they meet at the station they abandoned discretion, and kissed, spontaneously, oblivious to the wolf-whistles and envious jeers from a carriage packed with soldiers. Many, no doubt wishing they could exchange places. Weary, war-haggard faces, bobbed, higgledy-piggledy through gaping windows, Forage caps knocked askew, in an unconscious urge to hold a picture of anything beautiful, or normal. Then, as if by a magician's slight of hand, both lovers and soldiers became swallowed up in a ghostly, frothy grayness. The strangled coughs of the massive engine, accentuated its purpose of wafting all its passengers on to nebulous destinations.

Kissing her again, Philip told her, 'you look wonderful, Milliepead, absolutely wonderful.' He picked up her suitcase and observed the familiar stiffness of a brand new uniform. Millie smiled at his term of endearment. She was happy to be looking, once again into his enchantingly, lovely, blue eyes. Then with feathery shyness, she put her arm through his. It brought to mind the first time, that day back in Singapore, when casually, almost tritely, she performed that same action. Now it felt so different, such joy to touch him again.

Millie told him, 'you look wonderful too, fully recovered, I see.' He nodded. 'I'm so-so pleased to see you. I thought of you all the time, and then when I didn't hear anything, I—'

'I did write.'

'I never got—'

'No, I have them here.' He patted his pocket. 'There was a lot of confusion after we landed in India.' He threw a resigned glance at Millie. 'It didn't help us either, when we were separated almost as soon as we got off the boat. Anyway, I can tell you at the Indian army base, there was almost disbelief when I put in my report. Obviously they had heard about Singapore, but it took some of the top brass a while for the shock of losing the island to hit home. I think they were pretty fearful that the Japs might invade them. For some of us, it was a bit of a waiting game until orders came through for me and the wounded to return to England.' He didn't venture anything further, instead, suggested, 'I thought we could have lunch together.' Hoping Millie wouldn't think it presumptuous, he added, 'actually, I had a bit of time earlier, and I've booked a table. There seems a nice restaurant a street or two away, if you'd like that.'

'Yes, yes, I'd like that very much.'

Reassured, he squeezed her gloved hand. Seeing the FANY shoulder flashes, he said, 'so, you have decided to take up you nursing duties.'

'Um, mm, something-something like that.' She was fumbling around thinking what to say next, but luckily, for the moment, there was no need to elaborate.

Philip pointed, 'ah, here we are, this is the place. Hope there's something decent on the menu. We were rather indulged in Singapore, in some ways, I mean.'

'Yes,' Millie agreed. 'I know exactly what you mean.'

Concerned, the first question Philip asked once they were ushered to their table was, 'have you had any news of your father, or the old doctor, chap?'

'No, well, there's not very much information that's come through. The only scraps that Mother got from her constant trips to the Embassy, was that the Japanese had rounded up thousands of civilians and put them into Changi prison. They are presuming Father and Doctor Elder are among those poor unfortunates.'

'Yep, that's about the sum of what I heard had befallen the fate of the colonials. And the Japs have taken over the British Army's Selarang Barracks, and have banged up thousands of Australian and British soldiers, in our own bloody barracks! Christ, what a travesty.'

Philip was not going to mention the unofficial rumbling that had been circulating, on the grapevine, about the Japs setting up forced labour camps.

The waiter brought two menus printed out on cards not much bigger than ones used for playing poker. Attempting to study the food came as a diversion and gave them a chance to think on something else. There wasn't much of a selection, but they made their choice and ordered a flavoured fish dish, which most likely was the hermaphrodite snoek. When it came to it neither Millie nor Philip was particularly bothered about what food they ate, just delighted to be together.

'There's such a lot I want to ask, say,' said Millie, trying to disguise her emotion.

Philip had an overwhelming desire to kiss her again, to taste her lips. He wanted to hold her close, so close that he could feel her body, her pert little breasts and the curve of her hips. An evocative vision of the thin, cotton dress she wore on the *Dover Castle* suddenly sprang to mind. A vague hope he had earlier, that they might have gone to a hotel for the night, faded. It was out of the question. She had to be in Cambridge to start her nursing job. Philip thought, odd coincidence, that. He would like to have told her that he was at Cambridge University, only a few years ago, finishing off a PhD on the Relevancies of Ancient Language in Modern Times. But he had to be careful, it might complicate things, the need for secrecy was absolute, so he was told. On impulse, Philip reached across the table and held both her hands in his.

'You'll be so much safer up in Cambridge, Millie. Better to get away from London. The city has taken a terrible pasting, and we're left with all those bombed and unsafe buildings. The skies are quiet now. But we never really know what Hitler is likely to throw at us.' He wanted to know, had to ask, 'Millie, I-I do you mind me asking, are you, are you, you know, seeing anyone?'

He had such a pained expression that Millie couldn't help her misplaced sense of humour, and rather unkindly, started to giggle. Heavens, she thought, what time, and how in the name of God was it possible to be 'seeing' anyone? Philip took her unspoken response as a no, and breathed a sigh. Now he would be able to give her the letters.

Millie eventually drifted off to sleep, with Philip's declarations of love, drizzling deep into her psyche like a deliciously hot scented bath. Meanwhile, not far from Waterloo Station, Philip was spending a lonely night at the Union Jack Club. He lounged on top of the bed, finishing off his last cigarette before turning in. His thoughts were like tramlines, criss-crossing the nightmare events of that journey, a few months ago, yet still, indelibly fixed in his brain. That last day with McGregor, had started out so happy and carefree in Singapore. It was impossible to rein in McGregor from talking non-stop about Grace. What had become of his fellow officer? Philip could only speculate. He forced that memory aside, till he was seeing Millie, at work on the old *Dover Castle.* Her tireless efforts, in adverse conditions filled him full of admiration and love. The pretty frock she wore soon became smattered with blood and streaked in oil stains. Yet today, seeing her dressed in the sober FANY uniform, made him, inexplicably, anxious.

Travelling down from Doncaster to London had been a typical spring-like day. Interested, Philip even followed the fluttering, yellow splodges of daffodils, on railway embankments. With a lightness of heart, he couldn't help comparing England's lushness to the energy-sapping humidity of the Far East. He considered if, for an instant, one forgot about the war, it was the sort of day a poet, such as his old chum, Hugo Maitland, from Cambridge, might be inspired to write about. Philip was able to scoff at his own brand of romanticism, knowing his buoyant mood was down to the likely prospect of seeing Millie. And yet when he saw Millie, he expected she'd be dressed in something flouncy, feminine, not a dour military khaki. It disturbed him, somewhat.

He drew heavily on his cigarette before stubbing it out, and lay with his hands behind his head, staring up at a brown patch on the ceiling. He'd felt sheepish when Millie asked him how he came to be in London, but he stayed as near to the truth as he could. He told her that they (not elaborating upon who *they* were), weren't quite sure what to with him, once he'd got back from India, so they slotted him into the Signals. However, coming from living on a knife-edge, Philip felt a growing restlessness against the tedium and regimentation of military life in the Signals. So, he applied for a transfer.

Then just the other day, he was informed by the CO that there was some sort of a recruiting drive going on in London and he'd been ordered down to attend a selection board. After being put through a whole rigmarole of 'tasks,' his immediate future looked to be all mapped out. He'd been told that in a couple of day's time he'd join the Intelligence Corps based in Oriel College, Oxford. Here he would undergo a different form of training. This time the Army was to put to use Philip's university background as a language specialist, with a view to being recruited as an interrogator. It would seem his feet were set to remain firmly planted on dear old Blighty. He began to reflect on the probability that at least he'd get a chance to see a whole lot more of Millie.

CHAPTER SEVENTEEN

The sheer intensity of the course, and its long hours meant that there was no time to become acquainted on anything like first name terms, with fellow students. And as for socialising, well, their humourless tutor informed them, with undiluted relish, that that or any other form of frivolous entertainment was an obsolete luxury, while they were in the University's hallowed halls of learning. They were, he said, there to imbibe swiftly and accurately the language spoken by the "bloody Hun." A veteran from The Great War, he used this bilious spate when vehemently referring to the German soldier, and never once did he moderate in his vitriolic outbursts of hatred, for that old enemy.

The course wasn't exactly what Millie would have called a doddle, but as time went by, she was pleasantly surprised that her school girl German was not as rusty as she had feared. And at least she wasn't kicked out after the first week, which is what had happened to one shamefaced fellow. However, as fate would have it, Millie did not get to complete the German course. Just as the weeks were ticking by nicely, and with only a matter of days before its finish, Millie got pulled out of her studies. Irritated, she was on the verge of remonstrating with officials, which is what Millie might have done a few months back. But this student was learning, learning not just the language of the "bloody Hun," but learning discipline and self-control. So Millie held her tongue while waiting to hear the reason for her dismissal.

It was, therefore, not without a modicum of trepidation that she faced, yet again, Graham Bain and the SOE officer, whose name she still did not know, nor did she seek to ask. Summoned to a private closet, unnecessary chit-chat was dispensed with, as Bain came straight to the point concerning Millie's abrupt and untimely withdrawal.

He told her, 'we've read the reports on your progress, here, Miss Chance, which by anyone's standards is pretty good. So, you'll not miss out on much by not finishing the last few days.' He even managed the glimmerings of a congratulatory smile. 'The reason why we are here is to get you started on your first assignment.' By now, Millie was on full alert. Were they going to send her to France, so soon? She felt her stomach lurch. Bain noticed Millie's pallor. 'To set your mind at rest, in case you were wondering that we might have France in mind, the answer to that is no, it would be absurd, out of the question. You are nowhere near ready. The task we want you to undertake is much more doable, and it will give you practical hands on experience. And at the same time—'

Slap! Suddenly a set of documents landed in front of Millie.

'There are your papers.' The SOE officer coolly pushed them toward her. 'It's your security pass and travel warrant, and some money, not a lot, I know, but it should cover your expenses, provided you go easy and don't get too extravagant. If you are desperate for any more, or in an emergency, and I stress, an emergency, ring this number. Memorise it and then burn it. Understand?' Millie nodded and gathered up the money and papers. 'I shall need your signature.' While Millie duly signed to say she'd received the official papers and the cash, he told her what she had to do. 'Tomorrow, you will travel up to Oldham General Hospital. When you get there, report to what used to be the private wing. The hospital is now used for-for well, other things, but don't take any notice of the military goings on. Make your way to the second floor and show your pass to whoever is on security.'

Millie, for the first time, asked, 'what am I to do? Am I expected?'

Bain answered, 'yes, Miss Chance. You are expected. And what we want for you to do is to spend some time working on the wards.'

Before she had time to think the SOE chap, said, 'of course they are not the ordinary run-of-the-mill wards, as far as wards, in this day and age, can be ordinary.'

Millie felt she could be watching a game of tennis, for her head got swivelled from one man then to the other.

Bain drew closer, to agree with his compatriot. 'Quite. No, they are not, in any sense, ordinary wards. They are high security wards, units, housing wounded German and Italian prisoners of war. When the prisoners are classed as fit, they'll get shipped off to a transit camp, and we'll have no further contact, once they leave. But in the meantime, while we have them in our clutches, we want to discover as much about them as we can. Among the general riff-raff, there's bound to be some trouble makers, but it's not those blighters we're bothered about. No, it's the other little bastards we want to weed out. It's the possibility that the odd spy could have got hidden among the motley assorted rank and file.' He paused for a moment, to suggest, 'they might have got caught out with nowhere to go, once our chaps were rounding the prisoners up. They could have camouflaged themselves as ordinary soldiers.' He glanced at his colleague. 'It's a strong possibility, it has happened before, hasn't it?'

'Yes, yes it has. And on another important note,' Millie turned again towards the SOE officer, 'we strongly suspect, well, more than suspect, that a few of the high ranking officers know the exact whereabouts and numbers of German divisions based around Tobruk. It would be mighty helpful if we could winkle out that information. That would give us indications as to where the sites of their secret oil dumps are. Fuel is vital if they are to feed their extended supply lines. That is the type of information which would be really useful to the Allies.' He considered that was as much as Millie needed to know at this stage. 'Now, while you are going to be nursing them we want you to—'

'But I'm not a qualified nurse.'

Bain quickly reassured her, 'that doesn't matter. As far as we're concerned, the job is not about your nursing ability, that's only a front. For the medical and nursing staff we have concocted a cover story for you, and given you the name, Nightingale, Nurse Nightingale.' Millie groaned inwardly. 'It shouldn't ruffle anyone's feathers to see a new nurse.' Bain chuckled at his impromptu choice of expression. 'Because of the high number of prisoners that have arrived, the hospital will have had extra nurses drafted in. While this um assignment is absolutely hush-hush, you won't be entirely alone—'

'Thanks!'

Bain ignored Millie's ironic response. He was engrossed in unearthing another name among his various papers.

Pulling a slip out of a manila folder, he said, 'this chap, as you can see, is a doctor.' A cough pulled Bain up. He looked at his companion. 'Yes, well he is a doctor, of sorts. Not a medical doctor, he's a-a doctor of what is it, Philosophy? Well, something to that effect. Anyway, remember his name. He's been told you're coming, but he'll stay in the background, keeping his distance, until he judges the right time to contact you. Later you can pass on anything you get to him.'

The SOE officer told Millie, 'the important thing for you is to convince the prisoners that you are just a simple nurse doing her job, and one who doesn't understand any German. You can act as surly as you think fit, but listen very carefully to them talking; get them used to you being around, without giving the game away. See what you can pick up, even if it doesn't make sense to you. Don't disregard anything. You have an ideal opportunity to hone your skills, and it is a situation that could be very useful to our intelligence lot.'

Bain interjected, by stressing, 'they must never discover that you speak their lingo. Do you understand?'

'Yes, I understand perfectly.' And using a rather old-fashioned turn of phrase, she told him, 'rest assured I shall do my very best.'

'Good girl.'

That little flicker of warmth from Graham Bain gave Millie confidence to ask, 'where have the prisoners come from? Where were they captured?'

'North Africa, they were captured outside Tobruk. They are a bit of a mixed bag, though most are from Rommel's Afrika Korps.' Millie had no idea where Tobruk was until recently, when, in common with other people, had read the newspaper stories about the battles out there. 'They have a tough fighting reputation, the Afrika Korps, and are considered by some to be something of an elite bunch.' Bain went on, a mite enviously, 'especially the officers. We feel certain that a few of them will have information that could be really useful to Montgomery, if we can somehow get them to disclose it.'

'Of course they are not going to come clean and tell us,' the SOE officer added with his bit of derision. 'All we'll officially get is their name, their rank and number.'

It suddenly occurred to Millie that she'd need a nurse's uniform.

'What about my clothes, I came up in my FANY uniform. I'll need—'

'Yes, good point,' Bain told her. 'We nearly overlooked that. Wear civvies for the journey. You can collect your nursing uniform from the laundry supervisor once you get to the hospital.' He snapped his briefcase closed. 'Now, I think we've covered everything. Is there anything else you want to ask us?'

'Er, yes. Can you tell me how long this exercise will take or—'

Without hesitation, Bain told her, 'the plain answer is no. The figures that we've been given to date is twenty-two prisoners, some with serious wounds and some with an assortment of minor injuries, broken bones, gun shot wounds that sort of thing.'

'I see.'

'Anyway, to help speed your journey up, we've arranged for a car to drive you up to Oldham.' He now seemed keen to wrap the finer points up so he asked, 'do you-do you have any other questions?'

Millie shook her head, 'no, I don't.'

'Right, well,' the two men exchanged glances and Bain enquired of his companion, 'do you wish to add anything, old chap?' A shake of the head indicated no. Then almost as an after thought Bain offered, 'just one final bit of advice, Miss Chance. Perfect your cover story. And-and watch your step, and tread carefully. While any information you can get, however small could be very significant, we don't want any accident befalling you.'

While the two men headed for a quick drink at *The Black Pig*, before making their journey back to London, their parting comment kept repeating in Millie's inside, like an uncomfortable attack of indigestion.

CHAPTER EIGHTEEN

For the crew in charge of a barrage balloon, storms were feared, probably more than any other common hazard. And the accident that put Janet, and her runaway barrage balloon, out of action, happened during an almighty thunder storm. It certainly reinforced one of the first things they were taught, that steel cables attached to the balloon enabled lightening to travel down to earth. So, when driving their winch-mounted vehicle in such conditions, it was common practice for the crew to have to clamber on and then hop off sharply, to avoid being electrocuted. Sometimes, before an approaching storm, there was time to bed down the defence balloons, and that particular evening the weather did indeed look ominous. Janet and the team all watched the sky blacken. Then the decision was made to bring General Slim—as he was affectionately called, by the all female gang—down. However, the storm blew up so suddenly that try as they might to keep the balloon head to wind, he couldn't be controlled and he broke loose. In the ensuing struggle Janet sustained a wrist injury and burns to her neck.

Janet's wounds were not life-threatening, though they were severe enough to put her in hospital for a few days. This was followed by several appointments to the outpatients where her dressings got changed and fresh strapping applied to her wrist. Nevertheless, she was more fortunate than one of her colleagues, who fell heavily from the lorry and broke her femur.

Later on, in spite of Janet insisting she was well enough to rejoin the crew, her superior officer disagreed and she was transferred to lighter duties. It was a posting she was told that would be less strenuous, until she was fully fit. However, to Janet's, way of thinking, driving ruddy pampered army bods up and down the country was not as exciting as operating her beloved barrage balloons. Annoyingly, there was nothing that Janet could do, she had to obey orders.

Up to now, Janet had never chauffeured a female around. So when she read her instructions and saw she was to pick the woman up from Cambridge University, an image came to mind of some batty Margaret Rutherford type. Even the name, Miss Nightingale, suggested to Janet, a stuffy, intellectual eccentric. So feeling rather fed up, and with rain lashing down from the heavens, Janet was not looking forward to the drive up to Oldham. Her uniform was already damp from having to stop to fill up with petrol and now for the last twenty minutes she was kept waiting for the old gal. Through a blanket of rain, Janet at last spotted the woman, and got out and went round, smartly, to open the car door.

Janet asked, 'Miss Nightingale?' She could not see the woman's features, as she wore a scarf pulled down over her face, against the weather, and was cloaked in a long, beige mackintosh. She decided to get out of the rain fast and check her papers once in the car.

'Yes,' the woman acknowledged.

'Let me take your case, ma'am.'

'Thank you.'

'It's a shocking day, isn't it?'

'M'mm.'

To pass the time, once out of Cambridge, Janet tried to make small talk, but got no response from Miss Nightingale, seated in the back. Looks like its going to be a long drive with not much conversation, she thought. Some of 'her chaps,' as Janet called them, could become quite chatty. She even got asked out on one occasion. A rustling movement from the woman caused Janet to glance in the mirror. She was shaking her head to flick the rain off her headscarf. Janet became puzzled, and thought, why the heck doesn't she take it off?

Suddenly, after several more furtive peeps, realisation dawned and Janet forcefully, swerved off the road, screeching the car to a stop. Miss Nightingale was thrown forward, but scuttled back and wedged herself into the corner. Then Janet jumped out and ran to the rear of the car and flung the door open. She stuck her head inches away from her charge's face.

'It bloody well is you! I thought it was. Trying to hide under your scarf, were you? Why? Why for heavens sake?'

'I hoped you wouldn't recognise me. Sorry. I had no idea it would be a woman driver, let alone you. And anyway, why aren't you off somewhere flying your balloons?'

'Never mind that, why didn't you contact me to let me know what—'

Millie lied, 'I did telephone.'

'I've been in hospital.'

Alarmed, Millie said, 'I'm sorry, I didn't know. What happened? Are you OK?'

'Humph, as if you care, with you being a nurse I had hoped you might have visited me.'

'Sorry, I really didn't know. I've—'

'And what's with this name?' Janet scowled, '*Miss Nightingale?*' Millie didn't answer. Instinctively, Janet sensed something was up. She softened, and while watching little rivulets of water trickle down Millie's face, she said, 'here, let me take that wet scarf.'

'Thanks.' Millie smiled a big sigh. 'Such a lot has happened, Janet, and I can't utter a word to tell you what it's about.' She tried to make a joke. 'Not even to you, my bestest friend in the whole world. It's absolutely hush-hush, and I'm sworn to secrecy.' Millie shrugged, remembering the haste with which Graham Bain arranged for her to sign the Official Secrets Act. 'A sombre document, for one so young to put her name to,' was his remark, as he unscrewed the lid of the ink pot.

Gradually, it had stopped raining on the way up, and the mackintosh and scarf had got tossed aside in the back of the car. And several hours later, on the outskirts of Oldham, Millie and Janet said a fond farewell. Previously, they had taken a pub lunch at an inn that was off the beaten track, and their choice of location proved relatively quiet. There they fell to reminiscing on happier times. Laughing quietly at the school larks and silly pranks they got up to. They talked of old girlfriends and boyfriends, and touched on their families, but both steered diplomatically away from the taboo subject.

They agreed their parting would have to be formal, once they got to the hospital. So an affectionate embrace was made discretely away from the come-hither looks of two service men who had been giving them the glad-eye over tankards of beer. And as they arranged, once they got to the hospital, Janet officially handed over Millie's suitcase and without lingering, in order not to draw attention to anything out of the ordinary, she expertly turned the car around. To all intents and purposes, the hospital, Janet observed, appeared much like any other Victorian medical institution, except for coils of viciously looking barbed wire, fixed to the high security fencing surrounding the perimeter. Nevertheless, she couldn't suppress a cold shiver that ran down her back, and she pushed hard on the accelerator pedal to put as much mileage between Oldham and herself as she possibly could. It was, however, different for Millie. She was all hyped up for the task that lay before her.

Early the next morning, when Millie stepped into her nurse's uniform, for an instant she felt a sensation akin to being back in the hospital in Singapore. Mindful of her assignment, thoughts of Singapore vanished as rapidly as they'd come. Soberly, she tightened the navy-blue belt that accompanied the outfit, and with hairgrips slid along the seams, she secured the starched, outsized nurse's hat—so different to the small staid light-weight cap that she wore in the tropics. With a quick glance in the mirror to check her uniform was satisfactorily arranged, Millie set off to find the sister-in-charge of her designated ward.

What Millie found was a confusion of criss-crossing corridors that had to be negotiated after passing through the security check. She had all but got her bearings when the familiar wail of that dreaded noise heralded the onset of an approaching air raid. Nearing her ward she could see there was a bit of a flap on. She found porters and nurses moving some patients under beds for protection, and wheeling other less mobile patients in the direction of the basement shelter.

Suddenly, from behind her, a man's voice shouted in her ear, 'quickly, nurse, take the other end of this bed.'

She spun round and grabbed the upright rail. She asked, feeling slightly foolishly, 'where to, Doctor?'

'Just follow me, nurse, just follow me.' He tucked the ends of a blanket tightly under the mattress. 'Keep you arms in, Fritzee, me lado.' That was how he addressed the POW lying in the bed. 'That's your bloody mates up there. Mind you, we don't want any visitors calling right now. What do you say, nurse, aye?'

Millie couldn't speak. She was flabbergasted at his nonchalant manner in the midst of the crunch and thuds of exploding bombs.

'You're new here; I take it, just arrived? What's your name?'

Millie swallowed, 'Nightingale, Nurse Nightingale.'

'Nightingale, aye, ha, ha, hmm I see, just like the little song bird,' and he grinned.

Millie coloured. She wondered who this man was, to be so familiar. Damn cheeky thing. She thought, maybe he's not even a doctor, and her colour deepened while thinking he's probably a porter taking advantage of me being new to the place. Come to think of it, he did look on the scruffy side, with his tie skew-whiff, and his shock of red hair almost reaching his collar. Millie looked closer at him as they manoeuvred the bed into a corridor with some other patients. And those funny owl-like glasses made her wonder if he could even see properly. Nonetheless, this jolly, white-coated chappie was brazen, and sharp-sighted enough to give Millie a wink before he pelted at full speed in the direction from where he had come from.

Three hectic days had passed since the air raid—Millie's thunderous introduction to Oldham. Aside from the boiler house and laundry rooms, which had part of their roof blown off, and some shattered window panes to the east side of the building, the hospital escaped serious damage. After the clearing up, when everyone tended to muck in, Millie began to feel slightly uneasy. She had not heard from her contact, a Doctor Hugo Maitland. Not that it would have made any difference because she had nothing to report.

On an intuitive level, Millie sensed the prisoners were testing her reactions when they conversed among themselves. She found the German officers haughty, and they ignored her as she carried out her nursing duties. They were sullen, often remaining silent until she left. Some of the other ranks, though, gabbled away, in their native tongue, as if Millie was invisible. Millie hadn't much difficulty in following these brief snatches of conversations, which was, as far as she could make out, simple everyday grumbles about the lousy, English food, and constant quips tossed around cursing their bad luck in getting captured.

Following the example of the red-headed doctor or porter, she called all the Germans, Fritz. Some told her, Hans, I'm Hans, or I'm Otto, not Fritz, but she ignored their comic insistence and stuck to Fritz or even Fritzee, and generally they just laughed, calling her *dumm* or *dummkopf*—stupid.

A few of the men she was nursing had very bad wounds. Try as she might, Millie found she couldn't bring herself to hate them as such, or purposely inflict pain when she was treating them. However, it crossed her mind and made her think what if they had been Japanese…She even came off duty with one young soldier's pathetic thanks ringing in her ears. When caring for him, she had to force herself to remain distant and in control of her emotions. She had to steady a hand that could easily have trembled in pity as she bandaged his red-raw amputated stump. For the first time she began to question her motives and her strengths for volunteering into this uncertain business of-of well what exactly? She seriously wondered if she was up to it.

Millie had worked a ten hour day, all week and was hugely thankful to be given half a day off, at the end of it. The ward sister told her that there was a park, a little way from the hospital, if she felt like getting some fresh air. But Millie was so tired that she'd slept most of the morning away, and now there was just over an hour before she had to be back on duty. Eventually, she hauled herself up, quickly got washed and dressed, and headed for the park.

The long dead, Alderman, Mr G J Formby, who had bequeathed the only remaining intact bench in the park, would, Millie thought, be turning in his grave. The park had lost all of its lawns and flower beds, and was now transformed into one vast allotment, given over to growing vegetables. She watched a group of boy scouts diligently carrying water from an ornamental fountain to where they drenched rows of indistinguishable, leafy green things. Still feeling tired and with her muscles achy, Millie rested her back on the Alderman's tarnished name plaque. Watching the watery capers of the scouts, she soon became lost in her own thoughts, so much so that she didn't hear a man approach, until she felt a slight vibration of the seat, as he sat down. Just wanting her last half hour alone to relax and enjoy a pleasant bit of sunshine, she had no desire to talk to anyone, so pointedly she shuffled further the other way. However, out of the corner of her eye, she caught a flash of red hair. Her heart sank and she inwardly groaned, oh no, not him. He, on the other hand, remained quite oblivious to Millie, and didn't look at her.

Then he unexpectedly, said, 'good-day, Nurse Nightingale. I'm Hugo Maitland.'

Millie visibly sagged, then gasped, 'you, you're my—'

'Yep, it's me alright.'

'I had no idea—'

'Well, you weren't supposed to.' He still didn't move, staring straight ahead, from the end of Alderman Formby's bench. 'I've noticed you've settled in pretty well.' Again, he surprised Millie, as this was the first time she'd seen him since the air raid.

'Um, yes, I have, but I've not had a chance to-to you know—'

'It's early days, yet. All the same, I've a feeling in my water that things will liven up pretty soon.' He spun round to face Millie. 'By now, they'll have got used to your comings and goings. We're sending up some new boys, a fresh lot of prisoners. It should be interesting to see what you pick up when they meet their compatriots, and they get the chance to drop their guard.'

CHAPTER NINETEEN

The ward went deadly quiet. In full view of everyone, including the orderlies, a doctor, and the new batch of POW's, and without consideration for a young nurse's feelings, the sister-in-charge, loudly, and sternly reprimanded Nurse Nightingale, accusing her of working in a dirty sluice room that wasn't fit to be seen. She commanded her to clean it up and to clear up the soiled linen. Furthermore, the sister ordered all urinal bottles, and bedpans to be taken off the shelves and every single one washed again. With a hung-dog expression, and her face burning with shame, Millie slumped off to the offending room. She'd never felt so embarrassed since that day back in Singapore when she spilt the jug of water down the young Frenchman. Quiet mutterings both in German and English, followed Millie and the sister's exit from the ward.

When she was out of view from everyone including the patients, and other nurses, Millie, angrily, started to chew over the nasty scolding. Wondering where to begin the task, she stared around the sluice room. Her brow creased in a frown, and her jaw dropped, in disbelief. What was going on? Where was the dirty linen? There was no overflowing bins, no dirty bedpans. The sluice was spotless. Millie cursed, under her breath. What the heck was wrong with the bloody woman? She glanced up at the stainless steel urinals, gleaming and standing to attention like a line of regimental soldiers. Millie fumed; she's really got it in for me. She spun round to face the partly ajar door that she'd not closed properly. Then she held her breath. Slowly, slowly something clicked. She, the uppity sister, was the one that suggested Millie should go to the park, and that was when Hugo Maitland had turned up. The sluice got another examining. She looked again at its layout, in relation to the ward. Of course! Millie realised, this is an ideal spot for someone to stay hidden away out of sight, yet near enough to hear practically all of what went on in the ward. Here she could listen in and do just what she'd been sent there to do—spy. She began to understand. Sister had set this up. She had engineered the situation. *Sister* was the go-between. Millie had now a God given or sister given opportunity to secrete herself away for a couple of hours.

So the pretence began. A clattering of bedpans and urinal bottles was followed by Millie running the water taps full on. Then she took six or seven metal measuring jugs and put them in the shallow sink. She could pretend she was washing them, should anyone happen to walk in, which, Millie though was hardly likely unless one of the men needed a bottle. And on the plus side, those that had heard the sister sound-off, out of awkwardness would want to give Millie a wide birth to possibly spare her further blushes.

For sometime she stood tucked behind the door, popping out only to give the jugs a jangle, then nipping back to her hide-e-hole. Her ears started to prick up when a ripple of laughter broke out and she heard a POW reassure the new comers that in this hospital the British were soft, and they were left alone, no one gave them any hassle. They considered themselves lucky, for they could do what they pleased. Look, Millie heard someone declare, see what a time we have. We've got chess, and Hans has a mouth organ, and we play cards. There was a consensus of opinion that being in captivity was pretty cushy. And the stupid nurses can't speak German. We make fun of them, a raucous soldier bragged, and they just nod, like imbeciles. More laughter as someone else said something about giving Nurse Nightingale's arse a rub instead of the bedpans. Then, there was a sudden hush so Millie purposely clattered two bedpans together; it obviously told the Germans that Millie was busy cleaning. However, what Millie overheard in the next few minutes made the hairs on the back of her neck stand on end.

Checking her watch, Millie estimated that she'd spent enough time in the sluice. Any longer and it might arouse suspicion, or the chance that staff or patients may come in. The metal measuring jugs were rinsed then dried and hung back on their hooks. Then she splashed water down her apron and scrunched it up, and as an after thought, she pulled loose a few strands of hair from under her hat, to appear untidy. She was beginning to look as though she'd really given over the last miserable two hours to cleaning the sluice.

From the other end of the ward, sister was with two nurses, who were occupied in pushing back a set of screens. Seeing Millie emerge, sister marched, sergeant major-like towards her. Making a show of inspecting the sluice she looked Millie up and down, then said, stonily, 'go to the laundry, Nurse Nightingale, and change your apron, and smarten your self up.'

'Yes, Sister, of course, Sister, thank you, Sister.' Millie fled.

Materialising, as if from nowhere, Hugo Maitland slipped into the laundry, barely five minutes after Millie. He found her fastening closed her belt over a pristinely starched, white apron. And her hair was rearranged and tucked neatly under its hat. In spite of the seriousness of the situation, when Millie came close to Hugo, she put her two hands up to her face to smother uncontrollable laughter.

'Please, please excuse me, Hugo,' she eventually managed to say. 'Oh God, it's just this cloak and dagger stuff. I'm not used to it. And-and there's me banging those silly bedpans like I'm clashing the cymbals in a junior orchestra—'

The thought set Millie off on another fit of giggles. Then quite abruptly, Millie became serious, and looked as if she was about to cry.

'It's OK; it's OK, old girl. Its nerves-nerves do funny things to our emotions.'

Then he did a surprising thing. He took off his specs and kissed her tenderly on the cheek.

Millie swallowed. 'Thank you, Hugo, you are very kind.'

She had a great desire to be held in his arms, to be comforted, and she knew she wouldn't have resisted, if he had gone any further, but he didn't.

'Think nothing of it old dear,' he said, good-naturedly.

'Right, well, we'd better get down to business, before I forget all this bloody stuff.'

Hugo made notes of everything that Millie had committed to memory. Fresh news of the North African campaign was devoured by the longer term prisoners. There was a whoop of excitement when the old lags were told of Rommel's plan to feign a retreat in order to draw the British forward. They had been with their General and knew Rommel had tried this bluff before and it worked. If things went to form and with the Luftwaffe's easy access from its bases in Southern Italy, Tobruk was likely to be a carbon copy of a former success. Once the British made their move, Rommel would use the Italians to the South and his crack troops from the 5th Light Division would catch them in a deep pincher movement. One bumptious officer proclaimed boldly, an easy victory was anticipated by their magnificent General.

To the men of the Afrika Korp, this professional soldier, General Erwin Rommel, was their hero. He was admired more than any other leader. In a whirl-wind campaign, these incarcerated soldiers had earlier seen their idol push a depleted and weary Western Desert Force back from where it came. Now, they could only curse their dammed bad luck in getting left behind to get captured, rather than being able to bask under the umbrella of Rommel's successes. Even while the medical staff worked on the ward, the POW's made no secret in revelling in Rommel's victory at El Agheila, and the British defeat at Benghazi was openly talked over.

The final piece of information Millie gave to Hugo sounded somewhat confused. Nevertheless, he wrote that Rommel's intention was for the 15th Panzer Division to thrust forward to Gazala. Hugo wondered if Millie had maybe misheard the word Gazala as this was held by the British line of defence. The area around Gazala was strongly fortified with big guns, and heavily mined. Underlining Gazala, he wrote it down anyway.

Millie knew there would never be another chance to use the sluice room other than for normal purposes, or at the most just a quick dalliance. Later, the following night when Millie was coming off duty, Hugo caught up with her as she was heading for the nurses home. Talking softly, he told her, time was pressing as some of the POW's would soon be moved on. Hugo urged her to do what she could within the confines of pseudo-normality, but warned her not to take unnecessary risks by overplaying her hand. Millie thought Hugo expressed himself rather oddly. Nonetheless, returning on duty the next day, Millie, conscious of

Hugo's warning, found she had no other option but to stay in the ward, try not to look conspicuous and hope she could pick up something, anything amidst a slightly jaded undercurrent of unrest among the patients.

Sometimes screens pulled round a bed allowed Millie a degree of privacy, and a means of snatching a few extra minutes listening time. As the day went on, an opportunity presented itself while Millie was making evening cocoa for the patients. The kitchen was situated just off the main ward. It had two windows that were heavily taped up as a precaution against air raids, but there was also a tiny internal window which faced directly onto the ward. Millie hadn't though of using this window to eavesdrop as it was always closed, and usually overflowing with empty milk bottles, waiting to get collected. She carefully moved the bottles onto the other window sill, and with a bit of pressure, forced open the window. Unfortunately, this idea turned out to be fruitless.

A couple of days later, as Hugo had accurately predicted, four POW's were moved out of the ward. Frustrated, and agitated, Millie had learnt nothing new, except she had an uncomfortable sense of unease. She hadn't experienced anything like it before, but now she distinctly knew she was being watched. At first, Millie saw him as just another 'Fritz'. He was not among the original batch of POW's; he came in just a week ago, with the last group. He arrived, patched up, with a gun shot wound to his leg. It wasn't serious; a bullet had gone clean through the calf. Most of the other Germans had much more complicated injuries. The orderlies had given him a pair of crutches and he was mobile, fairly quickly. She did notice that he was able to help his compatriots by fetching and carrying cigarettes, playing cards and such like. Millie, however, didn't have to do very much for him, and one of the other nurses changed his dressing when it was necessary.

At first Millie thought she was imagining it, but then she suddenly became aware of him shadowing her, hovering near to her, too near for comfort. It was as if he was making a point of being with his compatriots when she was around. He was always prominent among the little huddles, listening and watching her face for tell-tale signs. When Millie saw him blatantly peering at her through the open kitchen window, she became certain he suspected her, so without further ado she shut the window. It was her intention to contact Hugo; unfortunately, she'd left it too late.

While Millie was closing the window 'Fritz' disappeared. She breathed a sigh of relief and prepared to leave the ward. However, he had followed her into the kitchen and had silently closed the door, behind him. As Millie turned, he threw his crutches at her. She ducked, instinctively. She wasn't quick enough and one of the crutches glanced off her head. The other missed, knocking several of the milk-bottles from the window ledge. Before Millie has a chance to put up any defence, worse followed. He was upon her, holding a knife inches from her throat, while he bent her arms painfully behind her back.

Unhurriedly, almost leisurely, he whispered down her ear, in German, 'I know you can understand, *Fräulein* Nightingale. I have watched you, I have been watching you for some time, and I know what you are up to. Those boys out there, they don't know. They haven't had my training. You think you fool them, yes? You think by your performance, and your little smiles, you hide what you really are, but I know—'

'You don't know as much as you think you do, Fritz, my lado.' It was Hugo's voice that Millie could now hear. He came in to the kitchen unnoticed. And with one lightening blow to the back of the German's neck, he dropped him to the floor, unconscious. Hugo retrieved the knife that had fallen from his hand, and then asked Millie, 'are you OK?'

Millie had gone a deathly grey-white. Clutching her throat in terror, she couldn't answer him. She wasn't even aware that by this time the ward sister was also in the kitchen.

'I'll take her into my office, Doctor Maitland, she's in shock. I've already phoned down to security they'll be here any minute.'

'Good, well done, Sister.' Then Hugo un-knotted his own tie and slid it from his neck. 'Just in case he comes to, I'll make sure he can't wriggle free.'

*

That was Millie's last stint on the ward. A few days later she was sitting in a secluded corner of the hospital canteen, waiting for a car to take her to the station. Hugo Maitland was coming towards her carrying a tray with large mugs of rust-coloured tea, and a plate with two current buns.

'Eat,' he ordered.

'I'm not—'

'Doesn't matter, eat.'

Millie still was very wane looking, and Hugo pushed the plate under her nose. Millie forced herself to comply and nibbled at the bun, and swallowed a mouth-full of tea.

She asked, Hugo, 'what will happen to him?'

'H'mm? Ah, the German. He'll get the third degree from our chaps at the cross-examination.' Hugo looked at his watch. 'He's probably under interrogation even as we speak.' Certain of the result, Hugo told Millie, 'he's a spy, alright. No two ways about it. But they'll give him a through grilling until they've wrung every scrap of evidence out of him. Then, he'll be taken to somewhere like the Tower, where they'll put a rope around his neck, and he'll be strung up.'

Hugo sunk his teeth into the bun. He wasn't wearing his glasses. Millie guessed he didn't really need them or used them only as a disguise. His eyes were steely grey and quite cold, as he spoke. She pushed her half-eaten offering aside. Now it was her turn to look at her watch.

'I'd better go down and see if my car has arrived.'

'Let me take your case.' They walked out of the canteen and down by a back staircase. 'You did tremendously well, back there, you know. We had no one else who could have come in at the last minute and done what you did. So don't feel badly that it didn't go quite as we expected. Things rarely do. But the fact is the information you gave me will be of great assistance in the right quarter. And besides, we've even got one in the bag who might have otherwise slipped the net.'

'Do many?'

'Do many what?'

'Do many slip the net, as you call it?'

'It's hard to say.' He gave her question a moment's thought, then as an optimistic response, Hugo told her, 'probably not, unless they had a really ace contact here they'd have a slim chance of surviving long on their own, without getting caught. You see, they'd require a base to operate from. A safe house, somewhere they could go to ground for months at a time, years even.'

'I see.'

The driver of the car was having a quick smoke while he waited for Millie. He stubbed the butt out on seeing her.

Hugo shook Millie's hand. 'Well, here we are, Nurse Nightingale, old thing. Chin up, and enjoy your spot of leave.'

'Thank you, Hugo. Goodbye.'

Millie thought it highly unlikely that her driver would be Janet, and of course she was right. There was probably dozens, hundreds of drivers even, ferrying people up and down the country, to God knows where. Clearly, it was neigh-on impossible that she should see the comforting presence of Janet, waiting for her. While the car made a u-turn Millie was about to give a final wave to Hugo when she stopped in mid-air. As Hugo threw Millie a half salute, he smiled farewell, then turned to acknowledge a figure behind him, in the shadowy recess of the doorway. The car was gathering speed, but by craning her neck, at the very edge of her vision, even in the gloom of the narrow exit, Millie could not fail to recognise the tall outline of Philip Hendry.

CHAPTER TWENTY

Grandma Chance was standing by the gas stove, totally oblivious to the kettle, which was puffing steam through spout and lid. She was deep in thought, and similarly, unaware that Millie had woken up and had come into the kitchen. Millie was wearing her mother's dressing gown, over pyjamas. For a moment Millie looked at her grandma's slightly stooped form, before going and gently guiding her to a chair at the table. A pot of tea was drawn and Millie poured them each a cup. They shared a smile over the gentler vapour, rising from a precious brew.

'What were you thinking about, just then, Grandma?'

The old lady swallowed. 'Oh, amongst other things, I was just thinking that it is almost two years to the day that Hitler strode around my beloved Paris, and planted the Nazi flag on the Eiffel Tower.'

She clunked the cup on its saucer, and pushed a two day old newspaper towards Millie. The headlines did not make for happy reading. A pained look came over Millie as she took in the plight of British ships braving the elements in the struggle to make the Atlantic crossing in one piece. Exact information on the number of ships sunk by U-boat packs was undoubtedly much worse than the press would publish. Millie guessed newspapers had a tendency to suppress the whole truth, not wanting to alarm the nation. Not good for morale, Grandma Chance had said. Millie tore her eyes away, and stirred her sugarless tea. She felt such pity for the poor Merchant Seamen, drowned, or left floundering in a watery wilderness, with only a slim chance of being picked up. She knew what it was like to be on an ocean, at the mercy of the enemy.

It was only a couple of days ago that the old lady had taken care of Millie, undressed her and put her into bed, just as she often did when Millie was a child. Earlier, when the train had left Oldham Station, Millie, tangibly felt her energy ebbing away as the rail-lines ate up the miles to St Pancras. She had fleetingly considered going to her flat, but she couldn't face the prospect of it being empty. She'd no notion of Janet's work schedule. So, using some of the leftover allowance money, that Graham Bain had given her, Millie got a taxi from the station and had come straight to the house in North London. She was in need of some family love.

As it happened, scatterbrained as ever, Millie found her mother rushing round in her petticoat to find a clean shirt. Then having pulled one from the clothes-horse, she had to iron it before dashing off to start her shift on the buses. She had barely time to kiss her daughter goodbye, let alone talk to her, and certainly she overlooked how pale and out of sorts Millie appeared. This fact did not escape the notice of Grandma Chance, who asked no questions while she held her granddaughter's hand until Millie downed a generous measure of brandy. And then before she sunk into the arms of Morpheus, the question Millie pondered on was, if this is what I'm going to be like after only a matter of weeks, surrounded by relatively tame German POW's, (she tried not to dwell on her close shave with death) how in heavens name am I going to cope with surviving in an occupied country, living with the enemy, for months at a time, longer, even?

Despondently, Millie dug her hands into the pockets of her mother's candlewick dressing gown. When the last of the cups of tea were squeezed from the pot, she wished with all her heart that she could confide in her grandma, confess her fears. But she dare not. Ever aware of the document which she had signed in front of Bain, who earlier had classified the job she would be doing as coming under the heading of 'highly secret and dangerous work.' She knew there was no advice that the dear lady could give her which could alter the road that she was headed for. Nor would Millie wish to make the family any more anxious than they already were.

Unexpectedly, it was just a few words, spoken so softly, that Millie had to ask, 'what did you say, Grandma?'

The old lady, with her eyes, shining, repeated, more forcefully, 'Millicent, darling, we can't let it happen again.'

Millie knew exactly what she meant. And this stoic resolve caused Millie to snap out of her introverted maudlin spell.

'Come on, Grandma, she exclaimed, brightly, 'let's you and me get dolled up. I've still got a few days of my leave left. So let's do something-something nice.'

'Oh, something nice, like what?'

Millie thought a moment. 'I know, let's go up West, and have dinner at some posh restaurant, and then take in a show. It will be my absolute treat.'

'Millicent, that sound's heavenly.' No one cheered her up like her darling Millicent. 'I'll go and put my nice blue dress on. Ah, but what about you, dear? I imagine all your pretty clothes are at the flat.'

'Don't worry, Grandma, I've heard that sometimes a girl in uniform can get tickets to see a show, for free. So, thankfully, there are some advantages to wearing a bit of khaki.'

Grandma Chance suggested her favourite little French restaurant, down a back street in Soho, and Millie knew the one she meant, having been there with her grandmother before. While they ate under its roof, only French conversation was spoken by everyone from the waiters up. Quite naturally, old Mrs Chance and Millie felt very much at home. Jokingly, she said to her grandma that she half expected to see the exiled French President de Gaulle pop in.

The restaurant had an abundance of jocular, Free French soldiers, smoking long Gauloise cigarettes, while knocking back copious bottles of wine as if there were no shortage of the nectar, whatsoever. A couple of attractive women were dressed in long, black sequined dresses. There was some sort of celebration taking place. Then generously, two glasses of wine were brought to their table. Surprised, Millie explained to the waiter that they hadn't yet ordered any wine, he pointed to a man standing to the left of the party. Catching Millie's eye, he bowed his head, and raised his glass to them; they did likewise, by way of thanks.

Millie and her grandma just gave pleasurable little shrugs when during their meal their glasses were refilled again, by the same gentleman. While the ladies were waiting for dessert, the French soldiers began drifting out in two's and threes. Calling, *bonne nuit,* to the waiters, as he went to leave, the gentleman who had bought them their wine, bent over their table, bowed again, and wished them good evening and good luck. He was a handsome, swarthy fellow, with a pencil-thin moustache. Had she but known it, his face was one that Millie would have good cause to recognise, later, down the line.

The lively Flanagan and Allen show had the crowd roaring with laughter. And everyone joined in singing and poking fun at the Germans with Flanagan and Allen's rendition of the song, Run Rabbit Run, for they changed the word Rabbit to Hitler. And of course more laughter and jollity followed. Then slightly more soberly, the likeable duo walked up and down the length of the stage singing sentimental songs that touched the heart of the London audience. Grandma and Millie found the whole outing thoroughly delightful. There was something about songs and music that uplifted the spirit and fed the soul, so old Mrs Chance said. Millie concurred, but felt sure the deliciously heady glasses of wine did much to enhance her grandma's enjoyment of the evening's entertainment.

It was well after one in the morning when the taxi dropped them off home, and they found Millie's two brothers were in bed asleep and so too was Mrs Chance. Their mother had placed them under strict orders to keep as quiet as mice so as not to disturb their sister while she was resting and recovering. Quite from what she had to recover from, the boys didn't know. Clive and Archie thought at first that Millie was ill, more dramatically, Archie came up with the idea that she was wounded.

The next day they were whisked off to school by their grandma, before Millie was up out of bed. Grandma told them that Millie needed her sleep but would come and meet them at the school gate when lessons were over. Meanwhile, a little later, Millie was able to have a couple of hours alone with her mother before she had to go on her shift. Clipping tickets on London buses was the last thing Millie would ever have thought of her mother happily doing. But she was wrong. Mrs Chance called it her therapeutic work. It kept her from falling apart, it kept her busy, she said, and stopped her mind from worrying all the time about what was happening in the Far East. The most the family heard was sketchy bits of information that dribbled in from the Red Cross. The last snippet of news they got was that thousands of prisoners were transported out of Singapore and into Burma. Depressingly, that too was confirmed by the

Embassy. The Japanese had rounded up both native Burmese and British soldiers to work on some kind of railway project that was being built by the Japs.

In the afternoon, Millie and her grandmother waited outside the school for Archie and Clive.

Dashing off, with a wave goodbye to his friend, Clive told Millie, 'Jimmy said you look spiffing, Millie. And he'd quite like to ask you out, as soon as he gets a bit older.'

Millie laughed, and gave him a hug. She thought how fast they were growing up. Archie, impatiently, had other things on his mind, and couldn't wait to show his sister the contents of his satchel.

'Millie, would you like to see my box of shrapnel?'

Millie kissed the top of his head, 'of course, Archie, I'd love to.'

It seemed Archie's toy soldier collection was demoted to the ranks of secondary importance. Precedence was now given over to a tin that contained charcoal-singed, contorted lumps of metal.

'Look at these Millie.' Archie blew on them and rubbed his cuff over a couple of cylindrical shaped objects. 'What do you think they are?'

Millie shook her head. 'I can't possibly think what they are, or where they could have come from.' All the while grandma Chance smiled. She knew they were 'hot stuff,' Archie's description of his latest treasure.

Filled with pride, Archie told her, 'these are caps from shells. And this is a lucky find from a machine gun, when the Messerschmitt got shot down last week.'

Millie tried to sound impressed. 'Heavens, how-where did you find them?'

'Well,' he sneaked a look at his grandma while she was speaking to Clive. Archie had been warned not to go there, 'mostly from old bomb sites. Sometimes I even get pieces on the pavement, but the best bits are around the bombed out houses and—'

'Bomb-bomb sites bombed out houses! Grandma, isn't that dangerous?'

The elderly lady shrugged her shoulders in resignation, 'boys will be boys.'

All too soon Millie had to get back to her flat. She would liked to have visited Mrs Elliott, but she'd run out of time. Millie could only ask her mother to pass on her regards and let her know she was thinking about her. The suitcase was considerably heavier than when she came. Grandma Chance had made Millie a cake, using some dried fruit and nuts that she had stashed away from the reserves that her daughter-in-law had prudently bought in South Africa. A pot of blackcurrant jam was got from the pantry. But Millie had no idea where her mother had unearthed the bag of ground coffee from. All the same, she was very grateful, and looked forward to sharing her goodies with Janet. Before leaving, Millie put two ten-bob notes on the sideboard for Archie and Clive.

*

Millie could hear music coming from the wireless, so she knew Janet was in.

'Hello, Janet, it's me,' she called, and closed the door loudly, in case Janet had company.

Janet ran into the hall to greet her friend. 'Millie, hello, oh it's so good to see you.' She gave her a kiss. 'Come into the kitchen.' She studied Millie for a moment. 'Mmm you're looking a bit peaky. Have they been overworking you at that hospital?'

Millie smiled, 'um, yes, it's something like that.'

Janet knew there was more to it. 'I was just going to get some tea. Fancy a cup?'

Millie saw two slices of unappetising looking bread on a plate. 'I've just come from grandma's house. They have turned the garden over to growing vegetables. But she saved a little patch where she now grows blackcurrants. She still likes to make a little jam. Look, she's given me a pot. Would you like some with your bread?'

'Oh yes, rather. How does she manage for sugar?'

'I've absolutely no idea.' Millie opened her case and handed Janet the jam. 'And, I think we can do better than that. Here we are. Grandma baked a fruit cake for us.'

'Oooh, that's absolutely lovely. What a darling! How is she keeping?'

They sat for a while facing each other across the small utilitarian table and Janet chatted away in between mouthfuls.

Eager to learn the latest, Millie asked, 'how's your love life these days? Still seeing Mrs Elliott's son, Christopher?'

Janet hesitated. 'Well, truthfully speaking, I haven't seen him for weeks. It's frightfully difficult. He's out on so many sorties. Lancasters, you know. He flies those bloody great Lancs. Bomber Command seems to delight in playing havoc with ones relations.' She sighed. 'We thought we had a dead cert date last week-end, then my rota changed and I found myself having to drive this bigwig major down to Devon. Mind you, he was quite a dish. We had a cosy dinner in this lovely old thatched inn.' She didn't add that she spent the night there, too. 'And anyway, you know me; I never was a stay-at-home girl.'

Millie did know, and she had to laugh. She remembered only too well the night they climbed out of the dorm window and shinned down a drainpipe to see some of the six form boys from St Aloysius Grammar School. Janet was the instigator of the prank, but Millie didn't need much cajoling. Along with another girl in the dormitory, the three went down to the village pub to meet the boys. They were discovered, of course. Wearing mufti and makeup, the girls might have got away with having a beer in the dim interior, but the fresh faces of three spotty teenaged lads didn't fool the landlord of the *Fox and Hound*. He telephoned their schools and one of the senior house mistresses promptly arrived to escort the miscreants back. Their punishment—which wasn't too extreme considering there was only two weeks left until the end of summer stretch—was that the threesome were confined to the school premises for the rest of the term.

With their tea finished, Janet went into the lounge and came back with some letters.

'Here's your post, Millie. I think you'd better take a look at them, in case there is anything urgent.'

Their eyes met. 'Thanks.'

Of the three letters addressed to her, only one shouted urgent. Dismissively, Millie dropped the other two onto the kitchen table then took the envelope stamped PRIVATE into her bedroom to read. Left sitting alone now, a surge of apprehension shot through Janet and she reached out for the cigarette packet. Inhaling deeply, for a few moments she realised there was nothing she could do nothing except wait, and follow the circles of smoke drifting inexorably upwards.

CHAPTER TWENTY-ONE

Steaming hot baths and a plentiful supply of freshly cooked meat took the edge off the miserably wet, Scottish weather. In spite of days of heavy rain, no one could complain that they didn't eat well. And, more times than not, they ate what they shot. Insofar as the shooting stakes went, Millie, however, lagged behind the others, especially Vanessa, the only other girl in the group at that SOE training school. And Vanessa was a crack shot, to boot. In the small weapons department, Millie found it hard going to hit anything still, let alone a moving target, for the only gun she had ever fired was Archie's toy water pistol. Frustratingly for Millie, Vanessa was also a natural athlete. Paired up together for this particular assignment, Vanessa could easily outpace Millie, who up to now had considered herself to be a fair sportswoman. She was the hockey captain at boarding school, and all the family swam like fish, including Clive and Archie who spent hours larking about in the pool of the family home, back in Singapore. And she easily thrashed Grace on the tennis court. But for speed and agility, she could see she would never be in the same league as the tall, lissom Vanessa.

Albeit grudgingly, Millie's admiration for her companion grew when she could see Vanessa was not an out and out glory seeker. She'd told Millie that she merely wanted to blend in and get through each part of the training with as little fuss as possible. Appearing unassuming, and modest with her talents, Vanessa was also a good team worker. She willingly took command of the job they were about to undertake, and Millie was happy to go along with that decision.

The pair had eight miles of wooded and hilly ground to cover. Although they were warned by their trainer at the outset, that it was a terrain strewn with hidden obstacles and traps set out especially to ensnare them; furthermore, this task had to be pulled off without them being seen by those labelled 'the enemy.' Apart from having to get across a river in a leaking, rickety rowing boat, the first few miles were easy going. Then their luck seemed to change. From a high vantage point Vanessa spotted their pursuers. Thinking on the move, she told Millie to keep watch while she planned a way to throw them off the scent. Vanessa appeared to be at home in the wilds of Scotland. She had a natural affinity with the flora and fauna in the area and talked about being up wind of ones prey and such-like terms. These expressions were all quite novel, to Millie. Though she did wonder, Millie had no idea where this girl hailed from. Anyway, they were explicitly warned not to become over friendly with their compatriots, so she never asked. Vanessa had no trace of any kind of accent, apart from an impeccable clipped, upper-class English enunciation.

With her concentration focused on a military vehicle some way away, Millie had momentarily lost sight of her companion. Getting worried, she made for the wood behind her. Tramping the undergrowth in panic, she really thought she was done for when she heard the sound of an approaching motor.

'Phist, phist, quickly, I'm over here, come quickly.'

Millie bent low, but could see nothing only a thicket of ash trees and blackberry brambles. Then a movement, as some branches wavered in the undergrowth.

'Oh, thank goodness! I thought I'd lost you. I felt sure they would be bound to see me.'

Quite buried under a tangle of greenery, Vanessa pushed aside the branches of a shallow dugout she had made for the two of them to hide in, until the danger had passed.

Vanessa hissed, 'quiet, no talking!'

Millie soon heard the reason for her partner's sharpness. A lorry drove past, just yards from where they were concealed, and pulled up alongside a fast-flowing burn. Camouflaged and barely breathing, the girls could hear the sound of the stream bouncing over craggy rocks, but they did not to know how many men had alighted. All the same, they did know that the men were searching for them. After what seemed an interminable time, the noise of the engine was heard being restarted.

Straining to listen, the vehicle didn't immediately drive away. Suddenly, Millie let out a stifled gasp. One of her calf muscles went into a spasm. She had to get up, straighten her leg, but Vanessa kept her pinned down. After a further five minutes of pain, Millie was on the verge of slapping Vanessa, she was in such discomfort. Eventually, Millie got a nudge to indicate all was clear. But with beads of perspiration trickling off her brow Millie was in the grip of agony. Quick thinking, Vanessa shoved up the trouser leg of Millie's pants and massaged the knotted ball of muscle. Such relief, Millie could have cried. But there was no time.

Rain which had eased for the earlier part of the morning now began once more as an annoying, persistent drizzle. It made the going tougher. Optimistically, they considered, whether the rain might encourage the men to stay in the dry and comfort of the lorry, for a while. They passed a few scatterings of old, tumbled-down bothies. Millie would have welcomed a rest in one of them. When she said as much, Vanessa advised not to risk it, as she was convinced there were blokes hiding inside waiting there for them to do just that.

Slicing the air across her throat, Vanessa quipped, 'come into my parlour said the spider to the fly.'

'OK,' responded Millie, 'not these flies.'

Cantering on, they had a further two miles to cover before they reached the manor gate lodge, the last point of the test. Millie was definitely flagging; twice they had to stop when she got cramp, again. Vanessa was also tiring, but kept pushing on, relentless. At the lodge they had to report in, and get their papers stamped. It would confirm they had completed the task, and reached the destination without being caught. At the check point, they were kept standing to attention while a dour sergeant took his time attending to the paperwork.

The relieved and satisfied glances Millie and Vanessa exchanged didn't go unnoticed by the sergeant. Hopeful of getting transport up at the manor, to take them back to their base, and with the sergeant's formalities completed, they put their documents away and plodded down the sweep of the driveway.

Behind them they heard the sound of a window opening. The sergeant stuck his head out, and barked at them, 'where the bloody hell do you two think you're going?'

They turned and Vanessa pointed in the direction of the manor house. 'We're going to the lorry, to get a lift.'

He growled. 'Sergeant, we're going to the lorry to get a lift, Sergeant!'

'What?'

'It's Sergeant to you!' He threw his thumb over his shoulder. 'And that's the way back. If you get a move on you might be in time for a mug of cocoa. Ha ha ha.'

'Oh, God,' Millie groaned at the prospect of another eight mile walk. All the adrenalin in her body seemed to have left her.

Vanessa swore. 'Fucking bastard!' Not caring in the least if the sergeant heard or not. Millie might have laughed if she had the energy, for the expletive sounded comical pronounced with her gravelly, upper class accent. Vanessa took out a handkerchief and wiped her cheeks. Millie ignored the rain and sweat that trickled down hers. Gloom descended on the pair as they about faced to tackle the trek back. A couple of hundred yards or so away from the gate lodge, Vanessa slowed down to a stand still, then glanced furtively round to make sure they had gone far enough to be out of sergeant's sight. Turning in the direction of the gate lodge, she said, 'come on, that shitty, jumped up little twerp won't get the better of me.'

'Oh, why, what-what have you got in mind?'

With hopeful anticipation of Vanessa pulling something out of the bag, Millie followed.

'Didn't you notice the bicycle under the porch? It could only be his.'

'Err, why yes, yes I did, what—'

'Right, they told us to use our initiative didn't they?'

'You mean we're going to steal it?'

'Yes, of course,' she replied, quite blithely.

Millie smiled. 'I wonder why I didn't think of that.'

'Because, you have to think as they think. You have become as devious as them, in this game. Then it's only a matter of finding the courage. Still,' she gave Millie a nudge, 'you're learning, old chum.'

Millie sat on the crossbar of the bicycle while Vanessa peddled. It was wonderful. Now able to use the roads without fear of being caught, the miles just flew by. Freewheeling down hills generated an extraordinary sense of exhilaration. But best of all was the tremendous satisfaction they got when they stood to attention and saluted, then each grabbed a wheel of the bike, and cried, in unison, 'one, two, three weeeeeeeee!' The sergeant's bicycle, with all due respect, and appropriate ceremony got flung into the murky depths of the river they had earlier rowed across.

Even though they weren't the first couple to get back, it left them feeling pretty pleased with things, as they tucked into a hearty dinner of venison, new potatoes, sliced green beans and young carrots. This was followed by deliciously thick slices of rhubarb tart and cream. It was probably true to say that no one in the training school gave much of a thought to outsiders, some miles away, having to live for a week, on lesser fare, than what they had just eaten. To round off the night the group headed for the lounge to get something stronger than cocoa. An hour or so later, from a desk in the hallway, everyone was told to collected a postcard and write a few lines to their families. They more or less knew what they could and could not write. In any case their messages would be read by a clerk in the office before being sanctioned for posting. After hot baths, Vanessa and Millie went to their own rooms.

Over breakfast, the next day, Millie saw Vanessa take a head count.

She whispered to Millie, 'two people missing.'

'Do you think they will have to do it again?'

'Mmm, it's very likely.'

'Thank heavens it's not us.'

Vanessa raised her eyebrows, and said under her breath, 'well don't rest on your laurels, just yet. Here comes Titch. I can tell by his grin that he's got some delights up his sleeve for us.'

Millie felt that at least in the close combat exercises, Vanessa started on the same level as her. They both got hollered at in equal measure by Sergeant Titchfield when they couldn't lift their male partner more than a few inches off the ground. Shown and demonstrated several times the art of unarmed combat, all the females could manage was to land in a sprawling heap on their backs. And then worse still, to avoid danger of broken bones, when Millie couldn't fall correctly the sergeant made quite a spectacle of her by making her practice and practice, even when the rest, including Vanessa, who just seemed to have the edge over Millie, had gone to lunch. After a while Millie felt confident that she had the hang of it. But it was still not good enough for the sergeant, who just put his hands on his hips and shook his head in exasperation. Paired up with a corporal, several more practice throws proved perfect. Yet she was still made to continue. By now, Millie was inwardly seething, and so exasperated that when he turned his back, instead of grappling the corporal to the ground, she crept up behind the sergeant, knocked him behind his knee, putting him off balance, grabbed his arm and tossed him, head over heels in the air.

Taken completely by surprise, this large, strapping fellow got to his feet. Then slowly and deliberately he picked up his cap, dusted it down and then looked Millie full in the face. She was almost quaking in her plimsolls. Surprised, she gulped as he put his hands together and started to applaud. He even broke into the minute glimmerings of a smile. A couple of windows got pushed open and more clapping could be heard coming from the canteen. Vanessa and the group had been surreptitiously following Millie's antics with interest.

Sergeant Titchfield shouted at them, 'go on you lot, get on with your lunch. And you Miss, you go and…go and sling your hook.' With as much energy as she could muster, Millie made a dart for the canteen. Titchfield looked at the corporal and exclaimed, 'women!'

For the more specialised unarmed combat exercises, the sergeant handed over to another training officer, bearing the rank of a major, who on the surface appeared to be the antithesis of Sergeant Titchfield. The major was a middle-aged, quietly spoken chap that—in the most matter of fact way—delivered a gruesome set of techniques for disarming and crippling the enemy.

'The soft flesh of the mouth,' he pointed out, 'will tear very easily if you insert a finger into the corner and give a nice yank outwards.' Thus he demonstrated by inserting his two index fingers into his own mouth. He followed that bit of artistry by placing himself at the side of a student. 'A sharp blow with the outside of your hand, aimed in the right place, here, just under the nostrils, will disarm the enemy by breaking his or her, nose.' Suitably impressed, the student gave a sniff and adjusted his tie. The major continued.

'And then ladies,' he nodded at Millie and Vanessa, 'though this action is not limited for the use of females alone, an accurate kick in the testicles will put your man out of action, and you can safely make good your escape.'

Plainly spoken, his procedures caused the students mind to boggle at the sheer choice of vicious and ingenious methods available for use in dire situations. All probably hoped they would never have to use any of them.

If, however, the students thought that they had seen the last of sergeant 'Titch', as he became commonly known, they were mistaken. Erratically, but at least three times a week, he took great pleasure in waking them up at two in the morning, to go for training runs.

'This is the place,' he'd say, watching them climb, bleary eyed into their uniforms, 'where we will get you physically fit by fair means or foul. So my hearty bedfellows, gird your loins and let's away.' Then with gusto, he'd blow a shrill blast from his whistle and the run would commence.

They would get hauled out of their comfortable beds at that ungodly hour many times before the allocated number of weeks of training in Scotland was ended. All the same, one thing was certain, keyed up and ready for their next assignment they were a fitter bunch of hopefuls than when they first arrived in that remote, and secret Highland training school.

CHAPTER TWENTY-TWO

They hadn't been told the whereabouts of the next destination, so speculation was not only inevitable, but occasionally wild, in the extreme. For covert purposes, they were made to travel through Scotland in a covered-in lorry; whether it was intentional or not, the windowless vehicle had the effect of creating a sense of disorientation. Regaining a modicum of equilibrium, once on open water, a suggestion was put forward by one in the group who thought it might be the Irish Sea they were bobbing on. But when a compass was produced it became clear Ireland was in the other direction. Someone else said he was confident they were secretly heading for France. At this being declared, worried murmurings circulated among a few in the party, though Millie thought the France theory nonsense. Vanessa, however, knew exactly where they were making for. A mile or so away, from what appeared to be their objective; she'd recognised the natural harbour and the causeway that connected the island to the mainland.

Out of earshot of anyone else, she quietly told Millie, 'I often went sailing round these islands with my father and mother, in our yawl, when I was a child.' Vanessa gave a derisive sniff, and stared into the distance. At that point, Millie wondered just how old Vanessa was. She tried to guess, possible three or four years older than me? The next moment, Vanessa added, 'I have to say the islands still look as bleak as ever.' Millie followed Vanessa's gaze. 'On the surface, the sea looks pretty tame, right now, but these waters with their fast changing currents, in this stretch of the North Sea, can be quite treacherous. It never seemed to bother my parents, though.' Millie was agog at the revelation, and a little uneasy that she should even be hearing this. If her guard had slipped, Vanessa went on, regardless. 'Father had a passion for yachting, and was into this bird watching thing. He did some work for an ecological organisation.

Seals were frequent visitors. I wonder if we will see any.' She thought hard, 'and Artic Terns. Yes, I remember now. Father would record the number of Artic Terns that arrived here to breed. Fierce little blighters they are too, when it comes to protecting their young. Apparently, some Terns can live from anything up to twenty-five, thirty years.' She turned to Millie. 'Amazingly long time, for birds, don't you think?' It was the first snippets of anything personal Vanessa had volunteered, and it was very illuminating for Millie to hear.

'Oh! Um, yes, yes it is, a very long time.' All the same, Millie decided to change the subject. 'That's um-that's all very interesting, but where the heck are we?'

Concocting an air of mystery, Vanessa answered, 'we are following in the steps of Saint Aidan.'

Vanessa's words got carried away by the strong wind. 'Saint who?'

'Saint Aidan. He had been dispatched, not unlike us, from the west coast of Scotland, to here, the Farne Islands to set up some kind of-of monastery, I think.'

Still none the wiser Millie decided to shut up so as not sound any more ignorant than she already was.

They spied two officers, who appeared to be waiting for them as they came to land on the jetty. Carrying their heavy packs, that included a radio transmitter, an ungainly scramble was made trying to alight from the boat. Once everyone was off, the motorboat turned about and sped away. One of the officers ordered the group to make their way towards a hillock, where humps of upturned rowing boats gave a sinister, mirage-like impression of bodies, long dead, sexless bodies. The island threw up an atmosphere of weather-beaten neglect. There was no attempt at conversation; each person seemed wrapped up in their own thoughts, most likely wondering just what they were in for.

They were treading on sticky, cloying sand, now, and their gait was that of a labouring plod. Millie brought up the rear of the party; for a few moments she got a little distracted by looking down thinking how pretty the shells were. She stooped and picked up a few, and blew the sand out of little apertures. She surmised that fishermen must come over from the mainland to catch fish, judging by the number of boats and fishing tackle strewn about; could it be that some of the islands were even inhabited? Out of the tail of her eye, she saw one chap kick aside what might have been a lobster pot, or maybe it was a beached log, she wasn't near enough to see exactly, but suddenly there was a terrific explosion. It scared everyone witless. Instinct took over, and they flung themselves flat, confused as to what had just happened.

They were still lying immobile when a voice shouted out, 'if that was for real you'd all be laying bloody dead by now.' Stunned, but more embarrassed than anything, people began getting to their feet. 'Pull yourselves together and get into the bloody house. What a bloody shower! You should have been watching out for bloody booby traps and not drooling over bloody crustaceans!'

The effect of the bang caused the shells to dig into Millie's hand. She threw them away and looked at the little frilly imprints left on her palm; piqued, she chose not to look at the instructor. At the same time, she was amazed that he'd spotted her collecting the shells.

The introduction to this round of training wasn't going too well. And it got worse when the trainee standing next to Millie asked the instructor where they were. He was ignored. Stupidly, he asked again. The reply he got was, 'Timbuk-bloody-tu.' Millie saw the chap redden. Clearly, they were not going to be told. Casually, he informed them that should anyone decide to throw in the towel they ought to check the tidal currents as the causeway floods at high tide and they'd have to 'bloody well swim for it'. Millie glanced at Vanessa who gave nothing away by her deadpan expression.

Once inside an old, dilapidated stone-built house, that was to be their base, the brusque instructor announced his name. 'I'm Captain Meene. Meene by name and mean by nature or so I'm told.' Having already had a taste of his lacklustre humour no one cracked a smile. Neither did Captain Meene. 'There are a few more army bods joining us tomorrow. And it's their job to hone the skills you will need to become guerrilla fighters. Sabotage and guerrilla fighting is what you're here on this island, to learn. Make no mistake, the organisation that you have signed up with, requires that you become capable of both acting independently in the field and working undercover in groups with resistance fighters, if there are any, that is.' He took a moment to let that sink in. 'As saboteurs, you will be trained to cause the maximum disruption to enemy forces. You will be taught detonator mechanics and how to use the latest explosive materials, without blowing yourself up, unless you want to.' His irony was not going down well. Millie wanted to tell him not to sound so bloody banal. 'You will get shown devises where you can hide and disguise bombs, as well as how to set booby traps. So, here's some simple advice for staying alive.' He squared his broad shoulders. 'Keep your mouth shut.' A perceptible flick from his eyes caught the still plainly smarting trainee. 'And use this.' He tapped his head, 'and when necessary, don't hesitate to use this.' With an astonishingly deft slight of the hand, he pulled out an evil looking stiletto. 'When those skills become second nature, and with luck on your side, then, and only then, will you have some chance of surviving among the enemy.' As if had all been rehearsed many time before he pushed home a final bleak bit of information. 'There's something else. You will quickly discover if you haven't already, and that is it's pretty basic here. There are no cushy amenities like those at your last port of call. We just have the essential requirements here, in order to complete your training. We do not have the luxury of running water. But, you will find there's a pump outside where you'll carry all your water in the canvas buckets. These are stored in the outhouse, look after them, our numbers are limited. Oh, and there's the dunny in that scrubby bit of garden.' Then with abrupt closure, he finished, by saying, 'right, that's our little jaunt wrapped up for this evening. So, get your gear off, and get yourselves organised. I'll see you lot in the morning.'

Later while the two girls were drawing water from the cranky pump, Millie remarked, 'he's Australian, I think.'

Vanessa said, 'I was trying to suss out the accent, between the bloody this and bloody that. He's a bit of a coarse brute, what?'

'Oh, I don't know,' returned Millie, teasingly, 'I wouldn't turf him out of my bed on a cold, dark night.'

Pretending to be aghast, Vanessa exclaimed, 'what a bold little thing you are becoming, darling. Why, upon my word, I can only put it down to mixing with all these rampant, testosterone charged fellows, that must be giving you ideas above and beyond the call of duty.'

They had to stifle their laughter, for just then Captain Meene and the other officer were climbing into their truck, leaving for the night. Millie, especially, didn't want them passing any remarks about getting too friendly. Oddly, it was something Millie thought about before falling asleep on rough floor boards, next to Vanessa. She liked this girl, admired her tremendously, and felt in other circumstances they could have become really good pals. But friends, forming friendships were a no-go area. It was one of the things that had been drummed into them right from the off, in Scotland, when sergeant Titchfield was preparing the trainees for what to expect, once behind the enemy lines. At this juncture he softened a tad, from his usual heavy-handed manner, and endeavoured to adopt a gentler approach. Nonetheless, the sergeant pulled no punches. He made it crystal clear, their lives would change, well, of course it would. It had to. Monkish, Millie remembered him calling it. Sergeant Titchfield warned them that it was quite likely they'd have to go into hiding, or at some point their survival might depend on them having to live off the land, with the certainty of thin pickings. The French, he said, were suffering great hardship in getting sufficient food supplies through, faring much worse than the British.

Living on one's wits all the time could make or break a secret agent, Titchfield solemnly, told them. He referred to the agent's life as that of a lonely, monkish entity. He warned them that some agents were caught through carelessness by making small, silly mistakes. And went on to furnish them with the example of one chap, who went into a café and rather loudly drew attention to himself by ordering black coffee, when milk hadn't been available for months. He reminded them of making small slips such as throwing away half-smoked cigarettes, because this was something no frugal French man or woman would ever do. Worrying, to hear, he also said for them not to expect to get a warm welcome by all French. His exact words were, '…you may even be resented. Many French openly collaborate with the Germans. Remember, the French people are an occupied nation. Survival for them is often down to their own conscience.'

It was profoundly clear to Millie that this private war of the secret agent was anything but conventional, and in such a war friends would be a luxury they could ill afford.

The next day a small band of soldiers from the Royal Engineers arrived. Millie couldn't help it, but she found she was scanning their faces intently. She knew of course it was simply wishful thinking to expect to see Philip, or even to hope that the familiar mop of Hugo Maitland's red hair might spring out among them. The soldiers were a rugged, tough looking bunch, who meant business by starting group training as soon as they stepped off the motorboat.

A dead rat was thrown at an unsuspecting trainee who nearly passed out at having to handle it. They thought it would have the same effect when it was given to Millie. To the instructor's amused surprise, it never fazed her, for she had watched much bigger rodents getting disemboweled and then cooked by the natives, out in Singapore. Vanessa confessed to Millie afterwards, she felt like throwing up when she had to yank the rodent's innards out for the purpose of stuffing the carcass with explosives. Yet again, when it became Millie's turn to practice, it never caused her to bat an eyelid.

CHAPTER TWENTY-THREE

Their stroke of good fortune started out simply by chance, during a weapons training exercise. A sand dune collapsed beneath the weight of one of the men. He took a tumble but wasn't injured. His aim though, was way off target and the grenade landed, exploding at the waters edge instead of reaching the simulated German HQ, ear marked for blowing up. It went without saying; he got a rollicking from Captain Meene. Afterwards, when they were gathering the dead and dying fish that had washed up on beach, Vanessa welcomed the accident, by calling it an ill wind. Isolated, for the course of this particular round of training, their food supplies—unlike the Scottish surfeit—always veered towards frugality. However, due to that fortuitous little fluke, they ate heartily for several days after it. Since then, as food stocks dipped on the lean side, someone would surreptitiously lob a grenade out to sea, and it usually sent forth a few tasty morsels, by way of the odd crab and some flat fish. These delicacies were easy to roast and cooked quickly over an open fire, and brought a welcome addition to their basic diet.

No civilians were encountered during their training on and around the Farne Islands. It was assumed that the military had commandeered the territory for the duration, though this was never confirmed by the powers that be. During the second week on the islands, the soldiers from the Royal Engineers chose the cliffs below Lindisfarne Castle for target practice and for laying booby traps. Then the trainees had to scale the cliff face to get access to the castle, which became established as a training ground for further exercises.

A short distance from the castle stood the old Lindisfarne Priory. Here they had spent a further two days carrying out various manoeuvres with the Royal Engineers. Towards dusk, when everyone was making their way back to base camp, Millie broke off from the rest, and said she'd scour the beach to see if anything edible had got washed up. Feeling pleased that her search wasn't in vain, she gathered up half a dozen tasty looking sole. Albeit, intent on the job in hand, she couldn't help wondered what her mother would think, if she could see her scavenging like this. With no further pickings to be had, Millie retraced her steps back to the priory, to where she had left her climbing ropes and tackle that she had used earlier. Outlined against a cloudy expanse of moonlit sky, the crumbling ruins of the priory, started to give her the creeps. Its decaying columns were shrouded in swathes of hoary shadows, which, despite the passing centuries, the ancient priory still persisted in ecclesiastical defiance by poking its gnarled-like fingers heavenward.

Millie had taken longer gathering up the fish than was sensible; with the result that daylight had practically gone. She began to dislike the feeling of being alone in such a chilly atmosphere, so finally, she cracked on and stashed away her gear as quick as she could. Suddenly, she stopped what she was doing, and became aware of an eerie sound. Millie knew she was the only one left at the priory. An uncontrolled shiver made the hackles on the back of neck stand on end. The noise came again. Fear gripped her entrails and she had an urgent desire to wee. Crossing her legs, she clung to the ruins of an arch. She could easily make out the Celtic cross; she remembered it was not far from there that a few seals were spotted by one keen observer, and Vanessa also watched them through binoculars. Millie posed the question, could the seals have reached this far inland? She wondered, did they snort like this when tending their pups? In all probability they would attack her, if she got too near. Should she make a run for it, leave the fish and equipment, and risk a dressing down from Captain Meene? No, she decided, hold fast, and not panic. Her soft plimsolls felt along the uneven ground, and luckily, their tread made no noise as she crept across the gaping structure of the snapping stonework. She was so pleased to have the moon's presence. Mindful, it was one of the things that an RE instructing officer talked about. He said that it was easier to remain unseen in the moon's shadows than to hide in a night without a moon. Millie looked up to see the orb's silvery beams break out from behind a passing cloud. It lit up the inside of the roofless priory as if it were a light bulb. Trembling, and hardly daring to breathe, she tentatively raised her head to where the muffled sounds seemed to emanate from. In no way did she feel as brave as Vanessa when it came to the seals. Then instantly, it was as if a thunderbolt had struck her, and she had to clap a hand over her mouth to stop herself from shouting out. There, revealed just yards from the arch she was crouching behind, was Vanessa—stark naked! Her unmistakable long, silver legs were wrapped around the equally naked silver form of a man, whose mobile buttocks rose and fell in rhythm with the grunts that Millie was hearing. Spellbound, Millie watched the sexy, bit of tomfoolery until her apprehension subsided, after which, it was all she could do to hold in her laughter. Some seal, thought Millie, and so much for fraternisation. She couldn't see who the man was—not that she wanted to—for his face was buried in Vanessa's breasts.

For a brief space of time, whenever the image of Vanessa's passionate clinch flashed through her mind, Millie couldn't help but smile, and she did wonder more than once who the man was. After a while though, she thought no more about *amour al fresco,* and kept focusing on getting through the rest of the training.

One hairy incident, nonetheless, affected everyone on the island, trainees and military personnel alike. It happened just the day before they were due to complete their training on Lindisfarne, or Holy Island as it later became know to the visitors. Things were winding down and they were given a rare couple of hours to themselves. The men had gone into their make-shift bar to enjoy some crates of beer sent over from the mainland. The weather was pleasant enough so Vanessa decided to take a stroll rather than joining a drinking session. Millie said she'd go along, and led by Vanessa, they ended up climbing the ridge of sand dunes where they had got their first taste of free fish. Lying flat on their stomachs taking advantage of a few hours of relaxation, they trained their binoculars out to sea, to watch a pair of seals, basking on a sandbank. Millie had seen enough, and she couldn't trust herself not to laugh so she set her glasses aside, turned over onto her back, and closed her eyes. Soon, Vanessa found she was talking to herself, for within a few seconds Millie had drifted off to sleep. Much as she had an interest in the creatures, it was getting slightly boring staring at snoozing seals and a snoozing companion. Vanessa breathed on her binocular lenses and gave them a clean with her cuff. She continued peering, nonetheless. Just then, she caught a movement on the sandbank. The seals were lumbering off their beds and making for the sea. They were truly cumbersome out of their natural habitat, and more than a little comical to watch, as their huge body mass waddled towards water.

Vanessa was sorry to see them go; she knew something must be up to set them in such a frantic haste to get off their comfortable patch. She swung her sights to the shore half expecting to see some of the chaps, but the stretch of land was empty. She got to her feet, awkwardly, sinking in the sand. The seals were gone; the reason was now clear for she saw something, an object, far more menacing than the harmless mammals. Excited, Vanessa pulled her leg from the sand, unaware that she'd kicked the powdery grains over Millie's face. Millie spat, and coughed.

Startled, Vanessa swung round towards her companion. 'Wake up, wake up, Millie. There's a-a there's a, Christ, Millie, that looks like a bloody great U-boat, just to the left of where the seals are-were.'

Brushing sand from her neck, Millie grumbled, 'I'm not in the mood for jokes.'

'It's no joke. Look! Look for yourself.'

Unwilling, Millie, nonetheless, stirred. Still convinced Vanessa was having a gag, at her expense. She told her, 'don't be daft, Vanessa. You must be seeing things. A German sub would never dare to come this near our shores.' Bleary eyed she fumbling for her own pair of glasses and made a wide sweep. 'There's the old wreck that we waded out to, is that what—'

'No! No! It's not that. Look more to the left of it.'

Then Millie gulped the air, 'wait, wait, yes, I can see something.' She twirled the mechanism that adjusted the sight vision. 'Good God! Vanessa, you're right. It is a U-boat, and on the surface too.'

'Of course it's on the surface—'

'What the hell is it doing?'

'That's what I'd like to know.'

Half-heartedly, Millie scoffed. 'You-you don't think it's some kind of-of, you know, some sort of mock up scenario for us to—'

Looking seriously worried, Vanessa scowled. 'Don't be silly. No one is going to such sophisticated lengths just for us to—'

Millie interrupted, with a gasp. 'There's a dingy being lowered.'

'Where?' Yes, I can see it. There are people-men, and they look like they are going to-' She tore her binoculars away and turned to Millie. 'Quick, there's no time to lose. We must let the army know. You go and get—'

Millie could feel her anger rising at the enemy's audacity. 'No, Vanessa, it's too dangerous for you to remain here on your own. We'll both go.'

They crawled on their bellies over the sand, just as if it were a practice exercise. Coarse tufts of grass swished them in the face, and following in Vanessa's tracks, sand got showered on Millie's hair. They felt nothing but the desperate need to get help. So as not to be spotted from the sea, it was only when they rolled over the ridge did they get to their feet. Then they ran full pelt, not stopping until they reached their base camp. There they burst open the door of the officers quarter. Bent double, and almost unable to speak, the pair had a wild look about them. Captain Meene rose to his feet. His second in command did likewise, as did another officer from the Royal Engineers.

Captain Meene demanded, 'what the bloody hell do you think you're doing forcing your way in like that? Stand to attention and explain the reason for this bloody, uncouth intrusion.'

'Ger-Germa-German U-boat...off shore,' was all the breathless, Vanessa, could spit out.

It only took a split second for Captain Meene to jump into action. Playing cards shot up in the air and got tramped, underfoot. The game was over.

The officer from the Engineers raced to the hut where most of the soldiers and trainees were quasi-socialising. Within ten seconds everyone was out and standing to. The only truck on the island was brought round and the engine kept running. A radio was shoved in the back, along with grenades, guns and ammunition. Captain Meene was in the driving seat and Millie and Vanessa squeezed in the front with the other officer. Most of the soldiers piled in the back or stood on mud guards. While the rest, along with the trainees, had to make it on foot, some grabbed the few available bicycles.

They were directed to the ridge by Vanessa and Millie. Once there, and having assessed the situation, Captain Meene immediately radioed their position and the position of the U-boat, using a top priority code signal. Impatient for a response, he kept repeating, top priority.

Meene was practically spluttering with contempt, as he told the officer next to him, 'do-do you-do you know, that-that bloody bugger wasn't taking me seriously, at first.'

The man swore in sympathy, and ran his hand through his hair. 'What are our orders, Captain?'

'We're to keep our heads down and not to do anything, just yet. The Navy and the RAF should be on their way. If they're quick they could drop one on the sub before it dives.' He began rubbing his hand with glee, picturing the scene. 'Then we can nab the Jerries in the dingy. Bag the bloody lot.'

Another officer wasn't quite so confident. 'Be that as it may, but what if the Navy and the RAF don't get here in time, what—'

'Damn it, man, I am well aware of that possibility,' Captain Meene interjected, angrily, 'but if we open fire too soon, we run the risk of scaring those bastards in the dingy off, and its as hell as likely that they'll abort their mission and get back to the sub.'

'So there's a chance we'll lose the lot of 'em.'

Under his breath the Captain mouthed, resolutely, 'not if I have anything to do with it.'

Spread out in the shape of a horseshoe, and camouflaged in the long grass dipping towards the harbour, soldiers and trainee SOE agents alike, were at the ready. Now they could only wait. All eyes were peeled on the submarine, and the dingy that had begun to distancing itself from its parent. A few minutes passed. Ears were strained for the sound of an aircraft, nothing was heard. Some stole a glance skyward, hoping to see the planes. Growing edgy now, Meene clicked his teeth.

The officer next to him said, 'she'll dive, if they don't get here in the—'

'Too late!' Captain Meene cursed. 'She's fucking-well going.'

Just then the roar of a plane engine was heard.

'Trust the bloody RAF, late as usual.' The other officer scoured the coast line. 'And still not a sign of Navy back-up, either.'

'All right, then.' Meene announced, determinedly. 'We'll deal with it. It's what we are trained to do after all.' He gave a sarcastic grin, to Vanessa and Millie, on his left. 'They don't know we're waiting for them. It's likely they've assumed the island is deserted otherwise they wouldn't have chosen this place to land.' He issued a command to a corporal from the Engineers. 'Get down the line and tell everyone to stay low till I give the order. We want them taken alive, at all costs. As soon as the Jerries get near enough to the harbour, we'll take the dingy and—'

Before he had time to finish his words were drowned out. The plane began to drop bombs on a vanishing submarine. Those on the shore, felt it was like closing the door after the horse had bolted, for bolt the sub did. The sea erupted as massive plumes of water exploded into the air. Another plane approached and joined in the hunt, flying low over the sea, dropping bombs in a futile effort of getting a hit on the U-boat.

With nowhere else to go, the Germans were furiously paddling towards the harbour inlet. As the dingy neared the shore it was possible to identify two people in it. Captain Meene's plan of action was to wait to the last possible minute, until the pair actually stepped out and started to wade ashore. All was going accordingly. The soldiers were in position, riffles at the ready to cut off any possible means of escaping, which is what would have happened if the navel motor launch hadn't been spotted off Castle Point. Paddling like hell, the Germans had also seen the launch. They appeared to be attempting to alter their course. Without hesitation Captain Meene decided to delay things no longer. He would not take any possible chance of the enemy slipping through his fingers.

Everyone knew Meene was the crack shot of the outfit and, therefore, the number one choice to pot the dingy. So, taking deliberate, unrushed focus, he fired several shots in rapid succession, just level with the water line. His aim was true. The dingy rapidly deflated, toppling its occupants into the icy water. At this point there was a flurry of activity from the Engineers nearest the shallows. Plunging in, the men surrounded the surprised and terrified Germans. There was a feeble attempt to throw a briefcase and papers into the sea, but these were quickly retrieved by Captain Meene, who handed them to Vanessa for safe keeping.

Millie stood at the water's edge with some of the others and watched the pair getting caught, red-handed. They were forcibly dragged through the water and unto dry land. For a few moments, Millie had nothing to do, she felt almost like a spectator. Then, with a sense of alarm, the clarity of what was taking place touched home with stark reality. All this training, practice, and exercises, tough though it was, undoubtedly it had an edge of safeness to it. And it had all been carried out on British territory. With trepidation, she asked herself, what if the roles were reversed. It might not be so different, in a few months time. A cold chill nipped at her heart, and more so when the Germans were getting searched, for it turned out that one of them was a woman.

CHAPTER TWENTY-FOUR

No one said anything. No one gasped, twitched a muscle, or moved in the slightest. No one looked anywhere other than straight at the man delivering the highly secret communiqué. Fifty yards, or so, away, the boat bumped against the jetty, impatient, it seemed, to take off from the island. This was their final briefing before returning to the mainland. It was not what they were expecting. However, they were becoming accustomed to expect the unexpected. The document was read out by Captain Meene.

Finally, when he flicked his lighter and put the flame to the paper's edge, he told them, 'remember, this never happened, understand? This never happened! You will never speak about what took place yesterday.' He waited for it to sink in. 'Should it become known that any of you has leaked out even the name of this island, you will be locked up for the bloody duration. And I will repeat again what I said to you when you first arrived, keep your mouth shut!'

Keep your mouth shut keep your mouth shut keep your mouth shut. With each jerky movement over the railway lines, Meene's command rattled and reverberated in Millie's brain. *Keep your mouth shut keep your...* until Millie eventually fell into a fitful sleep. It was a sleep that got broken by several interruptions, some at stations, and problems on the line meant the train had to remain in a tunnel for ages. And an hour later for those making the longer journey to London there was a train change before they ultimately got into the City. In all, it became an unsettling, and long journey back to the flat.

However, Millie's spirits lifted on opening her front door, she could hear laughter. The wireless was playing. She heard Janet laughing along with the background audience. Janet though, didn't hear Millie come in;

she had her hair wrapped in a towel and was having a smoke in between drying her damp curls.

Surprised, Janet exclaimed, 'Millie, darling! How wonderful to see you. I never know when you're going to show up. Come and take a pew and tell me how you are.' She secured the towel round her hair and gave Millie a kiss.

'Oh, you know,' Millie passed the comment, 'a bit tired. The blooming trains don't get any better.' Millie saw a dress hanging from the door. 'Are you going out?'

'Yes, yes, I am, but not for an hour or so. I'm meeting Christopher.' Janet tutted. 'Things aren't going terribly well with-but it's me really.' She puckered her lips. 'Actually, he's getting a bit intense. Wants to get engaged and all the married palaver—'

'Ah, ah I see, so—'

'The thing is I don't exactly feel…well that's not to say I don't like-love him, I do, of course I do. But,' she gave a sigh. 'The truth is Millie; I think it's reckless to commit to marriage at a time like this with everything so-so—'

'Then in all honesty, Janet, don't you think you ought to tell him?'

'Yes, yes I know I should. In-in fact I plan to tell him tonight. I had already made up my mind.'

'Is there anyone else?'

'H'mm? Oh, no, no! That is, I mean, there's no one serious. It's just that in my job I meet so many…and it's awfully hard to say no…' She gave a laugh and soon she had Millie laughing too. 'Oh dear, I think I'm turning into what my father would call, "a proper floozy."'

Millie put her arm around her friend and undid her towel and gently patted her hair dry. She wasn't exactly jealous of Janet, but she was envious of her freedom to make light of her love affairs, and to have the licence to indulge her feelings willy-nilly. Something which she knew she could never do. They chatted away while Janet got dressed. The time passed so quickly, and before Millie realised, Janet had her jacket on and was calling out, 'wish me luck.' Once Janet had gone Millie went through the small amount of post that had come in her absence. Her heart beat faster when she saw there were two letters from Philip. Oh, what joy! His first letter was over a month old. It said he was coming to London for a few days and he'd telephone. In his second one Philip wrote to say he'd got a new posting in London. It was his intention to telephone every night at eight o'clock in the hope of catching her. She looked at the clock, it had just chimed, quarter to eight. She got up from the settee and turned off the wireless set, and sat in the armchair next to the telephone. She read both letters again and studied the clock. The hand had only moved to ten to eight. Suddenly the telephone rang. It was picked up immediately.

'Hello, Millie Chance speaking.'

'Milliepead! Darling, love, you are home at last. How are you?'

'Philip, Philip, it's wonderful to hear from you. I was just reading your letters.'

'Good, well listen, Millie, I've only got a few minutes, but I'm off tomorrow. Will you still be in London?'

'Yes, I'm on leave for a few days.'

'Great. Here's what we'll do...'

Millie listened, knowing that the pips would go any second. She knew exactly what they'd do. She had other plans. Janet was leaving very early in the morning to do her chauffeuring stints, and she would most likely not see her until tomorrow night. Millie pushed aside her friend's overflowing ash tray, noting several half-smoked cigarettes and a few very long butt-ends. That definitely is not the way the French smoke. She smiled and thought; it's funny how one has become more observant these days.

Feeling enormously happy at the prospect of seeing Philip, Millie began rummaging through her wardrobe. She was being particularly choosy, as she wanted to wear something really nice for Philip. The weather was kind enough to allow something short-sleeved, and thankfully, she could get into a pretty cotton dress, instead of regulation service gear. She remembered the last time they met she had to leave in such a hurry that she had no chance to get out of her uniform. Lost in thought for a bit she was surprised to hear the clink of a key being turned in the door. She went into the hall, only to see a dazed and forlorn Janet.

'Hello, Janet, what-what's this, aren't you—?'

'It's Christopher,' she said, in a whisper. 'Millie, it's bad news, he's—'

Millie clung on to the door, 'oh God, Janet, he's not-he's not been killed, please say he's not—'

'Missing, they said he's missing.'

'How did you hear? Who told you?'

'His, um, um,' flustered, Janet said, 'sorry, can't remember. I waited for him for ages, but he didn't show up, so I phoned his base. I have a number; he gave me in case...' With tears running down her face Janet sobbed, 'they said his plane was returning from a bombing raid and got shot down over France. Christopher and the crew are reported as missing.' They looked at each other, and then Janet said, 'but Millie, missing, that's as good as...what if—'

'No Janet, it is not as good as, we don't know for sure. Don't think the worse, you mustn't, you mustn't, do you hear?' Millie held Janet tightly, and then her thoughts flew to Christopher's mother, Mrs Elliott.

'Millie,' said Janet, drawing apart, 'I wish I hadn't, you know, made up my mind to tell him.' She couldn't continue.

'But you didn't, that's the main thing, so there's no harm done.'

Rising after nine, Millie wasn't sure that Janet would be up to going to work. It was a surprise then when she read the note left on the kitchen table. *Millie, darling, you were such a comfort. It's marvellous what a few glasses of whiskey, a packet of fags, and a good night's sleep can do. I don't expect I shall get back until the late hours, be good, love, Janet.*

Buttoning up a favourite cream coloured linen jacket, it suddenly hit Millie; and the sick sensation was akin to the punch in the stomach that winded her, the time she fell from the climbing frame, on the assault course, up in Scotland. She was sure Philip had no idea that it was her driving away from the hospital. But why was he there? Ready to set off to meet Philip, another thought suddenly occurred. Could I have made a mistake? Am I absolutely sure it was Philip? Maybe it was someone else, the doorway was very dark. She toyed with these thoughts, yet remaining unconvinced she decided to put them out of her mind and take one thing at a time. So, in a more resolute frame of mind, she stepped into her most glamorous high heeled shoes, then grabbed her matching yellow clutch bag and gas mask, she hurried out of the flats to catch a bus into town.

Janet would have described it as, 'going weak at the knees.' She was always using that expression, especially when talking about a tall, handsome officer, whom she most definitely had a penchant for. All the same, it was exactly how Millie felt when walking along holding Philip's arm. And when they kissed butterflies danced around in her stomach, so that she could barely eat her lunch. Philip was continually touching her, he'd push back the strand of hair that fell over her face, or lovingly, caress her hand across the table. Millie felt her cheeks glow hot, she sensed the old waiter, shuffling back and forth, could read their thoughts. She'd given Philip an invitation, and with the prospect of an empty flat and a comfortable bed awaiting them, Philip threw down some money and left a generous tip for the waiter, and then they fled.

It the midst of hurriedly de-clothing, and without embarrassment, Millie suddenly exclaimed, 'Oh God, Philip. Have you got...you know?'

Breathless, he told her, 'absolutely, don't worry on that score, wouldn't want—'

Millie smothered him in kisses not needing him to say more.

Somehow Philip had managed to get a bottle of Claret, and they were well into their second glass when he said, 'I love you, Millipead.' Millie laughed; it always made her laugh when he called her that. He kissed her breast and told her with mock derision, 'no laughing. Laughter is *verboten, ja, verboten.*'

Suddenly Millie went cold. She sat up and pulled the sheet around her. 'Philip, why were you up at Oldham Hospital?'

'Why was I where?'

It had come out, and she'd said it, 'Oldham Hospital.'

'Yes, that's what I thought you said.' He pushed his glass aside and lit up a cigarette, and offered Millie one. She declined. 'I thought you were in Cambridge, nursing. How do you know I was—?'

'I-I happened to see you.'

'Ah.' He thought for a moment, with growing suspicions. 'Your job,' he said, timorously, 'your work, it's not just nursing, is it?' Millie looked away. 'No, I guessed not. No address to meet up. No way to phone you. The long silences, secrets'. He took heavy drags on the cigarette, and didn't speak for a while. He was almost afraid to say it. 'Secrets, why yes, of course, *official secrets*. Ah, I see. I take it we've both put our signature to *those* papers, signed our lives away, so to speak.'

'Don't say it like that, Philip, please.'

He hugged her tight. 'Sorry, darling, I didn't mean to upset you.'

'It's OK. I was worrying, have been on and off since then. But I feel better, cleared the air a bit.' With a sigh, Millie said, resolutely, 'still, it's best we don't...talk about it.'

Having got that out of the way she snuggled up and put her arm around Philip's neck. So Hugo Maitland was not in collusion with Philip. At least she was clear on that score.

CHAPTER TWENTY-FIVE

It had been cloudy and dull since the afternoon, and the onset of darkness crept in early. The room in use, however, was sufficiently lit by just one of the huge twin chandeliers, suspended, stalactite fashion either end of a long, seventeenth century oak table. Impressive, this sombre lump of furniture dominated the room. Of the same period, carved wood panels pressed the walls from floor to ceiling, stopping only to give way to two lofty, leaded-glass windows. In earlier times this church-like space might easily have been the hub of a religious order, the refectory, perhaps. Now, years of creeping fustiness intermingled with contemporary whiffs of *Old Virginia*. Hugo Maitland and Graham Bain were conferring. Hugo puffed away, unconcerned that the smoke from his pipe wafted up to get caught in the thatch of his resplendent wavy, red hair. He was thumbing through a list of prospective agents, when he paused. He leaned forward as his eyes stopped at a name he was familiar with.

'Ah,' he said, joyously, 'it's the nightingale girl!'

Hunched beside him Graham Bain was studying the duplicate copy. He asked, 'who? The next second, realising who Hugo meant, he responded. 'Oh, yes, Millicent, Millie Chance.'

'That's right.' Hugo added, eagerly, 'she's a bright young thing. You remember I worked with her at the hospital. She certainly knows how to hold a grip on the old nerves, I might say. And, she has done extremely well in her training, so far. Would you agree?'

Bain needed no reminding of his and Millie's first meeting. Without hesitation, he said, 'most certainly, I agree.' He had kept updates on Millie's progress right from the off. Concurring, though with a less effusive show than Maitland, Bain moved on to another page, where he circled a name. 'Then what about this fellow, as her radio operator?'

'Let me take a gander.' Hugo turned over a page. 'Yes,' he said, after a moment. 'I've boned up on his background. He's the oldest chap we've got here, at present, but, in some respects that's not without its advantages.'

'Mmm.' Bain's thoughts were running in the same direction, and he said, 'certainly, because of his age, there is less likelihood of him getting picked up and transported off to Germany, for forced labour. To strengthen this line of cover, we could arrange for the makeup people to give him a hump, or a limp, something along those lines.'

Hugo nodded. 'Our standard aids, which have got used before, and yes, they're good ploys. We'll agree then, there are strong possibilities for pairing them up for their first mission. By the way, what is Churchill calling this one?'

Bain informed him, 'Operation Rutter, or is it Jubilee? I'm not sure which they've decided on. Anyhow, Churchill wants the raid undertaken primarily to test the German coastal defences at this French harbour.' Bain jabbed his finger into the map. 'It may be some kind of stratagem conjured up to appease Stalin. We know he is pushing Winston to establish a second front, a full-scale invasion of Western Europe, no less.'

Hugo set down his pipe and gave a snort. 'Hitler will need assassinating, or at the very least made militarily impotent, and that's some years down the line, in my humble estimation.' He faced Bain. 'Look how grim our situation is in North Africa, for instance. The Eighth Army is well and truly buggered up, and is now pushed right back into Egypt. With troops spread all over the place, we haven't an earthly chance of pulling off a successful invasion for-for well, for God knows how long. Stalin must be made to see it will take a combined operation on a mammoth scale.' His brow became furrowed. 'Bloody hell, can you imagine all that coordinating between the Anglo-Americans and the Canadians, Eisenhower, Mountbatten, Eisenhower and Montgomery, Churchill and Patton, and the rest of the entourage?' Hugo exhaled. And then had a go at shrugging off his sudden dejection by picking up his pipe and continuing to read. Suddenly, as if he'd solved a cross-word problem he tapped his pencil, and said, 'aha, in the meantime, this is very useful.' Bain, interested in any new angle, drew closer. 'Do you see underneath his age?' Hugo scored in red the trainee's place of birth, and leaned over to point at the map in front of them. 'Our fellow grew up in a nearby town, so he should have a through knowledge of the area in question. They would make a good team, this pair, him, being the more mature, and possibly less headstrong than our young nightingale.' He threw the pencil down. 'They simply must get through this final round of training—the real toughie. This will soon sort the wheat from the chaff, so to speak. I don't know about you Graham, but I have much more admiration for the ones who attempt to brazen it out—'

'And don't take the easy option and call the emergency number.' Bain nodded. 'Once they get through this gruelling next round, I want those two going to France given sufficient time to learn their own cover story off pat. We can't afford any slip-ups. Churchill fights the SOE corner, with everything he's got. But we both know the dogs that are forever nipping at his heels, and complaining we are siphoning off the cream of the crop. Even Harris wrote a stinking memo to Winston, quite recently, complaining bitterly because we seconded one of his best men.'

Hugo laughed at that bit of common practice, and clapped Bain on back. 'Well, old man, the truth is there is never any coercion. We do always ask for volunteers, after all!'

'Hmm, true, but enough said on that. Anyway,' Bain went on, 'I'm standing firm on this. I want no corners cut just because they've given us a deadline.' He changed tack. 'I see their training at Ringway has got scrapped.'

'Yes, that's right.' Hugo explained, 'there simply was not time and as it's about priorities, they can do some practice jumps after this mission, when they get back. It's not a problem. For the operation they'll get taken over by plane, no parachuting business in this locality, far too dicey; they would be bound to get spotted. In any case, given the German military build up around...'

Hugo sucked on his pipe and Bain resumed staring at a map of the French coast. Their scheming, planning and jiggery-pokery would carry the two men well into the night.

To the villagers and locals, Beaulieu, set in the heart of Hampshire's New Forest, was synonymous with centuries of quintessential English stately living. The manor itself, and the scattering of smaller houses contained within Beaulieu's beautiful, verdant acreage, belied the inauspicious purpose of a deliberately contrived anonymity.

Millie's initial instructions were to go to Ringway, near Manchester, for her parachute training. Then, at the last minute, she got word of the change. Updated orders told her to go at once to the New Forest. When she arrived at Beaulieu she found she was in with a collection of seven total strangers. She was slightly unnerved to see that there was not a single familiar face among the bunch. Millie took it for granted that Vanessa would be there or at least a few of the group from the Island assignment. It was disappointing to find she was without Vanessa. And she felt she stood out like a sore thumb as she was the only female. Then a little later in the day she saw...well, she didn't know what his name was. She just used to think of him as the Timbuktu man. Unsure of the set up at Beaulieu, or what to expect, Millie decided to keep her distance, for the time being at least. However, after it was announced that luncheon was being served, Timbuktu suddenly spied Millie sitting at a table by the window. He gravitated towards her. A tall fellow in a navel uniform must have had the same idea, but Timbuktu wasn't having any of it, and elbowed him, neatly out of the way.

'Hello,' he said, cheerily, obviously pleased to see her. 'If I'm not interrupting, do you mind if I sit here?'

Millie attempted surprise, and answered, 'no, not at all, please do. How are you, Mr err-err?'

'Jack.' He didn't offer to shake hands, his being full with the food tray. 'Yes, well, I'm OK, now that I'm finally here.' Millie watched his pedantic care at arranging the cutlery, neatly, each side of his plate, while the tin tray was placed on a deep window sill. Then he gave the foodstuff a fine dusting of salt followed by hearty shakes from the pepper pot. Catching her eye, he said, 'it helps to disguise the taste.' He told Millie, 'I seem to have done nothing but get on and off trains for the last couple of days.'

Making conversation, Millie, asked, 'why's that, then?'

'The thing is they sent me to Manchester. Then once I got there they told me there was some sort of foul up with my papers and that I had to push off and get down to Hampshire.' He took a couple of furtive glances round the dining area. 'Didn't think I'd find anything quite so, well, you know, grand.' Quickly back to his plate Jack sliced into some pale, unidentifiable meat. 'Please excuse me tucking in; it's just that what with the trains only crawling along and then having to wait in a bombed siding for troop trains to pass, I didn't manage to get anything to eat all day.'

'Poor you, but do carry on. I am finished. And by the way,' Millie lifted her plate to take back to the serving hatch, then leaning close to his ear, said, 'you're right about the food. It's not a patch on our last port of call. Remember the crabs, and those delicious fat, blue lobsters that got landed?' He grinned, and munching on the chewy meat, gave a nod in agreement. 'I shan't be a tick,' she said, 'I'm just off to fetch us both some tea'

Millie was relieved, in a way to have Timbuktu, or Jack, for company. Yet despite the undoubted elegance and grandeur of the place that Jack was taken with, a gnawing feeling in the pit of her stomach told her this wasn't going to be any holiday camp. She knew that like her, Jack should have been scheduled in for parachute training. While pouring their tea, Millie was on the point of asking him if he noticed Vanessa, at Ringway, but then she thought better of it and didn't enquire.

Some hours later, when biding Millie goodnight, Jack told her he was looking forward to getting his head down on a soft pillow, and then with a mischievous glint in his eye he said he'd leave orders at the desk asking not to be called until ten o'clock. Come the next morning, however, with good humour Jack made a bit of a joke of it all. And in a way Millie could see the funny side of it, especially after he said something about sleeping the clock round.

All the same, Jack got a real shock, and so did Millie. Well, they all did, in those wee small hours of darkness. For some of the trainees it was not so comical at the time, and when Millie did a head count in the classroom, a couple of their number were missing. When the incident was dissected by an instructor, most found it hard to pinpoint the exact time it happened, so they referred to it as erupting in the middle of the night.

Looking back, Jack thought he was lucky, more than anything, for he was sluggish and disorientated when he woke to the piercing shouts of, 'Open up! Open up, Gestapo!' Wearing only his pyjama bottoms, he got out of bed and fumbled for the light. The lit-up room gave him the few seconds needed to clear his head, and he managed to grab his dressing gown. Repeated hammerings to the tune of, 'Open up, open up, *Geheime Staats Polizei*: Gestapo!' demanded he take action. He was about to open his mouth, and the door when by a strange quirk of his imagination, the voice of Captain Meene started to resound inside his brain. He could hear him saying, "Keep your mouth shut." This message saved Jack, because that was exactly what he did. When the uniformed Gestapo burst in he responded to their bullying and threats by never uttering a word. Unlike two hapless, sleep laden students who very foolishly answered, in English, 'come in!'

Millie's reaction was astounding, as well as unprecedented. After it was all over, though unknown to Millie, her handling of the situation did cause some amusement among the hierarchy. When her door was assaulted by the loud thumps and demands to open up for the Gestapo, Millie, fortunately, was not asleep. She had gone to bed and had indeed slept for a couple of hours, but had woken unable to get off again. So she was lying with her hands behind her head just staring into the darkness with irritating thoughts fighting to keep her awake. Now, fully alert, but nevertheless, horribly alarmed at the hammering and raucous demand, she jumped into a pair of slacks and shoved her bare feet into plimsolls. Then opening the window she started to climb out. Pausing, in mid-air for a few seconds, she thought she might have to jump for it, but found she was able to stand on tip-toes and use the narrow ledge below the window. Tentative support from an ancient Virginia creeper allowed Millie to inch her way to a drain pipe. Gingerly, shinning down the two stories she landed safely on soft earth. By this time the 'Gestapo' had burst in, seen the open window and seen Millie making a bolt for it. Calls to, 'halt! Halt!' followed her. Millie of course, ignored the shouts, and just ran. Blackout regulations were abandoned in many rooms as the manor got lit up. Millie's was a mindless flight, for she had no idea of her bearings, never as yet had time to see the grounds. Not knowing the terrain was perhaps her downfall, for fall she literally did, by crashing right onto the bonnet of the car that Hugo Maitland was in.

Such was his haste to see if Millie was badly hurt, Hugo flung the car door back so savagely he almost had it off its hinges, and whacking a 'Gestapo guard' into the bargain. When she didn't move, he became seriously worried. Then he switched a torch on and shone it into Millie's face. To his relief she stirred. She was stunned, and winded, but was able to recover her wits, after a few moments. Her puff regained, Millie was, however, left speechless when he lifted her in his arms, and strode purposefully back to the manor.

Hugo's voice rang with droll irony, as he declared, 'I say, old thing, we simply must stop meeting like this.'

Next day in the classroom, the remaining candidates listened carefully as the instructor went over the previous night's little fracas. They were told it was a planned exercise to test how they would react in an impromptu situation; it was not specifically carried out to see if they would crack under interrogation. It was done to show them that the unexpected was always the greatest danger for an agent.

*

'Life is full of little surprises, lately,' Millie told Hugo, a few days later. He thought that's an understatement, if ever I heard one. 'I didn't think I would see you again. How—'

He held up his hands. 'OK, confession time. I admit I did know you were here. It's just that I didn't expect to bump into you quite so soon.'

Millie couldn't help herself; he said it so seriously that she just fell about laughing. Her girlish giggling made him join in too, and he had an urge to put his arm around her. He didn't, he couldn't. And then she groaned and bent forwards, her ribs still aching from crashing onto the car bonnet.

'Come on,' Hugo said, 'let's make for that spot by the stream.'

A wooden bridge spanned the shallows, and they stopped in the middle, quiet for a few moments. Millie picked at the flaking bits of bark, and watched them float away. And then facing him, she said, 'there are all sorts of things I want to ask you about.' Hugo stiffened, noticeably. 'I won't of course. I shouldn't embarrass you by you having to refuse to tell me.'

Suddenly he couldn't help himself. Hugo took her hand and raised it to his lips. Millie instantly felt a pained twang of emotion. It wasn't anger, it wasn't passion, and then she recognised it. It was tenderness, and it nearly brought tears to her eyes. She blinked quickly to stop them from falling, and swallowed hard.

Hugo sensed her mood, and he instantly regretted causing her to feel sad. He murmured, 'there's a seat on the other side, where we can sit down.' A homely, familiar scent of tobacco clung about his person; it reminded Millie of the meerschaum pipe her father smoked. When they reached the bench Millie could tell he was on the verge of disclosing something. 'Like you,' he began, 'I am in the service—'

Abruptly, Millie stopped him, intuition warning her not to compromise his position. By way of skirting the issue she launched in with, 'this-this place, Beaulieu, they told us it's the final testing ground. The last point of call before...is that right?'

'Yes.' He fixed his eyes on her.

'When the time comes, will you, will you see me off, please?'

His gaze never wavered. 'Yes, of course I will...and I'll be waiting at Tangmere, when you return.' He wanted to appear blasé, so he said, 'anyway, it's my job,' and with a flippant gesture he lightly tweaked her nose, 'it's all part of the door-to-door service.'

CHAPTER TWENTY-SIX

Several nights of fog, then rain prevented the plane taking off. And again that night it was another nail-biting stand down. All the same, postponement of the mission was out of the question. This was the last possible chance for SOE agents to do first-hand intelligence gathering, so very vital for the impending Allied operation.

As though he were a magician set to pull a rabbit out of the hat, the onus was now on the weather man to come up with something. Teetering on the edge of uncertainty he forecast a small window of clemency, after midnight. It was the best he could give, he told them. Anxiously, they all watched the full moon slink, tantalisingly in and out through ribbons of cloud. Then ten minutes after the witching hour a definite thumbs up came from the pilot, and they got the long awaited go-ahead. There was a final hug for Millie from Hugo, and a formal hand shake for Jack. From the hanger Graham Bain observed the departure and watched as the plane finally took off.

To get them safely to France it all rested on the skill of the pilot who had the additional tricky job of navigating. Jack tried to give Millie a reassuring nudge; Millie could only mouth a grunt. They were squeezed in the rear cockpit of the tiny Lysander, which bumped and shook, and did nothing to help the contents of Millie's stomach stay down. It was traditional, apparently, that before landing, the agents would be given a hot toddy, laced with rum. Millie had already gulped it before she tasted the loathed rum.

So tight was the space, or lack of it that they were touching knee to knee. Jack's jacket was shabby, and he had on a pair of coarse, faded blue work trousers, that were patched, here and there. He'd been given the rig-out of a typical French farmer, even down to the black beret, fitting tightly on his head. He was minus their suggested hump, preferring to rely on his cover story and wits. Millie wondered if he had a spare pair of trousers, hoping she wouldn't be sick in his lap. Even if she was, Millie knew he'd take it all in his stride and not be disgusted.

Of all the trainees at Beaulieu she was glad he was with her. Jack had grown on her, and she felt comfortable working with him. Sometimes in lectures he would roll his eyes heavenward, or pull faces at her on things he thought were silly, or 'damn barmy,' as he called them. Aside, he once said to her, why go to all the bother of fiddling with messages on bits of paper only to get passed in a café in a box of matches, when a discrete whisper while drinking coffee, was every bit as good, and much safer. Jack was an ace with the radio communications side of things and both he and Millie excelled at map reading. Definitely when it came to picking locks, nobody came close to Jack. He was a natural. Even the lecturer, a locksmith, whom it was rumoured, was a cat burglar, in a formal life, said to Jack that after the war he must get in touch for they'd make the best safecracking team in the country—joking of course.

In spare moments Jack would help Millie, most frequently it was during weapons training. He'd watch her load and reload a .45 automatic pistol. Its recoil was so powerful it sometimes knocked her over. But he'd calmly encourage her to get up and fire at the target again, and again. It worked, because dedication paid off and quite soon she'd come up to scratch in the small arms department, including a high degree of accuracy when firing the sten gun. This weapon was popular with some, not so with others, due its tendency to jam. Though everyone was in agreement, including Millie, it was easy to dismantle and very compact for transporting and carrying around.

Millie and Jack were placed together when team training and on most other exercises, with the result a sound bond had formed. She knew she could rely completely on Jack. The last task; the initiative test, backed this up. She probably would have fluffed it if his quick thinking and skills hadn't kicked in at the crucial moment. Over the channel the weather was beginning to improve. In spite of still feeling queasy, when she thought about how well they had pulled the Pompey assignment off, it did make her smile.

Between the two of them, they discussed a plan of action on the train to Portsmouth; the journey gave them useful time for plotting. Once out of the station, they saw the pock-mark scars inflicted on Pompey and it horrified them. Steeped in centuries of history, the old navel town had suffered dreadfully at the hands of the Luftwaffe. However, it was here they had to infiltrate a munitions factory and plant explosives—albeit dummies. Dangerous in itself, because of the very nature of the work done there, they surmised that getting into a place like that wasn't going to be a piece of cake.

They ferreted out the factory's location and ascertained it was situated on the outskirts of the town. Buses ferried some workers to the site, and a quick reconnoitre told them that many workers also rode bicycles. Buses, therefore, was their chosen means of getting to the factory.

They made a snap decision to carry out the assignment there and then, rather than go back to a hotel for the night. They knew that to use the bus again would be too suspicious. Everybody seemed to know each other. At one point, it became slightly hairy when a female worker got chatting. Without hesitation Jack came up with the story they'd rehearsed—that he was an inspector and Millie was his secretary. Getting off the bus, they lagged behind the throng until most had gone through security. Millie made the pretence of leaving her handbag on the bus and they both retraced their steps. 'Bloody boffins,' someone jeered, 'they'd forget their head if it wasn't screwed on.' Titters of laughter died away, as workers hurried to clock in. Several buses were stacked up waiting to empty and turn around. That came as a bit of luck for the buses gave them the cover they needed to get away from the entrance and slip into a shed. That, however, wasn't so clever, from the comfort aspect, as the shed turned out to be full of coke. Still, they could do nothing about it, except stay put and wait until it got dark.

They learnt more about each other during those few hours than in all the time at the other schools. Each asked how it was they got sucked into SOE. Jack listened with interest, and admiration, as Millie recounted the leaving of Singapore. And Jack told her that after the fall of France he found the army boring, with nothing much to do. On manoeuvres they were sent to safe places such as Wales, and then Northern Ireland.

Like many other soldiers, he didn't get much time to be with his wife, and son, who lived in Coventry. He was with the Royal Corps of Signals when they told him his family had been killed in a Luftwaffe bombing raid.

After returning from compassionate leave the powers that be must have gone into his records, for the next thing he knew he was presenting himself at the War Office where a Major Gielgud, of the acting family, interviewed him. Jack thought it unusual that they spoke in French the whole time, but he enjoyed that part of it because his mother was French and he'd lived in France for many years, and enjoyed speaking in her native tongue. Major Gielgud explained what SOE was and then said to him, 'we'd want to send you to France. Of course, you don't have to go. But we would rather like it if you did.' Without thinking Jack told him, 'I'll go to France, and go willingly, if it gives me the chance to kill Germans.'

Millie had no doubt of Jack's sincerity, but all the same she had to suppress a shiver at Jack's blunt, yet apparently sole motive. She let it pass without saying anything, and just watched through the partially obscured window while one factory shift finished and was replaced by a fresh batch of workers. Millie commented to Jack that the men and women all wore a sort of nondescript dungaree and jacket uniform.

'We can't go through the factory dressed like this,' she was quick to point out.

'No, I know. We must get overalls from somewhere. Their clobber might allow us to go about without creating suspicion, depending on just what their security is really like.'

'And what if we're challenged?'

'Well, we'll have to think on our feet.' Taunting her slightly, he said, 'of course there is always the emergency telephone number we can ring should—'

'Not bloomin' likely!' Millie declared, though not altogether confident. 'If all goes according to plan we'll need to get bikes to get back into town.'

'That's not the problem; we can pick up a couple from the bike shed, over there.' They had seen the cyclists drop off the bikes before clocking in, and then later, collecting them when the shift was finished. 'Well, there's only one way, then, so agreed?'

Millie nodded, 'agreed.'

Jack unbuttoned his coat and pulled out his shirt-tail. Round his body he had a canvas belt with pockets that held the set of tools; he'd bought earlier from an ironmonger. He chose the wire cutters. Millie carried the dummy explosives. Jack made light work cutting through the wire fence with the powerful cutters.

'Money well invested,' he whispered to Millie, snipping away.

They climbed through the hole, and ran in the direction of the cycle shed. A quick scout around brought them to a solid, metal door. Because it was so heavily padlocked they guessed that this door must lead to somewhere significant, possibly a boiler room, which would be an ideal place to plant the explosives. They both hoped it wasn't bolted from the inside that would involve a longer job, should it be the case. The lock had to be opened by touch alone; they couldn't risk switching on a torch to open it.

Jack asked Millie, 'want to have a go?'

'No, thank you. I'll let the master demonstrate how it's done.'

He gave a soft laugh. Even in darkness, teasing open that great heart-shaped lump posed no difficulty, whatsoever, for Jack. Luck was running with them, no bolts to negotiate. Once inside they found themselves in a narrow, dimly lit corridor, which turned off to the left while a set of stairs dropped down to what they supposed was a basement. Of one accord, they headed for the stairs.

On reaching the bottom, Jack confirmed, 'there's nothing doing down here. It just looks like some sort of storeroom—'

'But-but couldn't we do something with all these shells!'

'Empty, they're all empty cases. That stuff's not going to blow up in a million years.' Millie looked puzzled. Jack hastily explained, 'they're duds. Didn't you notice how light they were?' She shook her head. 'They are most probably defectives, going back for scrap. And anyway, the Beaulieu bods will know we'd botched it up, if we plant explosives here.'

'So, back the other way, then?'

'Yep.'

They followed the maze of pipes and wires running along the ceiling. Some way along the passage, a hum of machinery noise indicated that they weren't far from the factory floor.

Cupping his ear, Jack said, 'now, this sounds more like it.'

Before they could go any further they had to squeeze round empty wooden pallets which were stacked higgledy-piggledy on the floor, while some were piled on a trolley. Millie wondered what Jack was going to do when he stepped up and started to throw sacks at her. Then he unearthed a bundle of rags and gave them a shake. Among the bits he found a filthy oil stained boiler suit that was shoved in one of the pallets.

'Hang on,' he said to Millie. 'This'll do for starters.' And he climbed into the overall.

Millie told him, 'God, you look and smell disgusting.'

Jack beamed. 'Good, so I'll pass muster then.' He looked at Millie. There was nothing that she could wear so he gathered up the sacks. 'You will have to improvise. Here, carry these till we can get something better, anything by way of a bluff, so as you don't look as if you shouldn't be here.' He rubbed his hands together. 'Right, let's get a move on and see what damage we can do.'

Her thoughts were interrupted. Unexpectedly, a crosswind hammered the fly-weight Lysander causing it to lunge, and then bank at a sharp angle. It sent her heart to her mouth. It was not unlike the sensation Millie felt when they were caught in the factory, just after securing the bundles of dummy explosives. They had placed a stuffed rat in an obvious position, as a decoy, and the rest got hidden, neat as you like, under a section of shells, live ones this time. Then just when they thought they had it all sewn up, two burly workmen were coming straight for them. Surprised, the conspirators quickly looked around for some means of getting out unseen, but it was too late, they had nowhere else to go, their exit was blocked.

'Oi. Oi!' This shout was followed by an ineloquent question. 'What the fucking hell are you doing down here?'

Gripped by panic, Millie shot Jack a confused look. He responded with a devil may care retort. Jack growled back at the man, 'you can see what we're bloody doing, having a bloody fuck, or trying to.'

'You dirty bloody bugger! Get the hell back to your work, both of you, or you'll feel my boot at your arse, never mind about feeling hers. I'll not have this sort of goings-on on my shift, I'm damned if I will. Go on, clear off back to work.'

Millie cringed and hid her face in Jack's foul coat while he removed his hand from her knickers, rather more slowly than she would have liked. Then, keeping his back to the men he pulled up the boiler suit from around his ankles.

She told him afterwards, 'you really rather enjoyed that, didn't you?'

'*Carpe diem,* sweetheart. Anyway, it's all done in the line of duty, our life of lies and the great art of pretence.'

Millie understood his Latin, but she wasn't going to try and fathom out what he was talking about. She was angry, not with Jack but at how lax the security was at the factory. It had been so easy to get inside. Almost anyone, an enemy spy; anyone with serious intent, she felt, could get into the factory and blow it up. She said as much to Jack, and he agreed with her. She was pleased then when he went along with her idea to leave a calling card.

'What do you say that we put our guerrilla expertise into action? After all, one could say we've been given *carte blanche.*'

Humouring her to an extent, Jack said, 'OK. I'm all ears. What have you got in mind?'

The stolen bicycles got propped behind the coke shed while yet again they slipped inside. Once Jack peeled off the old clothes Millie struck a couple of matches. The oil soaked material easily caught alight. They waited to make sure the coke had well and truly started to burn. Then they left and cycled down the road for Pompey. They only stopped once, turning behind them to gaze at the red glow streaking the night sky. Satisfied, that they had made their point.

Jack gave Millie a shake. The pilot was saying something, but she couldn't hear. Jack put his mouth to her ear. 'He said we're not far from Dieppe, a couple of minutes at the most. We're to keep our eyes peeled for a torch signal, from the ground.'

CHAPTER TWENTY-SEVEN

The gnawing emptiness Hugo felt was not entirely unexpected. It happened like that, every time, after an agent went out. Now, there were just awkward bits of conversation from Bain, as he tried to voice his thoughts. However, the veritable silent drive back from Tangmere didn't ease the tension for either of them. They were not far from Beaulieu when Bain, who was at the wheel, said, 'I've got half a bottle of Scotch in my room, want to share it with me?'

The leather upholstery squeaked as Hugo turned in his seat. 'Ah, thanks, Graham, I appreciate the offer, but um, no, I won't. I'll hit the sack. I have an early start back to London, tomorrow, got some loose ends to tie up. As you know, Millie left me with money, birthday money, for her brothers. I've got to see the Chance boys get it on time.' He uttered a croaky laugh and had to clear his throat. 'She was most adamant that I should get the dates right. Birthdays are apparently very important in their family. Funny,' he threw a glance at Bain, 'I don't know about you, but those sorts of anniversaries I find hard to remember. I suppose it's because it's not something we ever celebrated much. Anyway, she'll be away for one of them so…'

'Yes, well. I understand.'

Another silent intermission followed, until Hugo said, 'I take it you'll stay on here for a while?'

'Yes. I'll get the rest of the trainees processed. There's just two not quite up to the mark. You know the two I mean.'

'Yes, yes I do.' And without sympathy, added, 'they rather fouled up that last major assignment.'

Bain was more disposed to leniency. 'They got into a bit of a sticky wicket with the authorities, and couldn't talk their way out of it.'

Hugo fired back, disparagingly, 'so they succumbed to using the phone number we gave them, and had to get the police involved.'

'Well, when all's said and done, we have to give them something to fall back on, for emergency purposes, of course.'

Still being critical, Hugo said, 'Hmm, it doesn't say much for their ingenuity, what?'

'Um, yes quite possibly. But we can't have them coming to harm before they even get started. You probably recall there was a case some time back when the great unwashed took things into their own hands, and gave our fellow a jolly good hiding.' Hugo merely gave a grunt, which Bain ignored. 'Look, we have to avoid them getting duffed up and thrown in the clink, where we might never get hold of them in time.'

Effecting acquiescence, Hugo said, 'alright, maybe they will learn, but they will have to repeat the exercise at another location and we'll have to concoct a different scenario. Then, if they don't come up to scratch it's the cooler for them, and they're out.'

Bain dropped down a gear to negotiate a left hand turn. Happy to be on a more confident footing, he said, 'the rest look very promising.' Then he saw Hugo peering at his watch. 'She'll-they'll be alright, you know,' he said.

'Yes, of course they will. It's just the first time they go, kind of sets one's teeth on edge.' Flicking his cuff back he checked the time again. 'They should be down by now.'

In the hallway of Beaulieu Manor, the two men said goodnight. Bain shook hands with Hugo, and they went in different directions to their rooms. Wending his way wearily up the staircase, Bain took off his trilby. He patted his thinning hair, conscious of Hugo having the fortuitous advantage of youth and virility on his side. As he reached his room he was left in no doubt that Maitland was more than a little in love with Millie. He wondered if Maitland realised it himself. And rather scathingly, thought, for all his brilliancy, these academic types sometimes can't see what's in front of their noses.

*

The moth-like monoplane was on the ground for less than two minutes before it was taking off again. The moan of its single engine drowned out Millie's retching. Their contact, a thin, anxious fellow, paced up and down, impatient to get away from the naked strip of grass.

Jack said to him, 'give her a moment, it's just nerves.'

Wiping her mouth, Millie told Jack, 'it was my stomach that was upset, not my hearing.'

'What?'

'It's not nerves; it's that damn bloody rum.'

'What?'

'Nothing, Jack, never mind, I'm alright now, really I am.'

'Good girl. Then let's get going. Lead the way, *Monsieur*.'

They had no transport, so walking the three kilometres across the uneven country-side with a heavy radio transmitter was disquieting, as well as labour intensive. Nonetheless, their contact, Pierre, was unapologetic. He made it clear the need for caution was paramount. He stressed that unless one had a permit it was too risky driving a car, or truck after curfew. Pierre warned them to be very vigilant, as the Germans had mounted increased patrols in the region, especially in Dieppe, where military activity had intensified in the last few weeks. It made the townsfolk fearful. In the underground movement, the resistance fighters were saying it was as if the Germans had got wind of British interest in the area.

'Surely that's not possible,' said Jack, alarmed. 'We only knew the destination a few days ago.'

'It is possible, *Monsieur*, more than possible.'

Jack asked, 'how is that, double agents?'

Non-committal, Pierre shrugged, 'maybe.'

Not surprising, Millie felt instantly alone when Pierre left Jack at a farm house. Pierre said it was too dangerous for them both to stay in the same place. They trudged across several more fields and down a long lane which eventually led to another farmhouse. Pierre tapped the back door several times before it was opened by a middle-aged woman. Apart from an incongruously bright coloured floral head scarf, the woman was dressed in a garb that was as black as night itself.

Millie was hurriedly introduced by Pierre. 'This is Yvette,' he said. Millie blinked against the lamp light. She'd winced, at the time, when Hugo came up with the name, Gale. She thought it was his idea of a joke. Then he explained she had to get a code number, and a field name, every agent did. So he devised a shortened version of Nightingale. She scoffed, trust him. But he wasn't jesting. Hugo told her that for security purposes, Gale is the unique name, that Bain and himself, and others within the organisation would always identity her by. In a strange way, she felt a little caressed by his personal touch of delicate intimacy. For this mission, however, her cover name was Yvette. 'Thank you, Madame Etienne, for helping us.' Pierre said, and hastened to add, 'it will only be for a few days. Forgive me, but now I must go.' He kissed the woman on each cheek, and then hurried away.

Before uttering a word, the woman scurried to the windows on both sides of the farm house, to make sure no one had followed Pierre. Satisfied, it appeared none had. Relaxing now, she proffered her hand.

'You must be tired and hungry. I have kept some stew—'

'Oh please don't go to any trouble.'

'It's no trouble for me to heat you a little food, when you and your friend are taking the trouble to help us, and France.'

'Thank you, Madame.'

'Marguerite, Aunt Marguerite Etienne,' she rebuked, gently. 'Set your case in the corner and sit, please.' She began by reminding herself of Millie's ID. 'So you have had TB.' She thought it could almost be true, for the girl in front of her was thin and ghostly white.

'And now you've had to leave your nursing job at the hospital to convalesce here, with your old aunt.' Marguerite smiled at that.

Two bowls of stew were soon set on a bare wooden table with a small lump of broken bread. It smelt good to Millie, who, by now was feeling very hungry.

'Thank you, thank you very much, Aunt.' she said.

Madame Etienne took off her scarf, releasing a fuzz of woolly grey hair, and then sat opposite Millie. Without feeling any need to apologise for her living conditions, she plainly stated, 'all the water we use has to be drawn from the well. We do not have bath facilities.'

Millie just nodded more intent on spooning the stew from the bowl. She wasn't at all bothered. It reminded her of the same basic conditions that were on Lindisfarne, and similarly those at her French relatives' house, where she stayed as a school girl. And besides, it was most likely that she and Jack's stay would not be more than five days, a week at the most. There was great urgency for their information to be got back to Combined Operations Headquarters, just as soon as their mission could be accomplished.

It was early the next morning when Jack entered the kitchen. Millie was already up and waiting for him. He declined the coffee she offered.

'There should be a bicycle around somewhere for you,' he said. 'Try in one of the outhouses.'

'I'll fetch it.' They spun round. Coming downstairs, unheard, it was Marguerite.

'Good morning, Madame,' Jack said, a little awkwardly, at being spoken to unawares.

'Good morning.'

'I am Yvette's friend. Pierre has loaned me his bike. He said it's the best way to get to—'

'No need for more information than is necessary. The less I know the better.'

'Yes, of course, you are right.'

They watched Marguerite from the back door as she wheeled a rickety bicycle out of a shed and rested it against the wall.

Millie couldn't disguise her concern. The French woman laughed at Millie's expression.

'No need to fret, it is serviceable enough, if you don't ride over too many cobbles.' She told them to wait while she went to her pantry. There she wrapped a cheese in a cloth and unhooked a bundle of carrots which she put into a string bag. She gave them to Millie. 'Yvette, put these in the basket. More than likely you will get stopped by the Germans. And if they search you it will seem as if you have been shopping.' Madame Etienne took stock of the pair. Anyone, she thought, would take them as French, but a last minute scrutiny made her ask, 'have you all the proper documents on you, identification papers, and Yvette, are you carrying your hospital discharge certificate? And have both of you got your permit to ride the cycles?'

Jack tapped his pocket and Millie waved her little satchel and tucked it over her head. Madame Etienne wished them good luck as they climbed on the bikes. With arms folded across her body, her gaze followed them until the winding lane closed them from her sight.

CHAPTER TWENTY-EIGHT

They were dead, now, the two friends from Jack's childhood. Jack's memories of halcyon days became spoilt, and undoubtedly made forever acerbic by Pierre's dreadful disclosure. With his eyes reflecting the recent sorrow, Pierre told him they were executed, just last month, by the Gestapo. Recoiling in shock, Jack asked him to explain why and how it happened. Pierre revealed that they were working for the Resistance and got caught trying to derail a German troop train. He also had to tell Jack that the Bosch retaliated by taking ten hostages from the town and had them shot, too. For Jack, the little seaside resort of Dieppe—where the friends spent school holidays happily climbing among the long stretches of cliffs, or fishing on the banks of the river Scie—would never be the same again.

The plan, when Millie and Jack neared Dieppe, was to separate, then in the afternoon at the arranged time, they'd meet at the crossroads. They would wait for an hour and if either didn't show up the other was to go back to Madame Etienne's farmhouse. Millie took the route that veered in the direction of Puys. She was to suss out what type of fortifications, if any were at Puys. Jack would make his way into Dieppe itself. Before doing so Jack climbed into a field where a few cows were grazing. When he located what he was looking for he smeared the animal manure down his trousers and rubbed the surplus off on his jacket. He left his hands unwashed.

Ever conscious that each pedal revolution took him nearer the enemy, he knew that he had no other alternative but to keep going. There was no way to avoid the German check point. Pierre said it controlled the town. All the same, he had to get through it to reach the northern quarter. So assuming an air of confidence, that he didn't wholly command, Jack cycled up towards the barrier and then got off his bike. Waiting in turn were several other people, mostly women with shopping bags, and a few old men. He joined the resigned line that shuffled forward at an agonisingly slow pace. However, Jack didn't have to wait long before noses sniffed the air, and a few heads turned, in disdain. Quite soon the queue began to fragment as some people edged away to give Jack a wide berth. One woman held a handkerchief to her face and moved aside to let him go in front. The German guard noticed the line's irregularity and glared at the poor woman with instinctive suspicion, until the reason for her movement became evident. With his hands stinking and streaked with dung, Jack muttered a subservient apology, and held out his papers. It didn't do much good, for the guard, irritated that anything should disrupt his routine, snatched them from the disgusting specimen, standing in front of him. Then he took one reproachful glance at the papers, and rather than give them back to Jack he flung them into the road across the checkpoint. As he wheeled the bike through, Jack got a thump in the back from the guard's riffle butt. Jack remonstrated a little, a very little.

Up wind of Jack the second soldier soon curled his lips and edged away from the smelly body. Still bent on retaining rigid authority, he pointed the muzzle of his firearm at Jack and bellowed, threateningly at him, 'what's your business here?'

Gathering up the strewn papers, Jack replied, 'my shovel broke, look.' Pleading somewhat, he rubbed his hands down his trousers to suggest the reason for his muck covered state. 'I have to buy a new shovel to—'

'Get on your way,' the soldier snarled in anger, 'and be quick, your filthy swine!'

Satisfied with his progress so far, Jack found the town, as he rather anticipated from Pierre's warning, crawling with Germans. He had to exercise a degree of self-control in trying to cycle through the streets without undue haste. Located bang centre of the Town Square was the Headquarters of the German Infantry Division. It angered Jack to see that they had commandeered the largest, and grandest of Dieppe's houses. He made a mental note of the ease with which the enemy sauntered in and out of the Swastika decorated building, and the numerous striations of military vehicles that were parked—on the once beautiful green—like satiated fat, field-grey slugs. Passing them with care, Jack knew, provided nothing untoward occurred, he could soon take to the narrower turnings that would eventually lead him to the safety of *Monsieur* Blanchard's ironmongery shop.

The premises were shabbier than he'd remembered. Paint was curling, and had begun peeling off the façade. There too, was noticeably less of a display of wares sitting by the door. Jack recalled the shop as being a veritable hive of activity. The elders of the town would congregate to see the latest tools that arrived from Normandy. And a pipe or two got smoked when money changed hands, and customer and proprietor went away happy. Gentlemen farmers would walk their horses up the alleyway to get their shoes shod. As a youngster, Jack was kept enthralled by all the many farm implements that hung from rustic shelves, while galvanised buckets and tin baths were stacked at the rear of the shop near the counter. He knew ever nook and cranny of the shop as well as the owner's son did, he was there that often. Jack thought about those days, now, while he waited.

Jack began to feel apprehensive when no one came in answer to the ring of the shop bell. So he pushed the cycle out of the front doorway and up to the old forge where he could hear hammering. The thump-thum, thump-thum, so rhythmically timed it could be likened to that of his own heart beat. A man, alone, was hunched over a forge, in what appeared to be deep concentration. He pounded, with a purpose, intent in his work. Jack watched him for a time; he was sure the man didn't see him so he waited, patiently, not wanting to startle the man by springing upon him unawares.

Suddenly without looking up the man abruptly asked, 'what do your want?'

'I-I-it's Jack. *Monsieur* Blanchard, its Jack, do you remember me, Henri's friend from school?'

Slowly the man straightened his shoulders and moved his bulk round. He tightened his grip on the hammer, and the poker he was working on glowed blood-red. Goblets of perspiration dripped from his brow. *Monsieur* Blanchard tried to focus, attempting to draw a memory from the recess of his mind. At last, he said, 'yes, yes, Jack, of course I remember. Jack the sprat, Henri called you!' Still clutching his tools, he asked, bitterly, 'do you know they murdered my son, murdered my Henri? Did you know that?'

'Yes, I-I heard. I am sorry, so very—'

'Why then, in God's name, did you come back, don't you realise the danger you are in, the danger you are putting us in? The enemy is all around us, we're overrun. We're a conquered country.'

'Don't give up, *Monsieur* Blanchard; you mustn't think we don't—'

'That's easy for you to say. You don't know what you're talking about.' He tasted the salt on his lips. 'Ten. They took ten. My neighbour, next door, her husband…' He put down the hammer and doused the poker in cold water, it hissed and spat while *Monsieur* Blanchard asked with contempt, 'what do you want, Jack? Why are you here?'

Jack crept close. 'We have to get information back to London—'

'What?'

The loss of his friend and the sudden heat from the forge seemed to sear into Jack's soul, weakening his resolve. He knew what he had to do, but now Jack wondered if he was asking too much from the father of his dead friend. Nonetheless, he set about explaining.

'We have to get certain information back to London. We must let them know just how heavily defended Dieppe is. They have little idea that Dieppe has such a huge garrison of troops entrenched here. If we were able to get specific numbers of Infantry and Artillery Regiments, what Battalions are stationed here, that sort of thing, it would be of invaluable assistance to Combined Operations. You see, something-something is being planned, in London. I-I can't say anymore that than. *Monsieur* Blanchard. Can you help us, please?'

*

Meanwhile, in the opposite direction, Millie almost ran smack into a heavy battery emplacement. The guns were so well camouflaged they practically merged into the undulating terrain and hillocks. From the air and on the ground there was no mistaking the airfield she passed, a few kilometres back, but the webbing concealing artillery and anti-tank weapons would have been impossible for the RAF to spot from aerial reconnaissance photographs.

Recovering from a terrible scare, Millie pulled off the dirt track with such haste that she practically threw herself into a wooded hollow. To regain her composure she crouched in undergrowth, and let ten minutes pass before she felt sure she'd not been seen. With adrenalin pumping she knew she had to go very cautious now, and keep off any kind of a path. The bike, then, would have to get pushed through the wood. She had barely gone more than a few hundred yards when to her horror; she came upon her first German.

He had his back to her and was leaning against a tree. Millie guessed he was having a pee. Again, she frantically searched for somewhere to hide. She even contemplated taking a risk and dumping the bike, but whatever action she chose he would either see or hear her. Glancing around threw up a sudden flash of inspiration. She had an idea for a ruse. Within hands reach were mushrooms, huge flat bubbles, as big as the skullcap that Clive used to wear. Quickly, she started to gather them, putting as many as she could into the basket. As she expected the German soldier was alerted, and turned, in an awkward gait towards the rustling. Millie feigned a startled surprise, yet in a moment she sensed there was a strange aura about him, something queer. He spoke to her in German.

'Aaah, aaah,' he moaned, in breathless jerks. '*Frau-Fräulein*, help me please!'

She did not expect this, and for a few seconds all Millie could do was stare at his bedraggled state of dress. And as her eyes travelled down the length of his body she saw a long tear in his trousers which were stained with what looked like blood. Oh, God, what do I do now? Captain Meene's method for silent killing came into her head. She even started to work out the way to get behind him. Yet these wild thoughts, in this situation, didn't seem appropriate. For one thing, if his body was found, killing the soldier would reflect badly on innocent locals. As well as that, she thought of the possibility that he was attacked by someone in the underground movement.

Then he spoke again, breaking into her deliberations.

'I've fallen. I need help.' He clung to the tree, in obvious need of support. 'Can you come, please?'

Millie approached, gingerly, and then it became clear as to what had happened to him. She saw an empty wine bottle, and smelt the alcohol on his person. He looked so young, probably he was no more that eighteen or nineteen. She surmised he'd got drunk, fallen down the nearby ravine, and injured himself in some way. This realisation brought her unbridled relief. Millie also understood perfectly what he was saying, but she muttered in French to tell him to sit down while she looked at his leg. She put the bike aside and went towards the soldier. He hesitated, not understanding until she sat on the grass and implied, by patting the ground, that he do the same. She helped by easing him down, and began inspecting the leg. She found thick blood matted and dried around the gash. Guessing, with all the leaves stuck to his tunic, he must have fallen asleep. By which time, the numbness brought on by his inebriation, had now worn off.

He was very pale, and as far as she could make out, it was a bad wound, but she needed to get his trouser leg opened, further. With her fingers opening and closing, she signified scissors. He lent forward and touched his knife. She was thinking this is not real. What am I doing? She had this knife in her hand, she could easily...no she could not. She was a nurse. Her duty was to save life. But that was back in Singapore. What an ungodly dilemma. Pushing those dark ideas aside, Millie gently sliced some inches up his trouser leg, thus allowing her enough room to feel and see that the leg, although probably not broken, was very swollen and horribly gashed. There was no way she could clean it up, she would simple have to bandage it as best she could. He wasn't far from his base in any case, so he'd soon get proper medical attention. She removed her scarf and made signs for a handkerchief. He opened a top pocket in his tunic, and pulled a perfect white square piece of cotton cloth. At the same time his wallet and a photograph tumbled to the ground. Millie got the handkerchief and handed him his wallet and photo.

'My parents,' he said, looking guilt-ridden at the image. 'They are good religious people, Quakers, very correct. They would not be pleased to see me like this. I've never drunk wine before.' Millie clenched her lips to stop from smiling at the whole bizarre situation.

In spite of his childish shame, Millie thought him brave, for he neither flinched nor cried out, as she bandaged his leg, first with the clean cloth and then tightly with her scarf, to draw the edges of the wound together.

'What is your name, *Fräulein?*' Millie kept her head down, ignoring him. He asked her again, and then tapped his chest. He informed her, 'Helmuth.'

She nodded. Still keeping her head bent, she said, 'Yvette.'

Signalling, the soldier wanted to know what Millie was doing in the wood. She knew the question was coming and pointed to the fungus. He looked blank. Millie could do no more for him except try and find a stick that could help his walking. She was definitely not going anywhere near his base. She'd see him out of the wood and then she'd clear off, fast. He struggled to get up, until Millie firmly held him down. Picking up his knife she began searching about for some sort of a longish cudgel. She didn't need the knife for there were enough thick branches lying about from a tree, brought down by some storm or other. She selected a sturdy specimen that would do the job.

The next minute she was literally in the arms of the enemy. It was a strange sensation. He held her in what was akin to a lover's embrace. That was the first time he winced, showing pain. Sweat broke out and began running down his face, but he was standing, at least. Gently releasing him, Millie left Helmuth leaning against the tree, with the stick in his hand, while she quickly wheeled her bike up to him. Then she lifted his arm over her shoulder, and with the help of the stick he began to hobble. She could bear his weight easier than she imagined, and with her free hand she was able to push the cycle. After a bit, he spied the mushrooms in the basket, and pointed. Millie took one out and put it to her mouth, as if to eat. With as much force as he could summon, Helmuth knocked it out of her hand. She gasped, taken aback. For her own survival she becomes drawn once again towards the knife. He jabbered on, somewhat incoherently in his native tongue. Then she understood. He is telling her she must not eat them because they are poisonous. However, Millie is still confused, for in truth she thought they were the same as those large, flat mushrooms they had in Scotland. The German is beside the basket now, and struggling somewhat, he reaches in to grab another of the flowerless plant. He turns it over, and with his finger, he ruffles the snow-white gills of the fungi underbelly. The delicate, frilly fan crumples. A picture from her old school botany class comes to life. Of course, he is right, they are toadstools! However, Helmuth is convinced Millie still doesn't understand the danger. He gets round that difficulty by gripping his throat. Everything becomes clear. Millie nods, and makes grateful signs to show she knows what his violent diatribe meant. Immediately, the rest of the luckless toadstools are thrown away, and they share a rare smile.

CHAPTER TWENTY-NINE

Jack had to find a safe place to set up his radio transmitter. And so towards evening, from the relative safety of a derelict barn he had transmitted the information that Blanchard had given him to London. However, the enemy was on the alert. The increased radio traffic has not gone undetected by the Germans, and soon one of their radio direction finders was homing in on his radio signal. Fortunately, before they had time to get an accurate fix Pierre had seen the van with its tell-tale aerial cruising around, and drove at speed to the barn to warn Jack. With only minutes to spare they just managed to gather up the radio set along with its code book and give the detector van the slip. It was a close call. On the move now, Jack wondered where he'd end up before curfew.

As events worked out, one of Pierre's contacts, a priest, sympathetic to the Resistance cause, allowed Jack to shelter in his church. And in the crypt Jack rested his head on an uncomfortable wooden pew. Idling the time away reading the tomb stones, Jack got to know the names of long dead villagers, some more recently interned, he even recognised. Even so, it was something to do over the next couple of nights. Because of the build up of troop activity it was only then that Pierre was able to move Jack to the farm where Madame Etienne lived. It wasn't ideal two agents staying at the same place, but right now, there was no alternative.

Previously, Millie and Jack had missed one another at the crossroads. Once having got rid of the German, it took Millie several hours to make a hazardous detour, and so knowing Jack wouldn't wait longer than they had arranged for rendezvousing, she went directly to Marguerite's.

Having done a quick skate around the farmhouse, Jack was careful to take precautions to hide his radio set in Marguerite's empty piggery, which was well away from the dwelling house itself. In the evening, at the arranged signal schedule, Jack waited, somewhat anxiously. To his dismay he was sent a short, but urgent message from London. When he decoded the information he told Millie that a plane would pick them up on the 15th, three days earlier than was first planned. Jack took it that pressure was on London to pass on all available information to Combined Operations, fast. This meant it only gave him and Millie one more day to suss out the stretch of beach around Varengeville-sur-Mer, and Pourville. At first, the time factor worried Millie, but these were both localities that Jack knew well. To reassure her, Jack mentioned that Varengeville, especially, had good wooded cover with the cliffs running down to the sea. Secretly he hoped they wouldn't find too many changes, like cut down forests replaced by German gun emplacements. They studied a map of the area, closely, and then decided they would also give it a go and try and get to the other side of Pourville as well, see what sort of defences the Germans had in place.

Four wheels turned up this time, thanks to Pierre offering to drive them in his open top truck. To a large extent Pierre was making a legitimate journey, his early weekly run to Berneval market. Pleased though Millie and Jack were at the offer of a lift, they initially declined, on the grounds that it would be too chancy if they got stopped. They couldn't risk having their papers and cover stories looked into too closely at check points. It was vital for them to steer well clear of any German presence. Pierre had foreseen these concerns and insisted Millie get into the cab. Puzzled at his obstinacy, she watched him nonchalantly open up a slatted wooden cavity, under the passenger seat. Millie was satisfied at this, and smiled her gratitude. Intuition told her here was a bolt-hole that had obviously got used frequently for some sort of contraband, human or otherwise. Still, she was happy to tuck herself away.

Strangely, once in the dark, confined space it was like she was back in that Priest Hole. It reminded her so much of the time when she was at boarding school. She and Janet were invited for a long weekend stay at a friend's extraordinary and hugely grand family home. A few days into the visit and the friend playfully suggested that the girls try and discover a secret panel that led to the Priest Hole. Impressive though Hollsworth Manor was, Millie thought her friend was showing off, boastful even. Janet, on the other hand, always up for a bit of mischief, couldn't contain herself, and set about peeking behind tapestries and paintings. She also painstakingly tapped the panelling at the side of a life size suit of armour, which stood guard at the bottom of the stairway.

Of course they knew all about Priest Holes from their history lessons. They had long, sometimes boring sessions about Tudor Henry's dissolution of the monasteries, and of the times when the practice of Catholicism became illegal. Priests, they learnt, were exiled on pain of death, and were banned from performing the sacraments. Nevertheless, many aristocratic devotees still devised ways to worship and retain their Catholic beliefs. For protection, in case their homes were raided, many staunch religious families constructed secret hiding places to conceal their priest, hence the aptly named Priest Hole. And according to this family's historical records, or so their friend said, it was in the 1580's that Hollsworth Manor's hide-e-hole got built.

In spite of hunting high and low in the vast number of rooms, neither Millie nor Janet could find the secret entrance. After endless hours of trying, they had to give up. The school friend, with quiet satisfaction, stood her guests in front of a massive fireplace. Positioned in the centre, well above head height, was a brightly coloured shield which exhibited the family coat of arms. Just underneath and running the whole length of the deep mantelpiece were carved wooden flowers, and nuts. Millie could identify ivy leaves and mistletoe that intertwined with fleur-de-lys and roses. To give them a clue, but still keen to prolong the mystery, the friend ran her hand lightly along the flowers. As she fingered the ancient wooden carvings, she first asked Janet then Millie where she should stop. When they said, 'stop now, and now,' nothing happened. Milking the evident suspense and exasperation of Janet and Millie to the utmost, she finally stayed her hand at a cluster of acorns. Insignificant in itself, it was only when touched and pressed in a certain fashion, that one particular nut magically swivelled to open a small oak panel, half the size of a man, and so cleverly disguised in the timbered struts.

Amazed at the revelation, both girls were terribly excited as they climbed down through muted light to find the tiny space where the unfortunate priest might have had to remain, often for days until the pursuit was over. Before long, something quite unexpected and alarming happened. It was not the spider webs that spookily brushed their faces, or the icy blast of air emanating from within that seemed to want to force their bodies out, or even the gruesome crunch of treading on a long dead a rat that horrified them. No, it was none of these things. It was the shock of seeing the brave, lion-hearted Janet, flee, screaming hysterically, while desperately trying to claw her way up the footholds to escape. Millie didn't understand it at the time, but Janet had most certainly been overcome by a formidable ambience retained over the centuries, in the very fabric of the Priest Hole. She had experienced and succumbed to a contemporary attack of claustrophobia, easy to appreciate now, given the confined underground place the two girls had squeezed in.

Once Pierre's truck started up and moved off, Millie suddenly realised why Janet was so much taken when working with her beloved barrage balloons. It was that sense of freedom that she could relate to, where the balloons soared and floated through an expanse of open space. It jolted another distant memory, too, when the girls, at the close of their school years, had some flying lessons with Janet's uncle Percy. Millie fervently hoped Janet was back flying her great beautiful beasties once more, and not, like herself shut in the cab of some cramped vehicle.

Pierre also had a solution for Jack's concealment. He told Jack to climb on the back of the truck. When he got up, Pierre covered him with sacks of grain and vegetables, cabbages to be precise, that were destined for the good folk in Berneval market. Jack still had a concern about the Germans riffling through the produce. Pierre said he made the trip every Friday, and because most of the guards knew him they only made a cursory inspection. He casually mentioned that to keep the Jerries sweet, he sold fruit, and occasionally fish to them, cheaply, on the quiet.

Twice the truck got stopped, and each time Jack could hear some ribaldry guffaw, or a few guttural complaints from the Germans. He even felt cabbages bounced about. Thankfully, it seemed the enemy was too lazy to shift any of the heavy grain sacks. Some kilometres on Pierre pulled in as near as he safely could to Varengeville.

Pointing to the signpost, he told them, 'I will pass this place on my way home from the market in the afternoon at around three o' clock.

I'll pull over take a pee, and have a smoke. Don't be late. I can't hang around. *Bonne chance.*'

They thanked Pierre, and waved him off. Millie plucked a few stray bits of vegetable leaves from Jack's coat.

Watching them fall to the ground, he said, with a touch of humour, 'I do hope Madame Etienne isn't cooking up cabbage soup tonight. I don't think I could face leafy greens in whatever shape or form, for a while.' Millie gave a chuckle and Jack rubbed his stiff muscles. 'Anyway, enough larking about, we need to get off theses roads and head cross-country.'

It wasn't at all unpleasant striding out on the little cart tracks, sandwiched protectively between high-hedged fields. And when an aircraft flew overhead the dense shrubbery on thick banks hid them from sight without any difficulty. Then after an hour or so they could sense a weather change and quickened their pace. Grey clouds blotted out the sun to give way to an easterly wind that quite quickly came gusting along the coast. A sea mist developed, that fast changed into drizzling rain. Soon the dampness started to cling to their clothes, hampering their earlier progress, and making them feel miserable. The atmosphere too had changed to a dull silence.

Pourville was approached cannily. They were not taken unawares this time by the intense military activity. With numerous, cumbersome lorries being driven in and out, some filled with troops, some towing heavy guns, the Germans made no secret of their presence here.

'Jack!' said Millie, suddenly, 'what in heavens name is that?'

The next second Jack saw it too. 'Down, get down, for God's sake.'

Both flung themselves flat. Millie attempted a whispered, 'what is it?'

'It's a bloody great radar station, that's what it is.' Jack gave her a shove. 'Let's get into that copse.'

'Of course,' Millie said, her breath coming in spasms from a manic sprint. 'A radar station, of course, that massive dish, it makes sense positioned where it is.'

Jack needed to get an accurate map reading. To keep the map dry he sheltered it inside his coat and pencilled in a cross. 'And this is the best bit, somewhere in that direction,' he indicated with his head, 'Pierre said he's had reports of artillery batteries sunk deep into the cliffs with their sights trained out to sea. And apparently, so well camouflaged are they that they're invisible to the naked eye. The French are prohibited from going anywhere near this stretch of coast line, even for fishing, but the underground have ways and means, which is just as well.'

'If that really is the case,' said Millie, 'pray to God that the British Army is not going to attempt an assault by sea.'

With anxiety now telling in his tone, Jack said, 'I don't know about a sea landing, but when I made a recki of Dieppe, it was plainly evident only a fool would make an attempt to capture that heavily fortified port. Combined Ops could not possibly get a foothold there, quite, quite impossible.' Millie looked at him to elaborate. He leaned close, battling against the wind to say, 'there are huge numbers of the Wehrmacht defence force occupying the town. When we get back to England, I can give them chapter and verse if they want numbers.'

Millie groaned, and then asked, 'does it really appear that hopeless?'

Jack didn't answer. They were up on their feet moving through the coppice away from the radar station, noticeably well defended by German Infantry. Further along the coast at spots where Jack, as a youngster, used to play, they saw houses boarded up, and some buildings had even been demolished to make way for heavy gun emplacements. What Pierre and the underground had suspected, Jack and Millie's undercover intelligence work could now be confirmed, and taken back to London.

CHAPTER THIRTY

Much as he admired and respected the man, Graham Bain was beginning to get on the sergeant's nerves. There were just the three of them in a small ops room to the side of the hanger. Bain sat at a desk staring at the telephone, while his fingers, agitatedly twiddled with a mysterious envelope. A woman, in a corner, slightly out of view, seemed lost in the shadows. The sergeant, also seated, and to the left of the woman, took long drags on his cigarette and tried, unsuccessfully to shut out the monotonous tap-taping noise Bain was making with the letter. A dim light bulb, brown stained with nicotine, hung over Bain's head. It was impossible for the NCO to do anything else except keep his eyes fixed on the arcane letter Bain continually drummed with. The sergeant wanted to snatch it away, replace it, even with silence. Then, at last the shrill ring of the telephone punctured the air. Instantly Bain grabbed the receiver.

The only reply Bain gave was, 'OK.' Then stuffing the envelope into his coat pocket, he looked at his wrist watch, and said to the woman, 'right, drive me over to the runway.'

Startled at the abrupt order, she jumped to her feet. 'Yes sir.'

'Sergeant, you man the telephone, and if there is any change, find me, pronto.'

'Yes sir.'

Their car had been parked outside and the woman driver and Bain jumped in.

Mumbling, possibly to himself, Bain muttered, 'they're considerably overdue, bloody late in fact.'

Nodding perceptibly, the woman answered, dryly, 'yes sir.' At the same time she was thinking, I know they're bloody late, so does the whole flippin' unit know they are overdue. We've been waiting half the night, for heavens sake. I need a bloody cigarette.

At one point it was touch and go if Millie and Jack would even see England again. The pilot landed the Lysander with little or no difficulty. However, the plane looked doomed to never take off again. The rain that began the previous day fell continually throughout the night, without any let up. Unnoticed, until almost too late, this heavy rain saturated the improvised landing strip, and the field in places turned into a quagmire.

It took some organising, but help came, once again from Pierre and *Monsieur* Blanchard, and two of his compatriots. With winches and a hoist the Lysander was dragged to firmer ground, and with makeshift fences laid flat over the mud, the plane was able to take off. Even so, the exertion of helping to de-bog a plane had virtually exhausted the rookie agents. However, once safely airborne the pair sank back—as much as they could in the cramped conditions of the Lysander—utterly relieved to be finally off the ground.

Regaining her strength, somewhat, Millie said to Jack, 'look at the state of your shoes.' She had no sooner said it, than she felt she was sounding just like her mother.

Making an effort to stir himself, Jack eased forward, and retorted, 'look at the state of yours, they are positively filthy.'

They both doubled up in a hoot of laughter, causing the pilot to swivel round to see what the hilarity was all about, considering the dire straits they had just escaped from. He just shrugged, and shook his head, thinking there is no accounting for these bloody brave, loony agents. Seeing his perplexity, they laughed some more out of sheer joy to be safe. When their chortling abated, Millie said, 'back there, I was dreading that any minute we'd be surrounded by Germans.'

'The weather,' said Jack.

'What?'

'The weather, my love, it's something the British have in common with the Germans.'

'Jack, is the lack of oxygen addling your brain, because I have no idea what are you talking about?'

'They obviously don't like the rain.' He winked. Then after a few moments he became serious. 'Mind you, we'd have been rightly snookered if we'd got caught by the Jerries, before the plane got off the ground. Thank Christ they missed us.'

'We were lucky.'

He concurred. 'We were lucky. We had some fine underground people helping us.' He contemplated, before adding, 'and when you come to think of it, with just my little fracas in Dieppe to handle, I'd say, yes, we were damned lucky.' Was he being smug? For a second, it felt like that to Millie. And then when he carried on by saying, 'at least you didn't come face to face with any of the Bosch.' Millie felt a tad miffed. She thought, right, let's put the record straight, old chum.

Millie, was not the 'light under a bushel,' type of girl, so with as much verve as she could muster, she began to recount her tale.

'Well actually, now you come to mention it, there was one fellow; he even told me his name. Now what was it? Oh, yes, it was Helmuth…'

*

Aware that her training required control over ones persona, Millie tried very hard to mask her disappointment. Nevertheless, something reflected in her face. And this was picked up, by Graham Bain, simply because he made a singular point of checking out her reaction. Millie had assumed Hugo would be there. During the time in France their whole energy was given over to thinking of the moment, the task, and the danger. There was precious little time to think of anything or anyone else back home, except, just sometimes, sometimes she allowed Hugo to creep into her thoughts. And as they neared the English coast Millie experienced a giddy sense of euphoria because she believed that he'd be there. He assured her he would. She wanted him to be proud of what she'd-they'd accomplished for SOE. And now he wasn't there, and that lovely feeling evaporated. It hurt, terribly. But she had to swallow the let-down. She had to appear professional.

Heartily shaking Jack and Millie's hand in turn, while clinging onto his trilby with the other, Bain told them, 'it's good to have you back, safe and sound. What caused the delay?' He paused for a second, then, 'well never mind that now, we'll get you both over to the debriefing station, and you can tell me about it en route. A car is waiting over there for you both.'

It was still dark, and they had to focus hard to make out where exactly the car was. Then they got their bearings, and spotted a figure standing at the car door waiting to whisk them away. Bain went on in front, and helped Jack put their gear in the boot. Millie was hoping against hope that Hugo might suddenly spring out from somewhere and surprise her, like he did several times in the past. She brought to mind the time when she thought he might have been a tramp, when he sat at the end of the bench, in the park, near the hospital. And when he appeared in the kitchen and saved her from-well death, really. She furtively peered in the direction of the hanger, but instinctively she knew he wasn't coming. Millie turned away as the car door swung open for her. She took a brief glance at the uniformed female, and was about to offer her thanks, when to her complete astonishment, she saw that the driver was none other than her friend, and flat mate, Janet Marsh.

Despite being splattered in mud and disguised in the ensemble of a French peasant, Janet could not mistake her life long chum, as she clutched the door handle for support. And a croaked profanity was all the response Janet could manage at meeting this particular secret agent. Millie's attempt at professionalism was rapidly dissipating.

Janet would have remained there, frozen by shock, but for Bain, barking out, 'look lively, woman, we can't hang about here, all night!' He seemed unaware of any connection between the two girls.

It was difficult for the returning agents to judge how far they had travelled in the sleek black Wolseley. The soft purr of its engine and the distinctive whiff of leather upholstery oozed luxury. Truly, this vehicle was a world away from the bucolic travelling facilities they commandeered in France. Before Jack and Millie were hurriedly taken by Bain into the debriefing rooms, Millie managed to whisper to Janet, 'I'll see you back at the flat.' Janet mouthed back, 'damn right you will.' However, it was well into the afternoon of the next day when Millie found herself climbing the stairs of her old haunt in Stoke Newington.

Although they were both dog tired, Jack seemed to stand up to the rigors of the debriefing better than Millie. From the off, Millie thought the questions fired at them felt more like an interrogation session than the relaying of information on what they both felt was a job well done. Everything, every little detail of every single day during the whole operation had to be gone over and over; dissected and documented, and gone over again.

Jack and Millie passed on the detailed map references, and the rest of the intelligence they had collected. Uniformed personnel hovering at the ready stuck pins on charts to show the exact defences and fortifications the Germans now had in place along the coast line. Moving on to the town of Dieppe itself and surrounding area, they listened as Jack confirmed this was heavily defended and came under the control of the 302nd Division of the Wehrmacht. He could not have made it clearer to the debriefing committee that such was the German might; nothing short of a full scale combined air/sea/land attack could winkle out and defeat the enemy. His opinion was that at this point in time, the taking of the town would be impossible. To strengthen his argument Jack also pointed out the places where reinforcements of fresh troops could be sent in at a moments notice. The Wehrmacht, he said, had the additional support of the German air force whose airfields were just a few kilometres inland from Dieppe.

Disturbingly, tired and groggy though they were, Jack and Millie came away with the impression that Bain and his cronies weren't particularly interested in German air power, or the defences surrounding the town of Dieppe. Compared to coastal locations such as Puys, Pourville, Varengeville and Berneval, Dieppe seemed of secondary importance. This was a shock, and a bit of a blow for Jack and Millie, considering they put themselves, and the French Résistance in great danger to get all the accurate information that the London lot wanted. In spite of this, they were congratulated, and given hearty slaps on the back. It was only as they were leaving they heard a mention of something called Operation Rutter.

*

Millie gave the aspidistra leaf a little tweak then lifted the pot up to get the front door key. It felt good to be home. She dumped her case in the kitchen, and called out, but Janet wasn't in. Starting to unbutton her tunic she was grateful that at least they had been given facilities where they could wash off the French mud, and change their clothes. However, Millie was so weary that she barely got out of her uniform before falling into bed. Out like a light, she didn't wake until the afternoon of the next day when it was the rattling of tea cups, that woke her, and there was Janet standing over her, presenting her with fried eggs and bacon.

Yawning, Millie rubbed her eyes in disbelief. 'Where did you get all this from?'

A curt reply from Janet followed. 'Don't ask.'

After polishing off every morsel of the food, Millie said, 'thank you. That was absolutely wonderful, quite the best bacon and eggs I have ever had.'

Janet's attempt to pamper was genuine. She smiled. 'Have some more tea.'

'Oh, yes, please.' Millie sighed, contentedly, and sunk back into softness.

Janet took the tray away and poured out more tea. Then she climbed over the eiderdown, plumped up both pillows, and curled up beside Millie.

'Now, this feels nice and comfy,' Janet remarked, joining Millie in a cup of tea.

'Doesn't it just?'

Quite soon, Janet got propped up on one elbow. Then wearing a quizzical expression, she looked her chum straight in the face. Millie knew what was coming.

CHAPTER THIRTY-ONE

She may, or may not have been putting off the moment, but Millie told Janet, 'I have to answer the call of nature. Don't drink my tea! I'll be back in a jiffy.'

A quick sluice and a hair tidy, and with her teeth properly cleaned for the first time since arriving in France, Millie turned back to go to the bedroom. Then she caught sight of a suitcase, handbag and gasmask, all propped up purposefully, in the hall.

'What's with the luggage, Janet? Off on your hols?' Millie said, jokingly.

'No, not hols, not exactly, come and finish your tea and I'll tell you where I'm off to.'

Millie kicked aside her slippers and climbed back into bed. Janet gulped down the remains of her tea, wiped his lips, and said, 'I'm going to fly a plane, no, planes, to be precise.' Janet ignored Millie's spluttering. 'Hmm, maybe not straight away, but I'm definitely going to be a pilot. And then I want to fly a Lanc or-or a Spitfire or—'

'What! Fly a-are you mad?'

'No madder than you, Miss Chance.'

'What do you mean?' As soon as she said it, Millie knew she'd given Janet an open invitation to ask pointed questions.

'Well, it surely wasn't me flitting off to France.'

Touché, thought Millie. 'Yes, well that's another story.'

'And one we'll have in a moment. But first, are you listening?' She gave Millie a dig in the ribs.

Wriggling and giggling Millie answered, 'yes, yes I am. Proceed, proceed please do.'

Wearing a blasé air, Janet began, innocuously enough. 'A while back I answered an advertisement in the magazine, *The Airplane*. It was just by accident that I happened to glance through it while waiting in the car for some RAF official. The ad said ATA urgently require suitable candidates to become part of a team for Central Ferry Pool. It stipulated pilots would pick up and fly planes coming off the production line and deliver them to airbases around the country. Apparently, this would free up the RAF chaps for defence and fighter operations. Anyway, I applied and at the interview I was put through my paces by the old codgers er committee.' In spite of her *faux pas*, she gave a self-satisfied little sniff. 'Still, they must have been suitably impressed because I got a letter saying I'd been accepted for training into the ATA. That's the Air Transport Auxiliary.'

'I know what the ATA is, but I didn't know they took women?'

'They do now.'

'But you can't fly a plane.'

'Well, they don't know that, exactly.'

'Janet!'

'It's OK, it's OK. They were fine at the interview, fine. They asked me if I could drive. I said of course, it's what I'm doing at the moment. Could I ride, they asked. Though heavens only knows the reasoning behind that question. But my reply was yes, most certainly. I told them I used to belong to the Pony Club for years, well a year at least. And had I had any flying experience. Which—'

'Which, you haven't.'

'Which, I have!' And with indignation she told Millie, 'of course I have, you silly goose.'

'Janet, you don't—'

'I flew my balloons, didn't I?'

Millie stuttered, 'but-but that's not—'

'Well,' huffed Janet, 'that's their fault. They never asked what I flew.' Shaking off her moment of pique, she added brightly, 'what the hell, one shouldn't be deflected by such mere details.' With a great intake of breath she went on. 'Then again, you can't have forgotten my uncle Percy taking us up in his light aircraft.' Millie was too stunned to think of a reply. 'You know,' Janet went on, excitedly, 'that last summer of the school hols. He let us both take turns at the controls. Aaa,' she exhaled at the joyous memory, 'it felt quite wonderful and it's a feeling I shall never forget, absolutely bloomin' glorious.' She gave a snort. 'Remember how sick you were when we did loop-the-loop.' She nudged Millie and held her hand. 'Anyway, never fear, I can pick it up quick enough.'

Millie groaned and sank further down the bed. 'I am amazed at your audacity, really I am.'

'And,' with an impish grin Janet asked, 'what about *your* audacity?'

After a minute or two Millie heaved herself up, threw back the eiderdown and cleared her throat. Bearing in mind what Janet had already discovered, and what bits she had probably guessed, Millie knew she would have to choose her words cautiously. So, she only disclosed as much as she though would satisfy curious, but definitely nosy Janet, and give just enough of an over-view that could in no way compromise either of them.

When Millie had finished Janet became filled with admiration for this girl who after all she had gone through to get away from the Japs, now goes fearlessly off to beard another enemy in the den.

'Well bugger me,' Janet declared. 'You're a rum one and no mistake.'

Millie shrugged her shoulders. 'I just seemed to get drawn in. At first I imagined going back to Singapore, but that was never on the cards, at least—'

Millie was moved, considerably, when Janet begged, 'please Mills, please dear, take the utmost care, wont you?'

'Of course I will. And you too, you daft, crazy woman, fancy wanting to fly off into the wide blue yonder.' Forcing laughter, they gave each other a hug.

Then in a blink of an eye, realisation suddenly dawned and Millie pushed Janet away.

'Oh dear God, it's because of Christopher, Christopher Elliott. It's because of him that you're joining this mad scheme, on-on the-the off chance of flying to France to rescue him. That's it isn't it?' Janet said nothing, and then Millie jumped in with, 'I'm right, aren't I?' You've bloody well cooked up your own private agenda for joining the ATA.'

What an irrefutable sage you are, thought Janet, yet she didn't answer directly, instead she said, 'Millie, I'm so glad I didn't tell him at the time, tell him how I was feeling. You know me, how I blow hot and cold. I just got terribly nervous when he talked of marriage. So many people we know have bought it. Surely it would have been daft to wed in the middle of this awful war, wouldn't it?' Millie just looked glum. Janet sighed, and then stole an anxious glance at the clock. 'Darling Mills,' she said, 'I'd like nothing better that to stay gassing with you, but I must get a move on. I have a train to catch.'

Soon Janet had dressed and Millie had pulled on a flimsy, silk dressing gown. It was a resplendent, brightly coloured wrap-around. Each stitch in the material was hand sewn by deft fingers from a Far Eastern country. It showed exotic birds in flight, and flowers, found only in that part of the world were emblazoned on the sumptuous piece of material. A poignant memento, slung at the time, without thought, into a case before fleeing Singapore. Walking along the hall together, Janet paused at the half-moon table and pointed to some letters. 'Don't forget to read your post. You never know there might be news of your father. And I've taken some phone messages from your chap Philip.'

There was an emotional embrace at the door. By now Millie was resigned and fell in with her friend's decision, knowing she was motivated by the best will in the world. Millie said a quiet goodbye. Then she watched Janet clump down the flight of stairs. At the bottom, looking up Janet dropped her suitcase to give a last wave, and was gone. Millie closed the front door of a now cold and empty-feeling flat. In response to Janet's suggestion and for something to keep her occupied, Millie flicked through the letters. There wasn't anything from the Red Cross; she didn't really think there would be. The only thing relating to her father was a rent demand from the landlord. That was something she'd have to sort out when she went to see the family, in a day or so. She also had it in mind to find out where Mrs Elliott was staying and go and see her. She tore open another of the envelopes. Suddenly the letters reminded her of that other letter. She rushed into the bedroom and snatched up her handbag. With everything that had gone on since the debriefing, the letter from Hugo had totally slipped her mind.

Graham Bain had asked himself, was he really going to hang on to the letter, and not give it to Millie? He tried to reassure himself that he could always plead it was withheld for security reason. But Bain knew Maitland was too professional to divulge anything of a confidential nature. And besides, Bain felt uncomfortable from the twinges of conscience that kept stabbing him.

'Ah, Miss Chance, he said, dipping into his pocket. 'Just before you go off on your much deserved leave, I-a-I have a letter here for you.' He pulled out the envelope and handed it to Millie. 'It's from Maitland. He asked me to tell you he was sorry he was unable to meet you when you landed.' Millie took the letter, slightly bemused, as her initial disappointment had almost melted away. Bain continued, 'It was out of his hands, quite impossible for him to…um, he got called to the War Office, quite suddenly.' Covering him mouth, Bain noisily cleared his throat. 'You know how things happen, so quickly these days.'

Bain was put in the picture about the formation of a new unit, the SIG, Special Intelligence Group. It was an unconventional and secret intelligence unit, set up to infiltrate behind the German lines in the Western Desert, under the 8th Army. As well as the usual commando types, recruits, had among other things, to be fluent German linguists, and with Maitland's specialised attributes he was picked out and asked if he'd like to 'volunteer.' Bain had it on the highest authority that Maitland had, in fact, gone to North Africa with the SIG.

When Millie asked Bain where Hugo had been posted to, all he said was, 'he's gone to some hot place haunted by the lizard.' Millie took it that it was probably North Africa.

The envelope, however, cheered Millie up and made her laugh. Hugo had addressed it to, "The Nightingale from Singapore". She opened it slowly, careful not to tear the soft outer paper.

The letter began, *My dear, by the time you read this note I will almost certainly be out of the country. The powers that be took no account of our pre-arranged tryst. Rotten swine! So I'm very sorry old bean, couldn't do anything about it, though I did try! I did so want to be at Tangmere, when you landed. But as my old nanny used to tell me, what we want and what we get are two different things, and it just goes to show, one shouldn't make rash promises in war time! All the same, I know you will understand and forgive something said in the heat of the moment. Keep your chin up, my sweet, and God willing, we'll meet again soon, somewhere in dear old blighty when things quieten down—if not before.*

Fondest love, Yours, Hugo.

Well, for heavens sake, what did she expect? Surely not an open declaration of Hugo's love, no of course not, Millie thought wistfully. He's such a dear man, but so complex. Not, it seemed, like Philip given to wearing his heart on his sleeve. Philip! Philip! All those telephone calls Janet had taken. Must ring him back, will do it after a little more sleep catch up. Snuggling among the blankets, a doubt crept in when she began to think about Philip. She asked herself, what was he doing at Oldham Hospital, with Hugo? Was it really him, or was I mistaken?

CHAPTER THIRTY-TWO

Mrs Elliott was to be found up to her elbows in clothes. Just occasionally, now and then, however, she'd pause, raise her head, and look up at the sky or just gaze into the distance, her thoughts tumbling back to what had happened in the past. Undoubtedly, she would have remembered that it really wasn't so very long ago that she and Grace were doing much the same thing as she was doing now. Only then, the clothes—dresses, cardigans, shirts, shorts and socks—they were gathering up, were for the little orphan children, across the seas. Now, the blouses, skirts, knickers, shoes, pullovers, trousers and coats, she was sifting through, were for the little orphan children in London, who were also homeless, having got bombed out in raids over the City. The London County Council, and organisations such as the Red Cross, and the Salvation Army, which Mrs Elliott was now working for, had a massive task on their hands in trying to winkle out distant relatives. And on the more mundane level, the immediate needs such as clothing, food ration books and indeed accommodation, preferably houses that still had their roofs intact all had to be dealt with.

Mrs Elliott herself had no difficulty in finding a place to stay. The Missionary Head Quarters in Islington, on hearing of the terrible plight that overtook the hospital in Kuala Lumpur, along with the tragic deaths of their Minister, and Grace, offered Mrs Elliott a spacious flat situated in their grounds. Though not ungrateful, Mrs Elliott declined. She knew she would be unable to bear the impromptu questions and constant reminders from a cloistered, religious community, she once belonged to. And similarly, though for very different reasons, beautiful though Rose Cottage, in Kent was, and love in abundance that was showered on her, by the family, she knew she could not cope with the relative inactivity of a sheltered village life. In addition, the dear friends in North London, the Chances, begged her to take their empty attic suite of rooms, which even had its own bathroom, albeit a little antiquated. Clive and Archie both said they would dust and clean and make absolutely sure that not one spider would find a hiding place. Their kindly assurance warmed the cockles of Mrs Elliott's heart, but she had plans of her own that she felt compelled to pursue.

Mrs Elliott was well used to travelling light, unburdened with earthly possessions, and so without any bother she soon found a tiny, simple furnished flat, off the Mile End Road. It was adequate for the purposes she needed, that being near her work with the Salvation Army, and it had the added advantage of nestling in the heart of the metropolis, where she could enquire first-hand for information on her son.

When at last Millie awoke, lots of ideas were buzzing around her brain for just what to do with her leave. And she felt quite uplifted as she set off for her grandmother's house. When she got there instinct told her something was amiss. The front door was ajar; apprehensive, Millie pushed it tentatively open. Straining, she could hear muffled sounds and a hooting noise. She was almost knocked off her feet when suddenly, from behind, two boys charged past her and ran full pelt down the hallway, then through the open door into the garden. Once she had regained her wits, Millie followed the four flying heels out into the bright sunshine to be confronted by what could almost be described as a scene from the Mad Hatter's Tea Party. She pulled up sharp. Party, party! Oh, heavens! She remembered that's what it is. I've arrived on the day of Archie's birthday, and he's having a party. This was something which Millie had totally forgotten about. She stopped short, cursing under her breath. She'd not bought him a present. She was about to turn tail when Archie saw her.

'Millie, Millie, so glad you've come. Thanks awfully for the money. It was jolly decent of you. And I know exactly what I'm going to spend it on. Come and have a bowl of jelly and custard.' Archie clutched his sister's hand and pulled her over to a long trellis laden with a veritable feast of party delights. 'Grandma's made some scrummy gooseberry tarts, do try one, Millie.'

There was so much noise coming from around the table that she didn't hear what Archie was going to buy with his birthday money. She just laughed and nodded. Millie had forgotten she'd asked Hugo to deal with the family birthday arrangements. And today, it was heart-some for Millie to listen to the spontaneity of English children laughing.

*

Shading her eyes from the sun's glare, Mrs Elliott's care-worn expression suddenly lifted when she saw who it was that had called her.

'Oh, my, look whose here!' she exclaimed, throwing her arms around Millie. 'What a wonderful surprise. When I last spoke to your mother, she said you were nursing in a hospital up in Oldham. How are you, my dear?'

'I am very well, thank you, Mrs Elliott. And how are you keeping? They told me you couldn't be persuaded to say at Grandmas.'

'No, Millie, that's quite right. They were all very kind and helpful, but I knew I had to get stuck into some kind of work. After all, look at your mother, she is working so hard on the London buses, and then there are the night shifts that make for very unsociable hours. Dangerous too, given we don't know just when the bombs are likely to fall on us.' She smiled; 'it's a far cry from the genteel life of Singapore...' at her own mention of Singapore Mrs Elliott broke off. 'Look, just-just give me a minute or two to finish this little job and we'll go and get some lunch. We have such a lot to catch up on.'

'Yes, that would be lovely. Why not let me give you a hand? We'll get through it quicker together.'

The assortment of children's clothes got folded and boxed away. A littler later when the work was done they strolled arm in arm, barely taking in the yawning gap of a bombed out church, or rough planks hammered in to replace blown-out windows on shop fronts.

'Do you know,' said Millie, 'do you know what I really have a fancy for?'

'What, dear?'

'I have such a fancy for good old English fish and chips, with lots of salt and vinegar.'

'Yes, that sounds lovely, and why not? There's a cracking little café not far, and we can get a nice cup of tea, too.'

The fish and chip lunch was ever bit as tasty as Millie thought it would be. When their tea was brought over to them Mrs Elliott asked if Millie had any news of her father.

'Only a letter that Mother received from the Red Cross, months back, to say he was in Changi.'

'Ah, yes. She showed me that one. We, I mean the folk at the Mission, have tried all avenues of communication, but no one has any information about Dr Elder.'

Millie thought of the trousers and jumpers Grace had found for Archie and Clive, when they carelessly packed so little for the journey to Singapore.

She asked Mrs Elliott, 'will you ever go back to Singapore?'

Without hesitation Mrs Elliott answered, 'yes, dear, one day, when all this is over. I have to see…'

For a little while Mrs Elliott became reflective until Millie told her, 'I-I heard about your son, Christopher.'

'Did you?' Mrs Elliott was surprised.

'Yes, a-a friend told me. It was terrible. You haven't—'

'No. But I feel he's not dead. He can't be.' She clasped her hands. 'Well, it's not been confirmed, let's put it like that. They said there was a possibility that the French Resistance might be hiding him.'

'Oh! Well that's good. Yes it's good. Isn't it?'

*

Millie had planned to do all sorts of things, but by the end of a week she was starting to feel restless. She'd already given Mrs Elliott another two days help at the Salvation Army centre. And love them though she did, there was only so much of Archie and Clive's capers that Millie could participate in with good humour. And then, with her mother flitting in and our between shifts, it was not conducive to any heart to heart talks

Millie might have hoped for. With old Mrs Chance it was different. They'd sit comfortably side by side on a sofa, Millie with her feet tucked underneath, or at other times, across the breakfast table, before anyone else was up.

However much Grandma might have surmised, Millie's work with the FANY's was never touched upon. It was truly engaging, and Millie listened, in wonderment, while Grandma talked of friends still in France, especially mentioning the Blanc family, and her beloved Picardi. Then the old lady fell to talking of happier times when her husband was alive. It made them both nostalgic. The mood generally didn't last long before either Archie or Clive put in an appearance.

Once back at her flat, Millie continually tried to telephone the two numbers Philip had given Janet, but there was no answer from either of them. A few days later, while tidying the flat for the umpteenth time, the telephone rang, unexpectedly. Millie ran to answer it thinking it was Philip. Grabbing it, Millie was astonished to hear Graham Bain's voice. Even more surprising the call concerned an invitation for her to dine with him. Flummoxed, momentarily, Millie wondered if he was withholding bad news and was warming up to deliver it over dinner. She needn't have worried.

When they met in the foyer his eyes lit up as they travelled the length of the lilac sequined dress. It had a fashionable 'sweetheart' neck line, cut on the bias to reveal the merest hint of cleavage, and clung most seductively to Millie's shapely figure.

Bain told her, 'you look beautiful, Miss Chance, quite beautiful. Evening attire suits you.' Unused to delivering this sort of impulsive familiarity, he quickly added, 'a-and the rest has obviously done you good.'

Taken by surprise at the forthrightness of his compliment, Millie found herself blushing. Yet she smiled graciously at him, and took his outstretched arm. She almost wanted to say something nice about him for he was very well turned out in an unmistakably, expensive double-breasted pinstriped suit. But she couldn't quite gather her thoughts quickly enough before they were escorted to the table Bain had earlier reserved. Even so, he liked her gesture when sensitively she admired and straightened the large red carnation in his buttonhole.

Earlier, Bain ordered a taxi to collect Millie. She had taken care over the choice of frock and dressed accordingly as deemed appropriate for the rather exclusive Claridge's Hotel, in Mayfair. The dinning room was sumptuous, oozing opulent splendour at every turn of a table, despite war-time austerity. Great swathes of scarlet drapes flamboyantly hid the blackout roller blinds that adhered protectively compliant to windows. She'd remembered her father saying he and Millie's mother often dined at Claridge's, because it was hard to beat their delicious Scottish salmon. Millie doubted it would still be on the menu, now.

Bain gave a perfunctory glance at the list of dishes to be served. His voice rang with almost rehearsed authority when he told her, 'I can recommend the Scottish salmon, Miss Chance.' His knowledge of the fare caused Millie to swallow her wine too quickly, and she had to give a little cough.

'Let me refill your glass. There's nothing like wine from the Champagne region of France, would you agree?'

'Why yes, absolutely,' Millie said, truthfully.

So both had the salmon, and silently, Millie concurred it was every bit as good as the salmon they'd all had eaten on her first training course in the Highlands. Of this comparison she said nothing to Bain.

Small talk on topical war issues allowed a respectable time to pass after the meal. Millie, however, was by now starting to anticipate the worse. Thankfully, it didn't come. Instead, Bain asked her to dance. The band, mainly moustached, and silver haired musicians, in black suits and dickey bow ties, expertly played their instruments, as one, while the ivories on the baby-grand, like water trickling over smooth pebbles, gently tinkled away in the background.

Having not danced for absolutely ages, Millie found she rather liked being taken round the floor by a surprisingly good fox-trotter such as Bain. He on the other hand, basked in envious glances coming from his contemporaries. Perhaps it was the wine that had a mellowing effect on Millie. Though in truth, she was enjoying his company. And as the evening wore on, holding her, Bain recalled that other time when he was almost as close to Millie as this. She'd just arrived in London, from Singapore. It was in the air raid shelter. The crowds had jostled her so much that she dropped her handbag—an expensive crocodile one at that, he clearly recalled, having picked it up for her. Then, albeit feisty, she seemed a mere slip of a girl, while now, she was this bewitchingly beautiful woman…suddenly this remembrance had a sobering effect on Bain, and as the dance ended he led her back to their table to tell her of the other reason for asking her to dine at the exclusive Claridge's of Mayfair.

CHAPTER THIRTY-THREE

Graham Bain recognised the half smothered signs of panic; he had practically lived in F Section for the last few days, and for those listening in to the traffic, there was a good deal of nail biting going on in the background. Along with his SOE colleagues, Bain, too, was getting jittery because some transmissions from 'Prospero' were missed, and then replaced by an unusual amount of 'suspect' traffic. 'Prospero,' was the name of the network in the north of France, the largest F Section circuit that up until then caused them no real worry. One of the few, in fact, that tended to operate successfully under the leadership of a most experienced agent. Now, this group was causing them all concern. Recently, some of the decoded messages coming through from that section did not ring true; all were perfect, too perfect. No agent, Bain knew, ever sent continual error-free codes. The added security check within the messages was awry, as well.

Bain was well aware that the pressure on an operator to transmit on time was considerable; often they only had seconds in which to send. Understandably, agents transmitting without electric light were in a state of extreme tension. Part of his or her concentration might be given over to listening out for the fearful sound of the Jackboot on the stairs, or for the screech of a German vehicle, at the door of a barn. For some while Bain had a niggling sense that something was not right. Anxiety continued to mount, until growing suspicions that all was not well within the 'Prospero' network was soon confirmed—they had been betrayed.

Spring of '43 had started badly both for Millie and SOE. F Section's fears were verified when they learnt that disaster had befallen this underground circuit in Northern France, leaving it fractured and inoperable. Shortly before 'Prospero' was betrayed a last desperate message came through to SOE informing them that radio's were compromised, and the network had been penetrated by an enemy agent. After that message was decoded all contact with London abruptly ceased. Although the exact details were unknown to F Section, they had to assume that because of enemy infiltration the Gestapo would easily have rounded up those underground fighters working in that cell, including SOE's own agents. It was obvious the outcome was bound to be bad. Interrogation at the hands of the Gestapo was something that sent a chill of fear down Bain's spine. A bullet from a German gun would be a merciful end to their torture. More effective even, for a captured agent scared of talking under torture was to swallow their "L" pill containing fast acting cyanide.

The plain fact now was that SOE urgently needed to get one of their own people into the field to reorganise what if anything, was left of the cell. Bain sensed that it may require starting again from scratch. This situation was profoundly more difficult for SOE, because understandably, the French would be nervous and suspicious of any strangers suddenly turning up in the district. If mass executions were carried out, which from Bain's experience, was an odds on certainty, tension was bound to be heightened. This did not bode well for establishing French cooperation. The criteria that F Section had to fulfil was to get an agent who was not only bilingual but had specialised knowledge of the terrain in Northern France, Rouen and Paris and even Picardie. The task would not be easy.

After early despair, it was, however, agreed there was only one man for the job. Given the code name Charon, the agent was to be dropped by parachute from a twin-engine bomber at a remote spot on the outskirts of Rouen.

Charon, otherwise know as Philip Hendry, had hidden in the sole of his size ten shoe, a large amount of French bank notes. Some services, they understood, would have to be bought. A quantity of medical supplies and radio equipment floated with him from the sky, in sausage-like metal cylinders.

There was absolutely no way that Millie could have guessed that Philip Hendry had gone to France. She had tried and tried ringing both of the telephone numbers Philip had given her, without getting any reply. She stopped in the end as she had to move up to RAF Ringway, near Manchester, for the parachute training. That was the news Bain had given her, after their dinner at Claridge's. And Millie was so happy about it she could have kissed him, she was that glad to be back in circulation again.

Once up at Ringway, however, the weather changed for the worse with heavy falls of snow holding up progress, so that only inside activities could go ahead. Practice jumps from tall platforms and tumbles from long ropes were used over and over again to demonstrate correct leg positions when jumping from a plane. Instructors would show the trainee how to fall once they hit the ground. It was monotonous but that was what Millie and the others had to do. Planes were grounded and continuing filthy weather seemed to conspire to prevent any real headway. So, as it turned out it was well after Christmas before training in the air actually got restarted. Bad luck, though, seemed in pursuit of Millie. Only days into training proper, and attempting a second jump out of the plane, she landed badly and cracked a couple of ribs and broke her left arm. This meant she was well and truly out of action for a few months, at least.

At home alone at her flat, the weeks dragged on. Millie was down in the dumps and feeling rather sorry for herself. This lousy state of despair was about to be made worse. She had just got a letter from Janet saying what an exciting time she was having now that all the tests were finally over. 'I have passed out A1,' she wrote, 'and now at last I am allowed up in the air to fly real planes.' Selfishly, Millie wished Janet was still at the flat, to keep her company. The boredom could have got broken by a day spent up the West End, shopping or taking in a theatre show. In that part of London there was plenty of entertainment to choose from. Try as she might, Millie couldn't help but bemoan her bad luck. She was folding the letter back in its envelope when the telephone rang. It was Graham Bain.

'Hello, Miss Chance, how's the arm coming along?'

'Oh, you know...' fed up she may be but she had no enthusiasm for another dinner date with Bain. 'Really can't stretch to another turn around the floor though.'

'No, no, quite, I understand, wouldn't dream of suggesting it.'

She suddenly felt horrid. 'Sorry, Graham, I-I didn't mean to sound so rude. Please excuse me.'

'There's nothing to excuse, my dear. It's quite alright,' he said, convivially. 'I do understand. It can't be very pleasant humping that great lump of concrete around.' He paused. 'Ah. But now, the thing is, something important has cropped up, and I would like you to meet me at the Café de Paris, in Coventry Street. Can you do that?'

She couldn't say no to him, there was something akin to vulnerability in Bain's mien at times.

'Yes, yes of course I can. When and what time?'

'Tonight, seven o'clock.'

'OK. I'll be there. I can't promise to get dolled up, a bit restricted getting a dress over this darned arm.'

'You'll be fine.' He thought Millie would look good in anything.

Bain was waiting outside the Café de Paris to meet Millie as she got out of the taxi. He made a chivalrous gesture, and kissed the tips of her fingers just showing beneath the plaster.

That made Millie smile. 'Hello, Graham, it is good to see you again. Did you have a nice Christmas?'

He liked her calling him Graham. 'Christmas? Oh, it came and went, much as any other.' Millie was thinking, this promises to be jolly. In the lobby, he said 'let me take your coat.'

'Thanks.'

She had worn a three-quarter-length camel hair coat, draped around her shoulders. It was one of a couple of winter coats that she left in the flat when she went to Singapore. Now she was very glad of its warmth. Not wishing to draw attention, Millie discarded her sling, and used the sleeve of a leg of mutton cardigan to cover up most of her injured left arm, that was still in Plaster of Paris.

'Ah, here's our table.' He was being very solicitous. 'Allow me move your chair out.'

'Thank you.' Millie felt his kindness was almost a little worrying. 'What lovely flowers,' she remarked, trying to appear casual. A seasonal floral centre piece separated them. Millie sipped a glass of water that he'd poured, and noticed that there was another place setting, but she thought no more of it.

Bain had only just sat down when he looked at his watch and was on his feet again.

'Will you please excuse me a moment,' he said, 'there's someone... excuse me.'

As he left, a little impatient sigh escaped from Millie. A few minutes passed. She had no appetite, and couldn't be bothered to look at the menu. She plucked at the frayed threads of the now discolouring bandage. Just then a shadow fell across the table. Millie looked up. It was Bain back. She gave him a weak smile.

'Miss Chance,' he said, 'I have brought someone here to see you.'

When Bain stepped aside Millie gave a shocked gasp. She felt as if she'd got punched in the solar plexus. Standing in front of her was none other than Hugo Maitland!

Maitland grinned at her. 'Hello.' Pointing to her arm, he said, 'I see you've been in the wars.'

At a loss, Millie croaked, 'why, I-so have you.'

Slashed, down one side of his forehead, was an angry red gash, which stretched pirate fashion, past his eye, and then tapering as it ran down his cheek bone.

Bain quickly interrupted. 'Look here, I-I if you will excuse me, I must leave. Have an enormous amount of things to attend to. I-a-I thought you might like-anyway. I've told the man over there to put the bill on my account. And I've ordered that nice wine you like, Miss Chance. So, I'll bid you both a very good evening.'

Hugo turned and said something to Bain that Millie couldn't hear.

'The old boy arranged this.' He flicked his head in the direction of Bain's exit. Untidy red strands of hair escaped from under his cap.

She asked, 'how on earth-how did you get that?'

He sat opposite Millie, in the chair vacated by Bain, and took his cap off. 'What is it they say, all in the line of duty? And anyway, it looks worse that it is. It's only a flesh wound, got it messing about.'

Millie didn't believe that for a minute, for some grains of sand spilled from the folds of his cap onto the white table cloth. Millie made a circle in the little yellow specks. He followed her movements, and then whispered, 'I promise I haven't got any lizards tucked about my person.'

Smiling, she reached across and took his hand. 'Hugo, it's wonderful to see you. I had no idea. I think I was even rather offhand with our Mr Bain. And I feel bad.'

'Don't. In his eyes you can't put a foot wrong.' For ages Hugo sussed Bain was carrying a torch for Millie, just by the way he talked to, and about her. Hugo didn't entirely spell it out but he did say, 'I think he's got a soft spot for you.' He looked at her long and hard, then realised he was staring. 'Hum,' he cleared his throat, 'come to that so have I, old bean.'

Reassured, she said, 'Hugo, I have missed you.'

A waiter swooped by and filled their glasses.

Awkwardly, they drew apart. While sipping the excellent wine, Millie, mischievously, told Hugo, 'he dances divinely.'

'Who does?'

'Why, our Mr Bain.'

'Does he now? Well then, I'm certainly not going to be out done by *him*.' With care Hugo set aside their glasses of wine, and then he lifted her up.

Millie remonstrated. 'Hugo, I can't dance like this.'

'Nonsense, you only need feet on the floor, not arms.'

With that he clasped her good arm and enfolded her close. She giggled so much that a few couples stared. Hugo told them, haughtily, 'we've had an accident, fighting for King and Country.' Millie laughed some more into his chest. A shiver of excitement shot through her whole being. He had about him a faint scent of Lifebuoy soap and pipe tobacco, which she found strangely very sensual. She stumbled, he pretended to chide her. 'You're not taking this seriously. I can't be outshone by that Mr Bain fellow.'

She affected an effort but could hardly get her breath. 'Stop, stop. It's no good. You are crushing my ribs and making me laugh so much that it hurts.'

Hugo was pleased to see her spirits had lifted. A week ago, when Hugo had returned, wounded, from North Africa, Bain had visited him in hospital. The first thing Hugo asked was how Millie was. Bain said the couple's mission to France was a success even though the closely followed

Operation Rutter raid on Dieppe went disastrously wrong for the armed forces. It resulted in a tremendous loss of Canadian and British soldiers, with many being captured. Bain inferred Millie was to go to France, again, but it had to be put off due to her falling badly in training.

When they returned to their table Hugo asked, 'when do you get the plaster off?'

'I'm thankful to say in the next couple of weeks.'

Little attention was given over to the food, in spite of Bain's generous offer. A taxi was ordered which drove them all the way to Millie's flat in Stoke Newington. Climbing the stairs, a little giggly, Millie fumbled under the aspidistra pot for the door key.

Hugo asked, 'you're not anticipating any of your chums calling, unexpectedly?'

'No, Hugo. My friend Janet, whom I share the flat with won't be back for-oh months, probably.'

He grinned, raised his eyebrows and flung his cap on the sofa, 'that's good.'

Hugo may not have been in the same league at dancing as Bain, but he was a very good lover. He took her coat off and patiently helped to undress her. The cardigan was peeled down like the proverbial pre-war banana, and then, kissing her gently on the cheek, he positioned her injured arm so that it rested on his shoulder, while he unbuttoned her blouse.

Millie made happy little mewing noises as he kissed the black, blue and yellow bruise splodges on her breast. Breathless, she touched his face, 'darling Hugo.' He raised himself up, and kissed her tenderly on her parted lips, his tongue slipping in—their first heavenly kiss.

Then he whispered, romantically, close to her ear, 'how sweet are your words to my taste, sweeter than honey to my mouth.'

Millie gazed, longingly at him and told him, 'and you have the most beautiful, and inviting mouth that I have ever had the good fortune to kiss.'

Their love making was nothing short of divine.

Afterwards, she asked, 'how did you guess I adore poetry?'

Aware she was being satirical, he told her, 'at school there was a religious manic, who made us young fellows recite the Psalms, word for word. Fortunately, I have a very retentive memory, especially for Psalm one hundred and nineteen.'

Millie loved Hugo's sense of the droll.

Mostly, Hugo spent the next five days at Millie's. He'd pamper her with tea and breakfast in bed. And regularly he'd go out to get her a newspaper, or pick an early flower, or slip of a shrub to stick in a vase. One morning, he arranged her tray with his usual care, and then lifted up a letter that had come through the letter box. He set it on her breakfast tray along with the frugal edibles, and ambled into her bedroom. The bedroom held Millie's heady perfume, as well as frilly undergarments, and frothy night attire that lay carelessly strewn across the bed, as well as dangling, seductively from the wardrobe. Hugo watched as she stretched and rubbed the sleep from her eyes. He thought her incredibly beautiful, part naked, and with her hair all tousled.

'Madam's breakfast, is ready.'

'Oooh thank you. Thank you so much.'

'Well, it is only tea and toast.' He gave a chuckle, 'it's all I could find.'

She took the tray. 'Darling, darling Hugo, thank you. Oh thank you.'

Wearing a smile on his face, Hugo went back into the kitchen and poured another cup of tea. And with an air of contentment he felt in his pocket for his pipe. He had just struck a match when suddenly he heard Millie scream. Rushing back into the bedroom he saw her clutching the letter, having a fit of hysterics.

CHAPTER THIRTY-FOUR

Hugo's physical scars were already fading, as if they had never existed. Only the deeper cut on his cheek was just visible. And the MO had already passed him fit for active service. He didn't mind, on the contrary. After all, like Millie, he'd pushed hard enough to return to duty. There were moments over the recent few days when only the action in hand enabled him to blot out the emotional pain of their parting. This was his second secret mission behind enemy lines in North Africa. As things went, there were quiet times, such as now, when most of the men were sleeping, and the only sounds to be heard were their sporadic snoring which seemed to accompany the distant ra-ta-tat-tat of gun fire. Still, this lull in activity did nothing to stop thoughts of Millie racing once again.

Knowing for certain how Millie felt about him, gave him agonies of torment. In any other normal situation he'd picturing himself happily conforming to that often talked about courting period, when couples sought parents permission and would then get engaged, and set a date for the wedding, choose a honeymoon, buy a house, plan for the future. Of course times were anything but normal. In his mind, he even questioned what normal people would send young women to France into the jaws of the enemy, and into that dangerous world of spying. And yet, like him, each and every one of them had volunteered, willingly, none more so that his beloved Millie. He was not used to this churning up of his feelings. No other woman had ever had such an effect on him as Millie. Yes, he found out she was going once more to France, yet he didn't even try to persuade not to go. It would have been pointless in any case. She was even more determined to get back there, since her friend was killed.

Janet's death had pained Millie deeply; Hugo could tell it also made her very bitter. Hugo hadn't previously known much, well anything, actually, about their friendship, friends from their school days, she told him. After the initial shock, Millie became a little more composed on the drive down to Godalming. Mrs Marsh, Janet's mother, had written and told Millie as soon as she could, but the letter was delayed and the funeral was being held in the afternoon of the letter's arrival. Through his efforts, Hugo managed to cadge the loan of a car, from Bain, and wangle enough petrol to get them down through Surrey.

For a while they travelled in relative silence until Millie began to tell Hugo more about her friend. It was an outpouring of sorrow. He listened patiently, sympathising whole heartedly. He knew what it was like to lose friends and family. Who didn't theses days? Occasionally, Millie got angry, and through tears told Hugo she should have made Janet see sense, and stopped her from flying. It was at that point Hugo pulled the car off the road and headed for a village pub. A quiet word from Hugo to an understanding landlord magically produced two brandies. Hugo gulped his down, and told Millie to do likewise, and stop trying to blame herself. The gently reprimand helped, and they were both in a calmer frame of mind to watch as the remains of the young woman was laid to rest, in a quiet English country graveyard.

Poor Mrs Marsh was beside herself, and couldn't speak coherently about her daughter's accident. She was being comforted by Janet's uncle Percy, who no doubt recalled it was he that had first introduced his niece to the skies. Millie, though, learned from the Commandant of the women's section of the Air Transport Auxiliary, what caused the crash. No longer the novice, and with plenty of flying experience under her belt, transporting planes such as the Tiger Moth, Reliant, the twin engine Mosquito, the Hurricane, and after several trips delivering Wellington Bombers, Janet eventually had got her wish to fly Spitfires. On that fatal day, she had got the order to go up to Castle Bromwich, and pick up the single engine aircraft, one of many that came off the production line, at the Vickers factory. Then, Janet was to fly the Spit to the airbase at RAF Hornchurch, home of the Spitfire squadrons. Tragedy struck, somewhere over Essex, she was spotted by a lone Messerschmitt. Seeing the low flying Spit as an easy target the Me 109 opened up his guns, and hit the tail section of Janet's plane, causing it to spin out of control, and crash into a field. Undoubtedly, it would have brought Janet some sense of purpose had she but known that a squadron of spitfires had simultaneously taken off from their base in Hornchurch, and pursued the Messerschmitt, until in turn, he was shot down.

Among the solemn gathering attending the funeral were three young women, wearing the dark blue uniform of the Air Transport Auxiliary. They came to pay their respects since Janet was their comrade in arms, and they had all shared the same digs. Before Hugo and Millie set off back to London, Millie caught them up and spoke to them. In one way she wished she hadn't, in another it made her realise just how tremendously brave Janet was. Millie listened in numbed amazement, as they told her it was quite the norm for female flyers to fly without a radio, or with little in the way of instruments. As if they were not disadvantaged enough, Millie learned they always flew unarmed, and at the mercy of not only the elements but in Janet's case from an attack by an enemy fighter.

*

Weather conditions were perfect for a drop. A warm, moonlit summer's night, saw Millie parachuted safely onto French soil. She was met by a reception committee made up of a female SOE agent, code named Juliet, and two local Frenchmen, working with the Resistance. In her role as courier, Millie had personal documents, that if inspected would identify her as a student attending an agriculture research college, outside Paris. She also carried a letter from a friend, sympathising on the loss of an aunt. This would show Millie's reason for travelling so far from her college address.

Before leaving London, Millie had been given a large amount of French bank notes, and blank identity cards as well as ration cards. She also brought a small box of crystals, for radio sets. A wireless operator, or signaller, had to make sure his or her crystal was firmly in the set before they could transmit their messages to London. And these fragile pieces of equipment frequently got broken. Some of the money and all the ID cards she had to pass on to Juliet, the crystals she had to deliver to a contact in a district of Paris. Then she had to get to an agricultural college and collect secret documents that had been smuggled out of Oslo. Millie was charged with the task of getting them back to London, if not in person, then via the 'postman.' This was someone who collected agents mail from 'letter-boxes,' then they'd put mail or information on Lysanders, to be flown back to Tangmere. Other than that, she would have to wait for instructions from London, However, unbeknown to anyone in F Section she also had a private agenda—to find out the whereabouts of Christopher Elliott.

While one of the French men buried Millie's parachute, the other took the two women to a safe house were they stayed over-night. It was a bit of a relief for Millie when Juliet told her she would go with her as far as Paris. After that, though, she had to make her own way down to the college. In that certain knowledge, Millie ate the meal that was prepared for them, and slept soundly that night. She was called early next morning by Juliet, who was preparing for the short walk to the station where they would catch a train to Paris. If asked, they were travelling as cousins, having attended the funeral of their aunt.

At the station there were a few Germans smoking, and lounging about waiting for the Paris train. In any event, it was the French police that made Juliet nervous.

She told Millie, 'there are always French police at ticket offices, checking papers and sucking up to the Germans, so we'll wait till the last possible moment before buying our tickets. You leave that to me.'

Along with a few other women passing through the barrier, Juliet and Millie had to show their travel papers. While under the scrutiny of the policeman's cold, shark-like eyes, Millie could feel a shakiness coming over her with each passing moment. When he came to read the letter about her 'aunt's death,' Millie started to sniffle. She only had to think of Janet and it brought tears to her eyes. Apparently convinced, the policeman had no reason for doubting what he'd read, and hurriedly waved the pair through to get the train, which had just pulled in.

Wearing what seemed to be a permanent frown, a V shaped scar, on the bridge of her nose added to the earnest, slightly pained expression that was set on Juliet's countenance. Millie judged this new acquaintance to be about ten years older than her. When the carriage door was slammed shut, Millie did catch Juliet's hint of a smile as she put away her hankie. Because the carriage was full of an assortment of travellers there was no opportunity for much more than casual conversation. Juliet, however, had given Millie a through briefing of exactly where to go in case they got separated. Apart from one other ticket and document check the train arrived in Paris without further incident. It was when they were getting off the train Millie's heart began to beat fast. Two lines of police and customs officials were scrutinising passenger's papers.

Juliet whispered, 'try to appear normal. These checks can be through and time consuming, but they are usually random, unless they are specifically looking for someone.' Neither of the girls had suitcases. Millie had a small rucksack on her back, Juliet had only a handbag. She lent her head and quietly, asked, 'you don't have anything incriminating in your rucksack, do you?'

Millie whispered, 'no, I've only a few clothes and toiletries, the other things are around my waist.'

Neither, sets of papers were given more than cursory glances, and relieved, Millie and Juliet soon found themselves outside the station. Now they had to get across the city to the Montparnasse district. A short underground journey took them to the Metro Gaîté, where they got off. No further than a ten minute walk they passed the old Montparnasse Theatre. And when they neared a small market area, Juliet veered to the left and indicated with a nod of the head their destination was a perfumery shop. In spite of the war, business at *Parfums Mutel* was pretty brisk. Due to a combination of the close proximity to the theatre, and wealthy German officers wanting to impress by spending money on buying perfume for wives back home in Germany, or alternatively, recent French mistresses, the shop still managed to remain open. It was at this shop that Juliet stopped and peered stealthy into the window. Pausing, before they went in, they waited as a giggly young woman left clutching the arm of a German officer.

A fragrant, hazy mix of scents wafted towards them. Mistakenly, Juliet thought the shop was empty, but it was too late to turn and go out, it would seem suspicious. Towards the rear, two other German officers were being served by the proprietor. There were several perfume bottles on the counter, and it appeared a debate was going on between the officers as to which bottles to choose. The sound of the door bell chimes made them both turn round.

Seeing Millie and Juliet one slapped the counter and said, '*Mademoiselles*, would you be so kind and give us your opinion.' He picked up a bottle. 'Advise us, if you would, on the perfume. Which would you prefer? What would be your choice?' His French was good, if a little stilted.

Juliet approached, confidently, and said, 'but of course, *Monsieur*, with pleasure.'

A great show was made of smelling and cooing over the scents. Juliet would hand bottles over to Millie, for her thoughts. Opinions given, the girls discretely moved across the shop to look at boxed handkerchiefs, while the Germans finished their business. Before leaving one of them picked up a couple of boxes of the embroidered hankies, said something to Madam Mutel, and with their purchases made, they clicked their heels, touched their caps, and left.

Now alone in the shop, a unanimous cackle of laughter erupted, and when Madam Mutel told Millie and Juliet that they had each been bought a box of hankies by the enemy, they laughed even more. Needless to say, both girls put the pretty lace kerchiefs back on the counter, whence they came from. With the shop now empty the owner turned the closed sign round, then drew the blinds and bolted the door.

'Good perfume is so hard to get these days,' she sighed, 'and that's almost the last of my beautiful French fragrance, *Midnight in Paris*.' Disdainfully she held her hands up, 'and to think, it's for their whores, pffff.' The woman's lips curled down in disgust, and she made a spitting noise. Then in an instance her countenance changed, and with a charming smile she warmly greeted Juliet with a kiss on both cheeks. '*Bonjour*, Juliet.'

'*Bonjour*, Madam. This is Gale. She has brought the packet for you.'

Millie shook hands and went to unfastened a cloth belt from around her waist.

'No no, not here, *ma chère*,' Madam Mutel said, quickly. 'We must still be very careful. Come, we will go upstairs. You know the way Juliet.

Take Gale, while I close the shutters. No one will be any the wiser as I shut the shop about this time, anyway.'

Millie noted the familiarity with which Juliet lead the way upstairs to Madam Mutel's living accommodation. It was obvious to Millie Juliet had called here before. Very soon the aroma of coffee replaced the sweet smell of perfume. In the comfortable, spacious living room, Juliet flung herself down in an oversized sofa. Millie remained standing, patiently waiting to get rid of an uncomfortable belt that was starting to chaff. Without moving them, she looked through the net curtains at the streets, below. She dwelt for a while on the little stretch of open topped stalls. It was pleasant for her to see that even under the jurisdiction of an invader the French people could still ply their wares in seemingly much the same way as they would have always done. A vegetable barrow had a few customers queuing, and Millie smiled when a woman selling fish, flung some heads in the direction of a thin, orange cat. On another stall a man with one arm had an assortment of what appeared to be pictures, and picture frames, and there was even a book seller. Books! Suddenly the though hit Millie. I'm supposed to be a student, at college, and I don't carry a single book.

She was saying as much to Juliet, and then asked, 'is there a Mr Mutel?'

Just then Madam Mutel came in with coffee and bread and cheese. Now this is something that really smells good, thought Millie.

While she was pouring the coffee Madam Mutel had overheard the conversation, and said to Millie, 'to answer your question, my husband, was taken, along with dozens of the men folk from our district, to Germany. Packed off, almost at a moments notice they were, and flung into cattle trucks and put to work for the Germans, in their forced labour camps.'

'I-I'm so sorry, Madam I—'

The woman shrugged in resignation, 'what can we do, except…we do what we can.' She went on, 'that is a good idea to carry some books with you. Before the stallholders pack up for the day you could go and buy one or two.' Stepping in front of the window beside Millie, she added, 'have a look more closely at the stall with the picture frames. Do you see the man with the one arm?' Millie squinted through the nets, and nodded. 'That's your contact,' she said. 'He is called Marcel. When you have made the pickup from the college you are to pass it to on to him.' Millie assumed that she'd have to give the information to Madam Mutel. 'Since the Germans came the market people are only allowed to sell on two days, Wednesday, and Friday. So he will only be there on those days.' She repeated, 'please don't forget, Marcel will only be there on the two days. Do you understand?'

'Yes, yes I do. Only I thought you would—'

'No! You must not bring it here.' Her face clouded over, and she took on a frightened stance. 'Don't come back here. I must stress that. Once you leave for the college do not come here, to the shop. We might be watched. There are eyes everywhere. It will seem hard for you to believe, but there is always the *agent provocateur*, damned collaborators, willing to inform on us patriots. It is very dangerous for-for some of us, living here.' She took a deep breath and a different tack. 'It is vital that the package gets back to London. It must not fall into enemy hands. Should anything go wrong, in that you miss Marcel, go to Montparnasse Theatre. There is a 'letterbox' there. Ask for Madam Ariane, she's one of us. She works at the theatre, and you'll find her at the stage door. If, for whatever reason, the worst should happen, destroy the package, burn it, anything. The Germans cannot be allowed to find it. Is that clearly understood?'

'Yes, Madam, it is understood.'

The French woman smiled and the tension eased. 'Good and now let me have *your* package so that you can take your coffee and eat comfortably.'

Millie was glad to finally shed the contents of her body belt, and to see that all the precious radio crystals were unbroken. Revived now, with some lovely real coffee, and warm bread and cheese, Juliet and Millie carried the dishes into the kitchen. Millie saw Juliet checking her watch.

'The time of my next sched is in fifteen minutes.'

Puzzled, somewhat, Millie asked, 'where's your radio?'

'It's in the attic,' she gave a rare smile, 'with Madam Mutel's permission, naturally. I've had it stored up there for the last couple of days.' Millie knew very little about this agent, which was not uncommon, given the lengths SOE went to ensure secrecy. To them secrecy was the name of the game. Now, however, Millie grasped why Juliet was so accommodating in offering to accompany her to Paris. Juliet and Madam Mutel were as much involved in this mission as she was.

When the last of the dishes were put into a cupboard, Juliet pointed to the loft and said to Millie, 'I'll let them know you've got here safely, and that you will leave tomorrow for the college. But, I must be brief. I'm anxious not to stay too long on the air. Those bloody direction-finding units scare the life out of me. The Gestapo has got so wise to what's going on that to fool us their lorries are often disguised to look like a butcher's van, or a bread van. Still, mustn't dwell on that. Anything you want passed on?'

Remembering the first mission in France, and the risks Jack took, Millie was all too aware of the danger wireless operators faced when transmitting, and she didn't want to add to Juliet's consternation. Appreciatively, she said, 'no. Thanks all the same.'

Later in the afternoon, Millie purposely waited until the stall holders were almost finished for the day, and then she went out by the back door of the shop. In the little market area, she threw a glance briefly, at the one-armed man. He was intent on putting his frames onto a wooden carrier attached to the back of his bicycle. He never paid any attention to Millie. Being so crippled, she wondered how on earth he managed to ride the bike. Such courage, thought Millie. Further along, amongst the many intellectual works on poetry and literature, Millie was able to find only two books that had any relevance to agriculture, but, she felt they would, in a token sense, suffice. And at least they were to do with botany and insects. Having paid for them, she again passed Marcel. She did her best to blend in with the last few shoppers, and felt confident that she didn't draw attention to herself. It would have surprised her to know she was wrong. In fact, once she'd gone by, Marcel watched her very carefully, even observing the purchases she made. Then, as she returned via the back way up to the shop flat, and still keeping her within his vision, he put the last of his picture frames onto his bicycle, with a degree of quiet satisfaction.

With wishes of good luck ringing in her ear, Millie left the shop early Thursday morning for the agricultural research college. What Millie did not hear, however, was the shrieking horns blaring out from the military detector van, and trucks, disgorging loud, jack-booted Germans as they pulled up outside *Parfums Mutel*.

It was barely more than ten minutes after Millie had left, that Juliet set up her radio to be on time for her scheduled transmission to London. Settling down, she had only managed to send a few sentences when she stopped, abruptly.

Madam Mutel was just about to open her shop for the day's business when the van screamed to a halt. Slamming the door shut, she selflessly tried to warn Juliet, but was too late. Fully armed Germans burst in, and violently knocked her aside. While they stormed up through to the flat's living quarters, ransacking each room as they went, one plain-clothed Gestapo official kept Madam Mutel held at pistol point. By now Juliet was fully aware that they had been discovered. For her, she knew there was no means of escaping, other than to swallow her suicide pill. She chose one other option. Valiantly, she continued to transmit. Her 'fist' tap-taping even as the hatch to the roof was smashed open. In that next instant Juliet, her radio and the attic were sprayed with machine gun bullets.

CHAPTER THIRTY-FIVE

Penetration confirmed. That was *the* news Graham Bain did not want to hear. The message that came through to the signal room, in Baker Street, read, "Prospero's organiser and courier captured, along with thirty six French Resistance workers. Fear the worst. Only wireless operator, Madeleine, escaped." Soon more devastating intelligence followed. Philip Hendry, code name Charon, radioed that the whole Prospero circuit and the two sub circuits were compromised. And the sub circuit's arms dumps and food supplies were discovered. Bain's spirit sank lower when he heard their best and strongest network was practically non-existent. One high-ranking SOE officer spoke to Bain in confidence, expressing his concern on the validity of such reports. Bain, however, had no reason to doubt the information which came from Charon, the latest agent sent to Rouen.

Formulating a hasty plan, on the basis of the messages received, Bain ordered an SOE operator to radio a reply back to Charon. The message was, "will send assistance to rebuild network." Charon was informed to "expect a liaison officer, a courier and a wireless operator, as replacements." At the time of sending that message Bain had not heard about the raid on Madam Mutel's house, at Montparnasse.

It was late in the afternoon when Millie got to the agricultural college. There weren't any students about, and she was feeling slightly conspicuous. Now that she had reached this last hurdle, she knew she couldn't afford to mess things up. Anxious that time was pressing; it didn't help in that finding her contact—Professor Stroud—was proving difficult. She plucked up courage and asked an old gardener where she might find Professor Stroud. Pausing from snipping bits of the grass edge, he suggested she tried the greenhouses across the east grounds, as that was where he often took his students for practical work. When

Millie got there someone was in the long, middle greenhouse. If that was her man, he was the most unlikely looking professor ever to cross Millie's path. Bearded and bespectacled and probably pushing sixty, he was bent over watering some feeble, sickly-looking seedlings.

Giving a cough to attract his attention, she felt foolish talking about snow in August. However, he answered with the correct response, 'it happened last year, in Monte Carlo.' Then he growled, 'you're late. Have you thought where you're going to stay tonight?'

'No, I-I hadn't quite thought, though I hoped—'

Millie stopped under his scrutinising stare. He studied her for the first time. 'Hoped, hope, is there hope? Mmm, I'll speak to the Bursar. Perhaps there's an empty room in the students halls.' He threw the watering can aside, and muttered, 'these are a damn waste of time, won't come to anything, I shouldn't wonder.'

Eyeing the drooping specimens, Millie said, 'yes, I agree.'

Unexpectedly, he laughed. 'My students are not so impudent. They don't answer me like that.'

Then he grew serious. Cagily, he glanced up and down the lavender beds before pulling the greenhouse door closed. Sure now that they were alone, he indicated for Millie to follow him as he trod between rows of plants, almost to the far end of the greenhouse. Stepping sharply off the concrete walkway, Millie almost tripped over him as he stooped down. Then using a trowel he started to scrape away the earth around an inlet by the brick frame. Millie watched as the effort made his shabby, knitted pullover ride up around his waist, showing off his shirt tail. In a trice, though, he had unearthed a small oilskin packet. After coaxing the soil off, he put the item into his trouser pocket. Straightening his attire, he then pushed back his grubby sleeve cuff to get to his watch. He said, 'aah, nearly time to eat, I see. Would you like to join me, Miss, Miss, mmm Miss Hope?'

He was already out of the greenhouse before a bewildered Millie could finish saying, 'yes, yes, thank you, lovely.'

Later, in the Professor's study, Millie waited, impatiently, to be given the important papers. Naturally, she had assumed she was collecting papers, or documents of some sort. Professor Stroud moved aside a clutter of books towards the edge of his desk and produced a tiny cylindrical tube. It wobbled when he touched it. It took a moment for Millie to grasp what it was. Out of the oilskin, it then became clear that this was the object that he'd dug up in the greenhouse. Holding it now, between thumb and forefinger, he began to explain.

'This is what London wants, and God knows it was got at a price.' He didn't expound. Here, sitting in front of him was a mere girl, who looked like a puff of wind, would blow her over. He thought she can be spared knowing the exact cost in Norwegian lives it took to get it out of Norway. It should have gone via *The Shetland Bus* route, but it was deemed too chancy for such an important item to travel that way, because German patrol boats had made attacks on Norwegian fishing boats. On such missions, most of the little boats had to set out in secrecy, under cover of darkness, for Scalloway, in Scotland. He placed the small ampoule-like canister down on the desk, and let his gazed fall from her sober face. He rubbed his brow. Then squaring his shoulders, he charged her with the task.

Lowering his voice, he told her, 'this has to be got to London.' He felt she must, however, be made to understand its vital significance, so he said, 'inside the tube is a piece of film. A highly secret piece of film, and made at huge risk to those filming.' He handed the phial over to Millie. 'Take great care of it, guard it with your life, and do all you must, to ensure it is delivered to London. It must not fall into the hands of the enemy. It contains information that is of the utmost importance to the Allies.' Should he go on, he wondered. Inches now from Millie he did confide, 'the film shows drawings of a new weapon. It's a type of bomb, yet it is so advanced that it doesn't even need to be dropped from a conventional airplane.' This was beyond Millie's comprehension. 'Should the enemy ever get as far as launching this-this vile monster, England, no, the world will never know what has hit them. Some of us are acutely aware of the capabilities, and the technology that German scientists have at their fingertips. Their expertise is far and away beyond anything that our own boffins have come up with so far. At present, we know this-this weapon is in its embryonic state. One of our men working at the plant has managed to secure a copy of the prototype designs. These are contained in this film.' He took a deep breath. 'The Nazis have forced several top Norwegian scientists, and skilled technicians, to assemble this truly gruesome bomb at a secret location in Germany. They are working in a specially built factory, deep underground, to withstand air attacks. The Germans have an unlimited labour force to do the menial jobs, and they are working round the clock. If Hitler gets this weapon into production within the next four months the planned invasion of Europe will never take place.'

Millie felt a massive wave of responsibility wash over her. However, with an air of quiet confidence she told him, 'I'll keep it on my person at all times, day and night.'

The Professor nodded, gravely, and gave the tiny tube to Millie. She took it and put it inside her brassier. Once she got to her room she would secure it with sticking tape. The man sitting opposite looked visibly relieved that it was out of his possession.

Sensing the meeting was nearly over Millie decided to push for something else. She had not found the time or the place to talk to either Madam Mutel or Juliet, about escape routes for getting downed airmen back to England. She was vexed that she'd not made the slightest headway in her resolve to do this for Janet. Over dinner she was wrestling with her inner emotions as to whether or not to approach the Professor on the matter. It was on the point of leaving his study that she hesitated. She knew there'd not be another opportunity. She would be gone early in the morning, to get back to Montparnasse. Millie swallowed, and sought to ask.

Not at all sure how to start she began awkwardly. 'Professor Stroud may I-may I please ask you, do you have any knowledge of any group, or French Resistance people that would help RAF aircrew that get shot down?' His eyes narrowed, yet still she continued. 'Is there a unit, someone in the French underground or an organisation that I could contact, to ask about a-a particular pilot?' He didn't answer so she ploughed on. 'You see, he was on a bombing mission, and failed to get back to England. All the information that the family have is that he has been posted as missing.'

Abruptly, his chair scraped the polished floorboards, causing Millie to flinch. Then he delved deep into a desk drawer. Uncorking a bottle top, he took a swig of whatever was in the bottle, smacked the cork back in, and pushed the drawer closed with the toe of his boot.

Of course the well established, and much used 'Pat Line,' was unknown to Millie. This was one of the escape routes used by downed Allied airmen, as a means to getting back home. Nevertheless, it was an escape route that was well known to the Professor.

Wiping his hand across his mouth, he asked her, 'when was he shot down. What's his name and rank?'

*

In spite of having to shoulder the enormous responsibility of delivering the film, Millie left the college on a cheery note. She was feeling good on behalf of her friend, Janet, because she had made a sure-fire breakthrough. At the same time she couldn't help thinking what a strange man Professor Stroud was, and wondered just what else had he buried in those greenhouses. Still, that did not concern her, and she shrugged the notion off. The main thing was he would help. A *quid pro quo*, Prof had called it. He told her to be patient. It might take some time, but he would make enquiries for her, and leave word with Madam Mutel when he got any information.

Such was her happy mood that when Millie came to the little market, in Montparnasse, she didn't at first notice the absence of one of its stalls. It was only when ambling through the middle of the market that her heart started to pound. Where was her contact? Where was the one-arm man? She made pretence of rummaging through the second hand books, at the same time as looking along the line of stalls. She wasn't mistaken. To her horror he wasn't there!

Millie ventured to ask the book seller. 'Excuse me, please. I wanted to get a picture framed, and a friend said that someone in the market would—'

Brusquely, Millie was informed, 'he wasn't a regular; people come and go, selling this and that. Not like me. I have had my pitch twelve years, but business has never been so bad. No one wants to buy books these days. No one has money to buy books, it seems.'

Millie mumbled sympathetically, hitched up her rucksack and moved on. She considered going to the perfume shop, but only for a moment. She remembered Madam Mutel's warning. She told herself, something must have happened. With leaded legs, she started to walk to the theatre. In the event of plan changes, this is where she had to go, to contact a Madam Ariane, in an emergency. Millie kept to the tree-lined side of the boulevard, there were more citizens to mingle with, and from here she could get a better angle of the approaching theatre. Soon, she knew she'd have to cross the street to get to the theatre.

About to step off the pavement, she turned to check the traffic. Out of nowhere a gruff voice, close behind, said, 'keeping going, don't turn round and don't go to the theatre. It's a trap. Go to the metro and buy a ticket to Metro Vavin.'

If Millie's heart was pounding before, now it was racing! She could have sworn she'd heard the voice before. There was something familiar about it. She heeded the warning. Once seated on the train, Millie opened her rucksack and got out a book, to help her stay calm. She'd obeyed the man's voice. All the same, while waiting to get to Vavin station she found it wasn't easy to resist staring at commuters nearby to see who might be looking at her. It was all she could do to keep her eyes fixed on the pages. She thought it stands to reason, he's bound to make himself known to me, once it is safe to do so.

Soon the doors opened, and Millie got out. She handed her ticked in and made for the exit. Blinking, in the bright sunlight, Millie was confronted by an unexpected figure. She drew a sharp intake of breath. The one-arm man! For the first time she was able to see him at close range. He wore a typical French black beret, pulled well down to his eyebrows, and spectacles that she failed to noticed before. And he had a grubby, canvas satchel, slung over his head, which due to him not having a left arm looked like a hangman's noose. He gave her a slight nod, and shuffled out of the station, turning into Rue Brea. Millie followed a good few paces behind him. His walking speeded up. Millie wondered how far he was going for it was all of twenty minutes before he took the quiet, narrow side turnings. Doubling back, at times, as if to make sure make sure they weren't being tailed, he eventually knocked on a door at the side of a shabby, workman-type café. When the door opened he stood aside for Millie to enter, then he followed. An elderly man quickly shut the door behind them. He squeezed past and took them along the hall and down some steps into a cellar.

It was a well lit and good sized cellar. Wooden barrels were stacked at one side. A table and chairs were placed under an archway giving the impression that here was a place where black market deals would get done, or meetings of a clandestine nature might take place. For a few minutes the two men had their heads close together, talking softly; Millie could only make out snippets of their conversation, she heard the old man call her contact Marcel. Neither of them uttered a word to her. Then the old man left.

Suddenly, the man with the one arm cried out, in English, 'thank Christ you're safe!'

Millie's eyes widened, in disbelief. In the next moment the man proceeded to take off his glasses, his beret and satchel, and then his coat, exposing to an amazed Millie, a perfectly good second arm that had fingers, tightly clasped around a lively looking pistol!

'Jack! God almighty! Jack what in the name of heaven…how did you-was that-was that really you in the market?'

Silently affirming, he adjusted his waistcoat, set his pistol down, and rubbed his forearm vigorously, to get the circulation going, before putting both arms around her.

Releasing her, he said, 'come and sit down.'

Just then the door creaked open and the old man came in with a tray containing a little food and wine. He carried it to the table and left.

'Jack,' said Millie, when they were alone, 'Jack, I got an awful attack of the jitters when I couldn't see the man-you at the market.'

'The Gestapo raided the perfume shop, and I saw Madam Mutel taken away.'

Millie gasped, 'oooh no, no!'

'That's not the worst of it.' There was no other way of telling her. 'Our agent, Juliet, was killed, shot by the SS.' Millie clasped her hands over her mouth. Grimly, Jack went on, 'have you got?—'

She gulped, 'yes, yes it's safe. I-I have it here.'

He pushed the wine towards her, and he swallowed half a glass. Through clenched teeth he announced, 'the bastards were waiting at the theatre.' Hearing that, the glass shook visibly in Millie's hand.

Jack went on to explain how he had kept watch on the building, waiting for her to arrive. No one took any heed of a cripple. So unnoticed, he was able to observe the movements of plain clothes Germans, coming and going through the stage door. A German staff car also circled the block. All this heightened activity Jack clocked up. And then when he saw Millie not far from the theatre, he knew she was only minutes away from being nabbed, if she went there.

He gripped her hand to steady her. 'There's an informer,' he said, 'maybe several. We don't know. We don't know who they are, but we'll find out, and when we do—'

'Jack,' Millie said, nervously, 'how am I to get this,' she touched her breast, 'how do I get this back to London?'

'Well, as you can appreciate all the original plans have gone up the spout. You were to pass *that* to me and I was to take it to London, and you were to—'

'I don't understand. What's to stop that from going ahead?'

'As soon as the raid happened I contacted HQ and told them that our agent was dead, and the French woman captured.' He finished the rest of his wine. 'I have since received new orders. We are to get out of Paris, fast! I have made some arrangements, through the old man. He's sympathetic to the cause, and I've bunged him a wad of notes for his trouble.' Jack then gestured with his thumb. 'His son works in the café, next door. When his bread van comes round, to make its delivery,' he looked at his watch, 'he will put you in the back-'

'And you—'

'No. We go our separate ways. Me to Rouen and you—' Millie looked scared. Gently he patted her hand, and said, 'you will be fine. I know it wasn't pleasant, all that.' He lit a cigarette and drew heavily on it, offering the packet to Millie. She shook her head. 'But anyway, there's no point in going over and over…they are sending a Lysander, tonight. You and *it*,' he pointed to Millie's hidden packet, 'will be on that plane.'

CHAPTER THIRTY-SIX

Bain exhaled a blast of cigarette smoke, and loosened his tie. He was glad to get out into daylight and the fresh air, despite the autumnal nip. He found the cavernous warren of the London War Rooms somewhat overwhelming, not least to say depressing. The atmosphere down there was thick with gleeful gloating at Italy swapping sides and joining the Allies. 'They may be coming over to us,' Bain heard someone say, 'but we'll hardly give them our full trust or welcome them to our bosom.' As well as that, there was speculative mutterings from all corners on how soon the invasion would take place.

In the room Bain was ushered into, stark though it was, the majority of its walls were covered in maps of Europe and Russia and North Africa. Bain was a jumble of chairs away from Churchill, yet he was still able to observe the big man, cigar in his mouth, gazing, intently through his owl-like spectacles at two vast maps.

Significant maps were carefully laid flat on a boardroom table that yawned from one end of the room to the other. One map showed an area strung out in pink wool that marked the up-to-date 1943 Russian advance. By February, the city of Stalingrad, much to Churchill and the Cabinet's relief, was at last, firmly held by the Russians, and more recently, in July, the Germans were beaten back by the Soviets, at Kursk. Suspended at the Prime Minister's back, another chart showed Berlin, circled in crimson ink, and stabbed in a dozen or so districts by a variety of coloured pins. However, no one paid much attention now, to the once hotly contested regions of North Africa. The powers that be in the theatre of war had already consigned this dust bowl of a country to the nether regions of the vanquished, owing to the fact that the Germans had given up North Africa, in May.

Bain lit up another cigarette. He mulled over the way they'd slapped him on the back, while Churchill gave him a congratulatory hand shake, at the same time telling him what he already knew, that the bombing mission on the German factory was successful. Winston said his agent did a first class job in getting the piece of film into England.

Hailing a taxi, Bain believed the whole assignment, if Churchill did but know it, was nothing short of a miracle. If not that, then it was a damn close run thing. And since then he thought about the many unnecessary tasks he'd drummed up, and how he applied all sorts of tactics as a means of delaying Millie's return to France. He had insisted she have a spell away from ops, to rest up with her family. After that, he asked her to help train some raw recruits. That took a good few months. And then there was another bit of trivia that whiled away a period of time.

Eventually, someone in SOE's hierarchy must have rumbled Bain's motives, for they inferred, sarcastically, 'aren't you breaking the rules, old boy?'

Bain had retorted angrily, 'rules, what bloody rules, *old boy*? Does the right hand know what the left hand does here?' He curled his lips in distain. 'I tell you, there's a smell about this place, at times, and it's not entirely wholesome.'

Bain was a man with a lot on his mind. In spite of that, shifting sideways in the taxi he fell to watching the ease with which decent Londoners walked in relative safety, through the century old streets. All most likely had no idea of that other war going on in France—Churchill's Secret War. "Set Europe Ablaze," was his mantra, back in July of 1940. Bain and the select few, thought then, it had a fine and noble ring to it, especially when it gave birth to SOE. He stubbed out the cigarette in the metal ash tray provided. Worried, he asked himself the question, why were so many of our agents falling into the hands of the Nazis? They should not be thought of as dispensable. He rubbed his brow and his brain screamed; they are brave human beings, for God's sake! He recalled how that same clever dick came up with a stomach churning statistic— six weeks! Six bloody weeks was the life expectancy of a wireless operator. He hadn't exactly counted in terms of weeks, but it was a terrible fact that Bain was well aware of. He took a crumb of comfort knowing at least Millie would not be sent out in that role. Courier, as a courier, she was best placed in that field. She could move around the country easier that many of her male counterparts, who worryingly, created suspicion merely because of their age. A little smile crossed his lips at the thought of Jack disguised as a man without an arm. The smile was soon lost. He admitted it to no one except himself; however, it was true he had tried to keep Millie in England. But he was running out of excuses and time, and it did not do to cross the PM.

And he wasn't blind to the signs, her restlessness, and the odd question here and there, when was she going, again? Would it be soon? Then as if the decision was taken out of his hands, the order came from the top— from Winston himself. Get the French Résistance properly organised, he was told. And Churchill expressed it in no uncertain terms. He told Bain, he couldn't give tuppence if they were Communist, Maquis, or affiliated to the devil himself. Just get more of our people over there to arm and train the French. Knock them into shape, and quickly! We must be fully prepared when the all important day comes. Nothing, and I mean nothing, must go wrong to hold up the invasion.

Millie had not said as much in so many words, but when Bain read a copy of her report, and got it confirmed by Jack, it became clear she'd only just escaped being caught by the Gestapo. He shuddered. That was a close call. For nights he couldn't sleep after that. Things were not going well. He wondered how many rotten apples were in the barrel. Undoubtedly, bad luck played a part, but so many agents had copped it. He had no firm proof, but he was highly suspicious that some of the agents' radios were in the hands of German Intelligence, who were in all events playing a double bluff by transmitting on the captured sets. Or even worse, under torture and duress, were forcing some of his people to work for them.

So, Millie would go again, to France. SOE were desperately short of agents, and he had his orders. And tomorrow she was due at Orchard Court, to one of SOE's flats, just off Baker Street, for a final briefing, which was why he'd suggested meeting for drinks, this afternoon. Candidly she told him no drinks, but a light lunch would be nice. In a way, he was looking forward to seeing her, had been, all week. Of course since Millie returned from France he'd seen more of her than ever before. And for him, each occasion was uplifting. He enjoyed her company immensely. He laughed to himself when he remembered her arriving in London, after the fall of Singapore. The cheek she gave him, at those early interviews, at times, quite put him in his place. Yet he liked her straight away, she had an honest, straightforward no nonsense manner that she wore like a second skin. She was the prettiest, most endearing thing ever to breeze into his life, and within the last couple of years he'd seen her grow into a real beauty. He got a handkerchief from his pocket and quickly wiped the corner of his eye.

At least he would have good news for her—Christopher Elliott was home and back with his squadron. He was puzzled about this chap and wondered if Elliott was an old flame. He'd have to ask, subtly, of course, just to satisfy his curiosity. He hazarded a guess at them meeting out in Singapore.

Inside the restaurant Bain was surprised to see Millie, he thought he was late, and checked his watch. Then she gave a little skip towards him, and said, 'Graham, I have done the decent thing and ordered our lunch.' He started to remonstrate, but she would have none of it. 'Now, no arguments, this one is on me. I know what you like, I should do by now, you've bought our lunches often enough.'

She hooked her arm through his and smiled into his grey, wistful face.

They were drinking tea while waiting for their food to be brought. It was a quiet restaurant, and with no one sitting close by it was ideally private for Bain to feel comfortable enough to talk on intimate terms. He pulled his chair closer to the table and gave her the news.

'I have a message for you,' he said, 'from Professor Stroud.' Millie set her cup down. 'Some months ago, Christopher Elliott was taken through the Pyrenees. Arduous though the route was his guide led him safely into Spain. And I can confirm that he arrived back in England, and has since rejoined his squadron.'

'Oh Graham, that is the most wonderful thing to hear. He's really back?' Bain smiled at her and nodded. Millie clasped her hands and closed her eyes for a few seconds, as if in silent prayer. 'That is just wonderful. His mother will be so happy.'

'His mother…ah yes, that's the um-um the missionary woman; you met on the ship going out to Singapore.'

She said, brightly, 'yes, that's right. Gosh, you have a terrific memory, Graham, fancy remembering something like that.'

There was nothing sinister, or untoward about it. Graham Bain remembered everything about Millie Chance.

'And the RAF chap, Elliott, where did you say you met him?'

'Christopher? Oh I've never met him. No, it was Grace, Grace Elliott, his sister, who was my friend. Of course you know the Japs murdered her, and her father.' She said it without emotion, but her eyes told him differently.

Bain could have bitten his tongue. He leaned over. 'I'm sorry, that was clumsy, Millie. I hope I haven't upset you.'

She broke into a smile. 'Of course you haven't, it's the best news ever. Thank you, thank you for telling me, it's simply terrific.'

'Well now, if you're agreeable, do you mind if we talk shop for a few minutes more?'

'No not at all. Here, let me pour you another cup of tea.'

'Thank you.' This touch of kindness made him feel better. 'As you've already been told, you will continue to work mainly with Jack. He has had the job, and, it has, by no means been an easy one, but he's doing pretty well in liaising with a number of pockets of Résistance fighters. We have made several drops of weapons, ammunitions and a plentiful supply of explosives, so the French are now well armed and soon they should be well trained. The Maquis, according to Jack are veteran fighters who need little in the way of instructing. But they are an undisciplined bunch.' Millie gave a little laugh at them being called undisciplined. 'I gather there was no end of fighting between them and the Communists, and one faction and another.' He now gave a chuckle. 'The French can be hugely sensitive and temperamental at times. Still, they seem to realise now who the common enemy is, and things have got a little easier for managing them. Anyway, Jack will take you to Charon, the 'organiser.' And our other agent, Madeleine, is the circuit's radio operator. Of course

I know you know all this.' Bain hesitated; he saw the waiter was coming over with plates.

Lunch was set in front of them and Millie said, 'I hope you like what I picked from the menu, Graham.'

He glanced at the food, and smiled back at Millie. 'Thank you, my dear, a good choice, it looks very appetizing.' He paused until after the waiter had gone.

Bain agonised for ages over whether to let Millie know the true identities of Charon and Madeleine. He was aware there had been a love attachment (he preferred to think in terms of attachments or relationships, affairs to Bain, sounded sordid) between Millie and Philip Hendry. It was part of Bain's job to know everything about everybody, except if that really was true and he did know everything...In spite of his uncertainty, he had made a choice. And it was a decision that he judged to be the best one under the circumstances.

'In confidence, Millie,' he said, 'I urge you to be very...very wary. There is, there is, I'm-we're not certain about this, and we may be well off the mark, but we think someone is leaking information to the Germans.'

'You are not suggesting Jack! Why he warned me—'

'No, no! Not Jack. He's one hundred per cent, solid as a rock. But we suspect, only suspect mind, we have no proof and nothing to go on, other that instinct.'

'Graham, what are you saying, exactly?'

'What I'm saying is there could be a plant, a double agent, possible even more than one, in the Northern circuits.' Millie thought Bain was not a man easily ruffled. But she could see he was disturbed. 'It could even be someone in the French underground. The French are having it tough too. I know we've been at war since '39, but they have been under occupation since '39.' He sliced his fish. 'They're in the grip of food shortages, and some have resorted to collaborating with the Nazis, whom I understand pay well. We don't know we just don't...' Bain tightened his hold on the knife. His knuckles whitened. 'All I can do is to warn you to be on your guard and to keep your wits about you at all times.'

He was struggling. He wanted to tell her to be careful who she trusted, he wanted to tell her...but he felt there was no more that he could say.

He would leave her the element of surprise. It might catch someone out, a little slip, something. God knows they needed something. One thing Bain was totally sure of, and that was when all four agents, Millie, Jack, Charon and Madeleine, when they met up in France, they would, without a doubt, each know the other.

CHAPTER THIRTY-SEVEN

The only passenger to cross the Channel to France, in the small Lysander, this time, was Millie. Though relatively calm, she felt hugely excited after having being away so long. She was getting her things together as they neared, what she judged might soon be the drop zone. She couldn't see the pilot's face, only the back of him, which probably, was just as well for at that moment he was unable to disguise his unease. He scanned the ground, eyeing the darkness, aware too he must almost be above the location. Then to his relief, he spotted a flashing light on the ground, and took it initially to be the landing signal. But it was too dim, and inconsistent. Not the usual signal a reception committee would set up, which was normally two lines of torches or burning flares, that was what he'd come to expect. He circled round again, but his senses, or possibly intuition told him something was wrong. This was when fear set in. He couldn't, wouldn't risk putting her down. It looked as if Millie's mission was about to be abandoned. However, the pilot decided to drop his machine lower, give it one final shot to see if there were any other lights showing. There wasn't. He was getting ready to swing the Lysander round, and head back across the Channel when he picked up a ground to air signal. The reception was poor, but with a map between his legs the pilot could just make another reference for a different landing strip. This was definitely not the norm, and he inwardly debated whether or not to give it a try. He hollered to Millie to come up. She got as close as she could to the cockpit.

'What is it?' She shouted back to him.

'I'm not sure. Something's not right down there. I may have to turn back.'

'No!'

'There is one other possibility. I've just received radio contact from the ground. We can try and go further east. But you will be about five miles from where you should be. You'll be practically in Picardie.'

Full of confidence, Millie said, 'that's OK. I know Picardie like the back of my hand.'

It was not possible for the pilot to make contact with England. As it was, he had to fly dangerously low to keep under the German radar.

He was still dubious. 'I don't like it.'

She squeezed his arm, and said, persuasively, 'don't worry, you just get me down.'

Ten minutes later he saw the other torch-lit field. He indicated with his thumb to show her the new drop zone. 'Are you sure you want to do this?'

Unwavering, Millie nodded. 'Yes, I'm absolutely sure.'

As soon as the door opened Millie scooped up her suitcase and flung it out of the plane. Her feet had barely touched French soil before the Lysander was bumping away on the makeshift runway. She had not even time to watch it take off before someone appeared from out of the darkness, and grabbed her arm, and pulled her over towards the protective cover of bushes and trees.

She heard a woman's high-pitched voice order her to, 'stay here, and don't move.'

Millie squinted as she followed the female's nimble form run up and down the grass, extinguishing the burning flares, one by one. She thought, I could have gone and helped.

Accustomed now to the dark, Millie's eyes darted this way and that, expecting to see others from the Résistance. When the woman had snuffed out all the flames, Millie asked her, 'is it just you?' She was trying to keep incredulity out of her voice.

'Yes, it's just me! Who else were you expecting, General de Gaulle and the whole French army?'

Millie stifled a laugh. 'Why no I—'

'Come on, no time for talk. Let's clear off before the plane noise draws attention to us.'

Millie was ordered not to speak as they climbed through thick hedges and crossed a number of fields. Silence prevailed. When they came upon some farm buildings Millie was shown into a small shed that stored hay. The first thing that assailed Millie's nostrils was the pungent smell of tom cats. Her contact struck a match and lit a hurricane lamp. However, to her utter amazement Millie saw that the person, who had tramped the French countryside with her, for the last half hour, was none other than a young girl, no, more a child. Millie surmised she could be no more that twelve or thirteen.

'You will have to stay here,' the girl told her. 'It is only for one night. You can sleep on the hay. You'll get sacks from over there'. She pointed to an indistinguishable pile in a corner. 'This is my grandpa's place. He doesn't know anything of this. He's not well; I come and take care of him. At this time of the night I can't make noises in the house or he will get worried. In the morning I'll bring you some food, and show you the water pump.' She frowned and grew stern. 'Stay hidden until I come for you. The Bosch does not come here to see an old man, but you never can tell they may have heard the plane.'

At last Millie found her tongue. 'Right, OK thank you.'

'I have to give you a message, from Marcel. He'll meet you here in the morning, between nine and ten.' Millie felt happier, and thought, good man, Jack.

The girl had already blown out the lamp and was pulling over a door. It was badly warped so it wouldn't shut properly.

'Thank you. Goodnight.' Millie's thanks trailed off. The girl had already disappeared.

It was the roughest, coldest and most primitive place she'd ever had to sleep in. However, sleep she did, though when she woke up she had a stiff neck and was nearly frozen. She hoped the girl would bring something hot to drink and something to eat. With these thoughts going through her mind Millie suddenly heard a vehicle approaching. Wonderful! Here comes Jack. She threw aside the sacks she'd slept under, stretched and started picking off the bits of hay that clung to her clothes. Then the air was rent with the sounds of shouting and banging on doors. Twigging pretty quickly that it wasn't Jack, but the Germans, Millie flew into action. She rapidly gathered up the sacks and piled them with the others. She was truly thankful that she'd taken the precaution, last night, of hiding her suitcase under some empty wooden crates. With all due haste, she dived under the deepest mound of hay. It was only a matter of minutes before the old door of the shed was viciously smashed in by someone. Millie held her breath.

A German soldier tentatively lent into the gloom, then suddenly pulled back, and swore. 'It stinks in there. It's fucking stinking in that shit-house.' Angrily, he kicked the broken door completely off its weak hinges. But he never ventured a foot inside the shed.

By now, the young girl was out in the yard. All Millie could hear was her sobs, and her mumbling, 'Grandpa sick. Grandpa sick.'

Millie felt cold sweat trickle down her back. Through clenched teeth she was thinking, if he so much as touches a hair on that child's head, I'll kill him. I'll kill them all.

The sound of heavy boots thudding nearer told Millie he was joined by other soldiers. They had already been into the house. The soldier could barely look at the girl, who was a few yards away from him. He pointed, and spat out, 'imbecile!' 'She's a fucking cretin, an imbecile,' he told them. 'Look at her, look at it! In Germany we have places for them.'

Keen to get away from foul, farmyard shit, one of the others reported to him. 'We've been inside the house. There's no one in there, only the old man, in bed, and just that.' Turning his head he aimed his riffle at the girl, at the same time concurring with his mate. 'The place is only fit for bloody pigs.'

When the Germans had driven off, and all was quiet, Millie breathed again. Then there came a high pitched sing-songie voice. 'You can come out now, come out now, the bloody pigs have gone, pigs have gone, pigs have gone…'

Millie emerged looking every bit like a mad thing herself—hair sticking up on end with spikes of twigs poking out of it. She'd lost a shoe and the rest of her was covered in straw. Yet all she could do was to stare at the girl, and wonder if *she* really was 'all there'. She was dressed in a short, yellow frock that only reached her mid thigh, and wore the strangest looking purple bonnet that had peacock feathers, and wax flowers around its brim. She tried to run to Millie, clumping along in outsized Wellingtons, and was sucking her thumb.

Millie couldn't take in what she saw. Then suddenly, to Millie's astonishment, the girl kicked off her rubber boots, and flung her hat in the air. Then she spun round and round, laughing. She declared to Millie, 'I'm going to be an actress when I grow up.'

She had Millie in fits of laughter, as she danced around the yard. Oh you clever, clever little *mademoiselle*, thought Millie.

In spite of sitting and eating in a warm kitchen, Millie could see just how poor the grandfather's abode was. As the girl explained to Millie he was indeed ill upstairs. Along with her mother, they did what they could for the old chap, coming daily to see to his needs, because he refused to move from his home.

No names were exchanged. No questions were asked. Millie thought it best that way. All the same, wanting to help the girl's plight in some way, what she did do was to push a bundle of notes into her hand, as she was leaving. The girl got cross. Millie was insistent and pointed up to the ceiling, meaning the money was for all of them. She was coming round, and acquiescing, smiled with sweet innocence, and nodded. Millie thought she was a pretty little child, and so very brave and very talented. She felt sure with a gift like that, one day, hopefully in the not too distant future, France would be blessed and privileged to have this budding new actress in their midst.

Millie was looking forward to seeing Jack again, and recounting the little drama to him. He always listened patiently, and she liked to hear his approval. However, it wasn't Jack in the motor; it was two members of the Maquis. This was Millie's first encounter with the Maquis. She had of course heard of this mysterious band of guerrilla fighters, though she thought they lived in the hills, and only fought in certain areas such as Brittany, and the more southerly regions of France. Unshaven and muffled up against the weather, from their guise, Millie sensed these were tough, seasoned fellows. The guns they carried inside their coats did nothing to dim that image. As they drove along the narrow back roads and country lanes of Picardie, it was their anger and hatred of the Germans, and their passion for a free France that soon became evident.

And that was all they talked about. She tried asking about Jack and Charon, but they skirted the issue saying she'd meet them soon. Making no headway, Millie tried to relax and resigned herself to waiting.

CHAPTER THIRTY-EIGHT

Jack and Madeleine, the wireless operator, were hunched shoulder to shoulder, studying, or trying to study a pencil sketch of the prison. Jack was finding it difficult to concentrate. The racket didn't seem to bother Madeleine, but it annoyed Jack. He sighed, aware of an incessant jibber-jabbering from all quarters. He cursed. Would their squabbling never cease? Just a modicum of quiet, he considered that wasn't much to ask. Exasperated, he flung the pencil down. What a mix they were. He thought, to see them, bedevilled by infighting, one would wonder if they really were all on the same side.

Gathered together, in one of the rooms at the remote chateau, buried in the Picardie countryside, were a group of French Résistance fighters. There were also some men who belonged to the Maquis, and the number included a couple of staunch Communists, who made their political views quite clear from the off. There was even a glum Anarchist fellow, to boot. Distractions and the political wrangling were beginning to go beyond a joke. Jack crossed his hands and put them on top of his head, prisoner fashion, and viewed their crazy bickering. He was mighty tempted to fire his pistol in the air. If it hadn't been for the noise of a gun going off in a confined space, he would have done so. Then the door opened, and in came a bandoleer-carrying officer from the Maquis. Instantly the mood changed, and the room went silent. Here was a man in authority, and he oozed anger. Slamming the door behind him he went and said something in Jack's ear.

Jack got to his feet straight away, and gave an order to Madeleine. 'You wait here. Show them the drawing.' Then he shouted to them, 'study the bloody outlay, for Christ's sake. And have it memorised by the time I get back.' Then he left the motley gathering in the company of the Madeleine and the officer.

If the decision had have been left to Jack he wouldn't have involved the Maquis, at least not so early in the game. They were such a fanatical lot, who showing little regard for discipline, and frequently had their own and did their own agenda. It would be a different matter when the invasion came. And to that end they must work together, as one, for France would need every able bodied man and woman when the time came. However, the decision to engage the Maquis in an ill-fated sabotage mission was Charon's, the SOE's organiser, and now he was captured along with two other Maquis fighters.

The car that drove Millie to the chateau had pulled up at the back, and Millie wound the window down. Jack was glad to see her and gave a wave. He would need a few minutes alone with her, before she met the others. She'd need to be briefed and prepared. Wasting no time, Jack took her suitcase and showed Millie through a back door and into what would have been the servants' entrance. Most of the chateau was boarded up. The former occupants, being Jewish had fled. The family left a caretaker in charge. He lived in a cottage on the now overgrown estate, and for a sum of money, turned a blind eye, at these occasional visitations. The chateau was thought to be too isolated for the Germans to inhabit, and its lonely location well suited the Résistance as a secret meeting place. After all, as someone said, the Germans couldn't watch every kilometre of soil in France. Someone else's response was that the enemy was having a damned good try.

Jack greeted Millie with, 'hello, you're cold.' It was bitterly cold, and Millie was shivering. They had reached the kitchen. 'It's cold in here too, I know. We have to be careful burning too many fires. Anyone local passing by would think the odd bit of smoke is the caretaker at work. But we can't tempt fate too much.' He had to come to the point, quickly. Clearing his throat, he said, 'I have some bad news, and I want to give it to you here, rather than upstairs. There's a meeting going on, quite an ensemble actually.' He dug his hands into his pockets. 'Our agent Charon and two Maquis fighters were caught by the Gestapo.'

'No! Oh no, no. In God's name, will things never go right for us? When, how?'

He answered, 'it was a couple of days ago. And how?' Shrugging, he glanced down, and then scuffed the worn and uneven flag stones. 'They had a job on…it went wrong…bad luck. I suppose one could put it down to bad luck. I don't-we don't know. God knows.' Jack was evasive, and this created a little flicker of doubt in Millie's mind. Somehow she couldn't go entirely along with his 'bad luck' thing. Jack continued, 'what we do know is that yesterday, they were taken to cells in the town. Months ago, the Germans established a jail in what used to be the Government Welfare Offices. They got rid of most of the French clerical staff and put in their own people. Then they moved the lot to an annex behind the main building.' Millie looked dejected. Sensing this he said, 'however, all is not lost. We have a contact inside the building; she works there as a cleaner. She told us the big noise in the district, *Sturmbannfüher* Kieffer, drove into the town, yesterday. His presence suggests they must realise they've captured people of importance, in the underground movement.'

'Is that the reason for this meeting?'

'Yes. We are planning to break in and get them out. The jail itself is small but the facilities, or shall we say equipment to interrogate prisoners is much in line with the usual imaginative, implements of torture, that the Gestapo has a penchant for.'

'I see.' She grew pensive. 'You say they got captured a couple of day's ago?'

'Yes. There was a great deal of panic, as you can guess. We had to change your drop zone, because of what happened.' He never mentioned he too only just missed capture, by a whisker. 'That's why I had to arrange for the lads to get you over here.'

'I see.' Millie said, again.

Jack thought Millie seemed reticent, unconvinced, and almost suspicious-like. He didn't expect that reaction. It irked him, and he had enough to deal with upstairs. Putting these notions aside, he said, 'look, we'll go through now and I'll get you some hot coffee, and you can get yourself warmed up. You can meet the gang. They're a bit of a mixed bag, but well intended.' Jack gave a grunt. 'I think!' Then he added casually, 'by the way, you'll have a bit of company.' Jack began to take Millie upstairs. 'We have someone here you'll remember from the past. She'll cheer you up.' Millie was puzzled. 'It's the wireless op, Madeleine.' Obviously her code name, thought Millie. 'She's been working here-well a good while now, so she knows the form and her way around, pretty well. She's been an absolute brick in managing to get this bunch all together.'

The brick or Madeleine happened to be her one-time comrade in training, Vanessa. Cigarette smoke hung thick in the airless room, and Millie couldn't make her out at first, then she recognised the husky voice straight away.

'Good God! It's Millie! Darling, what an amazing surprise! Naughty Jack never said a word.' She threw a deliberately sly look in Jack's direction. He didn't notice he was busy getting the coffee heated for Millie. 'I suppose he's taken pleasure in not telling me you were in France. Wanted to surprise me, I dare say.' She beamed that charming Vanessa smile. 'This is not exactly the Ritz, darling, but hey, what the hell, we'll have a jolly time catching up.'

Startled at Vanessa's sudden, and unexpected appearance, Millie, nevertheless declared, 'Vanessa, it is wonderful to meet you again.' She thought, Jack had obviously not told Vanessa I was coming. I wonder why.

As it happened, there was no opportunity for that 'jolly time catching up.' Jack and the officer in the Maquis put an immediate stop to the group's desultory talking, by getting down to the serious business of springing the three prisoners from the jail. Jack stressed time was at a premium. His fear being that under torture, the captives would talk. When he said as much there was raucous shouts of 'never, never' from some of the fighters. All the same, in Jack's experience, nails ripped from fingers and toes, or having your head forced in a tank of water until one practically drowns, or that other delight, an electric currant passed through one's testicles, or a scalding rod inserted into the vagina, all of these means of torture on their own was enough to make any man or woman crack.

But he knew they knew that anyway, so he let their protestations pass. From past encounters, Jack told them, it was more than likely that the Gestapo would move the three men to Paris, or worse Berlin, for further interrogation. He practically pleaded with the group to act quickly. Taking as much into account as they could, it was finally agreed they had to break into the jail the following night, or it could be too late. And the best time to carry this out was just before curfew, when the guards changed their shifts and the evening domestics went into the building to work. Millie and Vanessa and Jack would go in as cleaners, with the 'inside' woman. There was only one male cleaner employed, so arrangements had to be made for him to be 'sick.' Jack would take his place for the main purpose of picking the cell locks.

Having gone over and over the layout, Jack was confident he knew exactly how get to the cells. And they knew they could call upon the help of the cleaner if anything untoward cropped up. The sketch showed the number of cells on the lower level. Three squares were pencilled in and each had red crosses to show where their compatriots were held. Jack said that if all went to plan the job could be done under the noses of the Germans without them even knowing what was going on. At first there was strong resistance from a couple of Maquis fighters who became very militant, and would have relished the opportunity to kill some of the Bosch. However, orders came from their commanding officer, and Jack, who was insistent that the Germans must not be killed, unless it could not be helped. He wanted to prevent the town's people being taken as hostages, or blame falling on the cleaning crew.

Later the next day, they filtered into the town in one's and two's. Some made for the cafés, a few headed for the bars. One fellow went to the library, and another even went to the barbers. A rendezvous was arranged for six o' clock at the church, where Jack would have a black Renault van parked by the railings that circled the graveyard. Another car driven by the Maquis officer would be tucked out of sight, ready to whisk two of the prisoners away. Charon was to go into the van with Jack and everyone else.

Having got a lift part of the way, Millie and Vanessa then caught a bus into the town. They still had an hour or so kill. Vanessa knew her way around the place and took Millie into a ladies boutique. She said it would help to take their mind off things. It didn't help, for Millie's mind was not entirely focused on what Vanessa was saying about garments. Her attention was elsewhere rather than what Vanessa was planning to wear. Once Vanessa had finished admiring hats and dresses, they went into a café, a few shops further along the mall. Millie sat at a table near the window so she could watch the goings on in the street, while Vanessa ordered and paid for two cups of ersatz coffee. Millie wished she'd shut up, and stop her silly non-stop chattering about the dress fashion, but it seemed she couldn't.

'Millie,' she said, 'I wish I had bought that green woollen dress, you know the one with the lace collar, that you said you liked, too.'

Millie wondered how on earth she could think of such a frivolous, mundane topic at a time like this, and was about to ask her to stop harping on about something as prosaic as clothing. However, it wasn't necessary, for in the next moment Vanessa clunked her cup down and said, 'wait here for me. I'm going back into the boutique. I must have that lovely dress.'

Before Millie could prevent her, Vanessa had grabbed her scarf and bag and was out of the door. Millie began to feel exasperated. It was typical of Vanessa's impulsive style. Millie watched her dart past the window and across the road. Her eyes widened in surprise at the speed with which Vanessa took off. It made Millie angry. She did not want to be sitting in the café on her own. She was carrying a knife in her handbag, and right now she wanted to leave. They had been lucky so far not to have got ensnared in random searches. Impatiently, Millie drummed her finger nails on her cup then made an instant decision to catch up with Vanessa. She picked out quite clearly, the tall form of Vanessa, scurrying along the street, and made a huge effort to catch her up. Suddenly Millie pulled up sharp in her tracks to listen to an odd thought that flashed through her mind. She turned round and looked back in the direction of the café. Why, is she going that way when the clothes shop is only two doors down to the left of the café? A cold sense of unease gripped Millie as she strained to keep Vanessa in sight. She began to question Vanessa's motives for leaving her on her own when they had strict instructions from Jack to stick together. Timorously, she asked herself, did Vanessa want rid of me? And if that was so, well why?

CHAPTER THIRTY-NINE

A little later, Millie knew exactly why Vanessa wanted rid of her. The knowledge brought a gasp and rooted her momentarily to the spot, and unable to think straight. In that same split second, she felt her arm caught in a vice-like grip. Before she could struggle, her feet were lifted off the ground and she was physically thrown into the back of a car. Her head was forced down onto the floor and someone had, what felt like their boot on the back of her neck. She could neither move nor breathe. The car was being driven slowly away, and at the same time Millie could feel herself slowly slipping away into unconsciousness. The next thing she was aware of was a light shining into her eyes, and then being roughly hauled from the car. Gasping for air, she felt as if she had been choked. Someone was shaking her. She blinked hard. Rough hands were pinching and shaking her by the shoulders.

Then she heard of a voice calling her name. 'Millie, Millie, it's me, Jack.'

'Whaat, ooh my neck.' Groggily she asked, 'did you...who did this to me?'

'Look at me, Millie. Look at me,' Jack said, with clipped urgency. 'We had to lift you. We thought you were going to go into the building, the German HQ.' He gave her another shake. 'Do you understand what I'm saying?'

'Yes.' She was conscious enough to say yes, for if she didn't she felt her bones would not stop rattling. 'Yes, yes I understand.' She could smell petrol. She assumed they were in some sort of shed or garage. She could now see three other grim faced men. She recognised them as the partisans, some of the ones from the chateau, the Maquis. Jack still had a tight grip on her shoulders. He feared if he let go she'd topple over.

She started to mumble. 'I saw…I saw Vanessa talking to…then she went into…' she paused unable to comprehend what she actually witnessed.

Jack saved her struggling with her thoughts. 'We know. We were watching her. We've suspected her for sometime.' He was thinking of Millie's last mission, when Juliet, a wireless operator was murdered at Madam Mutel's. 'Now we are certain. She was at the German Head Quarters to inform on us. To make sure that Kieffer could nab the whole bunch of us, when we attempted to get our people out of the jail.' Millie couldn't take it in. She stared blankly at Jack. 'Listen Millie, we can't go into it all right now. There's not a lot of time. But there is a way to convince you she is the traitor.' Something was obviously discussed, for the others versed their opinion by quietly agreeing. 'Then there can be no uncertainty. Just tell me this.' He cleared his throat. 'We saw you both go into the café. Why didn't you stay together, as planned?'

'She told me to wait there, in the café, while she went to buy a dress. But she didn't, she—'

Jack threw a glance at the men and with loathing in his voice, said, 'she went to tell them we were here. She went to warn her friends, the Germans.' Jack had a long memory, 'It was just like she did back on Lindisfarne.'

'Lindisfarne, what's Lindisfarne got to do with it?' Millie was totally confused.

'Never mind that now. This is what you must do. Go back to the café. Make it look as if you had never left it. Got that?' Millie nodded. 'Good. Then this is what is going to happen. And you must do exactly as I tell you. Everything depends on it.'

What Jack could not tell Millie was something so awful, that if he disclosed it at that juncture, he knew she would not have the strength to do what he wanted.

Millie's heart was pounding against her rib cage. She was worried that she'd not make it to the café before Vanessa. Luck was on her side with five minutes to spare. She even got the same window seat.

When Vanessa walked through the door Millie had rehearsed in her mind what she was going to say. And she began. 'So, you bought your frock, then.'

'Frock, what—? Oh, no. I-um, I tried it on again, but changed my mind. Anyway,' she glanced at her watch, 'we'd best be on our way. We mustn't keep the boys waiting.' Vanessa shot Millie a look. Are you alright? You look a bit pale.'

'I'm fine,' Millie lied. Her nerves were jangling.

The rendezvous was fast approaching. By now, the evening was drawing in and shutters on a few shops had been pulled across, and quite quickly people were disappearing from the town. The day's business was over for them. Millie's adrenalin was set racing when Vanessa took off at a brisk pace in the direction of the church. What lay ahead for her, Millie felt was fearsome. However, she braced her shoulders and deliberately sidled up on Vanessa's left. She knew what she had to do, and do it she must. It wasn't the most direct route to the church, all the same, after the barber's shop Millie had to make Vanessa turn right. They were almost there. Millie reached into her coat pocket and pulled out a weapon, and shoved the barrel into Vanessa's side.

'We turn off here.'

'What?'

'We turn off here.' Vanessa hesitated. Millie spat out, 'do as I say you or I'll shoot you here and now.' Prodding her, Millie said, 'move your bloody self!'

'For God's sake, have you gone mad? What do you think you're—?'

Millie hissed, 'shut up!' To show she meant it, the weapon got another hard push into Vanessa's ribs.

There was not a soul to be seen in the narrow side turning they had just taken. Millie prayed Vanessa didn't suddenly decide to do something alarming like punching her. She was taller than Millie, and Millie remembered her athleticism, and robustness. Inwardly quivering, she was thinking, how much further, please. Suddenly from the side of a building they were surrounded by a small party of German soldiers.

One of them shouted in German, 'halt! Put your hands up.'

Millie quickly got the weapon back into her pocket and put her hands in the air. Vanessa did likewise.

The same German strode forward and asked, in broken French, 'what are you doing here?'

'We're on our way home, just got delayed,' Millie told him.

'You,' he pointed his riffle at Vanessa, 'where are you going?'

She lowered her arms and replied in excellent German. 'Well, actually, I was just on my way to see your commandant, *Strumbannführer* Kieffer, when this silly girl way-laid me. I thought she was actually going to shoot me.' Vanessa shocked Millie by laughing. 'I have an appointment with the *Strumbannführer*.' Vanessa smirked, 'he is expecting me.'

The conversation proceeded in German. 'What do you want him for?'

'That's none of your damn business,' she answered brusquely. 'But since you ask, I'm bringing her in. She's working for the Résistance, and she is an English agent.' Scowling she added, 'so look sharp or you'll find yourself on a charge for delaying me.'

The German moderated his tone. 'Come. We'll take you.'

'Wait a minute.' Vanessa reached into Millie's pocket to get what she thought was a gun, only to discover it was a piece of wood. 'You bloody bitch.' Incensed, at being duped, Vanessa grabbed the stick and whacked Millie viciously across the face with it, sending her reeling and bloodied.

Unmoved, the German issued an order. 'Enough of this,' he said. 'Both of you are to come with us.'

CHAPTER FORTY

Silently, she had been congratulating herself. Vanessa always admired her own skills. Puffed up with a strong sense of accomplishment, she thought, what a record for a double agent, and to cap it all, a bulging bank account, to boot. Yes, she mused, dreamily, she'd done very well in the last few years, and she'd do very well when all this was over. She relaxed, sank back and closed her eyes as the car drove off. I'll make sure I come out on the winning side. Yes, she steadfastly maintained, it's all about winning. Stuff and nonsense this team work lark. Long ago, she'd mocked the ideals of her old school headmistress, who would have always dished out encouragement to pupils on the importance of taking part in the games, when the less sporty competitors couldn't keep up with Vanessa. It gave her a tremendous sense of pride as she remembered her silver cups were among the many family trophies displayed above the book cases in the library, at her parents' home. Oh yes, for me it's all about the winning.

Possibly, it was doing a little too much day-dreaming that caused her to drop her guard. For, as Vanessa soon discovered, she was not being taken to the German HQ. And then the truth hit her right between the eyes. She had made a catastrophic blunder of huge magnitude. With terrible clarity, Vanessa realised that she had been caught wrong-footed.

She spat sour bile that had bubbled from her stomach when she knew the game was all but over. Yet still she tried to bluff her way out, while the Maquis fighters were tearing off German uniforms and sneering at her. She fumed at her own stupidity, and for underestimating Jack's intelligence. They had set a trap for her, and she fell into it, hook line and sinker. Vanessa suddenly cottoned on it could only have been Jack who had conceived it. She could see it was a masterly *coup de grace.* Given any other circumstance and she would even have laughed at the part that little mouse played, pretending to have a gun, indeed! She recalled the time they were in Scotland, when Millie could barely tell one end of a gun from the other, let alone shoot straight. Bloody little bitch!

Now the odds were stacked against her. And in the light of what she had done, clearly she could not expect any degree of mercy. Vanessa knew, she had been hoisted by her own petard, and she had that idiom to mull over as she was driven to the chateau.

Meanwhile, Jack had the painful task of confronting Millie with Vanessa's evil work.

There would be no need for any jail break that night, Millie was told, no need at all. Of the group, it was just Jack and Millie left in the town, along with the van driver, who stayed at the wheel of his vehicle, and waited for them.

Resting beside a broken fence post, a little bunch of wayside flowers was the first thing Millie saw. Jack had prepared her, but even he could not have imagined her reaction. Just half an hour earlier, Millie was given the whole story, and told the raid on the German HQ was abandoned because their compatriots were already dead. Executed, early in the afternoon by Kieffer's men, and their bodies were left hanging in public view. A final insult, Jack called it.

Saddened almost beyond words, Millie asked, when she saw the flowers, 'were they shot? Was it a quick end?'

He wished she hadn't asked. He couldn't lie. Anyway, she'd see for herself. She'd have to. At first, all he said was, 'no.' And then he told her, 'strung up with piano wire on meat hooks does not make for a quick death.'

Millie's heart sank, and she felt sick. She was about to turn round, she didn't wish to see the bodies of three brave men, humiliated, and left dangling like pieces of meat from butchers hooks. He steadied her. Despite Jack holding her arm, gently, this time, he had to show her the evidence in order to prepare her for what was to come. They stopped for an old woman to cross the street. Oblivious to Millie and Jack, she sobbed into a handkerchief. They judged that by now, the terrible spectacle had been seen by all of the townspeople. Millie thought perhaps it was the old woman herself that had laid the flowers, she felt it a kind gesture, if a somewhat dangerous thing to do.

And so they came upon the scene. It was a pitiful sight. Jack was seeing it again for the second time. Millie creased her eyes, not really wanting to see. However, standing now before them, she had an overwhelming urge to look at their faces. She tried to blot out their soiled and blood-drenched torsos, and the puddles of urine below their feet. It was the faces she felt that out of respect she should remember. Of the three, there was one face that she was drawn to, as if by a magnet. She inched closer. Jack felt her begin to shudder. He truly sympathised, for it was a ghastly sight to behold.

Taking charge, he said, 'OK Millie, I think we've seen enough. Let's go.'

Then dramatically, Millie threw off Jack's arm, and let out such a shriek that Jack cursed. He had visions of a German patrol materialising from behind the church, to cut off their escape. The black Renault van was concealed there. He shouldn't have brought her. He had to get her away quickly before they were spotted. It wasn't that easy. She was losing control and becoming unhinged. He'd never seen Millie acting like this, and for a minute he was at a loss to know what to do. Then he did something that hurt him as much as it did Millie. He slapped her face. This had the effect of quietening her a little. But she was so distraught that he thought he was going to have to gag her.

All at once she pointed, and cried out in desperation, 'it's Philip! It's Philip! Oh God, they've hung Philip!'

He got her away by virtually carrying her to the van. He shouted through the window. 'Drive like hell!'

Only when she'd calmed down did Jack fully comprehend the awful truth—that the agent Charon was in fact Philip Hendry. He would later tell the French fighters that the two went back a long way, back to Singapore. The Japs sunk a craft Philip was in. Millie helped pull him out of the sea, barely alive, and she then nursed him back to health. When they landed in India, Philip had to remain there for a time with the army. Later, they met one another again in England, and became lovers. She loved him, and now she witnessed him having been betrayed by one of their own, and murdered by the Gestapo. The partisan and Jack shared her agony. Jack gathered Millie had no idea Philip was even in France. He wondered did they really know what was going on back in London.

They were well into the Picardie countryside now, and not far from the chateau. Jack had his arm around Millie, and while holding her was making little soothing sounds of 'there, there, there.' Gently, he used his spittle on a rag to wipe the congealed blood from the blow Vanessa landed her. She felt nothing of that. It was though, Millie's own thought process that helped to subdue her. Tumbling back, little images flitted through her mind like butterfly whispers. Happy ones like that balmy evening when she danced with Philip, at the *Lotus Hotel*, in Singapore. And the huge relief at finding him alive on the old *Dover Castle*, and the lovely romantic times they had spent in London. Then a crease formed on her brow when she recollected that it was quite by chance, she saw Philip at the hospital, in Oldham, and realised that by then he must have been recruited into the SOE. She became struck by a pang of guilt. Hugo came into her life and she fell in love with him. Things got complicated. She was away at different training schools and she and Philip couldn't somehow manage to get together. The war played havoc with relationships. Jack felt her shudder. 'There, there,' he murmured, again. It was at the training school in Scotland that she first met Vanessa. Now, Millie's thoughts quickened, and turned to ones of vengeance. She would make her pay dearly for what she had so treacherously done. She still had a knife in the handbag on her lap. Intent on what she was going to do, she gripped the bag, tightly.

'I was just thinking,' she lifted her head from his chest. The tears had got wiped away, along with the streaks of blood. 'Tell me Jack, you said something about Lindisfarne back there. Did you really have your suspicions about her as long ago as that?'

'Yes, I did, but I'll tell you later.' The driver was pulling up at the chateau. Feeling a thrill of triumph tighten his throat, he said, 'we're here.'

Millie said, 'right.' Her composure had returned. 'I-no we have a score to settle, so let's get on with it. There's no time to waste.'

'I'm with you on that,' declared Jack.

A figure of a man came out from the darkness of the doorway, momentarily startling them. Jack recognised him as one of the Maquis. He was obviously acting as a look out. He told Millie and Jack to go up the main staircase. He stayed at his post. Meanwhile the driver eased the van to the rear of the chateau, so that it was well out of sight. Jack led the way upstairs and along a gloomy hall. They saw another one of the bunch, leaning against closed double doors; he was intent on fiddling with the bolt of his riffle. He stopped, and nodded to Jack, gave Millie a grunt, then showed them in.

It must have been an elegant room, once, possibly where the family might have entertained. Shutters were flung back to let in a fading light, though the windows were closed. While the tiny, mezuzah on the door post of the main door, had vanished, a few paintings still hung on some of the walls in this room. Tell-tale signs of discoloured patches pointed to the owners having removed their most valuable pictures. Some pieces of quality furniture seemed at odds with the uncouth users. The intruders' boots left dirty imprints on a scarlet and gold fabric sofa, and an antique chair had its legs broken. Partly covered in dust sheets, a piano stood forlornly to the left of the wide windows.

Only minutes ago, while in the car, it had given Millie great satisfaction to imagine Vanessa on her knees, begging for mercy. And in her mind she devised ways to heighten that pleading. She even visualised some of the methods she'd use to make her confess the truth. The Partisans, however, had got there before her. An angry Millie stomped over to the middle of the room, ahead of Jack. Resolved to do what she'd been brooding on, Millie pulled out her knife. Vanessa was tied to a chair, with her hands behind her back. Breathing rapidly, and with bitterness in her heart, Millie studied her. She couldn't miss the blood trickling down Vanessa's chin, from a split lip. A torch was being shone in her face. Millie noted an eye was beginning to close over. Then one of the men grabbed her hair from behind and snapped her face upright to take a punch from his opposite number. A weird, gurgling noise came from Vanessa's mouth. There was a sense that they had established here was the traitor. And in dealing with it, two men poured out their hatred by inflicting further physical violence, and verbal loathing on the seated female form.

Millie was more than willingly to fire the gun. In fact she'd make sure she was the one to carry out the execution. But revulsion overwhelmed her when confronted with such barbarity. It made her feel that she was no better the Gestapo. In an instance, all her earlier intentions evaporated. She found she could not be part of this complicity; it turned her stomach to watch Vanessa subjected to this form of torture. Besides, there was an aura of hopelessness about what was being done, and it could not bring back the dead. She had to stop it.

Grabbing a fistful of shirt, Millie pulled one of the thugs out of the way. She bellowed at him, 'I want to interrogate her.' She would rather have said, 'speak to her', but that would have sounded too weak, too feminine, and these were tough blokes, and it was their men that they had seen hung. Automatically, there was an argument at Millie's demand, and others protested. Yet, there was an edge to Millie's tone that made the two fellows kowtow. Their commander was lounging against the piano, just watching the goings on. Millie shook him up by shouting, 'I want to interrogate the prisoner, alone!'

He thumped the piano keys in anger and slammed the lid shut. Fearing the whole thing would blow up into a damn awful mess, Jack practically ran to him while the rest stamped about, clearly, agitated. Jack signalled for them to come together and they gathered in a huddle to have some sort of an impromptu confab. Millie had no idea what was being said, she didn't care, she was staring at Vanessa. It didn't take long before the men dispersed though not before a couple of them made a point of loading pistols. Involuntarily, Millie shivered. Nevertheless, the room emptied and the door was shut, leaving Millie and Vanessa alone.

Outside, the men hung about, with only whispered exchanges taking place. This was when Jack put them fully in the picture regarding Charon. Jack could see by their faces they were shocked. He asked them to grant Millie some time with the woman. It was a tense moment. Tacitly, most nodded and some just grunted their approval. Jack heard a cork pop. Someone had got hold of a bottle, and it was passed round.

Inside the room, Millie dragged a chair over to face her captive. Still unable to comprehend Vanessa's actions, it puzzled Millie that this woman, who had shown a remarkable capacity to inspire trust, should have committed such atrocious deeds.

She addressed her in English. 'Why?' Millie asked, struggling to stay in control of her emotions. 'Why did you do it? Why have you betrayed us? Why did you betray everything we believe in?'

Vanessa lifted her head; sucked in her cheeks and through her injured mouth spat a great glob of blood streaked phlegm. It stuck to Millie's face. Sickened, Millie wiped the thick spittle off with her cuff. This enraged her so much that she wanted to strike Vanessa. She was almost on the verge of doing so when Vanessa unexpectedly hurled, 'you're a silly, stupid half-wit! You're mistaken if you think I'd tell *you* anything!'

Millie bounced to her feet, only just managing to hold back from raising her hand with the knife clutched in it. Furious, she paced round the room. She could sense Vanessa's eyes following her and felt her hatred sear into her very own soul. For a couple of minutes Millie said nothing, she was trying to rein in her anger. With every fibre of her being she endeavoured to think rationally. And then she came to the conclusion that Vanessa would never tell her why she did what she did. Millie thought, she will never tell me…but I'll try one last tactic, appeal, possibly to her better side—if she has one. Millie was still walking, round and round. Then with her back to Vanessa she said, 'for some time you and Charon have worked closely together, here in France.' She swallowed. 'You would have seen at first hand what a good man he is-was.' Vanessa said nothing. Millie continued, slowly now. 'Of course, I knew him much longer than you. I knew him out in Singapore…he used to call me Millipead…we fell in love.' She gave a little laugh. 'It sounds wet, doesn't it?' She wasn't expecting an answer, so she continued to talk. 'When he got back to England, he asked me to marry him.' Now she spun round, to see what effect this had on Vanessa. And it was a quite a knee-jerk of a response. She saw the woman visibly flinch, and little gasps, akin to sobs came from Vanessa's throat. At the same time Millie watched her chest heave while tears rolled down her one time colleague's face. Millie turned away, she'd seen enough. She went and leaned against the piano. For some minutes she gazed out of the windows, into the growing Picardie gloom. Satisfied now, just to hear Vanessa's pathetic whimpering. Then she squared her shoulders and put the knife back into her handbag, and marched to the door, without a backward glance.

Millie found the men not far away. 'I'm finished,' she told them, resolutely. 'There must be no more of this mindless violence.' They showed no remorse, but there were nods of agreement. That accomplished, she said, 'right, so, let's just get the rest of it over with.'

CHAPTER FORTY-ONE

Jack was left with a problem. What to do with Millie. They all agreed that it would be too risky to stay any longer at the chateau. By now the Germans were almost certainly on full alert, and hunting for them. The Maquis would put their usual plan of action in place by spreading themselves out and disappearing South, into the French hills. Jack would do what he always did, get on the move, and not stay in any safe house longer than one or two nights, at the most. Not only did SOE agents have to battle with circuit infiltration and collaborators, but as every operator knew, the radio was the organisation's Achilles heel. Their messages were so easily picked up by German listening devices. Nevertheless, Jack had to send London an urgent update telling them what had happened. They signalled back ordering him to get 'Gale,' in other words Millie, ready to come home. Clearly, the trauma of it all had taken its toll on Millie's nerves, and London wanted her pulled out. However, in quick succession there followed another message saying, 'regret no plane available for three or four days.'

What to do in the meantime. Jack was stumped. He had concerns for Millie's well-being, perhaps not surprising; after all she'd gone through. He thought again, over what had happened, and he knew he and the other officer had made the right decision; in fact it was a unanimous decision. Of course Vanessa was guilty; there was no question about it. She had to be executed. And it was carried it out quickly, within minutes of Millie completing her 'interrogation'. He could fully understand the Resistance wanted to exact revenge; it was unforgivable what the woman did. All the same, Millie was right to put an end to the inhumane treatment dished out by the French.

At the end of it all, if it hadn't have been so tragic it would almost have been sickly funny. No one would give her a pistol. Millie had gone round to each and every man, demanding a gun, including himself and the commander, whom she gave a hefty thump, when he too refused. She saw it as her duty to put the bullet in the traitor's brain. And she got angry at them not cooperating with her. Feelings of exasperation ran high, and brought her almost to the verge of tears. It was then Jack drew her aside. Even now he couldn't think how he explained it; how he explained to her the reason they all had for refusing her. All he knew was it would have been something that she'd have to live with for the rest of her life. That alone would not have been so terrible, but Jack had been at a botched execution, and with the state Millie was in he had no wish to witness another one mucked up. With the weapon placed at the nape of the neck, it took a steady, determined grip; a pistol in an unsteady hand resulted in a smashed skull with brains and gore exploding in all directions, and splattering the executioner, into the bargain. He did not want to see that again, and it was not something he was prepared to let her attempt to do. Of course, it fell to him to carry it out. With it being a woman, Jack did not relish the task, but it was inevitable. And it only took a single shot fired from his Colt .45, at close range, to deal with the traitor. Distasteful though it was for Jack, (though possibly not for the French) Vanessa's execution was carried out cleanly, and it was instantaneous. Which was more than could be said for the three men who had to endure an excruciatingly, painful end to their lives.

After the body was buried, the Maquis took off right and sharp, leaving only Jack and Millie at the chateau. Jack knew they too had to get away, quickly. He was not worried about himself, he already had that sorted, but he was racking his brains for somewhere to secrete Millie. As it happened, Millie came up with the solution of her own accord. Quite perfunctorily, she told him she would go and stay with a great aunt and uncle. At first Jack didn't know whether to believe her, he wondered if she was still in shock. However, she stated it in such a calm, matter-of-fact way, that when he asked her for some more details about this great aunt, it turned out that it was her grandmother's French sister, who coincidently, lived no great distance from the actual chateau.

When Millie came to the top of the little incline, the view that confronted her was exactly as she remembered it. There was the Blanc farmhouse. This was the home of her great aunt and her husband. From the outside it still looked every bit the same as the last time Millie was there and that was when she and Janet cycled through France, that lovely, long summer. Nevertheless, worrying concerns were beginning to play on her mind. Were they still living there? Were they still alive, even? They would both be quite elderly, now. She never said anything of this to Jack, she thought, why complicate things. She only wanted to curl up somewhere, and hide and sleep.

After Vanessa's execution Millie felt terribly empty inside, she had a great longing for Hugo, to be held in his strong, protective arms, and made love to. And strangely, for Graham's company, she so desired to hear his words of kindness and guidance. And then there was her dear grandmother. It was while she was thinking about her that she remembered how adamant her grandma was in getting Millie to remember where her French relatives lived. The Blanc's were her family, Grandma had said. Apparently, they were her only remaining family now left in Picardie. Good people, Grandma had called them. There was the inference that if ever Millie should find herself in need of a bolt-hole she would be assured of a sound one with them.

Millie turned back to see Jack arranging stones by the gate post. This gypsy-like hallmark would be their 'letterbox', a place where they would leave messages for one another. Jack told her he wouldn't go to the house except in an emergency. She only had to wait a few moments for him to finish a neat, unobtrusive little circle of pebbles. The job done, he gave a wave and she waved back, watching him cycle off. Millie had to be quite sure who was in the house, so instead of taking the path straight to the front door she made a detour across the field.

What Millie didn't see was Jack dumping the cycle and doubling back. He had to be satisfied she was OK. Not that he had any doubts about Millie's loyalty, but too much skulduggery had gone on and he had to make sure she was safe. When he heard voices and laughter he knew everything was well, yet again, to make absolutely certain, he stole in though the unlocked back door. His mind was set at ease when he saw Millie embracing an old man and woman. They never heard him creep away.

It was after lunch-time the next day that Millie woke to something of an epiphany. It all came flooding back so clearly to her. Because other things had taken precedence, she had pushed aside Jack's shattering revelation. His suspicions of Vanessa went back to their time on Lindisfarne Island, so he had said. Millie sat bolt upright. Of course, *now*, it was as plain as a pikestaff. They had almost completed the training on the island and everyone except Vanessa and Millie had gone for beers. Confident that she'd be alone, Vanessa had decided to go for a stroll. Millie, however, must have foiled her plans because she went on the walk with Vanessa. They had got close to the sea edge, and for a while had watched the seals, until bored, Millie fell asleep. What had taken place while she dozed off Millie didn't know. She had only woken up because Vanessa had made a disturbance walking over the sand. Once Millie thought back hard it became clear that Vanessa had set up a secret assignation, to meet the two spies that had been sent ashore from the German submarine. Millie's thwarting of the traitor's plans—albeit unintentional—meant Vanessa had to put on an act and go along with the sighting of the sub.

When Millie remembered the seals near Lindisfarn, she came to the conclusion that it could only have been Jack that was enjoying a sexy tryst in the moonlight with Vanessa. She had to smile at that thought. She made a mental note to ask Jack at some point about the nocturnal cavorting in the Abbey ruins.

A knocking on her bedroom door brought Millie out of a day-dreaming state. She called out, 'come in,' and in came her great aunt.

'Papa said, I'm worrying too much, but I had to come up and see if you were feeling well. You have been asleep for so long that I was getting a little worried.'

'No need to worry Auntie,' said Millie, stretching. 'I am feeling, just-just wonderful, and so happy to be with you both.'

The old aunt clasped her hands and drew nearer to the bed Millie had slept in.

'A neighbour has brought us a couple of rabbits. So I'll make a big pot of stew for dinner, and I have invited him to join us. He is in the shed skinning them.' The speed with which Millie got out of bed and started to throw on her clothes startled the old lady. Quickly she attempted to reassure Millie. 'No, no you mustn't be frightened, my dear, he's a good friend.' She whispered, 'he's with the Free French Army. Just before the Germans invaded us, he got away to London on a boat at Dunkirk. But now he has come back to-to well perhaps you know, or can guess.'

Millie might guess, but all the same, she was not taking any chances. Once she heard her aunt going downstairs she pushed her hand under the mattress and pulled out the gun Jack had given her *after* the execution. She ran a comb through her hair, grabbed a cardigan and wrapped it around the gun, and followed behind her aunt. By now the two men were in the kitchen.

'My dear,' the aunt took Millie's arm, 'this is Charles, and he is the man we have to thank for our dinner tonight. Charles, this is my great niece, Millie.'

'*Enchanté.* It is a great pleasure to meet you, once again, Miss Chance.' Millie's eyes widened, in surprise. Here was a stranger, yet he knew her name. However, there was something vaguely familiar about this swarthy, moustached man. He laughed aloud. 'Miss Chance, forgive me, I see you do not entirely remember. Well, why should you, it was some time ago, but it was in *Londres*. You dined at a most delightful French restaurant, in Soho, with your grandmother, I believe.' He winked at the old lady. 'They both looked quite charming, that evening.'

It suddenly came back to Millie. 'Why-I why yes, yes of course. I do recall. Grandma and I were sitting and…' She remembered the glasses of wine sent to their table. She also remembered she was in uniform. She cringed, thinking, how on earth anyone could look charming in heavy khaki serge.

Reading her thoughts, Charles told her, 'and you were very chic in your FANY uniform.' He pulled out a bottle of wine from his rucksack. 'We can drink this with the meal tonight.' He broke into a wide grin as he placed it on the table. 'It was liberated from the Bosch,' adding with derision, 'even though it is *our* wine.' Gathering his bits together, he said to everyone, 'please do excuse me as I must get on my way.' Millie followed him to the door. She had no idea from whence he came or with whom he was connected. She'd just have to wait and see. He whispered in her ear, 'and please, I assure you, there really is no need for the gun.'

He gave Millie a knowing look, bowed and was about to leave when he seemed to remembered something. 'Miss Chance I was asked to give you this.' He delved into his inside coat pocket and pulled out an envelope. '*Au revoir.*'

'Thank you,' Millie reached out, 'and goodbye'. She was trying to piece the puzzle together, why had he a letter for her. And then guessed the letter must be from Jack. Millie peeped into the kitchen where she saw the old folk busy with the food. She excused herself and went to her room and started to read. The weak sun had moved to the other side of the house, so Millie gravitated to the light of the window. When she saw who it was from, she staggered back to the bed for support. She had to look again. There was no signature, the letter merely ended with the initial *H*, and in the same simply way it was addressed to, *My dearest one.* She read it over and over knowing that as soon as she went into the kitchen she'd have to burn it. She felt her heart would break, she so wanted to keep the few beautiful lines written to her from her darling Hugo.

A couple of days passed, and each day Millie checked the little pile of stones. But there was nothing from Jack. Then on the third day Millie did unearth a message. She eagerly read his note. Jack had written that a plane would pick her up on the Friday. He would see her tonight, at seven, and give her the time and place to be at. However, even before she finished reading, she knew exactly what she was going to do. Predictably, Jack hit the roof when she told him.

'For Christ's sake,' he yelled, indignantly, 'you can't bloody well buggar-off, and do your own thing! I've had my orders from London. They want you back! And you're going! Have you got that?'

Millie was well prepared for his ire. Calmly, yet firmly, she hooked her arm through his and told him, 'let's take a stroll, preferably out of sight of the house. You can hear the rest of what I have to say, while we walk.'

Jack couldn't trust himself to reply, but thought, whatever she says, she's going on that plane, even if I have to chuck her on it myself.

They'd walked at a leisurely pace for half an hour or so, and by the end of their sauntering Millie had talked Jack round. Nonetheless, when he succumbed, he clearly saw the sense in what she'd said. When they reached the Blanc's wood shed she sat down on some logs, and after a few moments he lent against the pile close to her. He wasn't angry with her; at the worst of times it was hard for him to get angry with Millie. His respect and admiration for her, was too strong. And he could tell the rest she'd had with her aunt and uncle had done her good. She was her old self; she'd bucked up no end. Not only that, he knew she was right in her argument when she stated that there was a great deal of work for the Résistance to do in the build-up to the Allied invasion. And they needed every pair of hands they could get.

Somewhat more relaxed, now, Jack let his gaze drift over the peaceful Picardie fields that belied the horrors of war. Quite out of the blue, he asked Millie, 'do you remember our little sortie, into Dieppe?'

She smiled at him, pleased he'd accepted her decision to stay in France. 'How could I forget?'

With an air of fun, he smacked his fist into his palm. 'Indeed, indeed. How could either of us forget our first mission together?' He suddenly became serious. 'Christ! I hope the real *big* one is better planned, or it will turn into *the* most awful blood bath. Not just for the likes of you and me but—'

'It *will* be better planned and *we'll* be here doing our bit. We'll do everything we can to fight the Jerries. And we'll beat them, you'll see.'

Her optimism was infectious, and Jack couldn't help but get carried along with her courageous enthusiasm.

'Of course we'll beat the bastards. With the likes of us on board, how can we not?'

CHAPTER FORTY-TWO

Yanking in a parachute for all she was worth, Millie cursed out loud, while thinking this sort of carelessness was blatantly at odds with SOE's code of practice. All parachutes must be buried. That was one of the first things they were taught. And now, she scowled, greatly put out, we-no I have to do someone's dirty work. Who the hell do they think they are? And who or what was this so called Jedburgh outfit? Huffing and puffing, and much annoyed, she continued to inwardly seethe. Well, so much for secrecy and discretion, and she could not fathom out why they were in uniform. What is going on? Millie, like a good many agents and underground fighters guessed the Allied invasion of France must soon take place, but of course, no one knew when it would happen, or where.

*

When Millie met Charles Durant in the spring of '44, it was at her great aunt's house. He didn't let it be known to Millie exactly when he had arrived in Northern France. However, later she did learn that he underwent training at Milton Hall, near Peterborough, and was drafted into to a newly formed Special Forces unit. This elite outfit was code-named Jedburgh or the Jeds as the individuals in it became known. The forming of Jedburgh was an ambitious plan that saw the amalgamation of small units of British, French and Americans, who were specially equipped men entrusted with the job of creating a discernable presence in France, prior to the Allied invasion. SOE had flown Durant into the Picardie region ahead of his team primarily to liaise with Jack, and assist in rebuilding the fractured Prospero network. And, when some weeks later, intelligence filtered back to London informing them that their strategy was beginning to work, they were happy, or as happy as it was possible to be, given that the idiots within the confines of the secret service, had been fooled for long enough to let the 'Vanessa affair' continue to muddy the waters for such a length of time.

Charles Durant was now Jack's second in command. Durant brought with him orders and instructions for the Resistance, stating that they were to go all out in the effort to cause the maximum disruption to the Germans. This would be done by destroying communications, blowing up roads and railways, and sabotaging transport, in fact anything of that nature that would delay and confuse the German response to the invasion.

It soon became evident to both Jack and Millie, that Frenchman Durant had the way withal to inspire his countrymen's flagging spirits. He was totally fearless, with an attitude towards freedom from German tyranny that virtually teetered on the edge of madness. Jack put Durant's devil-may-care approach down to euphoric liberation fever. Though he mostly kept his opinion to himself, Jack sometimes confided to Millie that he thought Durant took unnecessary risks in order to get things done the moment he thought up an idea. In particular, when, on one daring raid into the U-boat pen territory, at Calais, Jack strongly advised caution, Durant replied, 'to hell with caution! Your country has not been occupied by the filth Bosch, like my France has for five long years…' Understandably, Jack had nothing to say that would stand up to that point of view.

Nevertheless, Jack couldn't ignore the fact that Durant had spent the best part of the war years in exile, in England, working under the jurisdiction of General de Gaulle. And what with having been out in the field longer than Durant, by comparison, Jack was cannier, or as Millie would say, Jack was more of a forward thinker. She knew only too well from working so closely with Jack that he planned his missions, meticulously. A fairly recent and very successful undertaking which involved blowing up railway lines took place when there was an RAF bombing raid. Jack synchronised the timing of the action to fool the Germans into believing it was the RAF who was responsible, and so no reprisals were taken against civilians. Durant on the other hand, was more of an opportunist. On another occasion Durant led a group that planted explosives under the arches of a bridge. He deliberately timed a detonation charge so that the structure blew up when a convoy of German troops were crossing the river. Yes, undeniably Durant was headstrong, but at the same time he got things done.

Millie's happy sojourn with her great aunt and uncle had come to an end. Jack had given her the OK to stay, and shortly afterwards, London sanctioned it. Obeying Jack's orders, (this time!) she had to say goodbye to her relatives as the group had to get nearer to the Pas-de-Calais. Plainly, with continual heavy bombing by the RAF the area around Calais was a dangerous place to be. They found the Port heaving with thousands of Germans, and ongoing reinforcements were pouring in daily. Jack grimly called it 'injin' country. Whispered rumours abounded amongst the French community that when the invasion came, Calais is where it would be. With so much speculation, and the intense build up of German military units, Jack and many in the underground movement were also coming round to the idea that the invasion would almost certainly take place at the Pas-de-Calais. Mindful, therefore, of such implications, steps were taken for Résistance activity to be significantly stepped up.

*

The parachute incident happened when they were heading off to a make-shift landing strip, a few kilometres from the outskirts of Calais, and it was thereabouts that Millie got separated from Jack and Durant. En route, they all had to duck for cover to avoid a convoy of German vehicles travelling towards the port. They got split up, and Millie lagged behind the two men, but she knew where the drop was to take place so they signalled they would go on ahead. Some time later, and in the confusion, Millie found herself alone at the drop zone with the discarded parachutes as evidence of a landing having taken place.

To cover the parachutists tracks Millie instinctively started to reel in the chutes. She was wondering if the ones that had just landed had anything to do with the Jedburgh crowd. The letter that Charles Durant brought from Hugo hinted that he was involved with a Special Forces team. While she was pulling in the billowing parachute she couldn't help wondering if Hugo was among this lot, or if it was just wishful thinking on her part. Suddenly, the sound of gunfire came from the vicinity of the trees. This stirred her to speed up what she was doing. Concentrating on getting the material into a tight ball for burying, she didn't hear a German soldier coming up behind her, until she felt the sharp jab of his riffle prang the small of her back. She almost jumped out of her skin.

He ordered her, 'put your hand's up!' Millie dropped the parachute and put her hands in the air. Once again she began to experience that horrible weakness in her limbs that she got when at the mercy of the enemy. She moved her head a fraction and caught sight of a flurry of grey figures, more German soldiers, running into the wood. She tried to think quickly. She had no gun or any kind of weapon with her. Jack had snatched the pack of equipment off Millie before they split up. Her being at the airstrip should have been a routine exercise. On this occasion, it wasn't as if they were desperately short-handed, she only went along to help with carrying things, and to assist with lighting the flares for the parachutists.

What should she do? Her innards seem to turn to jelly. She tried to think of what she'd been taught on unarmed combat. The kick to the testicles, two fingers drove into the eyes, but how far behind was he? He held the advantage. She'd learnt the procedures at training school; right enough, though she'd never had to put any of them into practice. Millie was hesitating. She wasn't thinking quickly enough. She could almost hear Vanessa saying, 'too slow, you're too damn slow,' just like she'd criticised her back in Scotland. Vanessa was always streets ahead of her in running, unarmed combat, riffle shooting: she prayed, please don't let me end up like Vanessa, with a bullet in my head. So, she'd have to opt for something else. Go for the little girl lost scenario, or try the poor French peasant act?

Before she had time to properly react he poked her again and demanded, 'turn round!' Her blood seemed to run cold. She had to obey him. Millie eased round slowly to face him. He barked, 'what are you doing? What are you doing in the middle of this field, with that?' He was now shaking his riffle up and down at the parachute.

'I-I'm sorry I-I.' Abruptly, she quivered to a stop. Instantly Millie recognised the German. 'Oh, H-H-Helmuth, it's you. Don't you remember me? Yvette, Yvette?'

He stared, and gawped until recognition set in. 'Aha, yes, it's you, the girl the little girl with the mushrooms.'

'Well, you knew they weren't mushrooms, and you saved me from getting poisoned.'

He lightened up. 'No, they were not mushrooms. *Pilz* as we call them in German. That was in Dieppe.' Then he became stern. 'Never mind that, what are you doing?'

She put on a sad countenance, and answered, 'Helmuth,' she knew she was taking a risk but she bent down quickly and grabbed a flap of the parachute. 'Helmuth, this is good material. It's silk, I think. We-I have not been able to buy new clothes, blouses or underwear, for years. When I saw these big balloons falling from the heavens, and-and men dropping from the sky, I ran and hid. But I-I got curious, and then I saw this beautiful material just lying, blowing about, going to waste.' Her voice took on a pleading tone, and sweetly, she said, 'Helmuth, I wanted it. Look Helmuth; look at the rags I have had to wear for so long.' She tugged at her skirt, and it lifted up to her thighs, to reveal the merest glimpse of her knickers. 'I've not had anything new to dress up in for ages.'

He came close to Millie, and studied her, his gaze drinking in the rise and fall of her breasts, before finally falling on her bare legs. He slung his riffle over his shoulder. Then, he ran his hands over her body, very slowly. She got a sense he was becoming aroused. Millie held her breath, telling herself he was feeling for a gun, and at the same time hoping he wouldn't ask to see her papers. Just then, more shots rang out from where the trees were.

Galvanised into action, he stepped back from Millie, and became the German he was. 'Go,' he said, 'and take the bundle with you.' He looked round furtively, then pulled his cap off and wiped his forehead, while Millie snatched up the parachute. 'I remember you were kind to me.' He touched the place where he bore the scar on his leg. It caused him to become thoughtful, and he told Millie, 'I should not like my sisters to have to scavenge in this way.' Keeping her head down Millie mumbled her thanks. 'Anyway,' he smiled, and flicked his cap on his head, 'I am ordered back to Germany. I leave tomorrow. With luck, maybe I will see my mother and father.' Then adding, with an amused sense of embarrassment, 'I have given up drinking your French wine.' Shrugging, and still wearing a smile, he said, 'so, what difference does a bit of cloth make?'

Without answering, Millie nodded by way of thanking him, again. It would take a moment or two before her thumping heart calmed down. Even so, Millie tried to walk away confidently, except she was uncertain which way to go, then she decided the trees might be the best bet. Tempted, she looked back at him and he raised his arm in a wave. She wanted to wave back but it took both hands to carry the chute. Wearing a satisfied little smile, too, she sighed and whispered, *quid pro quo*. No sooner was that said when abruptly, she faltered and almost fell as a loud shot rang out close to her. Then to her horror, Mille saw Helmuth fall, like a stone to the ground. Staggering, she cried out in disbelief, 'oh no, no!' She was stunned. Then she saw the man who fired the shot come in full view. He flew past her and went up to the body and fired again. It was Durant.

Once or twice, over the course of the last few years Millie had heard it said, 'no time for tears.' This was one of those occasions when she might easily have broken down and cried when she saw the corpse of the young German soldier—Helmuth—lying there. And yes he was the enemy, yet at that moment she knew the full meaning of that bandied about cliché, 'no time for tears'. Almost immediately Durant was at her side. Breathing heavily, he told her, 'he's dead, one less filthy Nazi. Let's get the hell out of here.'

As he was helping her away, Millie couldn't resist a last glance at Helmuth's lifeless body. And she could not she help thinking, with pinched sadness, one more day, one more day and he would have been safely back in his home town. Now, his Quaker mother and father would never see their son again. Would, she wondered, would anyone even bother to collect his dog tag? And his sisters, how many, two, three? There would be none to tell them that the last words their brother spoke were of them. This young German soldier's act of kindness had cost him his life.

Following on, another shock was in store for Millie. Whether it was all the emotional and physical exertions of the last couple of hours, she didn't know. What she did know was that her heart hurt, it hurt terribly, so much so that she barely had the strength to climb into the lorry Durant had steered her towards. Not surprising, what with everything going on, and it being so well camouflaged among the trees, she hadn't seen it before. Then strong arms lifted her into the vehicle and it began to move away. The lorry had a ridged tarpaulin cover, which made the inside pitch black. And with a mixture of cigarette smoke and booze and petrol fumes, it stunk like the devil's own armpit.

Cramped to one side against the rough, wooden slats Millie was feeling ill-at-ease, and claustrophobic. She sensed it was because there were a lot of people jammed in behind her that she couldn't see to distinguish who was who. As well as that, it became unsettlingly, for the arms that had lifted her in, continued to keep a firm grip of her. Millie told herself, I'm not going to keel over, if that's what this oaf thinks. She was about to try and brush the lout off when a match got struck, and the man that had hold of her started to speak in English, in a quasi-serious tone, just beside her ear.

He began, 'for a while, we were all rather worried back there, watching the German pointing his riffle at you. It was bloody frustrating, because no one could get a clear shot of him for fear of hitting you.' He was so close Millie could now feel his breath on her cheek. The touch of his moist lips made her senses spin. 'It looks like you've got our man Durant to thank for saving your skin.' Millie's heart leapt. She knew that voice like no other. Endeavouring to turn, she let out a cry which got suppressed by a kiss, planted full on the mouth. He wrapped his arms around her, and whispered, with infinite tenderness, 'hello old thing.'

She felt a flood of happiness wash over her, but for that moment all she could say was,

'Hello Hugo.'

CHAPTER FORTY-THREE

Caught off guard, they were all fooled that morning of the sixth of June, not least Field Marshall Erwin Rommel; who had professed to his cronies that no invader in their right senses would attempt to cross the English Channel in such foul weather as they had just had for the last two weeks. He had poured over numerous weather bulletins and was of the opinion there would be no let-up in the poor weather conditions for some days to come. Entirely convinced of the improbability of an invasion that month, the Field Marshall grasped the opportunity to enjoy a much overdue spot of leave. Rommel left Paris in high spirits, carrying an elegantly wrapped box which contained a pair of exquisitely crafted Parisian shoes, a birthday present for his darling wife, 'Lu'.

Called Operation Overlord, an impenetrable blanket of secrecy cloaked the largest invasion fleet ever to be launched. And when the Allied forces surprised the enemy by landing on the beaches of Normandy, many kilometres from the Pas-de-Calais—the site thought by the Germans most likely where the invasion would happen—Rommel was back in the heart of the homeland enjoying a cosy *tête-à-tête* with his beloved *Frau*. For a while, Rommel and many of the high ranking generals in Berlin were quite oblivious to the intensity of the battle being played out in the Normandy theatre of death. When intelligence reports of the Allied landings did begin to filter back through various channels to the German High Command, those closest to Hitler were all terrified to inform him. This was due to the fact that Hitler had taken a sleeping draught the night before, and left orders that on no account should he be wakened. And so, in spite of the urgency of the situation, combined with hierarchical frustrated in-house ranting, no one dared to contradict the dictator's orders.

This time delay gave the Allies a precious advantage to push on in-land. Some influential German generals were still, even at this late stage, convinced that the 'real' attack force must come from Dover to the Pas-de-Calais. Some, rather more academically inclined, even purported that any invasion would be launched from Scotland across to and through Norway. When the landings started, it was believed by the majority of these German militarists that the skirmishes at Normandy were nothing more than a feint. And so, to the mighty relief of General Dwight D Eisenhower—the supreme commander of Operation Overlord—the Allied deception had worked magnificently.

Jack was able to radio back to H Q in London telling them that the Panzer armoured tank division, along with the rest of the Wehrmacht army based in and around Calais remained firmly ensconced in their positions. Although intense fighting raged on for hours, days at some stretches of the Normandy beaches, initially, no additional German troops were brought in to reinforce their existing infantry along that stretch of the coast. Fortune indeed favoured the bold. The Allies were well and truly able to secure a bridgehead on the Normandy shoreline. Thanks to a well kept secret, the enemy had swallowed the big lie!

*

A few months later, in August, at the height of a glorious French summer, Paris was liberated. The Germans capitulated, and were driven out of the city. After five long years, Paris was no longer under German occupation.

Caught out in the growing retreat, here and there, pockets of German soldiers were taken prisoner, though frequently, summary executions were carried out by French freedom fighters. These men had long memories of the inhuman torture and executions mete out to their families and friends by the hated Waffen-SS. Jack and Millie witnessed some of these shootings but were powerless to do anything about it. From one man's mouth they heard how a whole village was destroyed: men and boys were separated, then lined up and shot, while the women and children were locked in a barn and then the barn was set on fire. Everyone inside were burned alive. The man told them he lost his entire family that day. Being a Frenchman, Durant's sympathy was for his compatriots. Nevertheless, Hugo and the Jeds were there to co-ordinate sabotage work amongst the Resistance, prior to, and during the invasion, and although they were sickened by first hand accounts of such atrocities they had more than enough to contend without becoming embroiled with personal issues of revenge.

Travelling from the North; the journey towards Paris was slow. Roads in part were clogged with civilians on the move, who were confused, and often unaware of what was happening. These delays caused the truck with the Jeds in it to have to make constant detours. Current lack of information on the situation in Paris was sketchy. Therefore, it was agreed by all that the easiest and safest way for Jack and Millie to get to Paris was by sticking with Hugo and the Jedburgh team for as long as possible.

They were not far from their destination when Jack got a radio message from London. It ordered both him and Millie not to go into Paris. Instead, they should wait at a particular hotel on the outskirts of the city. There, they were to rendezvous with SOE officers from London. This directive was disappointing for Millie. She was just getting used to having Hugo all to herself. It was the happiest of times she'd had for what seemed years, and she was falling in love all over again. Earlier, one evening, Hugo found a decent inn that had been hastily vacated by German officers, and they all bedded down there for the night. It was at the inn that Hugo and Millie managed to snatch a few precious hours alone, and over a bottle of wine Hugo proposed marriage to Millie. And now, she found out that Hugo and the Jed team had to push off in the opposite direction, into Belgium.

The radio message Jack got from London gave no names of the two SOE people. Therefore, it came as a marvellous surprise to meet up once more with Graham Bain. Millie was totally unprepared for this visitation, and of all places, in France! She was so happy to see him that she had to stop herself from hugging him. Yet in that split second of hesitancy it was evident he was different. His manner was not only restrained, but cool and business like. Quickly, Millie understood. Protocol reared its ugly head. Graham was in uniform, not just any old uniform. He was formally dressed as a British officer bearing the rank of major. Somehow, she had never thought of Graham in uniform, and she felt suddenly ill at ease. Intuitively, Millie put his standoffishness down to the fact that he wasn't alone. He was accompanied by an officious-looking woman. This formidable female, was a high ranking officer in the WAAF. Wasting no time, she began to explain that they had flown over to debrief Jack and Millie on the reported deaths of Madeleine and the agent Charon, in other words, Vanessa and Philip. As well as that, they were there to gather intelligence on other 'lost' SOE agents.

Although ultra polite, as always, Millie sensed Bain was nervous in the woman's presence, and he only ever referred to her as Vera. When they talked about it afterwards, Jack told Millie that he had met the woman, briefly, a couple of times. When Millie asked when that was, Jack said it was on two occasions when he was leaving England to go out on a mission to France. She processed his documents and checked his clothing to make sure there was nothing left in pockets that could link him to spying. Jack added that like Bain, he'd not seen her in uniform, until now. Annoyingly, he couldn't recall her other name. The WAAF officer had brought over Millie's FANY uniform. And Jack watched, slightly bemused as she then proceeded to open another suitcase. She pulled out a pair of brand spanking new army regulation shoes, his exact size. Then she shook a khaki tunic, and handed over a pair of trousers that looked vaguely familiar to Jack. He'd worn them when serving with his old outfit, The Signals. The only difference being back then, he was just an ordinary rank and file Private. Vera pointed out he'd now been promoted to the rank of Captain. While Jack was thus engaged with Vera in these formalities, Graham was able to draw Millie aside and have a few words, out of their hearing.

'Sorry,' he told her, 'sorry this is all so boringly official, Miss Chance. But this um this uniform business, it's for your own safety.' Because Millie seemed puzzled, Bain was quick to tell her, 'we don't want any of the natives getting you or Jack confused with collaborators. There are a lot of hot heads out there, intent on revenge. It's understandable in some respects. Still, this "act now and talk later" mood is worrying.'

Millie got the message, alright. She had already seen two pathetic women with their heads shaved and their faces black and blue, as well as a number of corpses hanging from gibbets. She glanced in the direction of the WAAF officer, who was busy writing notes on a clip board. Under her breath, Millie said, 'gosh, Graham, the old bird's a bit of a hoity-toity madam.'

He laughed, quietly, at her expression, remembering Millie never minced her words. 'Don't mind that,' he said, dismissively, and then with hasty sobriety, added, 'her work, the greater part of her-our work, one might say, is only just beginning. There has to be an investigation into the deaths of our people, and we have to get to the truth of it all by collating as much evidence as possible, while it is still fresh.' He said, with and air of hopelessness, 'many men and woman agents are still missing. For the records, and for their families, we have to find out what has happened to them.' He cleared his throat. 'You see, the role of the SOE in France will soon be over, and you and Jack and every other agent who is still free in France, will soon be sent back to England.'

'Still-still what?'

'Free. Yes Millie.' He spoke, looking at the ground. 'Some we know will never come back. Killed, murdered. Of others, we've got information, albeit sketchy, that they held are in German concentration camps.' Bain felt the need to loosen his tie. 'Some agents deep in Europe are still active. It will-it could be a long process to get it all—' Millie squeezed her eyes. 'I'm sorry, my dear, so sorry.' Bain was touched, saddened. He said, 'I-I'm so glad you aa-and Jack are...there were times...I-we've all had more than a few sleepless nights across the water. Not that that did anyone much good.' Bain was once again struck by a twinge of guilt as he took in her delicate features, which he knew from old, belied her strength and determination. 'I-I thought of you a lot.' There was a catch in his voice. Surprised, Millie blinked hard. 'When we first sent you, I thought I'd done the wrong thing.'

'No, you didn't, Graham. Don't ever think that.'

'What I mean is you-you were so young.' He gave a little embarrassed laugh. 'I am not a particularly religious man, but there were a few time when I prayed to God to keep you safe.'

Millie couldn't help it, she started to sob. 'Philip, poor, poor Philip, oh Graham, you don't know what they did to him.'

Bain reached out to Millie, and moved her aside so that an interconnecting door obscured Vera and Jack's view. 'Yes,' he said, 'yes I do know.'

She seemed not to hear. 'It was her, Vanessa.' Millie hissed, 'she betrayed us and heaven knows who else died because of her.'

He held her by the shoulders. 'I can assure you, I know it was her who betrayed Philip, and the others in Prospero.'

Blankly, Millie stared at him. 'Oh, how—' She didn't wait for an answer she was too angry. 'Graham, I could have killed her. I would have killed her. I would have done it. I wanted to. Damn and blast her. But they wouldn't let me—'

'No, I know. All the same...' Bain put his arm right around her, and felt her pain, and he hurt for her. After a few moments Millie tilted her face towards him. Her unheeded tears flowed. For a few moments Bain gazed at her until he became conscious that he was holding her in his arms. Then releasing her, and with tepid jollity, he said, 'we've come in an official capacity, to tell you, no, correction, *order* you, to take some leave.' He proudly told her, 'it's well and truly earned. We'll see you won't go short of money, and you'll be protected in your uniforms. Go with Jack, and enjoy Paris.' He smiled, and said, with all sincerity, 'I wish I could go with you.' Bain gave her his handkerchief, and she wiped away the tears. When she had finished with it he put it back into his pocket, knowing he'd never use it again. After a moment, he said, 'Millie, Germany is beaten. It is common knowledge; even the Germans must know the war can't go on much longer.'

'I hope you are right, Graham, really I do.'

'Hitler is finished.' Adding with as much resolution as he could muster, 'there's no two ways about it. It is only a matter of time. Why, Eisenhower and Montgomery even have a bet going.'

'What do you mean, bet, what bet?'

'Eisenhower has forecast that the war will be ended before Christmas. Old Monty disagrees.' Bain gave a chuckle. 'Monty argues German surrender can't be brought about before the spring of '45.' He leaned towards her. 'Still, whatever they say, I'm telling you with prophetic certainty, that one day, Millie, one day in the not too distant future, you will be able to tell your grandmother how you, and the brave people in SOE helped to free her beloved Paris.'

CHAPTER FORTY-FOUR

Not that they did, but even if Jack and Millie had felt otherwise inclined, such was the ubiquitous feeling of elation that it was impossible for them not to join the throng of wildly happy Parisians. It was a day when copious amounts of wine got drunk, and rare vintage bottles of champagne mysteriously appeared. Hidden, they heard it said, buried in the depths of cellars, or bricked up in cool loft spaces, carefully secreted away in the hope of such a time as this. That magic elixir once again saw the light of day, and oh how the corks popped. Oh how the ecstatic French people cheered amidst the noise of music, and horns blaring, and back slapping, and hugging and merry-making.

Trying to take this all in, Millie and Jack were astonished at the colourful mix of uniforms that sprung from all districts of Gay Paree. Not entirely ecstatic, however, Jack was considerably miffed to see the vast numbers of 'Yanks,' as he called the Americans, flamboyantly strolling down the *Champs-Elysees*, with smiling girls on their arms.

Remonstrating angrily to Millie, he said, 'you'd think them bloody gum-chewing Yanks won the bloody war on their own.'

Millie gave a laugh at that, then calmly, replied back, 'don't take it to heart, Jack, there really is no need. The people of Paris know differently.' She waved her arms at the massive crowds, and declared, 'today they don't care, so why should we care? After all, they have a lot to celebrate. They are free, free from tyranny, and what's more, we are alive, and free!'

She had talked him out of his moment of ire, and he shrugged off his ungracious spate, without too much further grumbling.

They saw Nazi flags torn to shreds, stamped on and burnt. And they watched war-weary French faces as *La Marseillaise* struck up and was played again and again. And they saw the tears streaming down many, many faces. Often, Jack stood to attention, and saluted and sang at the top of his voice. Millie tried to sing, but it made her too emotional and the words stuck in her throat. Nearing the end of a gloriously happy day, they gradually steered themselves towards the address of the hotel that Graham Bain had given them. Rather disconcertingly, it was as much as they could do to squeeze in through the melee of boisterous, intermingled bodies.

'Sit tight,' said Jack, when they eventually managed to grab a free table. 'I'll get us some wine. Are you hungry?'

Millie gave a wry smile, and nodded. While she watched Jack struggle his way to the bar, she thought, God in heaven, there was hardly a time when I haven't felt hungry in France. She was holding back the saliva in anticipation of getting something tasty. Jack wasn't that long, and she was glad, as it seemed ages since they'd last eaten. Then she saw Jack's face as he came to the table. Her eyes dropped to the meagre two plates of food that he presented.

'Sorry,' he said, tapping the half-stick of bread on his head, to test how stale it was. All the same, feeling duty-bound to apologise on behalf of the proprietor, he added, 'it's the best I could get. They've practically run out of everything. But, I did manage to wangle this.' He produced a bottle of wine from behind his back, and did a little jig. He made her laugh, as he so often did in the past, in spite of adversity. She'd never considered him what she would call stunningly handsome. Yet today, in uniform Jack did look dashing, and he was wonderful company, and his jocularity was infectious.

Picking up on her amused glances, Jack asked, 'so, when are you going to marry me?' His words were deliberately accentuated.

Of course Millie knew he was ribbing her, and with a twinkle in her eye, and a smile to match, she began, 'dear, darling Jack. Only we know how much we've been through—'

'Aaaagh, no-no-no-no!' He shook his hand in a very French way, a hand that would have to wear the scars of fighting for the rest of his life. 'I can feel a rejection coming on.' He affected a hung-dog look. 'And here's me thinking I'm in with a chance. Pooff. So I suppose it's this Hugo bloke that has stolen your heart from me, blast him!' Straight from the bottle, Jack swigged the wine.

After their laughter died away, Millie tucked into the all important business of eating. Then, bye and bye she grew thoughtful. Between mouthfuls, she asked Jack, 'do you-do you have any-any—'

He jumped in with, 'regrets?'

'Um, I was going to say…unfinished business.' Pausing to arrange her words she then started to explain. 'You see I-I have, I really have to get to Singapore…' Millie trailed off because Jack didn't appear to be listening. And then abruptly he shoved the chair back and was on his feet.

'Hells bloody bells!' He suddenly exclaimed. Shaken out of her wistful few moments, Millie followed the direction in which Jack had yelled the expletive. 'Well I'll be damned. It's Denise!' Megaphone-like; he put both his hands around his mouth and shouted. 'Hi! Denise! Denise my beautiful angel, I have long awaited your presence.' A big grin appeared on Jack's face. He turned to Millie and said, 'now excuse *me* but there's *my* unfinished business.' And with that he pushed his plate towards Millie and said, 'here, love, you have my grub. I've suddenly got an appetite for something really hot!'

It was obvious that Jack knew Denise, intimately. Millie though, had never met Jack's 'beautiful angel.' Yet a few hours later, Jack, acting the fool still had her smiling. He'd caught the red-headed, buxom Denise in a sexy clinch. And as if he was about to lead her into a Tango, he gave her a passionate kiss, causing a well-turned ankle to shoot up into the air. An eruption of loud wolf-whistles had everyone watching this bit of tom-foolery. And raucous roars of laughter broke out from the men congregating at the door, jostling to see what was going on.

It had been a long day, and tired now, Millie slipped away as soon as she had eaten, and went to her accommodation on the fifth floor. It was clean, and had a bath, but most of all it pleased her as the room overlooked the great metropolis. She flung back the windows and was able to enjoy a fine view of Paris, which, unlike poor London, escaped with negligible bomb damage, due to Paris being declared an 'open city,' in June of 1940. Millie rested her elbows on the sill, just gazing, happy to let her thoughts wander. She came to a point though, when her day dreaming stopped. Reality took hold and she realised that it could only be a matter of weeks, possibly days, even, before they would be flown back to England. And, she asked herself, what then?

Everything had changed, and yet for Millie, some things had not changed. She remembered, as if it were yesterday, that first formal interview, back in 1942. She could recall, practically word for word the conversation she had with Graham Bain, and the SOE officer, the one who asked her about duty. 'Miss Chance,' he'd said, at the time, 'now that you are back in England, where does *your* loyalty lie, and what do you consider is *your* duty?'

Loosening her tie and undoing her top shirt button, Millie almost scoffed as she recollected. Duty! In heavens name! To start off with, it was expected that whilst growing up, one had to learn to become a dutiful child. Then simultaneously, one learned about duty to one's King and Country. Duty! Millie knew it went without saying, because her parents, in common with most other parents, had instilled in Archie and Clive, and her, a lifelong sense of duty.

Millie knew, if they didn't, it was with duty in mind that she told the SOE officer, 'I'll do anything it takes to get my father and Doctor Elder home safely.' Yet for a moment, breathing in the sweet Parisian air, she became doubtful. She began to question herself. Had she been too bombastic? Too flippant, too reckless, or too ambitious, even, when it came to voicing her beliefs on this thing called *duty?* And as for making promises, Millie had made a promise to marry Hugo. With all her being that was what she wanted, and that was what Hugo wanted—to be together for the rest of their lives. Foremost, however, she had promised to do her utmost to get those two men—her father and Doctor Elder—home safely. Duty bound, she knew in her heart that she must honour that promise.

Night was falling, and the Parisian vista Millie had been looking out on, had grown dim, so that it was just a mere blur of patchwork lights. With her thoughts now quite free to flit hither and thither, Millie remembered one particular summer holiday, when her grandmother had taken her on her first visit to Paris. Old Mrs Chance called Paris a 'City of Artists.' Child-like, Millie asked, 'Grandma, where does an artist begin?' The answer she got was, 'the artist begins with an idea.' Millie knew she was no artist, yet an idea was forming in her head, and it was taking her across the sea, across oceans, and across the miles to that faraway island of Singapore.

A loud knocking at her door made Millie Jump. It went on and on. Cross at being disturbed, she judged, someone's damned impatient. Or was it something more sinister? Instinctively, Millie went for her pistol.

'I'm coming, just a minute.' Exercising innate caution, and with her weapon cocked, Millie inched open the door, only to see a thoroughly dishevelled Jack. Lowering the gun, she breathed a sigh of relief, guessing he'd probably had too much to drink. Or maybe the 'angel' Denise, turned into a devil in disguise, and had thrown him off. Before she could ask for an explanation, Jack brushed passed her.

'So,' he said, 'so would you like to know when we're going to Singapore?'

It was all she got out of him before he staggered over to the bed and flaked down on it.

'Whaaat? What did you just say?' Millie gave him a shake. 'Did you say Singapore? Jack, are you serious?'

'Course I'm bloody serious.' He started to fumble with his tunic pocket. Impatient, Millie went to help him. He pushed her hand away, becoming obstreperous. 'I've got orders,' he declared. 'Come right from the top, they have.' He thumped his chest. 'In here, for us, you me, brought and delivered no less,' his words becoming slurred, 'delivered f-from the fair hair-hand, hand, delivered from the fair hand of Denise, no less.'

'Jack, you're-you're drunk.'

'Not as drunk as I'd bloody well like to be.' Eventually, he retrieved an envelope, and flapped it at her. 'Here, read, you read.'

By the time Millie had read the communiqué twice, Jack was drifting off to sleep. Her hands were shaking as she unlaced, and eased off his shiny, new shoes. She rubbed a smudge of dirt with her cuff. Then she covered him with the eiderdown and kissed him lightly on the cheek.

Millie read the communiqué again. His words were a bit garbled, when he'd said it, but she was sure Jack had mumbled something about orders. He was wrong; there was no mention of orders anywhere in the document. She checked again. HIGHLY CONFIDENTIAL was stamped in red ink at the top of the page. And two lines below that was, SECRET MISSION TO SINGAPORE. There were two other names alongside Jack and Millie's, but no one person was *ordered* to go on the mission. The communiqué simply invited the persons named, therein, to volunteer their services for King and Country.

Millie set the shoes under the bed, and whispered, into his ear, 'you're wonderful.'

Jack answered, sleepily, 'Mmmm, I know.'

Lightning Source UK Ltd.
Milton Keynes UK
UKOW03f2252121014

239982UK00001B/36/P